THE
LITTLE
DEATH

BOOKS BY P. J. PARRISH

The Little Death*
South of Hell*
A Thousand Bones*
An Unquiet Grave
A Killing Rain
Island of Bones
Thicker Than Water
Paint It Black
Dead of Winter
Dark of the Moon

*Published by POCKET BOOKS

THE
LITTLE
DEATH

P. J. PARRISH

POCKET STAR BOOKS
New York   London   Toronto   Sydney

Pocket Star Books
A Division of Simon & Schuster, Inc.
1230 Avenue of the Americas
New York, NY 10020

This book is a work of fiction. Names, characters, places, and incidents either are products of the author's imagination or are used fictitiously. Any resemblance to actual events or locales or persons, living or dead, is entirely coincidental.

First Pocket Star Books paperback edition March 2010

POCKET STAR BOOKS and colophon are registered trademarks of Simon & Schuster, Inc.

For information about special discounts for bulk purchases, please contact Simon & Schuster Special Sales at 1-866-506-1949 or business@simonandschuster.com.

The Simon & Schuster Speakers Bureau can bring authors to your live event. For more information or to book an event, contact the Simon & Schuster Speakers Bureau at 1-866-248-3049 or visit our website at www.simonspeakers.com.

Cover design and illustration: Jae Song
Photograph of ghost orchid: Mick Fournier

Manufactured in the United States of America

10 9 8 7 6 5 4 3 2 1

ISBN 978-1-4165-2589-9
ISBN 978-1-4391-6923-0 (ebook)

For Barbara Parker,
writer, teacher, mentor, friend.

Let us alone. What pleasure can we have
To war with evil? Is there any peace
In ever climbing up the climbing wave?
All things have rest, and ripen toward the grave
In silence—ripen, fall, and cease:
Give us long rest or death, dark death, or dreamful ease.

—Tennyson, *The Lotus Eaters*

THE
LITTLE
DEATH

Chapter One

Something wasn't right. He could tell from the baying of the dog.

It wasn't the normal barking that came when the dogs had come across a cow mired in a mud hole. It wasn't the frenzied yelps that signaled the dogs had cornered a boar in the brush.

This was like screaming.

Burke Aubry shifted in his saddle and peered into the darkness. A heavy fog had rolled in before dawn, and it distorted everything—shapes, smells, but especially sound. The barking seemed to come from everywhere and nowhere at once, rising and falling with every shift of the cold morning wind.

A rustling to his left. He turned, ears pricked.

Just a cabbage palm. Its thick trunk, hidden by the fog, seemed to float above the ground. The wind sent the heavy fronds scraping against each other. It sounded like the rasp of a dying man.

Movement in the corner of his eye. The dark mass took shape as it came toward him, the blur hardening slowly into horse and rider.

It was Dwayne. Aubry could tell from the red kerchief he always wore around his neck. A second later, another, smaller shape emerged, a large yellow dog following close behind the horse.

Dwayne drew his horse up next to Aubry's. "You hear that?"

"Yeah."

"You think one of the curs got into it with a boar?"

Aubry didn't answer. He was listening to the baying. It sounded like it was coming from the south. But none of the men or their dogs were supposed to be down there.

He jerked the radio from his saddle. "Mike?"

A cackle of static. "Yeah, boss?"

"You working the east ten pasture?"

"That's where you told us to go."

"Are all of you there?"

A pause. "Yes, sir."

"What about the dogs?"

"Dogs?"

"Are all your dogs with you?"

"They're all—"

"Count 'em, Mike."

Seconds later, he came back. "Ted says his dog has gone missing."

A high-pitched yelping rose on the wind. It was coming from the south, Aubry was sure this time. He keyed the radio. "Mike, get the men down to Devil's Garden."

"Devil's Garden? But—"

"Just do it, Mike."

Aubry stowed the radio and turned to Dwayne. "Let's go."

Even in the fog, he knew where he was going. He had been working the ranch for nearly four decades now, and he knew every foot of the four thousand acres, knew every tree, every swamp, every fence. He knew, too, that no living thing, not even a dog, had any reason to be in Devil's Garden.

They headed south. They crossed a stream and entered a thick grove of old live oaks. The gray fog shroud wrapped the trees, softening their black, twisting branches and webs of Spanish moss.

The baying was loud now. It was coming from the direction of the old cow pen. The pen was one of the largest on the ranch but had been abandoned twenty years ago. Aubry urged his horse on. Suddenly, the yellow dog darted ahead of them through the tall, wet ferns.

Dwayne whistled, but the dog was lost in the fog.

The men prodded their horses to a fast trot. The dark wood of the pen's fence emerged from the mist. Two dogs now, barking and growling.

Aubry got off his horse, pulling out his rifle. He scaled the fence, and the barking drew him deeper into the maze of holding pens.

He reached the large central pen and stopped, rifle poised to shoot if the dogs were confronting an animal. But the mass that the dogs were hunched over wasn't moving. Aubry heard Dwayne come in behind him and then Dwayne's sharp command to the dogs to heel. Ears flat, fur raised, the dogs backed off.

Aubry approached the mass slowly, rifle ready.

The pale flesh stood out against the black dirt. At first, he thought it was a skinned boar carcass. Then he saw the arm. A step closer, and the rest of the mass took shape. A leg, and then a second one bent at a horrid angle under the hump of a bare back.

It was a man, naked.

Aubry stopped. There was no head.

"Hey, boss, what we got—"

Aubry heard Dwayne's sharp intake of breath as he saw the corpse.

"Jesus," Dwayne said.

Aubry pulled out his radio.

"Ah, sweet Jesus, where's his head?" Dwayne whispered.

Aubry keyed the radio. "Mike? Get back to the house and call the sheriff."

"What?"

"Just do what I say, Mike. Tell them there's a dead man. Give them directions to the old cow pen in Devil's Garden."

"Dead man? Who?"

"I don't know."

Aubry clicked off and pocketed the radio. He heard a retching sound and turned. Dwayne was leaning on a fence, wiping his face.

Aubry looked back at the body. He felt the rise of bile in his throat and swallowed hard. Shifting the rifle to his back, he squatted next to the body.

He could see now that there were deep slashes across the back, like the man had been cut badly. And it looked like the head had been cut off cleanly, almost like it had been sawed off. He scanned the pen as far as the fog would allow but didn't see the head.

He looked down. He realized suddenly that what he thought was black dirt was sand saturated with blood. The black pool spread out a good four feet from the body. He stood up and took two long strides back. The toes of his boots were black.

His radio crackled, but he didn't hear it. His brain

was far away, and suddenly, the memories he had tried so hard to bury were right there with him again. Another spread of blood, a different body. Once again, the outsiders would come here, men with guns, badges, and questions. Once again, he would have to stand silent and watch as the waves ate away yet more of his island.

The pain hit him, a knife to the heart, and he closed his eyes.

The wind died suddenly, and the quiet moved in.

He looked up, to where the fog had burned off, leaving a hole in the sky. He blinked rapidly to keep the tears away, watching the patch of sky until it turned from blue velvet to gray flannel.

An owl hooted. A hawk screamed. Then came the soft mewing cries of the catbirds. The day was coming alive in this place of death.

Chapter Two

The top was down on the Mustang, and the road ahead was empty. Louis Kincaid was not sure exactly where he was going.

He had never driven this road before. On all of his trips over to the east coast, he had taken Alligator Alley, which cut a straight, expedient slash across the Everglades from Naples to Fort Lauderdale. Always in the past, he had arrived quickly, done his job, and headed straight back home.

But this time, an impulse he did not understand had led him to the back roads.

The map told him he had to stay on US-80, but the highway had changed names several times already, narrowing to meander through cattle pastures and tomato farms, offering up a red-planked barbecue joint, a sunburnt nursery, or a psychic's bungalow. Three times, the speed limit dropped, and US-80 became Main Street, passing Alva's white-steepled church, La Belle's old courthouse, and Clewiston's strip malls. From there, the towns fell away, leaving only the vast flat expanse of the sugarcane fields, broken by a row of high power lines, marching like giant alien soldiers to the horizon.

The wind was hot on Louis's face and the scenery was a blur of color—the high green curtain of the cane and the denim of the December sky. The sun was behind him, and he had a strong urge to turn the car around and head back home. But he had made a promise and had to see this thing through.

Soon he reached the sprawling suburbs of West Palm Beach. The fast-food joints and gas stations grew denser the farther east the car went, ending in the pastel warren of old downtown West Palm Beach.

At the Intracoastal, Louis steered the Mustang onto a low-slung bridge that connected the mainland to the barrier island. He had the thought that the bridge looked nothing like the one that led from Fort Myers over to his island home on the Gulf. The Sanibel–Captiva causeway was a plain concrete expanse that leapfrogged across rocky beaches dotted with kids and wading fishermen.

This one looked like the drawbridge to a Mediterranean castle, complete with two ornamental guard towers.

The bridge emptied onto a broad boulevard lined with majestic royal palms and fortresslike buildings that looked like banks. There was no welcome sign, no signs anywhere. He guessed he was in Palm Beach now.

"Mel, wake up," he said.

No sound or movement from the passenger seat.

Louis reached over and jabbed the lump. "Mel! Wake up!"

"What?"

"We're here. Where do I go?"

Mel Landeta sat up with a grunt, adjusted his sunglasses, and looked around.

"Take a right on South County Road," he said.

"Where? There's no street signs."

"I don't know. I haven't been here in a long time. The island's only fourteen miles long and a mile wide. If you hit the ocean, you've gone too far."

Louis spotted the street name painted on the curb and hung a right. The financial citadels of the boulevard gave way to boutiques and restaurants.

"Where we meeting this guy?" Louis asked.

"Some place called Ta-boo. Two more blocks and hang a right onto Worth Avenue. You can't miss it, believe me."

In the three years Louis had been in Florida—despite the fact his PI cases had taken him from Tallahassee to Miami—he had never made it over to Palm Beach. But he knew what Worth Avenue was: the Rodeo Drive of the South, minus the movie stars. He slowed the Mustang to a crawl, looking for a parking spot. Some of the store names he recognized—Armani, Gucci, Dior, Cartier—but most didn't register. What did register was the almost creepy cleanliness of the street. From the blinding white of the pavement to the gleaming metal of the Jaguars and Bentleys at curbside, Worth Avenue had the antiseptic look of an operating room.

He pulled the Mustang in behind a black and gold Corniche. Mel sniffed the air like a dog. "Ah, the sweet smell of money."

The only thing Louis could smell was perfume. It took him a moment to realize it was wafting out on an arctic stream of air-conditioning from the open door of the Chanel boutique. A security guard, dressed in blue suit and tie, was stationed just inside the door.

Mel got out and stretched. He pulled his black sports coat from the backseat and slipped it on, then looked at Louis.

"Did you bring a jacket?" he asked.

Louis stared at him.

"A sports coat," Mel said. "I told you to pack one."

"It's eighty degrees," Louis said.

"Get it," Mel said.

Stifling a sigh, Louis popped the trunk and shook out his blue blazer. The Chanel guard had come out to stand just outside the door and was watching him.

"Hey, buddy," Mel called out. "Which way is Taboo?"

The guard's eyes swung to Mel, giving him the once-over before he spoke. "Two blocks back," he said.

They headed east down the wide sidewalk, pausing at a corner for a Mercedes to turn. Louis's gaze traveled up the imposing coral stone façade of the Tiffany & Co. building to the statue of Atlas balancing a clock. It was one-forty. They were late.

"You still haven't told me how you know this guy," Louis said as they started across the street.

"I knew him when I was with Miami PD," Mel said. "I helped him out once when he got in a jam."

This was certainly more than a jam, Louis thought. Reggie Kent was the prime suspect in a murder. A murder gruesome enough to have made the papers over in Fort Myers. A decapitated body had been found in the fields on the westernmost fringe of Palm Beach County. The head had not been found, but the mutilated corpse was identified as a Palm Beach man named Mark Durand.

The sheriff's department had connected the dots, and they had led sixty miles east and across the bridge, right to Reggie Kent's island doorstep.

That was all he knew, Mel had said. Other than Reggie Kent was scared shitless. And that he was innocent, of course.

"This must be the place," Mel said.

The restaurant's large open window framed two blond women sitting at a table sipping drinks. Inside, it was as cool and dark as a tomb, the long, narrow room dominated by a sleek bar. Beyond, through a latticed entrance, Louis could see a main dining room.

Louis knew that Mel probably couldn't see well. His retinitis pigmentosa allowed him to see blurred images if the light was bright, but at night or in the dimness of a bar, he needed help. Not that Mel would ask.

"What's this Reggie guy look like?" Louis asked.

"I haven't seen him in ten years. Blond, stocky. Nice-looking guy, I guess."

The bar was packed, mainly with more blondes, who

had given them a quick, dismissive once-over. There was a man sitting at the far end, waving a hand. Louis led Mel through a sea of silk and tanned legs.

The guy who had signaled them slid off his zebra-print bar stool. "Mel," he said, "My God, you haven't changed a bit."

"Neither have you, Reggie," Mel said, sticking out his hand.

Louis knew Mel couldn't see the guy well, but the lie brought a smile to Reggie Kent's face as he shook Mel's hand. In the blue reflected light of the saltwater aquarium behind the bar, Louis could see Reggie's face clearly. He was probably about fifty, but his round, pale face had an oddly juvenile look. His skin was pink and shiny, almost like the slick skin of a burn victim. Wisps of blond hair hung over wide blue eyes. He wore a pink oxford shirt beneath a light blue linen blazer and white slacks.

As Reggie Kent hefted himself back onto the bar stool he revealed a glimpse of bare pink ankle above soft navy loafers. The whole effect made Louis think of a giant Kewpie doll.

"You've saved my life," Reggie Kent said.

"Let's not get ahead of ourselves," Mel said.

"Yes, yes, of course." Reggie ran a hand over his brow. The bar was frigid, but Louis could see a sheen of sweat on the man's face.

"This is Louis Kincaid, the guy I told you about," Mel said, nodding.

Reggie focused on Louis. "You're the private investigator."

His voice had dropped to a whisper, and his blue eyes

honed in on Louis with intense curiosity before darting away. "You need a drink. How rude of me. Yuba!"

The bartender appeared, a tall woman with long, sleek black hair and almond-colored skin, wearing a white shirt and a black vest.

"You need a refill?" she said in a softly accented voice.

"Yes, another Rodnik gimlet. And whatever my friends are having. Just put it on my tab."

The woman hesitated.

"What?" Reggie asked.

"Don says I can't run a tab for you anymore," she said quietly. "I'm sorry, Reggie."

Even in the dim light, Louis could see the red creep into Reggie's face. Louis pulled out his wallet and tossed a twenty onto the bar. "Bring us two Heinekens and the gimlet," he said.

The bartender nodded and left.

Reggie was staring at something beyond Louis's shoulder. Louis turned and saw two women looking at Reggie and whispering.

The bartender brought the drinks and eyed the twenty. "That's fifty-six dollars, sir."

"What?" Louis said.

Mel laughed.

Louis dug out two more twenties. "Keep the change."

The woman took the bills and left.

"Nice tip," Mel said.

"It's all I had," Louis said.

Mel took a drink of beer. "All right, Reggie, why don't you tell us exactly what is going on?"

Reggie was still staring at the two women, and when

his eyes came back to Mel, they were moist. "Let's move to a table," he said.

They picked up their drinks and followed Reggie from the bar. He paused at the latticed entrance to the dining room, then veered right into an alcove. When they were seated, Reggie took a thin blue pack of Gauloises from his jacket and lit a cigarette. He nodded toward the other room.

"That used to be my table, that one by the fireplace," he said. "They're trying to slowly kill me. Who breaks a butterfly upon a wheel?"

Mel looked at Louis. "Who's 'they'?"

"Everyone," Reggie said. "This whole town."

"Why don't we start at the beginning?" Mel said.

Reggie took a big drink of the gimlet. "Well, it's like I told you on the phone. Four days ago, they found Mark's body out in the fields, and then they just showed up at my door and told me I had to come into the police station to answer some questions." He paused, shutting his eyes. "I had to go to that place and identify him. He . . . had no head. But he had this birthmark on his chest and—"

Mel interrupted him. "This Mark guy was a friend of yours?"

Reggie managed a nod.

"A good friend?" Mel asked.

Reggie picked up his glass and drained it. "Not really. I only knew him for a year, I guess."

"So why were the police so interested in talking to you?" Louis asked.

Reggie took a moment to meet Louis's eyes. "We were kind of in business together."

"What kind of business?"

Reggie looked to Mel.

"You have to tell to us, Reggie," Mel said.

Reggie blew out a long stream of cigarette smoke. "I'm a walker."

"What, like a dog walker?" Louis asked.

"Dog? Oh, good Lord, no," Reggie said. "A walker is . . . well, an escort of sorts." Reggie saw the look on Louis's face and held up a hand. "Not what you are thinking, I assure you. It's rather hard to explain."

Louis and Mel exchanged looks.

"Suppose you try," Mel said. "You know, like we're in fifth grade?"

Reggie looked to the dining room. "See that woman sitting by the fireplace? That blonde in the chartreuse Chanel suit?"

Louis and Mel swiveled to look. Louis focused on a woman in green with cotton-candy hair. Her face had the same taut look as Reggie's, and had the lighting been kinder, she might have been mistaken for being in her fifties. But her neck and hands betrayed her as somewhere past seventy.

"That's Rusty Newsome," Reggie said. "I was supposed to escort her to the Heart Ball on Saturday. Her husband, Chick, never goes to anything, so I always take her." He met Louis's eyes. "That's what I do. I take women to dinner or charity balls or the club. I pay attention to them if their husbands are too bored . . . or too dead."

"You make a living at this?" Louis asked.

Reggie gave him a small smile. "There's a lot of clubs in this town and a lot of widows in each club."

"They pay you?" Louis asked.

Reggie tilted his chin up. "Sometimes they give me a little cash. Sometimes they give me little gifts. It's not just about the money, you see. It's about having a door into a life I could not really afford on my own."

Mel took a long drink from his beer. "I always thought you were a hustler, Reggie."

Reggie looked wounded. "Some might see it that way. But there are good hustlers, and there are bad hustlers. A bad hustler is always trying to get something out of someone. I am always trying to give these women something. I am the first to admit I have no real talents or ambition. But I am a wonderful listener, I know about wine and food, and I am very good at bridge. I know how to make a lonely woman feel happy."

"Is sex part of this walker deal?" Louis asked.

Reggie's eyes shot to him. "Never. The women I know are not interested in sex."

Louis shook his head slowly. "Mr. Kent, I do a lot of work for wives whose husbands are cheating on them. Every time I find a guy's been charging escorts to his Visa, he claims he just did it for the pleasure of the lady's company."

"This is different," Reggie said, reddening. "What a walker offers is friendship. And sometimes a friendship is more intimate than a marriage. But it never, ever involves sex. We are not gigolos."

He picked up his glass and downed the last of the gimlet. Louis was hoping he wouldn't order another one.

"Your friend—what's his name again?" Louis asked.

"Mark," Reggie said softly. "Mark Durand."

"You said he was a walker, too?" Louis asked.

Reggie nodded slowly. "He was just starting out as one, and I was sort of introducing him around, helping him get connected. He would have been a great walker."

"But he turned up headless in a cow pasture," Mel said.

Reggie nodded and looked at his empty glass with longing. Louis wondered if Mel had a credit card.

"How many times have the cops questioned you?" Louis asked.

"Three times," Reggie said with a sigh. "It was in the *Shiny Sheet.* They even used my picture. Awful, just awful."

"Why?" Louis asked.

"Why what?"

"Cops don't question someone three times without good reason. Why do you think they're after you?"

Reggie was silent.

"Talk to us, Reggie," Mel said.

"I was with Mark the night before his body was found," Reggie said. "We had a dinner at Testa's and . . ." Another big sigh. "We had a fight. Everyone saw it."

"About what?" Mel asked.

"What does it matter now?"

"It matters," Mel said.

"Mark had been staying at my place, and he told me he wanted to get his own apartment," Reggie said. "I told him he should stay with me for a while longer."

"That's it?"

Reggie nodded.

"You two weren't—?"

Reggie stared at Mel. "Together? Oh no, no. Mark was quite a bit younger than me. No, there was nothing between us. We were just friends."

Mel drained his beer, set the glass down, and leaned back in his chair, crossing his arms. "Don't lie to us, Reggie."

"I'm not. Like I said, it was just a business arrangement. I was trying to help him. But Mark insisted he was ready to go out on his own and I knew he wasn't ready. This town will eat you alive, and I didn't want that to happen to him."

Mel was silent. Louis waited, watching the two men, wondering what the history was between them. Mel hadn't told him much about Reggie Kent, just that he had known him back in Miami. He wondered how the hell Mel had ever hooked up with a piss-elegant guy like this.

Reggie leaned forward. "You've got to help me, Mel. Please. I don't have anyone else to turn to."

Louis was afraid the guy was going to cry.

"They've hung me out to dry," Reggie said. "Even the police are against me."

"They're cops, Reggie, they're supposed to be," Mel said.

Reggie shook his head vigorously. "No, you don't understand. The police are here to protect us. When that horrible detective from West Palm Beach came here to question me, Lieutenant Swann came with him. They are my friends."

He picked up the pack of Gauloises, but when he pulled out a cigarette, his hand was shaking so badly he dropped it. Mel caught it before it rolled off the table. Mel looked at Louis, then back at Reggie. "So what do you want us to do?"

"Find out who killed Mark," Reggie said.

"Just like that?" Mel said.

"I told you, Mel, I have money. I can pay you. And your friend of course."

Louis was quiet. There was something about this guy he didn't like. His desperation was genuine enough, but something was slightly off. He was sure the guy was lying about something. Or, at the very least, leaving something out of the story.

"Please, Mel," Reggie said.

Mel held out the cigarette to Reggie. "Look, let us go have a little chat with your Lieutenant Swann and we'll get back to you."

Reggie looked to Louis, who nodded.

Reggie took the cigarette and grasped Mel's hand. "Thank you, thank you."

"Easy," Mel said.

Reggie nodded and sat back in the chair, running a hand across his sweaty face. His wide eyes were darting over the crowded room now. He waved at someone and tried a smile but it faded quickly and he dropped his hand.

"I think I better go home," he said softly. "There's a nicely chilled bottle of Veuve Clicquot in my fridge. I think I shall go home and get shit-faced drunk."

He picked up his cigarettes, rose, and held out his hand. Mel shook it. Reggie turned to Louis. "Forgive my manners. I've forgotten your name."

"Louis Kincaid."

Reggie smiled. "Thank you, Mr. Kincaid."

Louis gave him a nod. Reggie took one last long look around the dining room and walked unsteadily back through the bar and was gone.

Louis turned to Mel, who smiled.

"Welcome to Bizarro World," Mel said.

Chapter Three

It was nearly two-thirty by the time they left Ta-boo. Louis had called Lieutenant Swann, who said that if they came right over, he'd have some time to talk to them. The Palm Beach police station was only a couple of blocks away, so they walked. The curbs were bumper-to-bumper with luxury cars, the sidewalks a mix of locals and tourists. It was easy to tell them apart. The locals were whippet-lean in sherbet-colored slacks and sheaths. The tourists trudged along in Nikes and fanny packs, Nikon necklaces hanging from their necks, ice-cream cones dripping on their hands.

A tall woman was coming toward them. Louis's first thought was of a banana. She was thin, dressed in a yellow pantsuit, with sunglasses the size of grapefruits. She was dragging a spidery black dog that was determined to stop at a ceramic trough labeled DOG BAR.

Mel didn't see the dog, and as the woman pulled at the leash, it cut across his shins. Mel groped for balance, and Louis grabbed his hand.

"What the fuck?"

"Stop it, Phoebe!"

"Louis, help me out here, or I'm going to drop-kick the dog into the gutter," Mel said.

"You're hurting Phoebe!" the woman yelled.

Louis managed to free Mel, and with a tinkle of gold bangles the woman dragged the dog away.

"You okay?" Louis asked Mel.

Mel pushed his sunglasses up his nose and nodded. "Any more animals ahead?"

"You're clear."

They walked on. It was at moments like this that Louis considered asking Mel if he ever thought about getting a cane. But it wasn't the kind of thing even a best friend could do—force a man like Mel, an ex-cop, to acknowledge he was only one cockroach dog away from falling flat on his face in public.

They turned onto South County Road, passing more boutiques showing mannequins in fruit-colored capris and seascapes in heavy gilt frames. As they crossed onto a broad median dominated by a big fountain, Louis got his first look at the Palm Beach Police Department.

It was Aspergum-orange, with three roofed peaks of Spanish tile and wrought-iron trim. Except for the showroom-shiny police cruiser at the curb, it could have passed for a small Italian villa.

The station's small circular lobby had the hushed, cool feel of a hotel. Louis recognized the small dome in the ceiling as a security camera. The uniform behind the information window offered them a practiced smile as his eyes traveled over Louis's wrinkled khakis, blazer, and brown face.

It was Mel he addressed. "Can I help you?" the cop asked.

Mel just stared at the cop from behind his yellow-lens sunglasses. Louis stepped up to the window.

"I'm a PI from Fort Myers," Louis said, showing his ID card. "This is Mel Landeta, ex–Miami PD. We're here to see Lieutenant Swann."

"Ah," the cop said. "The lieutenant has been expecting you."

The cop picked up the phone, and less than a min-

ute later the door to the back of the station opened and
a man appeared.

Louis was surprised that Lieutenant Swann was not
in the standard blue uniform. He was wearing the same
kind of street clothes as Louis, but his blazer was pressed,
his khakis razor-creased, his loafers glossy, and his peach
polo shirt didn't look like it came from the sale bin at
Sears. His skin tone, build, and cropped blond hair were
those of a lifeguard, but the pillowed face gave him the
look of a man who ate too much rich food. Still, he had a
little cop in him; it was there in the cunning brown eyes.

"I'm Andrew Swann. Welcome to Palm Beach, gentlemen," he said, extending a hand to both Louis and
Mel. "Would you follow me, please?"

They followed Swann down a hallway lined with portraits of gold-braided police officers and men in dark
suits shaking hands. Swann's office was flooded in sunlight from two tall windows. Beyond, Louis could see a
small courtyard with stone benches set in a blaze of ma-
genta bougainvillea hedges.

"Can I get you some water?" Swann said.

"Yeah, thanks," Louis said.

"Me, too," Mel added.

After Swann had left the office, Louis went to his
glass-and-chrome desk. The spotless surface held a gold
pen stand with Swann's name engraved on the base, a
white phone, a blank desk calendar, a framed photograph of a big red dog, and a stack of papers. They were
the officers' daily log sheets. Louis turned the top one so
he could read the entries: lost dog in the vicinity of the
public beach; bike stolen from Publix; elderly person ill
in Bradley Park.

"Where's the ashtrays and dirty coffee cups?" Mel asked.

"There aren't any."

Louis positioned the log report back in its spot and turned to a bank of teak file cabinets recessed in the ivory walls. Above the cabinets on an otherwise bare wall, Swann had displayed his honors. There was a framed photo of Swann holding a trophy and clasped in a shoulder hug by a gray-haired man wearing the collar stars of a chief of police. Next to that was a walnut plaque for finishing first in a departmental training class on Beach Bicycle Patrol. Two certificates completed the display, the first one from the Optimist Club and the second an award for Departmental Officer of the Month.

Louis stepped closer to read the small type. Last August, an off-duty Swann had commandeered a tourist's air mattress and paddled out into the ocean to save Mrs. Clarence Wright's Jack Russell terrier from drowning.

The door opened. Swann stood there, holding three bottles of Evian. He noticed Louis looking at the certificate but didn't say anything as he came forward and handed him a bottle.

"So, did Mr. Kent hire you?" he asked as he gave the other bottle to Mel.

"Not exactly," Louis said. "It was just a preliminary interview. Kent's afraid he's going to be charged with this murder and asked us to work with the cops to make sure they don't develop tunnel vision, if you get my drift."

Swann's water bottle stopped halfway to his mouth. "The case belongs to the county, Mr. Kincaid," he said. "Our only involvement is to aid the sheriff's office as needed and monitor the interview with Mr. Kent."

"They needed your department's permission to interview a murder suspect?" Louis asked.

Swann opened a drawer and retrieved a cork coaster for his bottle. It was stamped with the Palm Beach city seal.

"It's to their benefit to extend us the proper courtesy whenever their investigations bring them across the bridge," Swann said. "To do otherwise wouldn't get them very far in this town. We're very sequestered here, if you get *my* drift."

Louis heard a soft crack and looked back at Mel, who had opened his Evian and was taking a long drink.

"To prove my point, I will let you in on something," Swann said. "We had already run your plate, driver's license, and criminal sheet by the time you walked into Ta-boo."

"You doing a little racial profiling?" Mel asked.

Swann looked quickly to Mel. "We don't profile here. We do run the plates of every dirty old car with a cracked taillight that crosses the bridge." Swann turned back to Louis. "Your Mustang qualifies on both counts."

Louis used the moment to take a swig from the bottle. He was beginning to understand why the sheriff's office needed an intermediary, a local cop, to open doors in this place. He understood, too, that he and Mel weren't going to get much information out of Swann, given his job as moat keeper. And it was probably a waste of time anyway. Mark Durand was murdered in the far western end of the county. His body was lying in the county morgue. Both places were miles and worlds away from here.

For the second time today, he was beginning to wonder why he had agreed to come here. He had never liked working for the rich. They tended to treat him not as a rectifier of their problem but as a distasteful reminder that something ordinary and sordid had touched their lives. Maybe that was why he was always so broke. He'd rather help some poor slob get his kid back for a couple hundred than sit surveillance on some rich dude's cheating child bride for five grand.

But Mel had asked for his help, and he had relented out of friendship. Now he had to make an attempt, at least.

"Lieutenant, did you know Mark Durand?" Louis asked.

"Just by sight," Swann said. "He hasn't been in town very long."

"Do you know Reggie Kent?" Louis asked.

"Everyone knows Mr. Kent," Swann said. "He's lived here for years and is a fixture here. People like and respect him."

"Do you think he's capable of murder?"

Swann blinked and raised a brow. It was an odd reaction from a cop who should have been used to making evaluations about anyone accused of a crime. But then, one look at the guy's wall revealed that it was highly unlikely that Swann had ever solved a serious crime, let alone worked a murder.

"I'd really like your opinion, Lieutenant," Louis said. "Have you ever seen a display of temper from Kent? Does he drink too much? Does he have a criminal history?"

"No, he has no record whatsoever, and he drinks no more than most people here," Swann said. "I've never seen him lose his temper, either. In fact, that argument Mr. Kent and Mr. Durand had at Testa's was about as angry as I've heard he's ever become. It was most unusual for him."

"Did this argument get physical?" Louis asked.

Swann hesitated, then went to the file cabinets and withdrew a paper from a manila folder. "One of our officers responded to a disturbance," he said. "It began inside, and according to witnesses, Mr. Kent followed Mr. Durand outside to the sidewalk. The summary illustrates the level of violence."

Louis took the report that Swann held out to him. It was written by a patrolman who detailed his intervention in what was described as a "minor verbal altercation." The last line read: "The only property damage was a broken flower pot. Neither subject was injured."

"Detective Barberry told me he was very pleased that we documented everything so thoroughly," Swann said. "He feels this argument will go a long way in showing motive."

Louis thought it was a little pathetic that Swann seemed to want this Barberry's approval so badly. But he could imagine that Swann would be impressed by the gold-badge guy from the big department tossing him a compliment.

"Did Kent tell you that Durand wanted to move out and get his own place?" Louis asked.

"I heard that's what he told Detective Barberry," Swann said, "but if you want my opinion, Mr. Durand didn't want to move out as much as he wanted to break up."

"Break up?" Louis asked. "You mean, Reggie and Durand were . . ."

When Louis didn't finish the sentence, Mel stepped forward. "Were they lovers, lieutenant?"

Swann nodded, amused at Louis's surprise. "Of course they were. Everyone knew that."

Louis looked to Mel before he addressed Swann. "Kent claims they weren't. You have any idea why he'd tell us that?"

"Well, this is just my theory," Swann said. "Like I said, I didn't know Mr. Durand, but I got the sense he was having a little trouble with the closet door. Mr. Kent was always open about his homosexuality, but maybe he was trying to protect his friend's wishes."

Louis looked back at the report. He knew that a domestic partner was always the first suspect when a dead body turned up. And the fact that Kent and Durand had argued the night Durand was killed didn't help Reggie's case. Louis also knew that when one lover brutally killed another, there was often a third person waiting in the wings.

"Did you guys pursue the idea that maybe Durand was seeing someone else and you might have a triangle here?" Louis asked.

"It wasn't our case," Swann said. "And I get the feeling Detective Barberry wasn't thrilled at the idea of hunting down Mr. Durand's other bed partners. He felt he had his suspect."

"But did the possibility occur to you?" Louis asked.

"Me personally?"

"Yeah, you."

Swann took a drink of his water before he answered. "Yes, it occurred to me. Briefly."

"I'll ask you again," Louis said. "Do you think Kent is capable of murder?"

"Maybe. But . . ." Swann said.

"But what?"

"You'd have to know Mr. Kent to understand," Swann said. "I think the idea of chopping off someone's head would simply be too repulsive to him."

Louis laid the officer's report on the desk. Swann had an interesting point. Not only was decapitation an indicator of extreme rage but the act required a taste for the macabre that normal people didn't have.

So why was everyone so quick to believe this mild-mannered middle-aged walker had committed this crime? Why were they, as Kent said, trying to set him up as some sacrificial lamb?

"I'm sorry," Swann said. "I have a meeting to attend. Allow me to walk you out."

Swann held the door for them and followed them back to the front lobby. He said goodbye and left.

"Batzarro's a polite little bastard, isn't he?" Mel said.

"Who?"

"Swann."

"Why'd you call him Batzarro?"

"Jesus, didn't you read comic books when you were a kid?"

"No. Just tell me, all right?"

"Batzarro was a character in the old DC comic books," Mel said. "He worked in Bizarro World and was the world's worst detective."

Louis looked back at the station door. "We're not going to get any help here," he said.

Mel held up his Evian. "But we got French water."

A door clicked open and a uniform came out. "Mr. Kincaid," he said. "Lieutenant Swann forgot to give you this."

Louis went to him and took the slip of pink paper. It was a ticket. On the right side was a list of possible violations, everything from speeding to jaywalking. The box next to "Vehicle Appearance" was checked with a small X, followed by the neatly printed words: "Dirty with cracked taillight."

"You're giving me a repair order for my car?" Louis asked.

"It's not a repair order," the officer said. "It's a ticket. Per city ordinance one-five-three-point-eight, all cars parked on the public streets must be in good working condition and inoffensive to the eye."

"You have an ugly-car law?"

"I'm not sure what you mean, sir."

"How much is the damn fine?"

"Ninety dollars, sir. You have ten days to take care of it. If you do not, we will ask a judge to revoke your driver's license."

Mel chuckled.

The uniform left. Louis jammed the citation into his pocket and looked up at one of the security cameras. He gave a stiff salute, then pushed out the front door. He was yanking off his blazer as Mel came up to his side.

"Why didn't you give him the finger?" Mel asked.

Louis managed a smile. "Let's go see some real cops."

Chapter Four

In Palm Beach, it was all about form. From the undulating eaves of the Spanish-tiled roofs to the precise placement of the potted geraniums on Worth Avenue, everything was designed to please the senses.

Here, five miles west of the ocean and on the ass end of the Palm Beach County airport, it was all about function. From the grab-a-Slurpee gas stations on every corner to the treeless tracts of multilaned boulevards, everything was geared to moving cars along as quickly as possible.

The Palm Beach County Sheriff's Office fit right into its surroundings. It was a huge, blocky complex painted a Crayola-flesh color, tarted up with waxy plants that could survive a decade's drought. A monolithic addition of the same pallid stucco rose in the back, its slitted windows identifying it as a jail.

Louis parked the Mustang near a white and green sheriff's cruiser, and he and Mel went inside.

The lobby was standard law-enforcement fare: yellow cinder-block walls and bulletin boards plastered with wanted posters and notices. The three rows of metal folding chairs were occupied by the usual sorry-looking souls watching *Wheel of Fortune* on TV while they waited for their numbers to be called.

After the sergeant behind the desk tossed Louis and Mel visitor's passes, he buzzed them through. The squad room was a maze of cubicles. There was a lingering odor of tacos and burnt coffee in the air, along with the steady ring of phones.

Louis had called ahead, and Detective Ron Barberry met them at the door to the Violent Crimes Division. He was a squat man with a lion's mane of white hair and a face made for a caricature artist: flat, apelike brow, ragged salt-and-pepper mustache, and horseshoe jaw. His bleary gaze, rolled-up sleeves—revealing a nicotine patch—and unkempt nails tagged him clearly as a cop who lived in the station and the local tavern.

Probably the strip joint Louis had seen at the corner of Gun Club Road.

"You got fifteen minutes," Barberry said as he waved them toward the back of the room.

Barberry parked his butt on the corner of a messy desk. His gaze lingered on Mel like he couldn't figure out what kind of man wore yellow sunglasses. His hard brown eyes finally swung back to Louis.

"You working for Kent?" he asked.

"Not exactly," Louis said. He felt Mel's eyes on him but didn't turn to him. "We're just checking things out right now."

"So what do you want from us?" Barberry asked.

"Kent's afraid you guys have already made up your minds about him and aren't going to look any further," Louis said.

Barberry rooted through the debris in a drawer and came out with a pack of Big Red gum. As he folded a stick into his mouth, he glanced at Mel, who was making his way through the desks toward an empty chair.

"What's wrong with him?" he whispered to Louis. "He got trouble seeing?"

"Yes, I do," Mel said, turning back. "But I can hear really well."

Barberry reddened and pulled out his own chair. "Oh. Sorry, buddy. Here."

Mel gave him a hard stare and came back to sit down, crossing his arms.

Barberry turned back to Louis. "Look, I'm gonna

make this easy for you. That fudge packer Kent is as guilty as a whore with the clap. He needs to hire himself a good lawyer, not a couple of out-of-work PIs."

Louis heard a squeak and looked back to see Mel slowly spinning his chair around away from Barberry.

"Detective," Louis said, looking back at Barberry. "How about a little cooperation here? Mel and I are both ex-cops, and we're not trying to make anyone here look bad."

Barberry glanced at Mel. "You worked in homicide?"

Mel nodded. "Miami."

"So what's wrong with your eyes?"

"Retinitis pigmentosa."

Barberry blinked. "My mom's got the same thing."

"That so?" Mel said.

Barberry nodded brusquely. "Yeah. Shit . . . that's tough. I mean for you being a cop and all."

Mel took off his sunglasses. His face was sunburnt, and he had two white circles around his eyes. "How's your mother doing?" he asked.

"She's got a nurse, but it still ain't easy for her." Barberry cleared his throat and reached for an accordion file on his desk. "Out of consideration for that, I'll throw you two dogs some bones. They found the corpse in Devil's Garden."

"What's that?" Louis asked.

"Some dot-on-the-map place south of Clewiston," Barberry said. "Lots of cattle farms out there. Anyway, some dogs sniffed out Durand around dawn. He was laying in a crappy old cattle pen, naked as a jaybird."

"Did you find his clothes?" Mel asked.

"Nope."

"What about a wallet, jewelry, anything?"

"Nope."

"Has the head turned up yet?"

"Nope."

"Did you find a weapon?"

"Nope."

"What about a time of death?"

Barberry plucked a set of stapled reports from the accordion file and flipped a few pages. "ME's best estimate puts the TOD between midnight and three A.M."

"How did you identify him?" Louis asked. "Prints?"

Barberry nodded. "We got lucky. The sucker was in AFIS."

"He had a record?"

Barberry grinned. "Don't they all? He was busted in Miami on a solicitation charge." He set the papers down and picked up his pack of Big Red. He offered a stick to Mel, who shook his head and pulled out a pack of Kools.

"You can't light up in here," Barberry said. "It's a new law. You gotta go outside with the other lepers."

Mel paused, Zippo lighter in the air, then pocketed the Kools. "How'd you tie him to Kent?" he asked.

"That's the address on record for Durand's driver's license. The boyfriend came here to confirm the ID. Once I met Kent, I knew exactly what I was looking at."

"Any witnesses to anything going on that night?" Louis asked.

Barberry swung his eyes back to Louis. "I guess you'll read this in the papers, so I might as well tell you," he said. "We don't have anyone who saw anything around the cattle pen, but we got a sighting of a car cruising through Clewiston around one A.M. the night before we found Durand."

"What kind of car?" Louis asked.

"Maybe a Rolls-Royce or something like it."

"Get a plate?"

Barberry shook his head, looking for something in the report. "The witness just described it as a 'big rich-guy car,' so we showed him photos of Rollses and Bentleys and shit. He couldn't say for sure what it was. Just that it was a big rich-guy car and it might have been light brown." Barberry closed the file and tossed it onto the desk. "Or maybe white or tan. Or gold."

Louis heard a metallic click and glanced at Mel, who was rhythmically opening and closing the Zippo.

Barberry watched Mel for a moment, then looked back at Louis. "The witness said he read in the *Clewiston News* that we found a body, so he thought he should report the fancy car," Barberry said. "He said he just thought it was weird to see a car like that in a place like Clewiston."

"A Rolls or a Bentley would have a very distinct kind of tire," Louis said. "Did you get any tracks from the area of the cattle pen?"

Barberry shook his head. "No tires. Only dog paws, cowboy boots, work boots, and bare feet that probably belonged to Durand. Oh, and horse hooves, too."

"Horses?" Louis said.

Barberry paused. "Yeah. It was some cowboys down there that found him."

"If the ground was soft enough for all that," Louis said, "didn't you wonder why there were no tire tracks?"

Barberry shrugged. "The main road going in is asphalt and then hard-packed gravel. Kent probably parked on the gravel and made Durand walk to the pen."

Louis couldn't quite envision things the way Barberry described them. He couldn't imagine that, out there in the middle of nowhere, there had been no tire tracks at all. The people who worked out there had to drive some sort of vehicles.

"What kinds of cars do Kent and Durand own?" Louis asked.

"Durand had some beat-up black Honda that's been in the garage for three weeks. The older fudge packer doesn't even own a car." Suddenly, Barberry's eyes shot to Mel. "Hey, do you mind not doing that?"

Mel paused, staring at Barberry, then snapped the Zippo closed. He set it on the desk, his eyes never leaving Barberry's face.

"Kent would have needed a car to transport the body out there," Louis said. "You're going to have to tie him to a vehicle to make your case."

"No shit," Barberry said, bristling. "But Kent could've borrowed a car. I'll place him behind the wheel of something, and once I do that, it's over for him."

"Swann told us Kent and Durand had a relationship," Louis said. "Did you consider there might have been—"

Barberry smirked. "Another man? Sure, I thought about that. But why should I waste my time hunting down some phantom fag when Kent won't even admit he was sleeping with Durand? Give me a fucking break."

The phone on Barberry's desk rang. Barberry answered it, turning his back. Louis looked at the accordion file. He wanted to see the crime scene and the autopsy photos.

Barberry hung up his phone. "Well, gentlemen," he said. "It seems I have somewhere to go. Can I walk you out?"

Barberry gestured toward the door, leaving them no choice but to head in that direction. Mel pushed from the chair, and Louis followed him out to the lobby.

"Tell the fudge packer I'll be over to see him soon," Barberry said at the door, and started away.

"Hey," Mel said sharply.

Barberry turned. "What?"

"Knock that shit off," Mel said.

Barberry stared hard at Mel, like he didn't get it. Then he gave him a hard grin. "Whatever you say, pal."

Outside, they paused as Mel reached for his Kools and stood there in the hot sun, patting his pockets for his lighter.

"Damn, I left my lighter in there," he said. "I'll be right back."

Louis slipped on his sunglasses. The whine of a jet coming in for a landing drew his eyes up for a second, then back to two uniformed officers coming up the walk. They didn't give him a glance as they went inside.

At home, in Lee County, he was used to getting nods of recognition from the local cops. His relationships with the sheriff and the chief were prickly but at least respectful. But here, in Bizarro World, as Mel called it, nothing felt even close to comfortable. Not only was he hitting brick walls with two different police departments, but their own client was parsing the truth about his sex life.

Client. Louis shook his head slowly. Despite his loyalty to Mel, he wasn't sure he wanted anything to do with Kent.

"They found the head," Mel said.

"What?"

Mel came down a step, lighting up a cigarette. "They

found Durand's head," he said. "It'll be here in about a half hour."

"How do you know that?"

"When I went back in for the lighter, I heard the phone conversation," Mel said. He blew out a stream of smoke. "We need to go see the ME."

"He isn't going to talk to us, Mel," Louis said.

"Why don't you call Vinny?" Mel asked. "See if he knows the guy and can get us a few minutes inside."

Vinny Carissimi was the Lee County medical examiner and a good friend of Louis's, and there was a fraternity of MEs across the state, just as there was for cops.

"Let's go find a phone," Louis said.

The medical examiner's office was located around the back of the building. Louis and Mel parked in the last row of the lot, next to a jail transport bus. They watched as a county van pulled up, letting out a deputy with an orange Igloo cooler.

A few minutes later, Barberry came around the corner of the building and disappeared inside. He reappeared forty minutes later, a little paler. Without lifting his head even to look around, he stuck his hands in his pockets and walked away.

Louis and Mel waited five more minutes before they went inside. The automatic doors opened with a wheeze, drawing the attention of a deputy standing farther down the hall, the same one who had brought in the Igloo cooler. Despite the NO SMOKING sign above his head, he was stealing a few puffs of a cigarette. He looked at Louis and Mel like a kid caught in the high school john, then managed to regain some sense of command.

"Hold up," the deputy said. "Who are you?"

Louis paused. As a favor to Vinny, the ME was expecting them, but Louis couldn't be sure the deputy wasn't assigned by Barberry to guard the head from outsiders. So he lied.

"Dr. Vincent Carissimi, Lee County ME," Louis said. "This is Detective Landeta. We're here about the severed head."

"Oh, well, then," the deputy said, gesturing toward the door closest to Louis. "You go right ahead. Dr. Steffel is right in there."

"Thanks."

Louis held the door for Mel and followed him inside. In the large tiled room, three stainless-steel autopsy tables, empty and shiny, sat under hooded lights. Below the shout of industrial-strength Lysol lurked the sour whisper of rotting flesh.

A door near the back opened, and a small woman in green scrubs came through it. She was about fifty, with a pretty pale face and a short, dark pixie haircut.

"Louis Kincaid?" she said, coming forward with outstretched hand.

"Dr. Steffel?" Louis asked.

"Sue Steffel," she said. She looked expectantly toward Mel, and Louis introduced him.

"I appreciate you letting us get a look at Durand," Louis said.

"Vinny and I are old friends," Dr. Steffel said with a smile. "If he vouches for you, then you've got to be okay, even if you are cops."

"Ex-cops," Mel said.

"There's no such thing," she said.

"Point taken," Mel said with a smile.

Dr. Steffel crossed her arms and leaned back against a steel table, giving them both an appraising look. "Vinny says you've got an open mind."

"A mind is like a parachute," Louis said. "It only works when it's open."

"Well, in this room, I work only with the facts," Dr. Steffel said. "And too often I find myself dealing with people who form their theories first and then try to make the facts fit."

"People like Barberry?" Louis asked.

Dr. Steffel held his eyes for a long time, arms still folded.

"We're just trying to find out the truth about Mark Durand," Louis said.

She pushed away from the steel table. "Which part of him do you want to see first?" she asked.

"Either."

Dr. Steffel motioned for them to follow her into a second room lined with freezers. She opened one, pulled out a gurney, and threw back the blue sheet.

The body lay chest up. It had been washed, and the skin was pale gray, the chest, arms, and legs knotted with muscle, the belly flat. Louis swallowed back a rise of bile.

There was something surreal about a body that was in perfect shape but had only a ragged stump of a neck. It looked like a toppled Greek statue.

"You'll notice a pronounced lack of color," Dr. Steffel said. "The blood loss was massive."

Louis stepped closer. There were no other wounds, except for some small lacerations just visible over the shoulder. But the kneecaps were bruised and torn.

"May I?" Louis asked, and nodded to a hand.

"Be my guest," Dr. Steffel said.

Louis took Durand's wrist and turned it so he could see the palm. It was shredded like the knees.

"His knees and palms are torn up," Louis said, for Mel's benefit. "Like he was crawling around."

"Take a look at this," Dr. Steffel said. She turned the body onto its side to expose the back. The red marks extended all the way around the torso. Thickest across the middle of the back, they formed a road map of welts, cuts, and tattered skin.

"It looks like he was whipped across the back," Louis said.

"How bad?" Mel asked.

"Bad."

Dr. Steffel lowered the body back to the gurney. Louis looked again at the bruised knees. The image of Durand groping around in the darkness with a whip cracking behind him was hard to stomach.

"Where is the head?" Louis asked.

Dr. Steffel moved to a smaller drawer. She paused before opening it and looked to Louis and Mel. "You want something to cut the smell?"

Louis and Mel shook their heads. Dr. Steffel pulled out the drawer and the smell spilled out into the cold room. Louis fought back the urge to gag.

The head was lying on its side, facing them. Unlike the body, it was well into putrefication, the flesh swollen and mottled. Part of the left jaw was missing, exposing the lower teeth, and the eyes were gone, leaving only sunken black holes.

"You guys okay?" Dr. Steffel asked.

Louis managed a nod.

"Peachy," Mel muttered from behind a handkerchief.

"The head was found three hundred yards from the body and was out there almost a week longer," Dr. Steffel said. "I'm pretty sure what you see here is the work of animal scavengers. I'll be able to tell more after I get in for a good look."

Louis drew in three shallow breaths, not wanting to risk one deep one.

"Come around to this side," Dr. Steffel said.

Louis and Mel joined Dr. Steffel on the other side of the table. He heard the snap of latex as Dr. Steffel pulled on some gloves. She carefully raised Durand's tangled, dirty hair from his neck.

"The first thing I wanted to know was if the head was cut off or chewed off," Dr. Steffel said. "To do that, I needed to expose the vertebrae and look for tool or teeth marks. It was definitely cut off. Grab that magnifying glass over there and I'll show you."

There was a fresh vertical incision from the base of the skull down what was left of the neck. The vertebrae glinted in the tattered tissue.

Louis picked up the glass and held it over the neck. Even before Dr. Steffel pointed them out, Louis saw two crevices in the bone—knife nicks. One was deeper than the other by a half-inch.

"Hesitation marks?" Louis asked.

"Or miscalculation," Dr. Steffel said.

"What do you mean?"

"The killer could have miscalculated the correct spot to place the weapon," Dr. Steffel said. "Or miscalculated the strength one needs to sever a human neck. Either way, your killer took three swings. The first two are evident here, and the third was complete and fatal."

Louis felt Mel pressing behind him and stepped aside so he could get a look. Mel bent low over the head, lifted his yellow-lens glasses, and squinted.

"Even I can see that," he said. He straightened and moved back quickly, taking a breath. "Any thoughts on the exact type of weapon?"

"I haven't had any time to check my catalogues and make any comparison," Dr. Steffel said, "but I can tell you it's going to be a long blade of considerable strength and narrow width. Something that allows a wide-arc swing that would give the killer the momentum needed to sever the neck."

"Like a sword?" Mel asked.

Dr. Steffel smiled. "That's the first thing that came to my mind," she said. "But it's important we don't jump to conclusions. There are many other kinds of weapons out there that could do the trick, and we need to eliminate them one by one."

"Do you have any idea what position Durand was in when he was decapitated?" Louis asked.

"Unless his killer is twenty feet tall, Durand was kneeling," Dr. Steffel said. "Again, I can be more precise later, but based on what I've seen so far, I'm estimating his killer to be between five-eight and six feet."

Reggie was about five-nine, Louis thought. But Reggie also looked like he had never seen the inside of a gym.

"Dr. Steffel," Louis said, "how much strength would it take to cut off a head?"

"Well, it's not easy to behead someone," she said. "In the old days, they used axes and broadswords, and you had to be pretty experienced to hit your mark. But then they invented the guillotine to make the task easier."

"So, an out-of-shape guy could do this?" Louis asked.

She nodded. "If the blade was sharp and the person swung it just right, he could lop the head off. Strength-wise, he wouldn't have to be Conan the Barbarian."

A phone rang somewhere in another room, and male voices carried behind it. Louis did not want to be caught here in an unauthorized interview and end up spending the next six hours in a jail cell on a trumped-up obstruction charge. But he had one more question.

"Do you know if any evidence was picked up around the scene?" he asked. "Cigarette butts? Candy wrappers? Anything?"

"I know they didn't find much," Dr. Steffel said. "You'd have to talk to the techs to be sure. But I doubt they'll be very forthcoming. Their supervisor is Barberry's cousin."

Dr. Steffel withdrew a business card from her pocket. "Call me if you discover anything worthwhile. I'll be glad to give you my sense of things."

Louis stuck the card in his pocket and started to leave, but a final question popped into his head. He turned back to Dr. Steffel.

"Doctor," he said, "have you ever seen anything like this before? A decapitation with torture?"

She shook her head. "I've been a medical examiner for fifteen years, some time here and some out west. I've never seen anything quite like this. It takes a mean son-ofabitch to whip someone when he's on his hands and knees and probably begging for mercy."

Dr. Steffel looked back at the head and slowly closed the drawer. The stench lingered in the air.

"I'd say this took a true monster," she said.

Chapter Five

After he left the medical examiner's office, the first thing Louis did was put the top down on the Mustang. Anything to get the smell of the rotting head from his nose.

They were heading west into the low sun. Louis slowed the Mustang to a crawl as the WELCOME TO CLEWISTON, AMERICA'S SWEETEST TOWN sign came into view.

"Is this berg as ugly as I remember it?" Mel asked.

Louis eyed the Dixie Fried Chicken joint. "It's a good place to pass through, I'd say."

"I was thinking that may be exactly what that tan luxury car was doing."

"What do you mean?"

"If you were driving from coast to coast, this is an easy route. The car could have been coming over from the west coast and just passing through."

Louis was quiet. Mel was right but only to a point. In the three years Louis had lived in Fort Myers, he had never once seen a Rolls-Royce or a Bentley. Even out in the moneyed neighborhoods on Sanibel and Captiva, the most extravagant cars he ever saw were Mercedes-Benzes and BMWs. Still, there was plenty of big money down near Naples, where a Rolls wouldn't have been out of place.

"We need to stop and ask where this Devil's Garden place is," Louis said.

"Go a couple miles west of town, then turn left when you see the sign for the airstrip," Mel said.

"How do you know that?"

"I asked the receptionist back at the ME's office while you were in the can."

They were out of Clewiston now, the stores lining Sugarland Highway giving way to the black dirt of the fallow fields. Louis spotted the sign for the airstrip and hung a left. They were heading due south, away from the cane and vegetable fields into pastureland divided by low wood fences. Clots of cattle stood motionless beneath the low branches of the live oaks, snow-white egrets perched on their rust-brown backs.

Louis knew there were cattle ranches in Florida, but he had always assumed they were somewhere north, maybe by the horse farms up near Ocala. It hit him again, as it had on the drive over, that Florida was many small unexpected worlds within its one large obvious one.

The road was deserted. Except for an occasional shed or other outbuilding in the pastures, there were no houses, no stores, no sign of human activity. It was, Louis thought, a good place to dump a body.

But the body hadn't been dumped. Mark Durand had been murdered out here. How had his murderer gotten him out here? And why bother to go so far from Palm Beach when any freeway drainage ditch or canal would have done the job?

They were coming to an intersection. A small state-issued green sign said: DEVIL'S GARDEN. Louis pulled the Mustang to a stop on the side of the road.

Mel sat up in the seat and adjusted his sunglasses. The yellow lenses maximized contrast, so Louis suspected Mel could see pretty much what he himself could see: a T-section stop sign, a cluster of gigantic live oaks swagged with Spanish moss, and miles of pastureland.

"Why'd we stop?" Mel asked.

"We're here."

"Where the hell is the town?"

"There is no town."

Mel surveyed the empty pasture and blew out a sigh. "Fucking Barberry. He knew there was nothing here. How are we going to find this damn cattle pen?"

Louis spotted a small sign in the weeds on the other side of the road. He got out and went to it. MARY LOU'S STRAIGHT AHEAD. He hadn't noticed any stores as they drove in. Back in the car, he turned the Mustang around and headed back north.

"We giving up?" Mel asked.

"Not yet."

A quarter-mile down the road, there was another sign with an arrow pointing right. The small cinder-block building sat back from the road in a dusty parking lot. There was an empty rust-pocked pickup truck at the lone gas pump.

"You coming in?" Louis asked as he parked.

Mel was squinting at the store. "Bring me a Coke."

The interior of the store was dark after the brightness of the sun, a cramped warren of shelves holding canned goods, cereal, motor oil, and baskets of mangoes and blackening bananas. A skinny girl of about ten in a dirty sundress and dusty bare feet was staring longingly at a display of penny candy. Louis spotted an old cooler in the back and got a Coke. As he passed the girl, he paused, fished in his pocket, and held out a quarter. The girl hesitated, then took it.

"Thanks," she whispered.

"You're welcome."

At the counter, Louis waited until the man behind the register was finished ringing up a six-pack of Tecate beer for an old fellow with a biblical beard.

"I wonder if you could help me out," Louis asked as the man handed him his change.

"You lost?" the man asked.

"Sort of. Did you hear about the body they found out here last week?"

The man glanced at the old geezer, who was staring out the door at the Mustang. "Everybody around here heard about it," the counterman said.

"Do you know exactly where it was found?" Louis asked.

"Can't say that I do."

"Why you wanna know?" the old man asked.

"I'm helping the police with the case," Louis said.

"That so? Then how come you don't know where the body was?"

"I'm not looking for trouble. Just a little help."

The old man held Louis's eye for a moment, then turned away. So did the guy behind the counter.

Louis picked up the Coke and pushed through the door. Back at the Mustang, he handed the Coke can to Mel.

"Any luck?" Mel asked as he popped the top.

"We're on our own."

Louis noticed the little girl coming toward the car,

carrying a small brown bag. She stopped before Louis, her jaws working a wad of bubble gum.

"I know where they found it," she said.

"Where?" Louis asked.

The girl looked at Mel and back at Louis. "Five dollars."

Louis laughed. The girl didn't break a smile.

"I tell you where it is for five dollars," she repeated.

"Mel, give her five bucks," Louis said.

"Forget it."

"Give her the money."

Mel grunted, dug in his pocket, and held out a bill.

The girl started to grab it, but Mel pulled it back, holding it just out of her reach.

The girl pointed south down the road. "Go past the sign for Devil's Garden. The next road you come to, turn left. Take the road to the end. The pen is there. But it's real old, and you have to look hard for it in the weeds."

"You gonna trust this little extortionist?" Mel asked Louis.

"Give her the money," Louis said.

Mel handed over the five. The girl stuffed the money into her dress pocket and ran off, her bare feet kicking up dust whirls in the still air.

Louis got back into the car and headed south. He almost missed the turn. The car left asphalt for rutted gravel. The trees grew thick overhead, an arching tunnel of live oaks. They passed a sign that read STATE LAND AR- CHER PRESERVE.

The gravel road ended abruptly in some high weeds. Louis stopped the car. About fifty feet ahead, he saw a spot of yellow—crime tape hanging limp on old wood.

"Why'd you stop?" Mel asked.

"The road ends. I don't need a flat out here. Let's walk it."

Louis shut off the engine. An overwhelming quiet surrounded them, as heavy as the humid, still air. Then came the metallic whine of cicadas.

"Watch your step, Mel," Louis said. "The ground's pretty rough."

The pen was a skeleton of rotting old wood. Its shape was hard to discern in the chest-high weeds, but it looked to be a series of fenced areas fronted by a narrow incline that rose about six feet from the ground, like it was meant for loading animals. Louis's only frame of reference for what he was seeing was a couple old westerns. *Hud* came to mind, and that scene that had always bothered him, the one where the cowboys were talking about having to shoot their diseased cows, and the stupid animals were crammed into a pit, bumping into each other with panicked eyes.

Mel came up to his side. He pulled a handkerchief from his pants and ran it over his glistening bald head. "Does this look as bad as I think it does?"

"Yeah. Looks like it was abandoned a long time ago."

They picked their way through the weeds and into the first section of the pen. The ground was sandy dirt, and the high sides of the gray wood made the space feel like a large wooden cage.

The cicadas stopped screeching. The quiet flowed in.

"See anything useful?" Mel asked.

"Not really," Louis said, his eyes scanning every inch of the fences and sand. "Just some rusted chains hanging on a gate."

They went into the next section, but it was the same as the first. A narrow passageway led to another pen. It was a maze of rotting wood, weeds, and sand. Then, suddenly, the space opened. They were in a large pen, maybe thirty feet square, with a small listing lean-to tucked in a corner. Another ribbon of limp yellow tape hung from the fence.

Louis went to the center. It looked like a portion of the sand had been scooped out with a shovel.

"This is where he was killed," Louis said.

"How can you tell?" Mel asked.

The sun was starting its descent. Louis figured Mel couldn't make out any details now. "It looks like the crime-scene guys might have taken soil samples."

Louis scanned the ground. It had rained during the last week, so there was nothing left of the prints Barberry had mentioned. There didn't even seem to be any evidence of blood.

Louis stood still, listening. No sounds now. Even the birds had retreated to their night roosts. There was no feeling, either. And he had always been able to get a feeling about a murder scene in the past. It was nothing he could put his finger on, nothing he could articulate. And he never told anyone about it. But he had learned to trust the weird vibration that sometimes came when he stood in the place where a person had taken his last breath.

But there was nothing here. Except for a strange feeling of something old and buried. Like an abandoned grave or—

"I can't see it."

Mel had spoken in a whisper. Louis turned to him.

"Can't see what?" Louis asked.

"Reggie. I can't see a guy like him coming out here and whacking off someone's head. A guy like him wouldn't even know this place was here. Shit, we barely found it."

Louis was quiet. He had been thinking the same thing. But how much did Mel really know about this Kent guy?

Louis went over to where Mel was and waited until Mel had lit his cigarette. "What are we doing here, Mel?" he asked.

"What do you mean?"

"Reggie Kent. Why do you care what happens to a guy like that?"

"A guy like what?"

Louis was silent. A hot current started up his neck.

"Gay," Mel said. "You can't even say it, for crissake."

"That's not—"

"And you're wondering how I even know a guy like that."

The way Mel had drawn out the last two words made Louis fall silent again. Mel took a long drag on his cigarette.

"I met Reggie about fifteen years ago, when I was a sergeant with Miami PD," Mel said. "One of my guys called me on an assault. It was Thanksgiving, and the only reason I was working that night was because I switched with a guy who wanted the day off to be with his family. When I got there, I saw Reggie sitting on the curb, all beat up. The uniform pulled me aside and said the two guys who attacked him were in a bar across the street. The uniform wanted my permission to no-action it."

Mel blew out a long stream of smoke. "The uniform said it wasn't worth the paperwork to go arrest them."

"What did you do?" Louis asked.

"I told the uniforms to leave," Mel said. "Kent said he didn't have anyone he could call, so I drove him to Jackson Memorial."

Mel tossed the cigarette to the sand and ground out the butt with his heel.

"I went back to check up on him the next day," he said. "Turned out he had a concussion. Almost lost an eye. He was in the hospital for a week. I went back and saw him a couple of times. The nurse told me he never had any visitors. No family, either."

Louis watched as Mel worked his jaw. It was the same agitated gesture he had done back at the sheriff's office, just before he told Barberry to "knock off that shit."

"So, you and Kent," Louis began. "You became friends?"

Mel shook his head. "Nah. But at Christmas, he sent me a fruit basket at the station."

Louis smiled.

Mel smiled, too. "Yeah, I took some shit for that."

"But you never saw him?"

"Nope. But every year, he sent a Christmas card to the station."

"How'd he find you after you quit?" Louis asked.

"Beats me. Somebody at the station probably told him I had hired on with Fort Myers PD. My home number's in the phone book." Mel took off his glasses and rubbed his eyes. "I was shocked as hell when he called me. Our paths crossed once a long time ago. That's all."

The sun was setting, great streaks of red. Louis wanted to start back so they wouldn't be caught out there when the dark came. But Mel had pulled out the Zippo and another Kool. The lighter flared and snapped closed with a sharp *clink*. Mel's face was lost in the dusk.

Again, the question came to Louis: What were they doing here? What was he doing here? Swann and even Barberry looked down their noses at him because he didn't have a badge. But he was used to that. He was even used to being the only black guy in a town of whites. What he wasn't used to was feeling like some kind of insect because he wasn't wearing the right jacket.

Face it, Kincaid, this isn't about Reggie Kent. It's about you not feeling like you fit in.

"I know you don't want to take this case," Mel said.

Louis looked at him. Mel was a silhouette, the tip of his cigarette glowing.

"I'm just not sure there's a case here, Mel," Louis said. "I'm not sure we can be any good to this Kent guy."

"Is it because he's gay? That's not like you to—"

"No," Louis said. "That's not it."

"What's bothering you, then?"

"Nothing. Nothing's bothering me."

Mel took a long drag on the cigarette. "Something's eating at you, Rocky. It's been going on for a while now. You aren't a barrel of laughs even in the best of times, but lately—"

"Gee, thanks."

"You know what I mean." Mel's cigarette glowed in the dark. "Is it Joe?"

Louis was glad Mel couldn't see his face. Truth was, it was Joe, in part. He hadn't seen her in months, and they had barely talked on the phone since Thanksgiving. He loved her, but he had the feeling now that they were drifting, and he wasn't sure anymore it was toward each other.

"All right," Mel said. "You don't have to tell me."

They were quiet for a long time. A cricket started up nearby. Louis could barely make out the yellow crime tape now.

"I want to try to help Reggie," Mel said. "And you know I can't do this alone anymore."

Louis heard the catch in Mel's voice, knew how hard it was for him to admit that.

"Let's give it a day, all right?" Mel said. "See how far we get."

Louis shut his eyes. No vibration. No feeling. No sense of what had happened in this strange place. His intuition was telling him only to get out of there.

"Let's go," Louis said. "You better take my arm."

Mel put a hand on Louis's sleeve, and Louis led him out of the darkness.

Chapter Six

L ouis voted for the Motel 8 in West Palm Beach. But Mel overruled him on grounds that if they intended to infiltrate Bizarro World, they had to be in the thick of it. A call to Reggie led them to the Brazilian Court, a couple of blocks off Worth Avenue. But when Louis discovered the rooms started at $250 a night, they retreated to Ta-boo to regroup. Yuba the bartender suggested they try a place nearby called the Palm Beach Historic Inn.

The small hotel had one double left, a Spartan but immaculate room with twin beds. It was $85 a night, but it was right next door to the police station. There was the bonus of a cozy little bar in the lobby.

That's where Louis left Mel around ten-thirty, with the last of the Burger King takeout and a second snifter of Rémy Martin. Feeling too restless to go back upstairs and watch the grainy TV, Louis set out on the deserted streets.

He found his way back to Worth Avenue, nearly empty now of cars and people. Drawn by the salty smell, he headed toward the beach, down a long block and under the watchful eyes of the mannequins in Neiman Marcus's windows. Alone on a bench at the beach, he found himself under new scrutiny, from a Palm Beach PD car that sat at the curb behind him for a full fifteen minutes before it finally pulled away. Louis was certain the cop behind the wheel had called in and someone had told him there was a black dude in town but he was okay.

After twenty minutes, he started back. The last thing he wanted was to listen to Mel snore, so he kept going down Worth Avenue.

The shops were closed, but most of the window lights were still on, some illuminating little velvet cushions imprinted with the outlines of the jewels that had been locked away in safes at closing time. The only sparkle now came from Christmas decorations.

A giant Christmas tree had sprouted in the intersection in front of Tiffany's, decorated with huge gold and white balls. The small palms lining the avenue had been strung with white lights and lit from beneath by aqua spotlights that made the trees look weirdly fake.

Louis paused. Christmas already?

He walked on. Three years in Florida, and it still took him by surprise. There was no set signal, no warning from the weather, that the holidays were coming. It always left him mildly depressed.

Joe was suddenly there in his head. And their conversation when she had called to wish him happy birthday last month.

Why don't you come up to Michigan for Christmas?

I don't know, Joe.

Don't you miss it?

She had been talking about the snow and all of the seasonal stuff. But he had heard: *Don't you miss me?*

Of course he missed her.

He paused in front of a flower shop, looking at a pay phone. It was past midnight, but he was sure she'd be up. She had never been the kind to go to sleep early, even when she was exhausted.

He used his phone card to dial long-distance to northern Michigan. Surprisingly, there was no answer at her cottage. He hesitated, then tried the sheriff's office.

As he listened to the phone ring, he had the thought that he had become too used to phones going unanswered. Busy . . . she was always so damned busy now.

She had gone back to Michigan almost a year ago, and spring was spent in a frenzy of campaigning for the sheriff's position in Leelanau. Their plan to meet in late summer had been postponed as the election neared. She won the election easily, campaigning on an ethics and crime-prevention platform. Because he hadn't heard much from her since Thanksgiving, he could only assume things were hectic. But a part of him always wondered what the hell the sheriff had to do in a quiet resort town like Echo Bay.

Finally, a woman answered the phone. He knew most of the dispatchers up there, but he didn't recognize this voice.

"Is Joe Frye there?"

"Sheriff Frye? Ah . . . yes, I think she's still here. Who's calling, please?"

"Louis Kincaid."

"What is this regarding, Mr. Kinsey?"

"Kincaid. I'm a friend. Just tell her it's Louis."

"Yes, sir, Mr. Kinsey. Please hold."

The woman set the phone down with a *clunk*. Normally, there was nothing in the background but soft voices and an occasional crackle of a radio, but tonight the line was filled with laughter, tinkling glasses, and Christmas carols.

A party. The department was having its annual Christmas party.

"This is Sheriff Frye."

"Hey, Joe, it's me."

She was almost shouting. "I'm sorry. Who?"

"It's Louis."

"Oh. I can barely hear you. How are you?"

There was a sudden burst of nearby laughter, and he waited until it faded before he answered.

"I'm fine," he said. "Say, listen, I was wondering . . ."

"Oh, Louis, hold on," Joe said. Her voice grew muffled, as if she'd moved the phone away from her mouth. "Enough with the mistletoe, Mike. Go pester your wife."

He waited for her to come back on the line. When she did, it was a shade quieter. She must have found an empty office.

"So, did you decide if you're coming up for Christmas?" she asked. "We're supposed to get ten inches. Should be beautiful."

"I'm on a case."

"Oh," Joe said. There was a long—disinterested— pause. "What kind?"

"Cleaning up rich people's messes. I'm in Palm Beach."

"Well, at least they'll pay well this time," she said.

"I'm not so sure this joker will."

Another pause. "Why take the case, then, if you dislike the client so much?"

It's not like you're driving a squad car that says TO PROTECT AND SERVE.

"Mel asked me to," he said.

"Mel . . . how is he? I've been thinking about him lately."

"It would be nice if you bothered to ask me how *I* am," Louis said.

What a lousy thing to say. What the hell is wrong with me?

"I don't have to ask how you are," Joe said. "I can tell by your voice. And I think we already talked about this at Thanksgiving, Louis."

He was quiet. The background noise was picking up again, and he heard someone launch into a drunken version of "Oh Christmas Tree."

"What do you want from me, Joe?"

There was a long pause before she spoke. "I want you to want something from yourself," she said. "And while you work out exactly what that is, maybe we should . . . maybe *I* should give you some space."

They were already fifteen hundred miles apart. How much more space did she think he needed? Still, even as he thought it, he realized he had known something like this was coming. Drifting . . . they were drifting. He was drifting.

"So, we're just ending it?" he asked.

Joe sighed. "Louis, this isn't a good time to talk about this."

"You're the one who brought it up, Joe."

There was a long pause. "I think we need to take a break," she said finally. "I think we need to find out exactly how we feel about . . . everything."

"Does that include other people?" he asked.

Again, quiet on her end. He leaned his forehead against the phone, closing his eyes.

"Okay, then," Louis said. "Have a merry Christmas."

"Louis, wait—"

He hung up and walked away from the phone. He went almost two blocks before he paused at the corner of South County Road. The sound of a woman laughing drifted out to him on the warm night. He headed toward the laughter.

Ta-boo was still open. Through the open window, he could see the crowd, two deep at the bar, loud and garrulous.

He squeezed in through the doorway and made his way to the far end near the waitress station. Yuba, the pretty Indian woman, was hard at work but gave him a smile as she strained a martini into a glass.

"Heineken, right?" she asked.

"You're good," Louis said.

Another smile, and she was gone, sweeping to the other end of the bar to deposit two drinks and returning a moment later with his beer and a frosted glass.

"Should I start a tab?" she asked.

Louis hesitated. "Sure."

A combo started up somewhere in the back of the restaurant. Through the latticework, Louis could see a couple drift out to the dance floor. The man was a slender white-haired gent in the requisite blue blazer setting off yellow slacks; the woman was tan, blond, and at least twenty years his junior. She wore a tight, low-cut pink dress, and Louis couldn't take his eyes off her huge breasts even though he was sure they weren't real.

Yuba returned and set a glass votive before him. She smiled when she saw him watching the blonde but said nothing. She pulled a purple Bic from her vest pocket. Her black eyes danced with the flare of the candle.

"Where's your friend?" she asked.

His mind was still on Joe, and for a second, he thought Yuba meant her.

"The tall fellow with the yellow glasses," she said.

"Asleep," Louis said. "Thanks for the tip about the hotel."

"You guys didn't seem like the Brazilian Court types," she said.

He had the feeling she knew exactly who he and Mel were and why they were on the island. He wondered if she lived here, but he had a feeling that, just like the gardeners and the maids he saw standing at the bus stop, she traveled back across the bridge at night.

"You're here to help Reggie, aren't you?" Yuba said.

"Yes," Louis said.

She grabbed a towel and ran it across the already spotless bar. She was looking for an excuse to linger, Louis realized, but was this about Reggie—or him?

Yuba nodded at his glass. "You want another one?" she asked.

"Yeah, thanks."

After she had brought the refill and made the rounds of the other customers, Yuba drifted back.

Joe was still there, cluttering his thoughts. He knew beer alone wasn't going to make her go away long enough for him to sleep tonight. He suddenly wanted a reason to keep Yuba in front of him, wanted the distraction of her lovely face, if only for the next hour.

"I'm glad you're helping Reggie," Yuba said, lowering her voice. "Reggie's a good guy. He's real. That's not easy to find in this town."

"I'm beginning to understand that. How well do you know him?"

She shrugged. "He comes in here almost every night. I've been here two years. We're not friends or anything, but in this business, you get a pretty good feel for people."

Louis looked at her skeptically over the rim of the glass.

"I went to a party at his place once," she said. "He has a nice house up on the north end." When Louis didn't respond, she added, "That's where the real people live."

"Ah," Louis said.

Someone called to her. Yuba waved to the customer to wait. "Reggie wouldn't hurt a fly," she said.

"You sure about that?" Louis asked.

She gave him a hard stare, then left to serve the guy at the other end of the bar.

The second beer went down more quickly than the first, and he suddenly wanted a third badly. But the bar was now three-deep, and he couldn't get Yuba's attention. He kept his eyes trained on her back, willing her to turn. No dice. That's when he felt the weight of someone's gaze and turned.

It was hard to miss her, even in the crowd. Turquoise silk. Milk-white skin. Carrot-red hair that could never be natural. And eyes below the soft sweep of her bangs that were trained on him like lasers.

A bare hint of a smile, and then it disappeared behind the rim of her martini glass.

Suddenly, Yuba stepped in, blocking his view. She set a frosty glass of beer in front of him. "From the lady in blue," she said with a half-smirk before leaving.

Louis found the redhead's eyes again, raised his glass in a salute, and took a drink.

The woman smiled back. Then she touched the arm of the man sitting next to her to draw his attention away from the conversation he was having with another couple seated nearby. She whispered something, and he gave her a quick peck on the cheek and turned away. She slid off the stool and picked up her drink and purse. Louis watched as she made her way toward him.

There was no vacant stool, so she wedged herself between him and the bar. She was tall, her body lush in the silky dress. A necklace of twisty turquoise glowed against her skin. Her face was taut, but as she smiled, a fine spray of lines at the edges of her eyes sprang into relief.

He couldn't guess her age. He couldn't even think of anything to say.

She leaned toward him and extended a perfectly manicured pink-nailed finger to the wet surface of the bar. She traced something in the spilled beer, a question mark that quickly faded.

The laser eyes found his.

"Louis," he said.

She traced another question mark.

"Scorpio," he said.

She smiled and traced another question mark.

"Democrat?"

She laughed. "I'm Sam."

The man sitting next to Louis tossed a fifty onto the bar and left. Sam slid onto the stool.

"Thank you," he said, raising his glass. "For the beer."

"You looked like a man in need," she said. When she crossed her bare legs, the front of the silk dress parted, revealing her thighs. Louis struggled to keep his eyes on her face.

"You're the detective I've been hearing so much about," she said.

"Word gets around quick here," Louis said.

"How's the investigation going?"

The last thing Louis wanted to do was talk about Reggie right now. He wanted—what? To take away the sting of Joe's words? He glanced over the redhead's shoulder and caught Yuba's eye. There was something in her expression, like she could read his mind, and for a second he thought of settling his tab and going back to the hotel.

He looked back to the redhead, looked right into her

eyes. "I can't talk about it," he said. "Client privilege, code of ethics, and all that."

The redhead smiled, then caught Yuba's eye and motioned for a refill on her martini before she turned back to Louis.

"Do you know Reggie Kent?" Louis asked.

"Of course. I live here."

He wanted to ask her if Reggie had ever been her escort but then realized it might insinuate that she was, what? Desperate? Alone? Or, worse, old? Reggie had said he never lacked for the company of widows. Up close, he could see she was maybe in her late forties. Beautiful, for sure, but not young. He snuck a glance at her left hand. She was wearing a wedding band of diamonds.

He allowed himself a small, wry smile.

"What's so funny?" she asked.

"Nothing. It's just not my night."

"Are you sure about that?"

Again, he met those eyes. They were dark, maybe blue. He couldn't tell in this light.

Yuba brought the fresh martini. Sam plucked out the toothpick and ate the olive, her eyes never leaving his. Then she picked up the martini and, with one quick flourish, drained it.

She slid off the stool, taking her purse. When she leaned close to Louis, he caught the scent of her perfume for the first time—cloves and something smoky.

"My Jag is parked in front of Tiffany's," she whispered. "Wait ten minutes before you come."

She left, swallowed up in the crush of bodies. He was so stunned it was a full minute before he finally took a drink. He sat there, staring at the yellow fish swimming in the aquarium behind the bar as he finished the beer.

Yuba wandered over and ran a towel over the bar in front of him. There were questions in her eyes, but Louis understood suddenly that she wasn't going to ask them. Palm Beach's weird code of discretion extended even to bartenders, maybe especially to bartenders. It was okay for a married woman to pick up a stranger in a bar. It wasn't okay for anyone to notice it had actually happened.

"Last call. Another beer?" Yuba asked.

Louis hesitated. Until this moment, he hadn't decided what he was going to do.

"No, just the check, please."

Outside, a cool breeze was blowing in from the ocean. The street was deserted. Louis paused, then headed away from South County Road. There was a black Jag idling in front of Tiffany's. As he approached the passenger side, the tinted window whirred down.

Sam leaned over. "That was fifteen minutes."

"My watch runs slow," Louis said.

"Get in," she said.

He slid into the cocoon of leather and orange dash lights. The door shut with a soft *shood* sound, and the tinted window went up. It was quiet, the outside world gone.

"Where are we going?" Louis asked.

"For a ride," Sam said.

The Jag pulled away from the curb. A couple of turns and a detour through a residential area, and they were on the road that ran along the beach, heading south.

The condominiums soon gave way to mansions

set on sweeping lawns on one side of the road, private beaches on the other. The farther south they went, the bigger and more isolated the huge estates seemed to become. Greek temples gleaming white in the moonlight, mini–Versailles palaces, sprawling Spanish villas glowering behind gates.

Louis strained to look back as they passed a huge place that looked for all the world like that onion-domed cathedral in Russia.

"So, where are you from?" Sam asked finally.

"I live on Captiva," Louis said.

"Really? Do you know where Marco Island is?"

"Over by Naples."

"I have a little beach house over there."

Louis had been to Marco Island years ago on a case. It was a rich playground, gated-community kind of place. He wondered what her definition of a *little beach house* was.

"This part of the island looks different from the north end," Louis said.

When Sam glanced over at him, her surprise was there to read in the soft glow of lights. "How do you know that?"

The lie came easily. "I've been to Reggie Kent's house." A pause. "Have you?"

She smiled as she shook her head. "No, I don't have much reason to go up there."

The car slowed, and she turned right. The headlights lit up an high iron gate. "We're here," she said.

"Where?"

"My place."

He didn't even see her push a button, but the gates

were slowly opening. He could see the lights of a small house on the left. But it was a looming structure far down the driveway that drew his eye. It was high and turreted, that much he could see. There were only a few feeble lights on inside and no outdoor lighting at all. Louis could only stare as one image came to his head: an old Spanish castle, like the one in the movie *El Cid*.

The car came to a stop.

"Yes, it's awful, I know."

He looked over at Sam.

"It's the oldest home in Palm Beach, a real Mizner, and we're restoring it," she said. "I'm staying in the guesthouse." She nodded to the house on the left.

There was no point in pulling punches at this point. "Where's your husband?" Louis asked.

"Rome."

She put the Jag in gear, pulled left into a gravel driveway, and cut the engine. The guesthouse was Spanish in style and looked new. To Louis's eye, it looked like it could comfortably house a family of ten.

He felt a flush of heat. He was out of his element. And Joe was suddenly there with him. What the hell was he doing here? Was this some stupid revenge thing?

"Is something wrong?"

He looked over at Sam. Sam with no last name. Sam with a husband somewhere in Italy. Sam with the soft white skin and smell of cloves.

Suddenly, very suddenly, it hit him. He felt off balance, out of place, off his game. And where that sort of feeling normally put him on guard, now he felt only . . .

"Louis?"

. . . liberated.

He leaned over the console and kissed Sam. Her lips were soft, the clove smell strong. The dart of her tongue into his mouth surprised him.

When he drew back, it took her a moment to open her eyes. "Let's go in," she said.

The details of the house registered in a blur. A beamed ceiling, living room of plush furniture, dark wood, and thick carpets. Paintings on dark green walls with dim lights over them. She led him down a hall and into a bedroom. Soft lights, odd straw wallpaper, dark furniture out of a rich man's safari dream.

A huge canopy bed dominated, ripe with white pillows and topped with a meringue of a comforter. Silky netting hung from the canopy, stirred by a paddle fan overhead.

She saw his expression and laughed softly. But she didn't say anything. She just came to him and kissed him deeply. Then she pulled his shirt from his pants and raised it over his head. Her lips were hot on his chest, and he closed his eyes.

Joe was suddenly there again.

It had been so long.

Her hands were urgent now at his belt. He started to help her, but she pushed his hands away. He let her do the rest, and when she stepped back to look at him, he didn't move.

"You're beautiful," she said.

Then, slowly, with a smile, she reached behind her back. He heard the zipper, then the turquoise dress puddled at her feet. She gave him only a moment to look at her—cream white skin, full breasts, long legs that met at a carrot-red thatch.

He laughed softly as his eyes lingered there.

She read his thoughts and laughed. Then she came to him and pressed her body against his.

Joe was there again for a second, then vanished.

It had been so long. It had been too long.

Her lips were hot at his ear. "Forget her," she whispered.

And he did. For the next hour, there was nothing but the feel of engulfing warmth, the smell of sweat and salt spray, the tangy taste of her skin, the sounds of her cries in his neck.

Then, suddenly, the game changed. She turned him onto his back and straddled him, taking control. Each time he was at the brink, she would pull back, teasing him, her hair damp with sweat on his chest, her mouth devouring him.

When he could stand it no longer, he threw her on her back and entered her with a ferocity he had never felt before. She clung to him.

"Die with me," she whispered.

Her body gave a final shudder that triggered his own. He collapsed on her, panting. It was a moment before the room swirled back. Another moment before he realized her arms had fallen from his back and she was not moving.

"Hey," he whispered.

Nothing.

He slid onto his side. Her body glowed with sweat in the candlelight, her head to one side, her eyes closed.

"Hey," Louis whispered. "Are you—?"

Her chest wasn't moving. He scrambled to his knees and gave her cheek a tap. "Sam, wake up!"

Nothing.

"Jesus," he whispered. His eyes darted to the phone on the night table, then back to Sam. Without thinking, he slapped her hard.

Her eyes sprang open, and she gasped, drawing in a ragged breath. She seemed dazed, and then her hand came up to her cheek as her eyes locked onto his.

"I'm sorry," Louis said. "God, I'm sorry, Sam. You were out cold, and I had to—"

Her eyes had gone as dark as a night sky. She turned her head away as she rubbed her face. "I think you'd better go," she said.

Louis didn't move.

"Just go," she said.

He was so stunned he didn't know what to say. Hell, what could he say? She had just ordered him out of her bed. He slipped out of the bed and found his clothes. When he was dressed, he looked back at the bed. Sam had turned on her side, away from him.

He went out to the living room and let himself out the front door. It was only when he saw the black Jag parked in the driveway that he remembered he had come there in her car.

Louis glanced up at the moon. It was probably only about three miles back to the hotel. He went down the driveway and scaled the gate. He turned north on the beach road, and started the walk back.

Chapter Seven

The roads narrowed, the lots shrank, the towering hedges disappeared. As Yuba had said, the north end was different from the rest of the island.

This was where Reggie Kent's home was, up on the far part of the island where the "real people" lived. The people who ran the bookstore, the florist, the dry cleaner, the people who might not have inherited their millions but had socked away enough to stake a small lot in one of the modest neighborhoods of older bungalows that made up the north end.

Two days ago, Louis might not have been attuned to the difference. To his eye, the homes they were passing now as the Mustang drove along North Ocean Boulevard were pretty damn nice. But after being in Sam's bedroom last night—lying in her soft Egyptian cotton sheets, sated and sticky with salt spray, listening to the ocean hiss in the blackness—Louis understood with a sensory clarity that there were two worlds within this larger Palm Beach one.

"I heard you banging around in the dark last night," Mel said. "Where did you go?"

Louis glanced over at Mel, then back at the road. "I couldn't sleep. I went for a walk on the beach."

"At four in the morning?"

"Yup."

Louis was glad Mel let it go. He didn't want to have to tell him about Sam. Or about the phone call with Joe. He didn't even want to think about it too much, because he knew if he did, he would overthink it and overanalyze it. He would maybe start listening a little too closely to that voice gnawing at his ear.

You cheated on Joe.

Screw that. She's the one who ended it.

You love her.

I'm not a fucking monk.

None of this had been in his head last night. Sex with Sam had been just a white heat of need, not just of physical desire but to cauterize the wound Joe had left.

"What road am I looking for?" Louis asked.

"Reef Road," Mel said. "Reggie said to look for a white house with portholes."

Louis spotted the white house on the corner by the small round windows. He pulled into the circular drive and cut the engine. Reggie came out through the front door. He was wearing crumpled white linen pants and a loose shirt the color of the ocean. He was barefoot and holding a tumbler of what looked like lemonade.

"Welcome to my humble little castle," he said with a smile. "Come on in. I hope you haven't eaten lunch yet. I've set out a little snack."

Louis followed Mel inside. It wasn't a big house by any Palm Beach standard, and though it had none of the overwrought luxury of Sam's guesthouse, it was a place designed for comfort and with great taste. The living room of white tile and walls opened up to a small dining room with a rattan dining table and chairs. Beyond that, the open sliding-glass doors offered a view of the ocean. The furnishings looked slightly dated—a light blue sectional sofa and Danish modern chairs and teak tables. The place smelled of salt spray, mustiness, and French cigarettes. The walls were covered with paintings, gaudy Technicolor tropical landscapes.

Reggie noticed Louis staring at a painting of two panthers surrounded by fruit trees.

"Do you like it?" Reggie asked.

"Yeah, it's very . . . colorful," Louis said.

"It's by Jean-Claude Paul," Reggie said. "He's Haitian. These are all Haitian. I've been collecting them for years."

Mel was standing close to a painting of a nude, squinting. "Nice," he said, turning back to Reggie.

Reggie shrugged. "People here wouldn't be caught dead with this sort of thing on their walls. But I love them." His eyes lingered on the panthers for a moment, then he smiled. "Let's go out on the lanai, shall we?"

Reggie led the way out onto a small patio. It was surrounded by orange bougainvillea hedges and crowded with potted flowering plants. Over the top of one hedge, Louis could see a construction crane and the skeleton of a three-story mansion.

"What are they building over there, a bank?" Louis asked.

Reggie turned back from the buffet table, a pitcher of lemonade in his hand. "Oh, that," he said. "It's my new neighbors. I think they are Russian. They bought four lots, tore down the houses, and are putting up that monstrosity. What can you do? Some people have all the money but absolutely no taste."

Louis thought that it didn't look any worse than some of the other places he had seen on the south end of the island last night, but he kept quiet.

"What can I get you to drink?" Reggie asked.

"A beer?" Louis asked.

Reggie grimaced. "I'll have to check. I might have—"

"Lemonade's fine," Louis said.

"Same here," Mel said from the chaise in the corner where he had stretched out.

Reggie handed them each a slender tumbler, and they took seats near Mel. Louis took a drink of the lemonade. It was heavy with vodka.

Reggie's mini-buffet was set up on the table between them. The centerpiece was a glass bowl set in ice and filled with what looked like mud. Also on the table were tiny cups of minced onion and chopped egg and a carefully arranged assortment of toast wedges.

"Please, help yourself," Reggie said.

Mel sat forward and picked up one of the tiny pearl-handled spoons and began to heap some caviar onto a toast wedge. Louis watched him, surprised. Louis had never seen him eat anything but bloody steaks, grouper sandwiches, and tacos.

"Is this osetra?" Mel asked.

Reggie's face reddened slightly. "Yes. I'm sorry, but beluga is a bit out of my price range these days."

"Don't apologize," Mel said, helping himself to another toast wedge. "It's good. Tastes like nuts."

Reggie smiled. "I'm glad you like it. This one is from Iran. I first tasted it at a birthday party for—"

"Excuse me," Louis interrupted. "If you two are done comparing culinary experiences, can we talk about the problem at hand?"

Reggie stared at him for a moment, tiny spoon in midair. "Yes, you're right, of course," he said. He carefully spread some caviar on a toast wedge. "Where do we start?"

Louis leaned forward. "We start, Mr. Kent, with you. You're not exactly leveling with us."

"What do you mean?"

"I mean that we aren't going to take your case if you don't start telling us the truth."

Louis felt Mel's eyes on him but didn't look at him. They hadn't talked any more since yesterday in the cattle pen, and Louis had decided he needed to push Kent before he agreed to take this on.

Reggie looked at Mel, as if he expected him to intervene on his behalf.

"Louis is right, Reg," Mel said. "I want to help you, but if you don't tell us what we need to know, we're out of here."

Reggie sighed. "Okay, ask me what you must."

"Let's start with your relationship with Mark Durand and why you lied about that," Louis said.

Reggie shifted in his chair, an unlit cigarette dangling from his fingers. "I didn't really lie," he said.

"Were you lovers or not?" Mel asked.

"We were," Reggie said softly. "But it ended months ago."

"How and when did it start?" Louis asked.

"I used to occasionally go to a club over in West Palm," Reggie said. "I had been alone for quite some time, and when I saw Mark that night at Kashmir's, I knew he was someone I could fall in love with."

Reggie stared out at the ocean, a sad wistfulness in his eyes. Louis let him have a few more seconds, then prodded him.

"He felt the same?"

"No," Reggie said. "Like I told you, he was a lot

younger. And at the time he was seeing this rich lawyer from Fort Lauderdale. The man was married and used to drive up to West Palm looking for anonymous, one-night encounters. He was paying Mark money for seeing him on a regular basis."

"So Durand was a prostitute," Louis said.

Reggie cringed. "Well, he was arrested in Miami for that once," he said. "But to me he was simply a beautiful young man in need of direction."

"How did you convince him to leave the other guy and hook up with you? You're not rich, are you?"

"Heavens no," Reggie said. "In fact, I usually rent this place out during the season to make money." When he saw the look on Louis's face, he went on. "I rent it out, pocket twenty grand a month, and go live in someone's guesthouse until Easter."

Louis glanced at Mel, who shrugged.

"But when this whole thing hit the newspapers, my tenant backed out," Reggie said. He looked around, shaking his head. "I mean, between the lawn man, the pool, the maid, the taxes, I have no idea how I'm going to get by if I don't find someone—"

"Mr. Kent, please," Louis said. "You were talking about how you and Durand got together."

Reggie nodded. "Yes, I'm sorry. Well, Mark wanted to leave the lawyer, so I told him he could come stay with me. He was living in a ratty little efficiency by the turnpike, so you can imagine how excited he was when he saw Palm Beach."

"So what went wrong?" Mel asked.

Reggie was silent for a long time. "The age thing, of course," he said softly. "That, and Mark realized I wasn't really rich. At least, not rich enough. But I didn't want him to leave." He gave a wry smile. "No fool like an old fool, they say."

He drew deeply on the cigarette and blew out a slow stream of smoke. "I knew I couldn't afford to keep him happy, and I had no illusions about him being faithful. So we struck a deal."

"What kind of deal?" Louis asked when Reggie didn't go on.

"I need a refill," Reggie said. He rose, picking up his tumbler. "Anyone else?"

Mel held out his glass. Louis hadn't touched his. Reggie went to the bar and returned with two more lemonades, handing one to Mel. Reggie sat down, staring glumly into his drink.

"What was the deal?" Louis pressed.

"This is so sordid," Reggie muttered.

"So is prison," Mel said.

Reggie took a big drink before he went on. "The deal was that if Mark stayed with me, I would leave him alone. And I would help him become a walker."

"He agreed?"

"Not at first. But I was able to convince him it was an easy way for him to have the kind of lifestyle he wanted, and that he could be a great walker if he tried."

"So you trained him?" Louis asked.

"You don't train to be a walker," Reggie said. "You either have it or you don't. Mark was very handsome, and he had a certain *avoir la gueule*." When he saw their blank looks, he added, "A certain animal appeal."

He snuffed out the Gauloise. "All I did was help him round off the rough edges. I got him to a good tailor, taught him how to order wine. Then I started introducing him to my ladies. I was determined to transform him into the kind of gentleman who could escort the richest women in the world. I didn't want him to have to depend on men to pay him for sex anymore."

"You're a regular Pygmalion, Reg," Mel said.

Reggie's gaze drifted out toward the ocean. The sunlight was making his eyes water and in them Louis could see both grief and love. But there was something else stewing in them, too. Betrayal?

Reggie seemed to feel Louis's eyes on him and he reached for a pair of sunglasses and slipped them on.

"What happened?" Louis asked.

"Well, things were good at first," Reggie said. "He was starting to get some requests for functions. As I watched him blossom, I took great solace in the idea that, if nothing else, I saved him from the awful life he had before."

Louis couldn't see Reggie's eyes behind the sunglasses but he could tell the man was having trouble not breaking down.

"But after a few months I knew something was wrong," Reggie said. "Mark started drinking heavily and disappearing for days at a time. He was moody and restless, like he was looking for something that he couldn't find here on the island. God knows what that was. There isn't anything you can't get here."

"Did you talk to him about it?"

Reggie nodded. "One night I got a call from Rusty Newsome. Mark didn't show up to take her to a party. When he finally came home the next day I asked him what was wrong. He wouldn't talk about it. And he wouldn't call Rusty to apologize. It was so embarrassing."

"That was it? He broke one date?" Louis asked.

Reggie shook his head. "There were others. And he just kept pulling further away from me. I was desperate to keep him, so I started smothering him, nagging him about where he was and who he was seeing. I started buying him all these gifts. For his birthday, I gave him a beautiful monogrammed robe from Kassatly's. I found it the next day wadded up in the bottom of his closet."

Reggie fell quiet. The silence was broken by the screech of wild parrots taking flight from a palm tree, streaks of acid green against the vivid blue sky.

"Tell us about the fight at Testa's," Mel said. "What started it?"

Reggie took another drink. The ice cubes tinkled against the crystal as he set the glass down. "I found a Patek Philippe in Mark's bedroom," he said.

"What's that?" Louis asked.

"A watch," Mel said.

"Not just a watch," Reggie said. "It was a brand-new Calibre anniversary model made just this year. I could only imagine the price."

"So what? You said you got gifts as a walker," Louis said.

"Not like that," Reggie said. "God, even low-end Pateks are twenty grand."

"Did you ask him about it?"

"I was afraid to tell him because he'd know I had been snooping in his room. So I asked him to meet me at Testa's for dinner. I was hoping that in a public setting, Mark would be civil and calm."

"How did he explain the watch?"

"Well, when he showed up I could tell he had been drinking." Reggie shook his head slowly. "When I showed him the watch, he got very angry. He grabbed it and put it on, saying he had worked hard for it."

"He was prostituting again?" Louis asked.

Reggie looked miserable. "That's what I thought, so I asked him. But then he told me that he wasn't even gay."

"What?" Louis said.

Reggie put up a hand. "I know, it sounds crazy. He told me he was really straight and only did it to make some easy money. Like I said, he was obsessed with money."

Louis's mind churned with questions—all of them too delicate and, hell, maybe too stupid—to ask someone like Reggie. But he had to admit that he didn't understand a man like Mark Durand. Either you were straight or you weren't, and if Mark was straight, Louis couldn't imagine any amount of money that would entice him into a man's bed.

"So, where did he get the watch?" Louis asked.

Reggie closed his eyes.

"Mr. Kent," Louis pressed. "You have to tell us."

"I kept asking him," Reggie said softly. "Finally, he just exploded and said that he was—pardon my language, these are his words, not mine—that he was 'fucking some of hottest bitches on the island' and making more money than he ever thought possible. He said one of them gave him the watch."

"He swung back to the ladies?" Louis asked.

"Not just any ladies," Reggie said sharply. "My ladies. My friends."

Louis sat back in the chair. "You sound angry."

"I am angry!"

"Why, because he betrayed you?"

Reggie wrenched off his sunglasses. "He betrayed the profession! Don't you get that?"

Louis just stared at him.

Reggie suddenly rose. "If you'll excuse me for a moment." And he disappeared into the house.

Louis heard the tinkle of ice and looked over at Mel. "What the hell is his problem?" Louis said.

"He's angry," Mel said, and took a sip of the lemonade.

"I'd say that's a pretty good motive," Louis said. "Durand led him on."

Mel slowly set the tumbler down and sat forward, resting his long hands on his knees. "Forget about the personal shit for a moment," he said. "Reggie took this guy under his wing and trained him in a profession. Now, we might think it's a pretty weird profession, but to Reggie it's a noble calling. And it wasn't supposed to include sex."

Louis shook his head.

"Think of it this way," Mel went on. "How would you feel if you were a cop—"

"I was a cop once, Mel."

"I know, I know. Okay, you're a cop, and you have to train a rookie. But the rookie disregards the rules, screws up protocol, has no respect for the badge, and is generally an asshole. How would you feel?"

"It's not the same thing, Mel."

"It is to Reggie."

At that moment, Reggie reappeared. His face was red, like he had scrubbed it hard. He had a fresh tumbler of lemonade. He sat down in his chair, spotted his sun-glasses on the patio floor, and scooped them up. He put them on and tilted his chin up toward Louis.

"What else do you need to know?" he said calmly.

"The police report said you and Durand got physical outside the restaurant," Louis said. "What happened exactly? And don't leave out any details."

Reggie drew in deep breath. "I told Mark I didn't care what he did to me, but I was not going to let him get away with trashing my reputation. He told me to go fuck myself and left. I followed him out."

"And what happened?"

Reggie was silent.

"What did you say to him, Mr. Kent?" Louis asked.

"I wish you'd call me Reggie."

"What did you say to him?"

Reggie glanced at Mel before he spoke. "I told him that all I had to do was whisper in the right ear, and he'd be dead in this town."

"Dead?"

"I didn't mean it literally," Reggie said. "I meant that he would be a pariah. No more lunches, parties, or pretty watches. I told him that with one word from me, he would be escorted off the island and dropped off at the nearest Greyhound station."

"Why did the cops come?" Mel asked.

Reggie looked miserable. "We argued, and he pushed me. So I pushed him back. I didn't mean it, but I was so angry. I wasn't trying to hurt him, but he was so drunk he just fell. He hit his hand on the sidewalk and broke the watch's crystal. He lost it, just lost it, screaming at me about the watch and calling me ugly names."

Louis remembered a detail from the police report. "There were people seated outside who heard you."

"I suppose," Reggie muttered. "And then the police came."

"What did they do?" Louis asked.

Reggie shrugged. "They just told us to behave ourselves, and they left."

"What happened to Durand?"

"I don't know," Reggie said. "The last I saw him, he was walking up Royal Poinciana."

Louis glanced at Mel, who was spreading caviar on the last toast point. He wondered if Mel was thinking the same thing he was—that when Detective Barberry heard this whole story, he would be even more convinced of Kent's guilt. If that was possible.

"We're going to need the names of these women Durand was with," Louis said.

"I don't know who they are," Reggie said. He gave an indignant tip of his chin. "Ironically, I would have been the first to know this sort of thing before. Gossip is currency in this town. But now—"

Before Louis could reply, a delicate ringing drifted from the house. Reggie perked up like an English pointer, then pushed his chair back.

"My phone," Reggie said. "It hasn't rung in days. Please excuse me."

Louis watched Reggie until he disappeared, then leaned over toward Mel. Mel's face was turned toward the salted breeze, his eyes closed.

"Mel, your friend is in deep shit here."

"He didn't do it."

"The level of rage in this crime points to someone the

victim knew," Louis said. "Give me another theory that jibes with that kind of senseless torture."

"A hate crime. Maybe Durand was still cruising the bars across the bridge."

"Good news!"

Louis looked up. Reggie was walking toward them holding a white cordless phone. "That was Margery," Reggie said, smiling broadly. "She wants me to take her to the ballet tonight." He glanced at his watch. "Oh, dear, I have to get to the cleaner's. My best tux is in there."

Louis stood up. "Look, Mr. Kent, I think it might be better if you laid low for a while."

"You don't understand," Reggie said. "This is Margery Leigh Cooper Laroche. You don't say no to Margery. She's one of the core people."

"Core people?" Mel said.

Reggie's face was lit with excitement. "I knew they'd rally around. I knew they'd help me. Margery must have put in a word. The dear, dear lady . . ."

"Reg, I think Louis is right," Mel said. "I don't think you should be going out right now."

Reggie ignored him, gathering up the plates and silverware. "I know this is very rude, and I know we have things to talk about, but you'll have to excuse me. I have a million things to do."

He stopped suddenly, turning to Mel.

"Wait, wait!" he said. "I just had the best idea. Do you have a tux?"

"What?" Mel croaked.

"A tux, do you—?" Reggie frowned slightly. "No, no, of course you don't. What am I thinking." He set the plates down. "We'll have to find a rental. Horrifying, I know, but I think there's a place—"

"Reggie, what the hell are you talking about?" Mel asked.

Reggie stared at them. "Well, you're coming to the ballet with me, of course."

Louis laughed.

"And you," Reggie said. "You have to come, too."

"Get serious." Louis was still laughing.

Reggie's expression had gone slack. "I'm quite serious," he said. "As you keep telling me, my life is at stake here. If anyone knows the women Mark was sleeping with, Margery does. And if you're ever going to get any doors to open for you in this town, Margery is the key." He paused. "Now, do you want to meet her or not?"

Louis looked back at Mel, who had taken out the Zippo and was lighting up one of Reggie's Gauloises.

"Looks like we're going to the ballet, Rocky," he said.

Chapter Eight

Louis thought it was damned ironic that they had to go to West Palm Beach to rent tuxedos. But as Reggie pointed out, every man who lived on the island owned his own formal wear.

"Renting a tux is like . . ." Reggie curled his lip. "It's like wearing bowling shoes. You don't know who has done what in them before you."

They were in Reggie's living room, sharing a quick

glass of wine before they left for the ballet. Mel was sitting down, one patent-leather shoe propped on a knee, long arm draped over the back of the sofa. He looked like the rented tux had been custom-made for him.

Louis turned and caught sight of himself in a mirror. He, on the other hand, looked like he was going to a prom.

He felt Reggie staring at him.

"What?" Louis snapped.

"That tie. You can't go out wearing that tie."

"Why not?"

"Didn't they have one that wasn't a hook kind?"

"What do you mean?"

"One that ties, like the kind Mel has on."

Louis looked at Mel, who just shrugged.

"You said it had to be black. This was the only black one they had left," Louis said through gritted teeth.

Reggie sighed. "I'll be right back."

He disappeared into a bedroom. Louis looked at Mel. "You start up again, and I will deck you, I swear."

"I didn't say a thing," Mel said. "I think you look swell."

Reggie returned with a tie. "Here, but make sure I get it back."

Louis took it but didn't move. The tie dangled like a dead snake in his hand.

"Don't tell me you don't know how to tie a bow tie," Reggie said.

"No, I don't know how to tie a fucking bow tie."

Reggie snatched the tie from Louis. Before Louis could react, Reggie reached up, unhooked the rental tie, and flung it to the sofa. He wrapped the black silk around Louis's neck and started to fumble with the ends.

Louis raised his chin, his eyes going to the ceiling. The starched collar of the shirt was digging into his neck. Reggie's wine breath was warm on his face.

"Stop fidgeting," Reggie said.

"Just tie the damn thing," Louis muttered.

Finally, Reggie threw up his hands. "I've never done this from this side before!" He looked at Mel.

"You're on your own, boys," Mel said.

Reggie grabbed Louis's shoulders and spun him around so he was facing the mirror. Then Reggie lined up behind him, and his hands came up around Louis's neck from the back.

"Hey!" Louis said.

"Hold still! This is the only way I can do this!"

Louis shut his eyes, steeling himself against the soft touch of Reggie's hands on his neck. Finally, he felt Reggie back away.

Louis opened his eyes. He didn't think the tie looked any different from the other one, and it was crooked. But he was damned if he was going to give Reggie a second chance.

Mel was laughing.

"Let's go," Louis muttered.

He got his revenge when they went outside. Reggie stopped cold in the driveway when he saw the Mustang.

"That's your car?" he said.

"Yeah," Louis said. "And it's not a rental, so I know exactly who has done what in it."

Louis opened the door, flipped the passenger seat forward, and gestured to the backseat. "Mel rides shotgun. You get the back."

But Reggie's eyes were focused on something over Louis's shoulder. And he was smiling. Louis turned just as a black Rolls pulled into the driveway. The car was so quiet Louis hadn't heard it coming.

A stout guy in a dark suit and cap got out and opened the back door.

Louis was amazed to see tears brim in Reggie's eyes. "She sent the car," he whispered. "The dear thing sent the car."

He wiped at his eyes and turned to Louis and Mel. "We'd better go before it turns into a pumpkin."

The Royal Poinciana Playhouse was a small jewel box of a theater with red velvet flocked wallpaper, gold sconces, and a view of the Intracoastal Waterway from its terrace. As soon as they got inside, Reggie told them he had to meet Margery Cooper Laroche at the private party for the ballet patrons. He apologized that he couldn't take them along but stuffed two tickets in Mel's hand and pointed them to the lobby bar before he disappeared.

They got some wine and found their way to the terrace. It was crowded with men in tuxedos and women in gowns. The temperature had taken a dip into the sixties, giving the women an excuse to drag their furs out of storage. Diamonds glinted in the mink like animal eyes in headlights. The air smelled of expensive perfume and a coming rain.

Mel took one of the tickets from his pocket and peered at it. "I can't read this," he said, handing it to Louis. "What's on the bill?"

Louis took the ticket. *"Swan Lake."*

Mel grimaced. "Going to be a long night."

"You've seen this before?"

"Sure," Mel said. "Great love story. The dashing young prince Siegfried is seduced away from his true love, the white swan Odette, by the evil black swan Odile."

Louis took a drink. "How's it end?"

"He's eaten up with guilt, so he throws himself in the lake and drowns."

Louis finished the wine in one gulp and looked out over the water. For a second, he thought about telling Mel about Sam. A part of him felt bad because she was married. But that wasn't what was really bothering him. It was the fact that with one act of sex with a stranger, he was admitting it was over with Joe. She had been the one who opened the door to the possibility. But last night, he had been the one who shut it.

Mel was his friend. He wanted to talk to him, but he couldn't, because Mel and Joe had once had their own relationship, and he wasn't sure whose side Mel would take.

"Speaking of swans," Mel said. "He's going to be a problem, you know."

Louis turned back, glad for something to take his mind off Joe. "He's just a guard dog."

"Yeah, but he's like that cockroach dog that tried to take me out yesterday. It may be small, but you don't want to get between it and its master."

It started to drizzle. In a rush of taffeta and tittering, the women were ushered inside by their men. Louis and Mel followed, staking out a corner by the front door in the suddenly packed lobby. There was nothing to do but stand there and take in the crowd. It was the same mix he had seen at Ta-boo: blondes with pneumatic cleavage squired by old men with gleaming teeth and clots of brittle matrons wearing golf-ball-size jewels.

There was an odd desperation to the laughter and chatter. Louis watched as everyone went through a weird choreography of kisses—quick pecks on the lips, full-court mouth presses, European air kisses, double air kisses moving from cheek to cheek. Louis had the feeling that behind each kind of kiss, you could somehow read a person's status.

A flash of red hair caught Louis's eye. He strained to see, and then, suddenly, the crowd parted for a moment, and there she was.

Sam—lovely Sam with no last name—standing near the bar. Her hair was twisted up on her head, her shoulders white against her emerald gown.

She was talking to a guy with dark slicked-back hair and a tangerine tan. It was the guy Louis had seen her with at Ta-boo, the one she had sent on his way with a kiss to the cheek.

The guy took a drink of champagne and leaned in to hear something Sam said. But all the while, his eyes, with the hard sheen of his onyx cuff links, wandered around the room.

Louis stared at Sam, willing her to turn.

Finally, she did. Their eyes met. Louis gave a discreet nod and a smile.

Sam turned away. She said something to the man. He put a hand at the small of her back and led her away.

Louis felt a hot flush travel up the back of his neck. *Well, fuck you, too, lady.*

"What's the matter with you?"

Mel's voice didn't register for a second. Finally, Louis turned to Mel. "Nothing."

The lights dimmed, and a soft bell sounded. The ushers were trying to herd people inside the theater, but no one seemed interested in moving. A sudden crack of thunder drew gasps. Beyond the double doors, rain began to pound down, and the awning billowed and flapped in the wind.

Mel pulled out a handkerchief and wiped his sweating head. "Where the hell is Reggie?" he said.

On cue, Louis spotted Reggie's pink face in the crowd. He had a white-haired woman in gray on his arm.

Reggie's face was shiny with sweat, but he was smiling broadly as he drew up before them.

"Gentlemen," he said, "may I present Margery Leigh Cooper Laroche."

The woman was more than six feet tall, stick thin, and straight-backed, wearing a severe gown of gray satin set off with long strands of gray, white, and black pearls. There was no way to tell exactly how old she was, but Louis was guessing somewhere north of seventy. Whatever her age, she had been a beauty in her day. Her sharply chiseled face was accented by a slashing red mouth and deep-set gray eyes heavily outlined in black. As she slowly raised a bony hand, Louis thought of one of the majestic blue herons he often saw prowling the beach in front of his cottage.

"Hello," she said.

If she hadn't been so stunning, Louis would have thought she was a man, her voice was that deep. Shit, the way things were here in Bizarro World, maybe she was.

Mel stepped forward to take her hand. He didn't shake it, just held it gently like a medieval courtier. "Ma'am," he said with a smile.

"You're Mr. Landeta." She smiled. "Thank you for being such a good friend to Reggie."

Reggie blew out a breath that lifted his wispy blond hair.

Margery Laroche focused on Louis, extending her hand. "And you must be Mr. Kincaid."

Louis held her hand the way Mel had. Her eyes bored into his. Over Margery Laroche's shoulder, he saw people staring and whispering.

"Maybe this wasn't such a good idea," Reggie said softly to Margery. "I don't want to put you in a bad—"

"Ishkabibble!" Margery Laroche said.

The lights dimmed again, and the bell sounded. The ushers once again tried to move the crowd, this time with raised voices, like teachers admonishing children to take their seats.

"We should go in," Reggie said.

Margery Laroche was still staring at Louis, still holding his hand. The crowd eddied around them, the whispers rising.

Margery Laroche finally let go of Louis's hand. "Fucking Philistines," she murmured.

Mel laughed. Reggie turned beet red.

The lights dimmed again. The bell pealed. Finally, the crowd was thinning out.

Margery Laroche's hard gray eyes went from Mel to Louis. "I'm not going to let these high-hatters destroy Reggie," she said. "What can I do to help?"

Louis looked to Reggie. He was staring at the floor, no longer trusting himself to speak.

"Just tell us the truth," Louis said.

Margery's large red mouth tipped in a wry smile. "The truth," she said. "*Quel* interesting. Be at my place tomorrow at ten. We'll do breakfast."

She turned sharply and started away. Reggie mouthed a quick "Thank you" to Louis and Mel and hurried to catch up.

"What do you think?" Mel asked

Louis watched Margery Leigh Cooper Laroche disappear into the darkness of the theater. "I think that woman knows where all the bodies are buried."

Chapter Nine

Last night's rain had lingered, turning the morning as dark as dusk. Louis kept one eye on the curbside street signs and the other on his rearview mirror looking for cops. He hadn't had a chance to get the Mustang's broken taillight fixed yet.

Worse, Mel wasn't along to help. He had begged off the breakfast meeting with Margery Leigh Cooper Laroche because of a blinding headache. Louis was worried, because the headaches, a symptom of Mel's eye problems, seemed to be coming more frequently.

Margery's home was "on the third El" off South Ocean Boulevard, Reggie had said. Louis spotted a curb sign: El Bravo Way. He slowed. The next one was El Brillo Way.

Another block, and there was El Vedado. Three Els. He swung a right.

Reggie claimed he didn't know the house number. "I've never had reason to mail anything to her," he said, adding that it was "the big pink house on the right. You can't miss it."

It was a three-story monster of a Spanish villa. And as Louis leaned forward to peer through the sweep of the wipers, he realized the property extended the width of the island from the ocean to the Intracoastal.

Louis turned into the broad circular drive, killed the engine, and jogged through the rain to the massive door under the portico. There was no doorbell, just a tiny security camera tucked into a corner above the door. He stared up at it and finally, feeling ridiculous, gave a small wave.

A few moments later, with a loud click, the door swung open. A small, stoop-shouldered old man in black stood aside to let Louis in. "Mrs. Laroche is waiting for you, sir," he said in a hoarse, British-accented whisper.

Louis followed the shuffling fellow through a drafty entrance hall of high arches and marble and down a long corridor of polished tiles and mirrors. It was very warm and moist, like there was no air-conditioning. Huge palms in blue ceramic pots sat motionless in the still air. The place looked like an ancient Spanish castle, and Louis's mind clicked back to the *Palm Beach Life* magazine he had thumbed through last night back at the hotel when he couldn't sleep. There was an article on an architect named Addison Mizner, who had single-handedly left his imprint on Palm Beach back in the twenties—everything from Worth Avenue's little alleyways to oceanfront mansions.

Sam was suddenly in his head, along with her brush-off at the ballet. And Joe was there with her, the sting of her words still in his ears. What did it say about him that he had to read an article about a dead architect three times before he fell asleep?

"Madame is in the loggia," the old fellow said, gesturing to an archway.

Loggia?

The first thing that registered was the bracing sweep of rain-scented air. Two of the room's walls were open archways with views of the gray ocean. From the high concave ceiling, painted sky blue, two paddle fans moved in lazy circles. The room was furnished in rattan, its blue cushions gently worn and dotted with limp yellow throw pillows and one needlepoint pillow with a dog's face on the sofa. A glass coffee table was heaped with art books, glossy magazines, and newspapers, and two table lamps, with bases shaped like squatting monkeys, held out against the gloom. Off in the corner, a wrought-iron table was set with blue and white china, sparkling glasses, and a bouquet of white calla lilies.

"You're right on time!"

Louis turned. Margery Cooper Laroche floated in on a swirl of rainbow silk. Her bony face was framed in a hot-pink turban. Big white hoops dangled from her ears. Four pug dogs circled her like chicks, snorting and barking.

"I love a man who's punctual," she said. "So many people today forget about manners." She frowned. "Where's the big bald fellow, Marvin?"

"Mel," Louis said. "He's a bit under the weather."

She waved toward the open window. "Yes, vile, isn't

it? *Quel sale!* But at least it's nice and cool out here. You don't mind being out here, do you?"

Before Louis could answer, she went on, "I don't use air-conditioning. Bad for the sinuses, and don't even get me started on what it does to the skin, dear. I mean, why should I pay a hundred bucks for an enzyme peel and then have air-conditioning freeze my face like I've been entombed in dry ice like a six-pack of Bud—"

She stopped suddenly. "Listen to me. I'm beating my gums again. I know I do it. Reggie tells me all the time that I do." Her wide red mouth curled up into a smile. "Next time I do it, you just tell me to shut up."

Louis smiled as he kept one eye on the dog sniffing at his ankle.

"Can I get you a drink?" Margery asked.

Again, before Louis could answer, Margery yelled, "Franklin!"

The old fellow in black materialized.

"Shampoo, please," Margery ordered.

The fellow nodded and left. Margery spun back to Louis. "Sit, please," she said, waving at the rattan.

Louis settled into the cushions of the sofa. Margery arranged herself on a lounge across from him. Three of the pugs bounded into her lap, and she drew them to her like babies. The fourth dog jumped up and positioned itself at Louis's thigh, staring up at him with baleful brown eyes.

"So, Reggie tells me you want to know what our little island is really like," Margery said.

What he wanted were the names of any women Mark Durand had slept with. But Louis had a feeling that the only way into Margery's confidence was via the long and winding scenic route.

"This is a strange place to an outsider like me," Louis said.

Margery's hard gray eyes seemed to be taking stock of him.

The butler or valet or whatever he was returned with a tray holding an ornate ice bucket and two stemmed glasses. He set the tray on the table in front of Margery and left.

"Shampoo?" Margery asked, raising the dripping bottle of champagne.

"Please." Louis accepted the glass and took a drink. He had little to compare it with—just the pink André in a plastic glass Frances let him sip on New Year's when he was sixteen and some other stuff over the years that tasted like carbonated kerosene.

But this—he snuck a glance at the label that read Heidsieck—this was great, like someone had crossbred pears with Pop Rocks.

He drank down half the glass. Margery was smiling at him as he lowered it. "Swell stuff, huh?" she said.

"Not bad."

A phone was ringing somewhere in another part of the house. It had been ringing for at least a full minute now, Louis realized. He noticed an old rotary-dial yellow phone on a table in the corner, though it apparently had its ringer off.

Margery seemed not to hear the phone. "Now," she said, "let's talk about Reggie. I adore him. He's like family to me. But he's a helpless old thing in many ways, and some people here take advantage of his good nature. So, before we go any further, I want to make sure you are a right gee."

"Ma'am?"

"A good guy. Excuse me, I slip back into the slang of my youth sometimes. I get away with it because I'm so old, and when you get old enough, you're allowed to mutate into an eccentric."

The phone finally stopped ringing.

She eyed him. "You're very young. How old are you?"

"Just turned thirty."

"How old do you think I am?"

Louis smiled. "I know better than to answer that question when a lady asks it."

She let out a low-throated guffaw. "Tell me about your background. I want to know what kind of man is going to be helping my Reggie."

Louis wasn't sure where to go with this. "I'm an ex-cop. I've been working as a private investigator for three years."

Again, the eyes bored into him. "But who are your people, dear?"

He had been in Bizarro World long enough to know what she meant. Family and name were everything here. He'd be damned if he'd let her intimidate him into spilling his guts about his messed-up childhood. But before he could answer, Margery waved a dismissive hand.

"Never mind," she said. "That was rude. Lou would have skinned me for asking that."

"Who's Lou?"

The wide smile came again but this time tinged with melancholy. "My late husband, Louis," she said, pronouncing the name "Loo-EE." "I guess that's why I told Reggie I would talk to you, because you have the same name. That, and you seem like a right gee."

"Thanks."

The phone started up again. Margery leaned forward, sending the dogs flying. She yanked the champagne bottle from the bucket and topped off his glass.

It was ten-thirty in the morning. There was no sign of food coming yet.

What the hell. He took a drink.

"Maybe we should start with me," Margery said, lying back against the cushions. The little dogs quickly reclaimed her lap. Except for the one at Louis's thigh. It was still staring at him like he was lunch.

"I've lived here forever," she said. "Well, since I was thirty, anyway. Before that, Lou and I lived in Paris—that's where he was from, being French, of course—but he was living in New York when we met, in this big old town house on Fifth. He was fifteen years older than—"

She stopped, smiled, and wagged a finger. "You didn't stop me."

Before Louis could answer, Margery jumped up, sending the dogs scrambling again. "Franklin! Bring me my book! And the Sears catalogue, too!"

Margery and the dogs resettled into the cushions. "Unlike most of the people here, I wasn't born into money," she said. "My people were farmers in upstate New York, and it about killed my momma, so I sure as hell didn't want to live the rest of my life with dirt under my fingernails."

Franklin appeared, cradling a large red book and a small black one. He set them before Margery and left, without bothering to pick up the extension of the still-ringing phone.

Margery brushed the dogs from her lap, swept the

newspapers off the coffee table, and opened the red scrapbook so Louis could see it.

"Now, where's my cheaters?" she muttered, looking around. "Ah! There you are." She snatched up a pair of pink glasses and perched them on her long, thin nose.

"I left home when I was eighteen and went to Manhattan," she said, flipping the pages. "I got work as a cigarette girl at the Trocadero, and then—" She pointed a long red fingernail. "*Voilà!* That's me!"

It was a large black-and-white photograph, creased with age, a full-length portrait of a young woman posed seductively on an ornate cushion. An elaborate peacock-plumed headdress framed her short, wavy hair and lovely face. Other than the headdress and a coy smile, she wore very little else, just some strategically draped pearls and scarves over her chest and long legs.

"You've heard of the Ziegfeld girls?" Margery asked.

"Sure."

"I was one. For ten fabulous months," Margery said. "I was eighteen, with long legs—that's my nickname, did I tell you? Legs, that's what they still call me. Everyone here has a nickname—Buffy, Rusty, Bunny, Hap, Bobo—although Bobo hates it when people call him that."

Nicknames? For one second, Louis thought of asking her about Sam.

But Margery was still speeding down memory lane. "I wasn't a star, of course, but I could fake a little dancing, so I got a spot in the chorus. In a jungle number, I got to ride a live ostrich. One night, the damn thing panicked and carried me right out onto West Forty-first Street."

She laughed. "Lou used to hang around the stage door of the Amsterdam, and finally I gave in and went to dinner with him. A week later, we were married."

She flipped a page of the scrapbook and pointed to a photograph of a dark-haired man in a bow tie. "That's Lou. My sheik."

She sighed and sat back, pulling one of the dogs to her breast. "We lived like royalty for a year. Did I mention that I posed for Guy Pène duBois? You know who he is, dear, right?"

Louis shook his head, but Margery was already off and running again. "Well, then the Crash came, of course, and everyone was jumping out of buildings. Lou had most of his money in gold—God, he was so smart— so we went to live in Paris until it all blew over."

She stopped abruptly. "Lou died in 1935. A heart attack. Of course, I never remarried. I was goofy for that man."

Her eyes teared, and she pulled the other pugs close. They began to lick her face.

"How did you get to Palm Beach?" Louis asked.

Margery drifted back. "Well, things were getting a little dreary in Paris, so I went back to New York, but I was all grummy, so I came down here to stay with friends, and, well, I just never left."

She stroked one of the dogs. "I wanted to start my life over. That's what people do here. They come to Palm Beach to reinvent themselves. It's just Vegas with better clothes."

The phone started ringing again. Louis couldn't take it any longer. "Should I get that for you?" he asked.

She frowned.

"The phone. It's been ringing for a while now."

She cocked her head like a dog hearing a whistle, then leaned closer. "I think Franklin is going deaf. I'd get a new man, but Franklin's been with me forever, and it's really hard to find someone who speaks English these days. It's so hard to understand those Spanish accents and all."

"Don't you have an answering machine?" Louis said.

She waved her hand in the air. "It's bad for the image. I don't need to hear from anyone. The world comes to me."

The phone finally stopped. Margery poured out two more glasses of shampoo.

"Now, what exactly is it you want to know?" she asked.

Maybe it was the champagne, but Louis decided there was no point in beating around the bush anymore. If he did, he'd be too shit-faced to remember anything.

"Reggie told me that Mark Durand was sleeping around," Louis said. "With women. Rich women."

Margery's eyebrows almost disappeared into her turban.

"Reggie said you know everything that goes on around here," Louis said. "I need names."

"My, my, my, my, my," she said. "I thought Mark Durand was a dew dropper."

Louis assumed she meant gay. "Mark told Reggie he was sleeping with women who paid him or gave him gifts. If I'm going to help Reggie, it's important I find someone who might have a reason to kill Durand."

"Like a jealous husband? *Quel* lurid!" Margery said.

"Can you help me?" Louis pressed. "Have you heard anything?"

"My dear," Margery said, "the kind of information you're asking for does not come lightly, not even from someone like me."

"I can appreciate that."

Margery rose from the chair, again dislodging the dogs. Three of them scampered from the room, as if they'd heard a silent dinner bell. The fourth kept its place next to Louis's leg, tongue out and panting.

Margery had moved to one of the arches and was staring out at the gray ocean. Her silk caftan fluttered in the breeze. Louis wondered if he'd blown his chance. How could he have expected this woman to turn on her friends to save a guy like Reggie Kent?

"It's not as if affairs and, God knows, even one-night stands don't happen here," Margery said as she took off her glasses and turned to look at him. "It's just that they don't happen as you might think."

"What do you mean?"

She floated back, standing over him with hands on hips. "Well, everyone sleeps around, dear. Well, almost everyone. There are a few people who don't, but most of them have cheesy little provisions in their prenups that keep them faithful, if not dreadfully miserable. But for the rest of us . . ."

Margery paused, her brows knitting in deep thought. "To put it bluntly," she said, "you can screw upward, and you can screw sideways, but you don't screw down."

"So, you're saying someone like Mark Durand would never get a second look?"

"Oh, he'd get the looks," she said. "He was a succulent specimen. But I just cannot imagine any of my friends passing him around like he was a sexual gimcrack."

She downed the remaining champagne and looked at Louis with a granite gaze. "And besides, if this sordid little game of stud-boy poker was going on, certainly I would have heard about it."

"Reggie Kent didn't know, either, until Durand told him," Louis said.

Margery held his eyes for a moment, then slipped back into the chair and reached for the bottle of champagne. She poured herself another glass, then grabbed Louis's wrist and filled his glass.

She crossed her legs and leaned close to him. A cloud of flowery perfume circled his head, but he didn't pull back. Her voice was almost a whisper, and he wondered why. The only other person in the house was Franklin, and he was apparently going deaf.

"Are you sure that Mark Durand is the only dead boy?"

"Excuse me?" Louis asked.

"I had a thought," Margery said. "I had a lawn boy once who was a living doll. Tall, golden, and sinewy, like Fernando Lamas in that dreadful 3-D movie about the slave who inherits a cotton plantation and has to tame the woman he loves, all the while fighting off the carpet-baggers with his sword."

Louis suppressed a sigh.

"Anyway," Margery said. "One day, Emilio simply stopped showing up."

"Your lawn boy?"

Margery nodded as she took another drink. "And I was absolutely shocked that he would do that to me. I mean, he was such a nice boy. Very hardworking and serious. I mean, he barely spoke English, but he was always so courteous and sweet to me. I really liked that young man . . ."

"Mrs. Laroche, what does this have to do with Mark Durand?"

She stared at him. "Emilio disappeared! Vanished! Poof! Well, I am thinking that maybe something bad happened to him, too."

Louis sat back. It was a preposterous assumption, and he had the feeling she was just miffed that she didn't know the gossip about Durand, so she wanted to stir up some dirt of her own.

"Mrs. Laroche," he said, "your yard man—"

"Emilio. His name was Emilio."

"Emilio," Louis said patiently. "If he was a day worker with a landscaping service, it wouldn't be unusual for him not to show up for work."

"There's something I haven't told you yet," Margery said.

"Which is?"

"I heard a rumor about him," Margery said. She frowned, tapping a red fingernail against her turban. "Now, when was it, exactly? Had to have been during the season, of course. I'm thinking it was around the time of the Red Cross Ball—no, it was the Retina Ball at The Breakers, because it was after my last face-lift, and I couldn't go because I was all blown up like a puffer fish and—"

She stopped suddenly. "Beating my gums again."

Louis gave her a tight smile.

Margery took a drink of champagne. "I was so worried when he didn't show up for work for weeks, and then—"

Margery glanced at the doorway and, satisfied that Franklin was not lurking behind the wall, turned back to Louis. "That's when I heard that he was caught in flagrante delicto," she said in a low voice.

Louis shook his head. "I don't—"

"In bed, dear," Margery said. "The rumor was he had been caught by the husband and chased from the house." She shook her head. "I never believed it, of course. He was such a good boy, and I always had the feeling he had a wife somewhere."

"Whose home?" he asked.

Margery shook her head. "I'm afraid I couldn't tell you that," she said. "It just wouldn't be ducky."

"Mrs. Laroche, you said you wanted to help Reggie," Louis said firmly.

The head shaking grew more vigorous. "This is a small island, young man. I have to live here."

"Reggie could go to jail if you don't help," Louis said.

She stared at him, then her eyes widened. "I have an idea. You can be Robert Redford, and I'll be Deep Throat, and you can ask me initials, and I can just nod."

"What?"

"That movie, dear," Margery said, touching his wrist affectionately. "My goodness, don't you watch movies? The one with those two reporters, Carl Woodstein and—?"

Louis had had enough. "This is not a movie, Mrs. Laroche," he said.

Margery set the pug aside and leveled her iron gaze at Louis. "Young man, you needn't be so patronizing. I am just trying to help. I may be eighty years old, but I still know my onions."

Louis nodded. "You're right. I'm sorry. But this is a

homicide investigation, and Reggie's life is on the line. I need names."

Margery shook her head fiercely. "Bank's closed on that one. I can't spill on my friends. You're just going to have to find Emilio—if the poor boy is still alive, that is."

Louis set his glass on the tray. The champagne was bubbling in his brain, but he was sober enough to know it wouldn't do him or Reggie a damn bit of good to push this woman. He had apparently pissed her off, and he had no badge here, no legal right to force her to talk.

"Do you remember the name of the company Emilio worked for?" he asked.

"Green something," Margery said. "They're over in West Palm somewhere."

"And about how long ago did he disappear?"

"I told you, about five years ago."

Margery reached for the champagne bottle, but it was empty. "Dead soldier," she muttered, turning the bottle upside down in the cooler.

She stood up, wavering, holding the pug. "Oh, my, I'm rather splifficated." She gave a delicate belch. "What time is it?"

Louis looked at his watch. "Almost eleven."

"Oh, futz, I have fitting at Martha's, and I am going to be late." She staggered to the door, the pug tucked under her arm like a hairy football. "Franklin!" she yelled.

She turned back to Louis. "You'll have to forgive me, dear, but I am going to have to get a wiggle on. We'll do breakfast another time, okay?"

Franklin materialized, along with the other dogs, yapping and bouncing. But Margery didn't seem to notice. She had gone back to the lounge, where she deposited the football dog on a cushion. She gathered all of the newspapers up and stuffed them into a Saks bag. She hesitated, then picked up the small black book that Franklin had brought in earlier with the scrapbook.

She came back to Louis. "Take these," she said, thrusting the bag at him. "This is a month's worth of the *Shiny*."

"Ma'am?"

"Oh, for God's sake, dear, it's time you called me Margery, please," she said, rolling her eyes. "The *Shiny*, the *Palm Beach Daily News*. We call it the *Shiny*. Think of it as your road map."

Apparently, she had forgiven him.

Margery held out the black book. "And you'll need this, too," she said.

"What's this?" Louis asked, taking the book.

"The Sears catalogue, dear!" When she saw his puzzled look, she added, "It's the *Social Register*. But we call it the Sears catalogue because nowadays the most awful people can get in it."

She put a firm hand on his arm and started leading him to the door. "But that's a story for another day. I must fly now. Franklin!"

"Here, madame," the old gent said.

Margery blinked, trying to focus on him. "Oh, there you are, you utter ghost of a man. Show Mr. Kincaid out, Franklin."

Franklin shuffled toward the door, Louis following, carrying the Saks bag.

"One more thing!"

He turned back to Margery.

She waggled a red fingernail in his direction. "I don't

like being pushed up against the wall, but I think you mean well, and I think you will be able to help my Reggie. I'll just have to trust my instincts with you, and, like I said, you seem like a right gee."

"Mrs. Laroche, I need those names."

But she didn't seem to hear what he said. The red mouth widened into a smile. "Louis, I think this is the beginning of a beautiful friendship."

And with that, she was gone through one of the archways, the pugs in her wake.

Louis followed Franklin to the front door. It was only after he was outside in the rain that he realized Margery had called him "Loo-EE."

Chapter Ten

It was just after noon when Louis saw the cruiser swing into the parking lot of the Palm Beach PD. He had spent the last half hour sitting under the awning of an art gallery, watching the rain and thinking about Margery's Fernando Lamas murder fantasy. It was probably the most far-fetched lead he had ever pursued, chasing down a lawn guy based on a five-year-old rumor that he had been caught in some woman's bedroom.

But what else did he have right now?

Swann exited the cruiser, jogging through the rain toward the station entrance. He was working his arms into his navy blazer and didn't see Louis until he was only a few feet from him.

Swann stopped abruptly under the entrance's overhang. "Mr. Kincaid," he said. "Are you waiting for me?"

"Yeah, I need your help."

Swann pulled a Tic-Tac dispenser from his pocket and popped one into his mouth. "I've already given you all the help I could. Reggie Kent's fate is in Detective Barberry's hands."

"Yeah, we met."

"I take it he blew you off?"

Something in Swann's voice made Louis realize that Barberry had done the same to Swann. He wondered if Swann had more of an interest in Reggie Kent's case than he had led them to believe.

"Yeah, he blew me off, more or less."

Swann nodded. "Well, I don't mean to be rude, but I really need to go, Mr. Kincaid."

Louis thought about asking Swann to go across the street to Hamburger Heaven. God knew he needed something in his stomach besides Margery's champagne. But he realized there was probably no place on the island where Swann would not feel the curious eyes of the people he was expected to shield from the outside world.

"Look, Lieutenant," Louis said, "I've learned something about Mark Durand that I think you need to know. And you need to know it before Barberry does."

Something sparked in Swann's eyes. "I know all I need to know about Mark Durand," he said. "I know it would take more than an Armani suit and capped teeth to get him entree into these people's living rooms."

"I don't know about living rooms," Louis said. "But it got him into some pretty exclusive bedrooms."

Swann's jaws stopped working the Tic-Tac. "What exactly are you saying?"

"Mark Durand was not just a walker. He was screwing wealthy women for money and gifts."

"Who told you this?"

"Reggie Kent," Louis said.

"It's obviously a lie to deflect suspicion from himself," Swann said. "Even if it were true, why didn't he tell Detective Barberry this the first time we spoke to him? It would certainly add a multitude of suspects to the list."

"He was embarrassed that his protégé had sunk so low."

Swann cocked an eyebrow.

"I also think he wanted to protect his lady friends," Louis said. "Strangely, he still seems to think more of them than they do of him."

That seemed to register with Swann. He ran a hand across his mouth. "Could Mr. Kent provide any proof?" he asked. "Any names?"

"He says he doesn't have names."

"Then why should I be concerned?"

"Because Kent's scared shitless," Louis said. "And if Barberry presses him, he'll spill his guts. Barberry will dig up everything he can, and he won't give a rat's ass about being discreet. Within days, you'll have an army of reporters crawling over the tops of your nice fifteen-foot hedges, trying to take pictures of horny old widows."

Swann looked down at the sidewalk, arms crossed, jaw working the Tic-Tac like crazy. He might be the island's gatekeeper, Louis thought, but his department was no different from any other—the shit rolled downhill.

"We need to make Kent feel safe," Louis said.

"How?"

"We need to let him know that between you and me, we can keep him out of Barberry's sights."

Swann rubbed his brow. "I can't help Mr. Kent," he said. "I've been told to stand aside and let the county investigation take its course."

"In other words, turn a blind eye to an innocent man going to jail."

"You don't get it, do you?" Swann said. "These are powerful people who will do anything to protect their privacy. Anything."

"Including taking this cushy little job of yours away, right?" Louis asked.

Swann stuck a finger in Louis's face. "Screw you."

Louis pushed Swann's hand away. "Look," he said. "You're not part of their world. You're a cop, for crissakes, and whether you believe it or not, that makes you better than them."

Swann had taken a step to go inside, but he stopped and turned back. His cheeks held a rush of color, and his eyes were snapping, but Louis didn't think it was from anger. It was something closer to a wounding. Louis gave the feeling a few seconds to settle in before he spoke again.

"All I need is some information," Louis said.

"What kind?"

"You ran my plate and name when I came on the island," Louis said. "I'm guessing you guys also keep track of the service people who work here. Maids, gardeners, people like that."

"Why do you care about service people?"

"I got a lead on another guy who was doing the same thing as Durand."

"So?"

There was nothing to do but lie. "He's missing."

Swann stared at him. "What's his name?"

"I only know his first name. And that he was a lawn guy."

Swann looked like he had just bit down on something sour.

"Do you guys keep track of service people or not?" Louis asked.

Swann held Louis's eyes for a moment, then looked around, like he was scouting out eavesdroppers. "All right," he said. "About a year ago, some of the residents got together and told us to videotape everyone coming across the bridge and run checks on them."

Louis shook his head slowly, thinking about those turrets out on the bridge. What a nice, convenient place for cameras.

"We didn't do it, for God's sake," Swann said. "The lawyers told us it was probably unconstitutional."

"No shit."

Swan hesitated, like he had something else he wanted to say. Louis could tell the guy was struggling with something deep inside.

"You have something to tell me, Lieutenant?" Louis asked.

Swann blew out a slow breath. "We used to make all the workers carry ID cards. We even fingerprinted them," he said. "We stopped it four years ago."

Margery had said Emilio had been around the island about five years ago. That made it 1984. Could he be this lucky?

"Do you still have these cards?" Louis asked.

Swann nodded toward a large Spanish-style building half a block away on the median behind the fountain. "The station used to be over there, too. We have them stored over there."

"Can I take a look?"

"I can't let you in our storeroom alone."

"Then go with me."

Again, one of those strange frozen moments where it was almost possible to see the rusty grind of Swann's courage.

"I have to go inside and check in," he said. "Wait ten minutes, and meet me around back of that building at Devil's Door. Look for the gargoyles."

Swann went inside. Louis stayed where he was, a little surprised at Swann's quick pivot from dickhead to detective. Maybe it was just another dimension of this strange place, where people saw nothing and knew everything, and doing the right thing required walking through something called the Devil's Door.

Louis went across the street and around the building to the far side. The rain had finally let up, and he waited at the odd-looking door. It was heavy wood, framed by elaborate stone scrolling and two stone devil heads.

Swann came around the corner a couple of minutes later. "Why the weird name?" Louis asked.

"I don't know," Swann said as he unlocked the door. "Before my time. Probably because they thought they were bringing the prisoners into some kind of hell."

Swann pushed open the door and quickly ushered Louis inside. When the door closed, a dusty gray light settled down around them. The place was stuffy and long abandoned, but it was far from hellish.

The walls were celery-green stucco, the archways and baseboards edged in colorful painted tiles, the terra-cotta floor chipped and scuffed. It looked more like a hotel lobby in Key West than a jail.

Swann led him down the hall and around a corner to what had once been two jail cells. The doors had been removed, and the cells were filled with plain white boxes neatly labeled with dates and the words GUEST PROFILES.

"Profiles?" Louis asked.

Swann gave a wry grin. "Better than labeling the boxes 'people to talk to if someone is robbed.'"

"Very funny. Where's 1984?"

Swann pointed to the bottom box in the tallest stack. It was partially crushed. "Right there, 1980 through '85, when we stopped."

Louis stepped into the cell and started shifting boxes. When he finally dragged the one needed to the middle of the cell, he was standing in a cloud of dust, and Swann was gone.

He sat down on the floor and took off the lid. Inside the box were hundreds of five-by-seven index cards, neatly filed in perfect rows. Given the meticulousness of the clerk who had been assigned the task of preparing these for storage, Louis was sure he would find 1984 in the back right-hand corner. He did.

Each card was exactly the same. A small photograph stapled to the upper left corner, the worker's name printed across the top, and the individual's data—age, address, place of employment—typed below. He had sifted through almost all of the cards when he realized nearly every face in the stack was black or brown.

And there were thousands more in this box and others. People with interchangeable faces who had moved unnoticed through the resplendent ballrooms and the safari bedrooms. People who often performed the most intimate of services yet remained strangers. The kind of people you pretended not to know when you met them on the street.

"You find your guy yet?"

Louis looked up. Swann was standing at the cell door, hand on the bars.

"Not yet."

"Hurry it up. I have to get back."

Louis went back to the cards. He was almost finished with the stack for 1984 when a name stopped him.

Emilio Labastide.

He was twenty-five years old, six foot one, and 170 pounds. He was a gardener, and his employer was a company called Clean & Green, located in West Palm. There was no social security number—something that would have made it easier to trace him.

Louis stared at the small photograph. Labastide was handsome in an earthy, unkempt kind of way. Black hair, hooded dark eyes, and an insolent half-smile probably directed at the cop taking his picture. Louis could imagine the bored rich women, sitting in the shade of their patios, watching the shirtless gardener sweat in the white-hot sun. It was something right out of a Harlequin novel.

Swann knelt down next to him. "That our guy?"

"I think so," Louis said. "You recognize him?"

"No."

"Why no social?"

"Probably an illegal," Swann said. "They come and go like the weather."

Louis pushed to his feet. "Can I keep this?"

"Let me make you a copy," Swann said. "If Labastide turns out to be a witness or something, we're going to need evidence of an investigative trail."

Louis heard the "we" Swann had used but decided to let it go for now. He pulled his notebook from his pocket and wrote down the information, just in case he was wrong about Swann's interest and Swann decided at some point to destroy the card. When he finished, he was surprised to see that Swann had picked up the open box and returned it to its stack. Swann dusted his hands and faced him. Suddenly, he looked like a kid caught behind the church with a cigarette.

"You'll be real discreet when you talk to him, right?" Swann asked.

"Sure."

"And you'll let me know if there's any truth to what Reggie Kent said?"

"Sure."

Swann looked down at Labastide's index card, then back at Louis. "I guess I'll just have to trust you."

Louis smiled. "Andrew, this could be the beginning of a beautiful relationship."

Chapter Eleven

I t was hotter inside than out. The sun was out in full Florida force, and after the rain, the glass walls of the orchid house were steamy with condensation. Louis was just inside the door, and already he could feel the tickle of sweat down his temples.

He had never been inside an orchid house before, but he suspected the moisture and heat were what the flowers needed. After all, they grew in jungles, didn't they?

The kid outside had told him this was where he could find Chuck Green, owner of Clean & Green Landscaping and Lawn Service. "Look for the big guy in the Dolphins hat," he'd said.

Louis made his way down a narrow aisle, ducking under hanging baskets of orchids and their long, stringy roots. He spotted a barrel-chested man in a dirty Miami Dolphins ball cap near the back, stacking empty baskets under a table.

"Mr. Green?" Louis asked as he approached him.

The man grunted and pulled himself erect. His face was round and sunburnt, his dirty skin cut with lines of sweat.

"That's me," he said.

Louis introduced himself. Then, without mentioning Durand's murder or Reggie Kent, he told Mr. Green he was looking for Emilio Labastide. He figured Green probably saw a revolving door of immigrant workers and that he would need a reminder to be able to place the kid. But Green surprised Louis with a quick nod and a half smile.

"I remember Emilio," Green said. "He's not in trouble, is he?"

"No," Louis said. "I think he may be a witness to something, that's all. Does he still work here?"

"Hell, no," Green said. "It's been a good four or five years. One day, he just stopped showing up, and I haven't heard from him since."

"Do you remember what time of year it was?" Louis asked.

"Not exactly, but I know it was the middle of the season. I had a full crew and more business than I could handle."

"When's the season?"

"Thanksgiving to Easter, give or take."

"Would you have kept any personal information on Labastide?" Louis asked. "Home address? Phone number?"

Green's eyes skittered and finally settled on something over Louis's shoulder. Louis turned to look. Green was watching a young Hispanic man hang baskets.

"Mr. Green?"

Green blew out a breath scented with Mexican spices. "Look," he said. "I do the best I can. I pay my guys good, and I treat them with respect. But I got no way of knowing if the information they give me is accurate. The government says that if the ID looks good, I can take it."

"I'm not Immigration, Mr. Green," Louis said. "I just need a lead here. Somewhere to start."

Green hesitated, then gave a small nod, indicating that Louis should follow him outside. Green led him to a small cinder-block building. The office walls were papered with schedules and flyers written in Spanish. Green gave one of the file cabinets a sharp kick in the side, and the middle drawer popped open. It was stuffed to the brim with papers.

Louis waited while Green dug deep into the mess. From somewhere outside, he could hear a DJ chattering away in Spanish. A few seconds later, a song came on. It sounded a lot like that Mexican Christmas carol . . . *"Feliz"* something. The song had ended by the time Green pushed to his feet.

"Here it is," he said.

Green handed him a Xerox of a form. Like the index cards in the old Palm Beach jail, it contained only the basic information: Emilio Labastide. Farm Workers Village, building 6, apartment 8. Immokalee, Florida.

"Can I keep this?" Louis asked.

"Sure," Green said. "It's been five years. Don't see what I'd need it for."

"You said he just stopped showing up for work one day. Is that normal for these guys to just disappear from the job?"

"Normal for most but not Emilio," Green said. "He was reliable and steady. Didn't have that chip on his shoulder many of 'em have."

"I was told he worked over in Palm Beach," Louis said. "Was that his regular route?"

"Hell, they all wanted to work on the island," Green said. "Ocean breezes and lots of T and A. But the people there are damn picky, so I only send my best guys over there. Only send the honest ones, too, so they wouldn't steal nothing—or get accused of it. Emilio worked there steady for over a year."

"Did you ever get complaints on him?"

"Not a one."

"Did he ever talk about his personal life?"

"The kid never said much about anything except his sister, Rosa. He worried a lot about her."

Louis looked back at the paper. Labastide had listed a Rosa Labastide as the emergency contact at the same address in Immokalee. Louis had been to Immokalee once before. Set in the middle of state land and vegetable fields, it was a dusty, nondescript town of rough-and-tumble bars and immigrant camps. It was a place where people came and went with the seasons but also a place that had the feel of a close-knit family making do in a hostile, foreign land. Louis hoped that if Labastide had moved on, someone there might know where he had gone.

"Did he ever talk about any of his customers in Palm Beach?" Louis asked.

Green shrugged. "Probably bitched about 'em once in a while, like they all do," he said. "Not that I'd understand much of it, since his English was kinda bad and my Spanish ain't good. But I don't remember anything specific."

"Is there any way to find out exactly whose yards he worked on?"

Green shook his head. "I have five or six different guys working the island at any point, and I wouldn't have kept daily route sheets from that far back, so there's no way I could know."

Louis folded the paper, thanked Green, and headed toward the door. When he got outside, he paused and looked around. Three men were loading sod onto a flatbed. Another was carting potted palms across the lot.

Two more were pruning pink bougainvilleas in the shade of an awning. All were Hispanic. All were sweaty and dirty, with whisker-stubbled faces. From the sounds of it, most didn't speak English.

You can screw upward. You can screw sideways. But you never screw down.

"Mr. Kincaid."

Louis turned to Green, who had come up next to him. "I just remembered something," Green said. "Don't know if it will help or not, but there was one time Emilio asked if he could work the Emerald Dunes golf course in West Palm instead of the island."

"Did he say why?"

"No. Just came to me one day and asked real politely if he could transfer crews."

"Did you reassign him?"

"I couldn't right then," Green said. "Landscaping those places over there takes a special kind of talent, and Emilio had that artist's eye. I couldn't just stick anyone over there, so I told him it would be a few weeks."

"How long after did he stop showing up?"

Green scratched his chin. "Now that I think about it, it was only a few days later. He wasn't the type to get mad, so now I'm wondering if someone over there was giving him a hard time and he was afraid to say something."

"Afraid he'd be discovered and deported?"

"Yeah," Green said. "These guys live in fear of that. That's why they slink around here, taking whatever shit people heap on 'em. They got no choice. They speak up, and they're gone." Green snapped his fingers. "Just like that."

The idea that Labastide was back in Mexico was depressing. He was the only solid lead he and Mel had at this point, maybe the only person who could firm up the sex connection to Mark Durand.

The question was too big to ignore: Why had Labastide wanted a transfer away from the work—and the easy sex—of Palm Beach? It had to have been quite a powerful drug for a young guy like Labastide.

Had he been threatened by a jealous husband, as Margery had said? Or had he gotten himself in too deep, maybe fallen in love with one of the women? Or had he gotten himself mixed up with a man?

Green interrupted Louis's thoughts.

"If you find him, you let him know he's welcome back to work here anytime," Green said. "He was a real nice kid. Real nice."

It was late afternoon by the time Louis got to the Farm Workers Village. It was just a few miles outside Immokalee, set in the vegetable fields, just off the sun-bleached main highway that ran through town.

Louis parked next to a rickety pickup and got out of the Mustang. He had the feeling he had stepped back in time, onto an abandoned military base where everything had been torn down but the concrete barracks.

There were six two-story, boxy buildings with peeling paint, stairwells littered with plastic toys, and balcony railings draped with laundry. Children with dirty feet and long black hair played in the yard. A few men had found shelter from the sun under a mango tree, hats pulled down over their eyes, fingers wrapped around Tecate beers.

Like in the nursery in West Palm, there was a peppy tune playing somewhere. Faded numbers painted on the buildings led Louis to the farthest building in the compound. He was acutely aware of the attention he was drawing from the folks on the second-floor balcony as he approached.

Building six stood in the shade of a gumbo-limbo tree. Apartment eight was on the second floor, last in a line of four doors, three of which were open to capture the cool air. But as Louis passed, the doors slammed shut, followed by the hurried closing of curtains.

At the last door, Louis ducked under a hanging red-flowering plant and knocked softly on the freshly painted blue door. From inside, he could hear a baby crying but no indication that anyone was coming to the door. He knocked again. A pair of beautiful brown eyes appeared suddenly in the gap of the yellow curtains. Louis had no reason to think Labastide's sister still might live here, but he tried.

"Rosa Labastide?" Louis called.

To Louis's surprise, the door opened. A lovely woman with flowing dark hair stood in front of him, a baby propped on her plump hip and a bold tilt tipping her chin upward. She and the baby were dressed in bright orange cotton dresses.

"¿Porqué usted busca a Rosa?"

Louis shook his head. "Do you speak English?"

She pursed her lips and shifted the baby to the other hip. He caught a glimpse of the inside of the apartment: blue sofa, brown throw rug, a gold-framed picture of Jesus dominating a wall of family pictures. A female voice, from a radio or TV, murmured softly in Spanish.

"I am Rosa," the woman said. "And I am not afraid of you. I am Rosa Díaz now. All legal."

"I'm not Immigration," Louis said. "I'm looking—"

The door of the apartment next to Rosa Díaz's opened. An older woman stuck her head out and spoke excitedly to Rosa in Spanish. Louis was sure she was asking Rosa if everything was okay. Rosa barked back at her, and the other woman quickly retreated. Rosa turned back to Louis, her eyes still wary.

"What you want, then?" Rosa asked.

"I'm looking for your brother, Emilio," he said.

"Who are you?"

"I'm a private detective," Louis said.

Rosa put a protective hand on her baby's head and reached for the door. Louis gently held it open.

"Not *policía*," he said. "A different kind of detective. Private, like . . ."

"Like Mr. Magnum PI?" Rosa asked.

Louis smiled. "Yeah."

Rosa returned his smile with a small one of her own, but still, she kept her hand on the door.

"I mean Emilio no harm," Louis said. "I'm not going to arrest him. I just want to talk to him."

Rosa glanced behind her, then motioned for him to come inside. A portable fan stirred the air, which was thick with the smell of baking cheese and baby powder. The blue sofa was draped with cream-colored things that looked like big doilies. A tiny TV sat under the picture of Jesus, its screen filled with the snowy image of that Latina talk show lady, Cristina something.

"I not know where Emilio is," Rosa said. "I not see my brother for long time. Almost five years now."

"Fall 1984?"

Rosa laid the baby down on the sofa and lowered her head. The bodice of her cotton dress rose and fell. "*Sí.* Eight-four. It was Halloween. I remember because I give out candy to the little ones. Since then I have no word. No letters. *Nada.*"

"Can you tell me what happened?" Louis asked. "Did he just stop coming home? Did he say anything about leaving?"

Rosa dropped to the edge of the sofa and placed a hand on the baby's back. Its eyes closed at the touch.

"One time, he just not come home," Rosa said. "He never speak of going away. He would not do that. We come here to this place from Santa Teresa, Mexico. I sixteen, he twenty. He not want to work here, so he get job in Palm Beach, for Mr. Green, working on pretty houses."

"When was this?" Louis asked.

"That summer before he go away," Rosa said. "He only work for Mr. Green short time before he got new *trabajo.*"

"A new job?"

"*Sí.*"

The baby drifted off to sleep. Rosa brushed a few strands of hair from her eyes and looked up at Louis. It was obvious that she had gone on with her life, marrying and having a baby, but in her soft brown eyes, he saw a profound sadness, the kind that came with being suddenly abandoned and not knowing why.

"Did he tell you what this new job was?" Louis asked.

"No," Rosa said. "But he . . . *ganó mucho dinero.*"

Louis shook his head and raised his hand to indicate he didn't understand.

"He make much money," Rosa said. "I show you."

Rosa pushed from the sofa and disappeared into the bedroom. She returned with a gold chain and crucifix and held it out to Louis.

"Emilio give me this before he stopped coming home," she said. "My friend, Juan, he . . . *mi amigo Juan me dijo que vale más que cien dólares.*"

Louis guessed she was saying that the friend told her it was expensive. He took the necklace and held it up to the light. The chain and crucifix glimmered in the sunlight. It was impossible to guess its value with an untrained eye, but it did not look cheap.

"Did he tell you what his new job was?" Louis asked.

Rosa took the necklace back, folding it in her fist. "He say it good job but maybe not one he want to do for long time. Say it is . . . *muy degradante.*"

"Excuse me?"

Rosa sighed in frustration. "Oh, how you say . . . not so good."

"Did he say why?"

Rosa moved away from him and sat down on the sofa. Her hand went back to the baby's head, smoothing its black, sweat-soaked curls.

"He not talk about it," she said.

Rosa hung her head, her face hidden behind the veil of dark hair as she began to cry. Louis was quiet, looking absently around the small apartment and wondering what else there was to say to this woman. Emilio was her brother, her partner in what had to be a frightening journey to a new place and a new life. And all she had now was a wall full of pictures.

Louis stepped over to them.

The insolent face he had seen stapled to the index card did not look like the same man Louis saw here. This man—with his brightly colored shirts, funny hats, and engaging smile—this was a man who had found joy not only inside himself but in this place.

Louis took a close look at the other pictures. Most of them had been taken at festivals, at picnics, or in the courtyard below. Most had Labastide as the centerpiece of a happy group, often men. But none offered a clue to what Labastide's sexual orientation was. And that was something Louis needed to know if he was going to connect Labastide to Mark Durand.

"Mrs. Díaz," he said, facing her, "can you tell me if your brother had a girlfriend?"

Rosa looked up. "No. *No tenía novia.* No girl."

"Are you sure?"

"*Sí,* he would tell me," she said. "We share everything we feel."

"Did he have a best friend?" Louis asked. "A guy I could talk to?"

Again, Rosa shook her head. "His only friend, Manuel, go back to Mexico three years ago. No one else close."

Louis looked back at a photo of Labastide with two other men about his age. They were lounging around a picnic table, holding beers and apparently sharing a joke. He could read nothing in the body language or gazes. And he could not ask Rosa that kind of question.

Louis took one of the smaller photos off the wall and studied it. It was of Emilio and Rosa, standing under the gumbo-limbo tree down in the courtyard. His arm was around her waist. Her head was against his shoulder.

"Mrs. Díaz, may I take this?" Louis asked. "I'll make sure you get it back."

Rosa nodded. "I have others."

Louis turned the frame over and started pushing back the clips that kept the photo in place. Rosa turned back to her baby and started humming softly.

It was good that she had a family of her own, but he had been an investigator long enough to understand that when a loved one simply vanished, it left a special emptiness that could maybe be eased but never filled.

There was no doubt in Louis's mind now that Emilio Labastide was dead. If he had been deported, or even imprisoned, he would have found some way to contact his sister.

"Thank you for your time, Mrs. Díaz," he said, setting the empty frame down. "Could I leave you my phone number, just in case you hear from him or remember anything else?"

Rosa waited while Louis wrote his home phone and the hotel's phone number on the back of one of his business cards.

"You are more nice than the man on the beach," she said.

"The man on the beach?" Louis asked. "What man?"

"When Emilio not come home for three days, I ask Juan to drive me to the beach, and I speak to *policía* about Emilio."

"The police on the island, near the ocean?"

"*Sí,*" Rosa said. "I try to make complaint about Emilio missing, but *policía* not listen. He tell me Emilio probably go home to Mexico, but I know he didn't."

"This policeman, do you remember his name?"

"His name was . . . *Cisne*."

"Cease-nay?"

Rosa raked her hair. "In English is . . . like white bird. I know . . . is swan. Yes, swan."

"Tall guy with blond hair?"

"*Sí.*"

"Thank you," Louis said.

Rosa nodded and retreated again to her sleeping baby. Louis had learned not to offer false hope to someone who was in the process of moving on, since in some ways that was crueler than never knowing. But he could give her one thing.

"I know Officer Swann, Mrs. Díaz," he said. "I'll talk to him about your brother. I promise."

"You will find Emilio for me?" she asked softly.

Find him. How was he supposed to answer that?

Rosa didn't wait for his answer. "*Usted es muy amable.* I know you find Emilio for me. I look for you to come back soon. *¿Sí?*"

Louis gave her an uncertain nod. "*Sí,*" he said. "I will come back."

Chapter Twelve

The choice was simple: Domino's pizza or Captain D's seafood. Louis couldn't imagine how a hook-'em-and-cook-'em fry shack like Captain D's stayed in business in a place like Florida. But he did know that once you ate fresh grouper at Timmy's Nook, you just didn't—as the folks in Palm Beach would say—lower yourself to beer-batter fish in a bag.

Mel would just have to eat pizza and like it.

The sky was pink and lavender as he parked the Mustang in the lot of their hotel. Louis grabbed the pizza box, the Styrofoam cooler he had filled with beer back at the 7-Eleven in West Palm, and the photograph of Emilio that Rosa had given him. As he hurried upstairs to the room, he wondered if Mel was feeling better and hoped he had forced himself to get out for a walk.

Mel didn't look as if he'd gone anywhere. He was sprawled on his bed, one knee up, arms behind his head, eyes closed. He wore only a pair of baggy jogging shorts and a set of headphones. His cherished CD player sat on the bed next to him.

Louis set the pizza and cooler down and nudged him. Deep in either sleep or Coltrane's jazz, Mel jumped. He propped himself on one elbow and reached for his glasses. It took him a moment to focus.

"What time is it?" he asked.

"Almost eight. You been asleep all day?"

Mel pushed to a sitting position and discarded the headphones. His chest, arms, and face were so sunburnt the color looked painted on. And it looked painful.

"You go down to the beach?" Louis asked.

"Just for a few minutes."

"Must've been longer than a few minutes," Louis said. "You look like a lobster."

"I am a sensitive man with sensitive skin," Mel said.

"You're a stale, pale male who lives like one of those underground creatures in that movie *The Time Machine*."

"Morlocks."

Louis snagged a beer from the cooler. "Why didn't you buy some sunscreen?" he asked.

"Why are you nagging me?"

"Well, don't bitch to me all night when you can't sleep."

"I won't have any trouble sleeping."

Louis flipped open the pizza box. There were no plates in the room, so he grabbed a couple of Domino's napkins.

"How many slices you want?" Louis asked.

"Not hungry," Mel said.

Louis started to ask where he'd eaten but paused when he saw a plate sitting on the nightstand between the beds. He picked up the linen napkin that lay on top. The food was a partially eaten bacon cheeseburger. The plate had the Ta-boo logo on the edge.

"You're getting takeout from Ta-boo?" Louis asked.

"Sure, why not?"

Louis threw the napkin down. "A little pricy, isn't it?"

Mel shrugged and started to put his headphones back on. Louis reached down to stop him.

"What's your problem?" Mel asked.

"Have you gotten any money from Kent?"

"He says he'll have some in a few weeks."

"How much?" Louis asked.

"He didn't say."

Louis went back to the pizza box. "I don't know how you expect us to get by here," he said. "Eighty-five a night for the room, a couple hundred for tuxedo rentals, and now you're laying around here eating takeout from the most expensive place in town."

"It's not the most expensive place," Mel said.

"That's not the point," Louis said. "We haven't even decided if we're going to take this case yet, and we're already five hundred bucks in the hole."

Mel swung his feet to the floor. "You going to bail on me here?"

Louis had a slice of pizza to his mouth, but he stopped and lowered it. Despite his increasing blindness, Mel was the most independent and get-out-of-my-face guy Louis knew. But his voice now had an edge of panic, a don't-quit-on-me kind of panic.

"I'm not walking away," Louis said, "but I'd like to know if it's going to be worth our while. This isn't going to be an easy investigation."

"There are no easy investigations, you know that," Mel said. "It's just a lot of begging and digging, and if you're lucky, you sniff out a lead that cracks things open."

Louis sat down on the edge of his bed and bit into the pizza. Mel started to pick at the cold French fries on the plate. For a couple of minutes, there was nothing but the soft crunch of their chewing.

"So, what did you find out today?" Mel finally asked. "Does this Emilio fellow exist?"

Louis nodded. "Yeah. His last name is Labastide. He's a Mexican illegal who worked for the lawn company in 1984."

"You found him?"

Louis rose, grabbed Rosa's photo off the dresser, and tossed it to Mel. Mel turned on the lamp and held the picture under the bright light.

"I found his sister, Rosa," Louis said. "She hasn't seen him since October of eighty-four. Says one night he just didn't come home."

"Does she think he went back to Mexico?"

Louis was chewing, and he shook his head as he mumbled an answer. "No. They came to this country together, when she was sixteen. She says no way would he desert her."

Mel was quiet, and Louis let him think about things while he finished a second slice of pizza and pulled two beers from the cooler. He set one on the nightstand for Mel.

"Do you think there is a connection between Labastide and Durand?" Mel asked.

"I don't know," Louis said. "Five years between murders is a long time in the killing business."

"Then let's lay it out," Mel said. "Grab that pad of paper over there, and start writing."

Louis pushed the remaining pizza crust into his mouth and picked up the legal pad. Mel started reciting the commonalities between Labastide and Durand, something any detective did when looking at the possibility of a single killer for multiple victims.

Both were young, dark-haired, and handsome.

Both had little money.

Both were looking to improve their financial situations.

Both had personal contact with rich married women.

"We're missing what could be the biggest link," Mel said. "Did you ask Rosa if her brother was gay?"

"No," Louis said. "It seemed like a lousy thing to throw at her, so I danced around it and asked about a girlfriend. She said she was sure he had no girlfriend, so I asked about a buddy. She said his best pal had gone back to Mexico."

"So, we don't know which way he swung," Mel said.

Louis rose again to get another beer. "First time in my life I ever needed to know something like that about someone."

"We need to know, Louis," Mel said. "If Labastide was gay, that will indicate a very likely hate-crime connection."

"Hate crimes are spontaneous and not usually planned. Hard to consider someone killing like that five years apart."

"Maybe it wasn't five years apart," Mel said. "There was a case up in Virginia a few years ago where a married man who hated gays was picking up young guys in bars and taking them home and killing them. He got away with it for eight years, because the bodies in between didn't turn up."

Louis took a drink of his beer. Mel's hate-crime theory was not one he was comfortable with. It felt farfetched, almost as improbable as believing that Emilio had become some kind of boy toy who spent his afternoons lying on Egyptian sheets and sipping mimosas.

And there was still the fact that as far as they knew, Durand swung both ways. Was it possible that Labastide did, too? And if so, who was more likely to kill him? A jealous male lover or a jealous husband?

"We need to find out what happened to Labastide," Louis said. "If he's dead and it was a homicide, then we'll know where to go."

"We could call Barberry and ask him to research his database of John Does."

Louis shook his head. "I don't want to let that asshole know what direction we're looking. I'll call Dr. Steffel and see what she can dig up. If Labastide was murdered, it's likely he was dumped in Palm Beach County."

"If that doesn't work," Mel said, "we may have to resort to begging favors from Lance Mobley."

Louis sighed. Mobley was the Lee County sheriff on the western side of the state, their home territory. Sometimes friend, sometimes adversary, but always a man looking for a microphone and a camera. Also one who did not know the meaning of the word *discretion*.

But if they had to play nice with Mobley, then so be it. There was no way to make a connection to Durand or Palm Beach until they knew what happened to Labastide.

Even if the cases turned out not to be related and Labastide had met some other kind of tragic end, Louis had still made a promise to Rosa Díaz. He said he would come back. And he didn't intend to do that until he had something to tell her.

O'Sullivan's was a cop bar. Conveniently located within walking distance of the Fort Myers police station, it had become, over the years, much like a married guy's cherished den. Stale, smoky air, cigarette burns on the tabletops, shelves of softball and bowling trophies, a floor of crushed peanut shells, and a big-screen TV permanently turned to ESPN.

And like all primitive habitats, it had a pecking order.

City detectives had staked claim to the back end of the bar; county detectives, out of legendary necessity, owned the three tables near the men's-room door. The slew of small round tables arranged down the center of the bar belonged to the rank-and-file officers, usually two kinds: those who dropped in only long enough to feed their egos by telling embellished stories of near-death experiences and those who had nothing else to go home to but dried-up cartons of Chinese takeout and an empty bed.

Lance Mobley, Lee County sheriff, sat in the back booth on his throne of tattered green vinyl, a vision of leonine golden hair, golfer's tan, and an oppressively starched white uniform shirt. With one arm across the back of the seat and a booted ankle on his knee, he looked like a sultan surveying his realm.

As Louis and Mel had feared, Dr. Steffel had not turned up any medical examiner's records for an Emilio Labastide, nor could she find any John Does matching the physical description. Late yesterday afternoon, Louis had resorted to calling Mobley. Louis gave him Labastide's general information and, to reel him in, added something to whet the sheriff's investigative appetite: "See if you have any decapitated corpses."

It had taken Mobley less than two hours to call back and tell them he didn't have a deceased person by that name, but he did have a young, headless John Doe, found about thirty miles east of Fort Myers, just this side of the Lee/Hendry county line.

When Louis pressed him for details on the cause of death, Mobley told him he would have to come back to Fort Myers and buy him a drink. That was Mobley's way of saying, *I got what you need, and I want a piece of this.*

Mobley spotted them and waved them over. He didn't rise when they got to the table.

"If it isn't the Lone Ranger and Tonto," Mobley said.

"Nice to see you again, too, Dudley," Mel said.

Mobley grabbed a chair from the nearby table for Mel. Louis sat down across from Mobley, taking note of a thin manila folder on the table between them.

Mobley saw Louis's gaze and slapped a protective hand down on the folder. "So, what's this case all about?" he asked.

"Just a routine homicide, Lance," Louis said. "Missing man with suspicious circumstances."

"Nothing is routine in Palm Beach, Kincaid," Mobley said. "Tell me the truth. Who is this Labastide? A Spanish count or just some piece of Euro trash who OD'd in The Breakers and was dumped out in the middle of nowhere to cover it up?"

Louis smiled. "Labastide was a twenty-five-year-old immigrant gardener."

The glint in Lance's eyes dimmed. "But you told me this guy was from Palm Beach."

"I told you he might have disappeared from Palm Beach," Louis said.

Mobley sat back and crossed his arms. "I can't believe I had guys digging around in our records room for a fuckin' Mexican."

"Jesus Christ, Lance," Mel said, "clean up your mouth. You're a public servant, for crissake."

"Fuck you, Landeta," Mobley said. "You don't like the talk in here, don't let the door hit you in the ass."

"Shut up, both of you," Louis said, reaching across the table to grab the folder. He didn't care about the reports. He wanted to see the fingerprint card. Every unidentified body was fingerprinted before it was buried. The card was usually stapled to the inside cover. And it wasn't here.

"Lance, where's the print card?" Louis asked.

"It's not there?" Mobley said.

"No. Where is it?"

Mobley shrugged. "Looks like the ME forgot to do one." He stood up. "I'm getting another cup of coffee," he said, pushing from the booth. "You want anything, asshole?"

"Coke," Mel said.

Louis flipped through the folder's contents. It was pretty thin, but it said the body had been found November 3, which matched Rosa's memory. The autopsy report revealed the John Doe was between eighteen and thirty-five, weight 170, height six-one.

"Read it to me, man," Mel said.

"Same height and weight that was listed on Labastide's Palm Beach ID card," Louis said. "Manner of death was seven stab wounds to the chest, one right to the heart."

"Any signs he was tortured or beaten? Any whip marks?"

"Nope."

"Clothed?" Mel asked.

"Yeah, jeans and a T-shirt. Pockets rifled, probably to remove money or his identification. Here's something interesting. His hands and nails were clean and trim. I wouldn't expect that of a guy who did lawn work."

"Maybe the women he was screwing expected it," Mel said.

Louis nodded and read on. "The ME didn't offer much on the weapon used to sever the head, just that it was consistent with a large blade." His eyes dipped to the name on the autopsy. It was signed by somebody named T. Cartwright. It had to be the ME who ran the Lee County office before Vince Carissimi took over.

His friend Vince would have never neglected printing a body.

"Got any pictures?" Mel asked.

Louis shifted through the crime-scene photos. There were just four showing the headless body from different angles. None of the corpse taken in the autopsy room. Sloppy work all around.

"How long had he been out there before they found him?" Mel asked.

"He was found Nov. 3," Louis said. "Rosa told me Emilio disappeared on Halloween."

"That area out near the county line is all state land, right?" Mel asked.

Louis started to nod again, then stopped when he saw a short note written by the responding officer to the dead-body call. The John Doe was discovered by a guy who worked for Archer Ranch.

Archer . . .

Where had he heard that name before?

He remembered. There had been a sign out at Devil's Garden near the cattle pen where Durand had been found. Something about state land and a preserve.

Mobley slid back in the booth, sloshing coffee as he set a can of Sprite in front of Mel.

"I asked for a Coke," Mel said.

"That's all they had."

"What kind of bar runs out of Coke?"

"Tell it to the owner."

"Lance," Louis said. "Do you know a family named Archer that lives out near Hendry County or Lake Okeechobee?"

"No, why?"

Louis didn't want to tell him that there was another headless body dumped in the same general area. The idea of a decapitating serial killer operating in Mobley's backyard was not something that needed to be pinballing around in the sheriff's brain. Right now, Mobley had no interest in the John Doe, and it was better for everyone if it was left that way.

"No reason," Louis said. "Just thought I recognized the name."

"Did the head ever turn up?" Mel asked.

"Not in my county." Mobley's beeper went off. He looked down at the number, then back at Louis. "If you don't need anything else from me, then clear out," he said. "I got a couple of DAs coming by in five minutes. Got that triple murder case on the burner next week."

Louis closed the folder and slid it back to Mobley. "Any chance we can dig this John Doe up and try to ID him?"

"Not on my dime," Mobley said.

"What if we can get some TV cameras out there to film you pushing the casket into the hearse?" Mel asked.

"Get out of my bar," Mobley said. "Both of you."

Louis and Mel rose together and paused outside. It was only a few minutes after noon, and the sun was high and warm. Louis pulled his sunglasses from his shirt pocket.

"Why'd you ask about the print card?" Mel asked. "What good would that do us?"

"I forgot to tell you something. You know those ID cards I told you about, the ones Swann kept on the workers? They had fingerprints."

"Why does that not surprise me?" Mel said.

Louis put on his sunglasses. "It would have been nice and easy just to match up two sets of prints."

"What was that stuff about Archer?" Mel asked.

"Mobley's John Doe was found by a guy who worked for the Archer Ranch," Louis said. "That's the same name I saw on a sign near the cattle pen."

"But the Hendry County line and the cattle pen are at least thirty miles apart."

"I know," Louis said. "Which makes the coincidence too big to ignore. You up for a trip to a ranch?"

"As long as I don't have to ride a frickin' horse," Mel said.

Chapter Thirteen

It didn't take much effort to find the Archer Ranch. Louis and Mel had stopped off at the bar in the old Clewiston Inn to grab a burger. The bartender, overhearing them talking about the case, lingered after he brought them their beers.

"What you two want with the Archers?" he asked.

"We're with the *Florida Livestock Journal*," Mel said. "They sent me to do a story." He jerked a thumb at Louis. "This is my photog."

Louis gave a nod.

"You know anything about the Archer Ranch?" Mel asked.

"Sure. Everybody around here knows the Archers," the bartender said. "They own half of Hendry County."

By the time they finished their burgers, Louis and Mel had found out that the Archer family had been raising cattle on their four thousand acres out near Devil's Garden for three generations. They were the only ranchers operating south of Lake Okeechobee, and, like the sugar barons, they were regarded as royalty in the towns that rimmed the lake.

As Louis paid the bill, his eyes traveled over the murals that decorated the bar's walls. Paintings of Everglades scenes with egrets in flight, marshlands with Seminole Indians and alligators. And over in one corner, a cowboy on a horse leading cattle across grasslands. The murals had a softly faded quality, like old Polaroids.

Outside, they paused under the inn's white portico for Mel to light a cigarette.

"*Florida Livestock Journal*?" Louis asked.

Mel shrugged as he pocketed the Zippo. "It was either that or Publishers Clearing House."

They headed south out of Clewiston, retracing their route to Devil's Garden. The bartender had said the family home was on a road heading west off the main one. He said to watch for a "big AR arch." The arch was easy to spot. It spanned the width of the road, an impressive iron thing with AR spelled out between cutouts of steers.

There was no gate, so Louis swung the Mustang into the drive. Live oaks bordered neatly fenced pastures dotted with horses. It reminded Louis of the tunnel-tree entrances to the historic antebellum homes in southern Mississippi. After a final bend, a large two-story white house came into view. The plain house was old but well maintained, with wood siding, a peaked metal roof, and a wide veranda complete with rocking chairs. It was a

style Louis had heard someone once call "Florida plantation cracker."

A new Ford pickup and an old canvas-top Jeep with
no windows were parked in the coquina-shell driveway.
Two saddled horses were tethered to a post in the shade,
their long tails swatting flies.

As they pulled up next to the Jeep, a man came out
onto the porch. He was a barrel-chested guy in jeans and
denim shirt. His face was hidden below the wide brim of
his cowboy hat.

"Can I help you fellas?"

The man's deep voice carried in the quiet. Louis
waited until Mel had gotten out of the Mustang and
then approached the porch.

"Mr. Archer?"

"Nope. Who are you?"

Mel had come up beside him. "We're investigating
the homicide of the man found on your land."

"That so?"

Louis had a better view of the man's face now. Skin
like old leather, a scraggly gray mustache bracketing a
hard mouth. No way to read the eyes hidden behind mirrored sunglasses. The man was probably in his sixties, but
he was huge, at least six-five and solid. He was standing
with legs apart, hands held out from his sides, like a bear
guarding his den.

"Can we speak to Mr. Archer, please?" Louis asked.

"I'm Burke Aubry, the foreman. You can speak to me."

Louis came forward a few steps. "We understand the
body was found by workers here. Can you tell us anything about it?"

"I already talked to that county cop," Aubry said.

"You talked to Detective Barberry?" Louis asked.

Aubry hesitated and gave a curt nod.

"Mr. Aubry," Louis said. "We're not working with Detective Barberry. We're private investigators. If we could—"

"I told you, I got nothing more to say," Aubry interrupted. "Now, I'd appreciate it if you would just go away and leave us be."

He started for the door.

"Mr. Aubry," Louis said.

Aubry turned back, one hand holding open the screen door.

"Why didn't you tell Detective Barberry about that other body five years ago?"

For a moment, Aubry didn't move. Then he slowly let the screen close and came out to the edge of the porch.

"Five years ago, one of your men found a headless body just over the county line," Louis said. "Why didn't you tell Barberry?"

Aubry tilted up his chin, and the sun caught the mirrored sunglasses. "I didn't tell him because he was disrespectful to Mrs. Archer," he said.

Mel came forward. "Mr. Aubry, Barberry is a sonofabitch. He's trying to make a case against a man we believe is innocent. These two murders might be related, and if they are, we might be able to prove our case. We could use your help."

Aubry was silent, just staring down at both of them. "Thought you cop types all stuck together."

"We're not cops," Louis said.

Aubry considered this for a long moment, then slowly came down off the porch. Up close, he was even more imposing. His jeans were worn to white at the knees, his boots cracked with age. His denim shirt looked new, and there was a logo above the left pocket of a cowboy with the stitched words HUNTER WHIPS. Around Aubry's meaty neck hung a handsome multicolored scarf that Louis recognized as a Seminole Indian pattern.

"What do you want to know?" Aubry asked.

"Who found the body at Devil's Garden?" Louis asked.

"Me and my other man," he said. "We were rounding up some calves nearby."

"Is that state land?" Louis asked.

Aubry nodded. "Yeah, Mrs. Archer sold off that parcel to the state about ten years ago. It's about ten acres. They're going to make a park out of it someday, I guess."

"So, you wouldn't normally be in that area?" Louis asked.

Aubry shook his head. "Nope. My men were just southwest of it. But one of the dogs smelled something and took off. We followed, and we got to that old cow pen down there, and the dogs were going crazy. I figured it was a dead boar, so we went in to pull the dogs away. That's when we saw it."

"You saw the body yourself?"

Aubry nodded tightly. "I told my man Dwayne to get the dogs out of there, and I radioed back to call the police."

"Tell us about the first body five years ago," Louis said.

"Not much to tell there," Aubry said. "One of my men, Ron, was hunting down a cow—they wander far sometimes—and the dog had a scent, but it was just outside our property and onto some state land. The state's okay with us going, so Ron did. He found the body and called the Lee County folks, since that's where he was."

"The Lee County sheriff?"

Aubry nodded. "They asked Ron some questions for their report. We never heard from them again."

"Does Ron still work here?"

"Nope. He passed on a few years back."

Louis looked at Mel, but he didn't seem to have any other questions, either.

"Is there anything else, Mr. Aubry?" Louis asked. "Any small thing you can remember might be helpful." When the man didn't say anything, Louis took a step toward him. "Mr. Aubry, the man they found five years ago—he had a sister. She's still looking for him."

Still, the man didn't move.

"Thank you for your time, Mr. Aubry," Louis said, and started away.

"Wait." Aubry cleared his throat. "There's something I didn't tell the Lee County folks. I don't know if it means anything now. I mean, I read in the papers that they never did find out who that man over in Lee County was, so I figured who would care?"

"His sister cares," Louis said.

Aubry dropped his head for a moment. "Okay," he said softly. "It was about a week after Ron found that body, and we were sitting around one night drinking. Ron got pretty drunk and broke down. I thought it was just, you know, having to see that body. I mean, I saw the one . . ."

His voice trailed off, and he wiped a hand over his face. "Anyway, the next morning, Ron came to me and said he found a necklace near the body. He took it, and he said he felt real bad stealing something from a dead man."

"Did you tell the police?" Louis asked.

Aubry shook his head slowly. "Didn't see the point. I didn't want Ron to get in trouble. The man was dead and buried. I didn't know he had kin."

"What happened to the necklace?" Louis asked.

Aubry hesitated. "I kept it. I don't know why I did. But if you think it might help, I got no problem handing it over."

"Thanks."

"It's at my place. It's not far from Devil's Garden. Why don't you two ride over with me? We could stop at the old cow pen if you want."

Louis was about to say that he and Mel had already seen it, but he realized suddenly that Burke Aubry could tell them more than any half-assed report Barberry had produced.

"We appreciate your help, Mr. Aubry," Louis said.

It was only a mile or so to Aubry's bungalow. They waited in the Jeep until Aubry returned. Aubry got in, uncurled his big fist, and dropped something in Louis's hand.

It wasn't just a necklace. It was a crucifix. And although Louis couldn't be sure without checking, it looked like a match to the one Rosa said Emilio had given her.

"What's the matter?" Mel asked from the backseat as Aubry started up the Jeep.

"I'll tell you later," Louis said, pocketing the crucifix.

They set off for the cattle pen, leaving the gravel roads

for the kidney-jarring terrain of the pasturelands. The warm air that rushed over their faces was thick with the smells of fresh earth, swamp water, and manure.

There didn't seem to be any road, not even ruts. But Aubry obviously knew where he was going. As they bounced along, the landscape morphed from flat, yellow grass to clusters of humpbacked palmetto palms and then a gathering of live oaks. It was as if they had passed through three separate states in a matter of minutes.

"How much farther?" Mel shouted from the backseat.

Aubry pointed to a stand of trees in the distance. He said something, but his words were smothered by the wind. Finally, he pulled to a jarring stop.

Aubry hopped from the Jeep with the spryness of a much younger man. Louis and Mel followed. They trudged through heavy brush and waded across a shallow marshy river, its banks rimmed with cattails. The sun was low in the sky, giving Louis his only bearings. From what Louis could tell, they had come to the abandoned cattle pen from due south. There was no sign of the gravel road he and Mel had taken on their first trip here. From this direction, it looked very different from the rest of the land he had seen so far on the Archer Ranch. It was heavily wooded, mainly with the same live oaks he had seen back at the ranch house. But these trees were even larger, great, twisting black things swagged with Spanish moss, so thick and high that they blocked out the sun. It was like they had entered some strange primeval oasis.

"Where's the road?" Louis asked, trailing Aubry through the high weeds.

Aubry pointed west. "Over that way. I brought us in the back, by way of one of the cow trails."

"Cow trails?" Louis asked.

"Yeah, the ranch is cut through with scores of them. But you have to know where they are."

"So, all the cowboys who work for you know how to get here without using the road?" Mel asked.

"Cowmen," Aubry said.

"What?"

"Cowmen. We don't use that word 'cowboy.' It takes a man to do this work. Got no use for boys here."

They were at the back end of the old cow pen now. There was a small structure that Louis had noticed on their first visit. It was made of the same bleached wood as the fences, and its tin roof was rusted red. It looked like one good wind would blow it away.

"What was that for?" Louis asking, pointing.

"That's where we did the branding, but this pen ain't been used for near twenty years now," Aubry said. He ducked under the rails, and they followed him into the large central pen strung with the yellow crime-scene tape.

"This is where we found the body," Aubry said, pointing to the depression in the sand.

Louis couldn't see the man's eyes behind the sunglasses, but he heard the catch in his voice. Still, he had to ask.

"Can you describe things for us, Mr. Aubry?" Louis asked. "It might help."

Aubry cleared his throat. "Well, like I said, we had to pull the dogs away first. That's when we figured it was, well, it was a human we were looking at. There was blood everywhere. I mean, I've seen cows slaughtered, so blood doesn't bother me. But this was . . ." He stopped, took off his sunglasses, and ran a hand over his face. "The head was gone, and at first we thought one of the dogs had got it. But . . . well, it was just gone."

"They found it later," Louis said.

Aubry gave a tight nod. "That's good, I guess."

"Is there anything else you can remember?" Louis asked.

Aubry seemed to be staring at a spot on the ground. "The man, he was laying facedown, and he was naked. His back was all cut up like he'd been whipped."

Louis flashed back to the two horses he had seen tied up outside the Archer house, to something coiled on the saddle.

"Mr. Aubry, do your men carry whips?" he asked.

Aubry nodded. "With all the trees and brush, ropes are about as good as skis in a desert. We use dogs and whips."

"Did Barberry ask you about your whips?" Louis asked.

His clear blue eyes didn't waver. "He saw that we carry whips, so he took the five we had. Then he asked me how many other men I had working for me. I said we had twenty all told. He ordered me to call them all in."

"You were questioned?" Mel asked.

"Yeah, we were questioned." He almost spat out the last word. "They made us all go in the bunkhouse, and they took statements. We were there all afternoon. Lost a full day's work. Then about sundown, Barberry got a call. He came back and lined my men up and started yelling at them."

"Yelling? About what?" Louis asked.

"Stuff like 'You hate queers, boy? That why you whipped that little faggot to death?' And then he—"

Aubry paused to draw in a deep breath. "Then he started in on Lee Marion, started accusing him of being queer. Lee's kind of a little guy, but he sure . . ." Aubry paused. "Anyway, I almost had to pull a couple of my men off Barberry. Now, I had a tussle or two with the law when I was young, so I know you can't win with those types. But that Barberry, he had no right to disrespect my men like that."

Louis could pretty much imagine what had happened. Barberry had scored a lucky hit with Durand in the fingerprint database, and Durand's record had popped up, complete with his prostitution arrest. From there, Barberry's primitive brain needed little help in making the leap to hate crime. And Barberry was certainly mean enough to take it a step further and try to bait Aubry's men with innuendo.

Emilio Labastide hadn't been whipped, but the whip connection to the Archer men was too powerful to ignore. "Mr. Aubry," Louis asked. "The twenty men who work for you now, were any of them here five years ago?"

"Almost all were. Except Ron. I told you that he died."

Louis was quiet.

"I know what you're thinking," Aubry said. "But I know these men. These men work here and live here, some a long time. Some of them were here when Jim Archer ran things, and when Jim died back in sixty-five, they stayed on out of loyalty to Libby Archer. We're like a family here."

"People do things that surprise even their families, Mr. Aubry," Louis said.

"I know that," he said. "But you gotta understand

something. This place, this ranch, it's almost like an island. We watch over each other here, and what happens in the outside world is almost foreign to us."

Louis caught Mel's eye.

"My men wouldn't do something like this," Aubry said. "And they sure as hell wouldn't do it here."

"Here? What do you mean?" Louis asked.

"Devil's Garden," Aubry said. "It's Mrs. Archer's special place—sacred is what she calls it—and all the men know it." He shook his head slowly. "Not here."

Louis watched him walk away, then turned to Mel. He could barely see him in the quickening dusk.

"Well, if nothing else, this trip got us twenty more suspects," Mel said.

"Not if you believe that Aubry knows his men," Louis said.

Mel shrugged and turned his face toward the faint ribbons of orange and pink resting on the dark blue horizon. Louis wondered if Mel could see the colors or if he simply sensed the beauty.

"You're good at getting feelings about things," Mel said. "What do you think happened here?"

Louis turned and looked back at the cow pen. The dark had descended, leaving only the black shapes of the fence and trees. All he could see now was a fluttering yellow tail of crime-scene tape.

There was no "feeling," as Mel called it. There was nothing. Just cool air and silence.

Chapter Fourteen

The clock chimed, its sweet sound carrying in the stillness of the house. She waited until she counted twelve chimes, then slid from the bed and went downstairs.

The marble was cold on her feet as she went quickly through the rooms. The white lights of the Christmas tree glowed in the dark. At the front door, she opened the small box and punched in the code to deactivate the alarm.

She hurried to the back of the house, passing the closed door of the study without a glance. At the French doors, she paused, looking out over the patio. The pool lights cast shimmering shadows on the swaying palm trees.

She switched off the lights, and the pool went dark. She unlocked the door.

Her heart was beating too fast, and she thought briefly of her doctor and his warnings. But she didn't care. It felt good. And it had been a while since she felt good.

She retraced her steps through the house and up the sweeping staircase. All of the rooms were dark; she had made sure of that. There was no one in the huge house but her; she had made doubly sure of that, even sending Greg on his way early with the excuse that she was too tired to work.

Back in her bedroom, she paused. Everything was just right. Fresh new linens, the lights on dim. The candle, smelling of orange blossoms—*was that a cliché?*—glowed on the night table. She felt a twinge of guilt over the candle—*what kind of woman spent $300 for one candle at Neiman's?*—but she didn't care. She had simply wanted it.

She went to the dressing table, looked down at the selection of perfume bottles, and picked up the small, square crystal bottle. She removed the stopper and ran it over the skin between her breasts, then put the bottle of Jicky perfume back in its place. She paused, looking at the larger bottle hidden behind the others. She picked it up, pulled out the stopper, and brought the bottle up to her lips. She closed her eyes as the scotch burned down her throat.

After wiping her lips, she replaced the stopper and put the bottle back in its place.

She moved to the French doors and opened them. She stepped out onto the balcony. A wafer-white moon hung over the ocean, and a cool wind was blowing in. She closed her eyes at the feel of her nipples hardening against the silk of her nightgown.

"Carolyn?"

She turned. He was standing in the doorway, as if waiting for her permission to come in. Which is exactly what he was doing, she realized suddenly.

How sweet. How different from the others.

"Come here," she said.

As he came forward, his features were a blur. But that was as she had planned it. That was why she hadn't bothered to put in her contacts. That is why she had broken her promise to herself and had the scotch. She wanted all of the edges to be gone. She wanted nothing but softness.

He held out the ceramic pot. "I was told to give this to you," he said.

The accent . . . she had not heard him speak much that first time, and she hadn't realized how lovely his accent was.

She took the ceramic pot and set it on the night table, then turned back to him. He was wearing jeans and a plain white dress shirt. He smelled like soap. Simple and clean, just the way she wanted it to be, just as she had requested.

"You're English?" she asked.

"Irish."

"What kind of name is Byrne?"

"It's Gaelic. I think it means raven."

His smile touched her.

"Byrne," she whispered. And she closed her eyes.

She was grateful that he understood that it was a signal. She was grateful that when his hands encircled her waist, they were gentle. She was grateful that when his lips touched hers, they were soft.

His breath was warm at her ear. "Your husband?"

"Not here," she whispered.

Then it was a dance as he firmly but slowly led her to the bed. She so loved being led. It was such a relief from the rest of her life.

She lay back in the fresh sheets. He was a beautiful blur as he undressed, just candle-gold skin and dark hair. When his body covered hers, she groaned and moved against him.

"What do you want me to do?" he asked.

"Whatever you want," she said.

She closed her eyes and felt his hands at her neck and then moving down under the silk to her breast. As he removed her gown, his hands were rough, and she had a vision of him as he might look when he was at work—tan and hard, pulling on the ropes.

"Tie me," she whispered.

"What?"

"There's rope . . . there by the bed. Tie me, please."

She closed her eyes and raised her arms over her head. He was gentle as he looped the rope over her wrists and around the bedposts. His hands were trembling.

"Tighter," she said.

"I don't want—"

"Tighter."

She cried out as he pulled the rope snug. Then he was kissing her, and she clung to an image of herself riding a sleek white yacht over huge blue ocean waves.

But it wasn't enough. She was too nervous, she was *thinking* too much, she was always *thinking* too much. Why couldn't she just let go? He would lose patience, just like the last one did, and it would all be ruined.

Tears formed in her eyes. She had to try it; she had to be brave and try it.

"Your hands," she said. "Put your hands at my neck."

"What?" he panted.

"Put your hands around my neck."

"Listen, lady—"

"Carolyn, I'm Carolyn, oh, please." She was crying.

"Don't cry. Jesus, don't cry. I . . . okay . . ."

She felt his hands encircle her neck.

"Tighter," she said.

His hands pressed into her throat. "More, tighter . . ."

"You tell me when it's—"

"Yes, yes," she gasped. "Do it, do it, please."

When he entered her, she cried out. And as he came,

his fingers closed tighter in a reflexive grip. The instinct to fight was there, but her hands were tied. When the orgasm came, she felt the world slipping away.

The next thing she remembered was the feel of something soft and wet on her face. She opened her eyes with a start. He was kneeling over her, sweating, holding a towel.

"Are you okay?" he asked.

She nodded.

"Good God," he said. And he fell back against the headboard in relief.

She couldn't move. Her head hurt. Her body felt like liquid. He undid the ropes and pulled her to his chest. He kissed her bruised wrists and her neck over and over.

She drifted into sleep, and when she woke, he was gone. She heard the clock downstairs chime twice. She picked up the phone and dialed the number.

"It's Carolyn," she said when the person picked up.

Her eyes fell on the red orchid on the night table.

"He was beautiful," she whispered. "Thank you."

Chapter Fifteen

M r. Kincaid?"

Jesus, what time was it?

"Mr. Kincaid?"

"Hold on a sec."

Louis moved the phone to his other ear and snatched his watch from the nightstand. Eight-fifteen in the morning.

"Mr. Kincaid? Are you there?"

"Yeah, Kent, I'm here. Start over. I missed what you said."

Reggie's voice dropped to a whisper. "The police are here," he said. "That detestable man Barberry and Lieutenant Swann. But they brought others with them, and they're everywhere."

"Calm down. Did they show you a search warrant?"

"They showed me a piece of paper. Can't you and Mel just come here and do something?"

Louis put a foot against Mel's mattress and shook the bed. Mel grumbled and rolled to his side.

"Do you know a lawyer you can call, Kent?" Louis asked.

"I know a hundred, but they all cost money," Reggie said. "Please. Are you coming?"

Louis wanted to tell him private eyes cost money, too, but he didn't. "Yeah. Sit tight, and don't get in Barberry's way, or he'll arrest you. Do you understand?"

"Yes. Thank you, Mr. Kincaid. Thank you so much."

Louis hung up and grabbed his jeans, kicking Mel's bed two more times before he finished dressing. Mel finally came to life, crawled from the bed, and stumbled to the bathroom. Through a crack in the door and over the sound of gargling, Louis told Mel about the search warrant being served at Reggie Kent's house.

Fifteen minutes later, they pulled the Mustang to a stop at the end of Reggie's driveway, behind a Palm Beach police car. One of Barberry's deputies stood on the porch, arms crossed, eyes shaded by mirrored sunglasses.

Louis was debating how to get past the guy when Reggie emerged from the house. He was barefoot and still in his robe, a white terry-cloth thing haphazardly tied. His wispy yellow hair was electrified with static. He stopped in front of Louis and thrust the search warrant into his hand.

"They're tearing apart Mark's room," Reggie said. "Can they do that?"

Louis scanned the warrant. It was standard stuff—the right to confiscate any and all possible evidence related to the disappearance and homicide of Mark Durand. It went on to list every conceivable thing human beings could have in their homes.

Louis gave the warrant back to Reggie and looked at the house. The front door was open, but Louis couldn't see much inside. It looked like Barberry had a full team of officers and techs.

"Have they taken anything of interest?" Louis asked. "Anything you think might look bad for you?"

Reggie shook his head. "How could they? There is no evidence. I didn't kill Mark. I told you that."

"Calm down."

Barberry came out the front door. He wore a mustard-yellow sports coat and chocolate-colored pants. Louis's eyes locked on the items he was carrying.

In one hand, he held a clear plastic evidence bag that contained a pair of men's work boots caked with dried mud. They were the kind of heavy-treaded boot that left a distinct print in soft ground. In his other hand, Barberry held an exotic-looking sword in an elaborate gold scabbard.

Barberry came down the drive, stopped near Reggie, and held up the plastic bag. "You recognize these, Mr. Kent?"

Reggie seemed to have a hard time tearing his stunned gaze from the sword. Louis wasn't sure how to read his surprise. Did he not know that either of these things was in the house, or was he horrified that he hadn't thought to dispose of them?

"Answer me, Kent," Barberry said. "Do you recognize these boots?"

"You don't have to answer anything, Reg," Mel said.

Barberry looked at Mel. "When did you become a goddamn lawyer?"

Reggie suddenly found some courage. He straightened his shoulders, pushed out his chest, and pointed to the boots. "Lots of men I know wear those kinds of boots," he said. "On any given night of the week, you can go over to Kashmir's and find half a dozen. But those are not mine. I've never even owned a pair like that."

"Maybe you borrowed them the night you took Durand for a ride out to the middle of nowhere and chopped off his head with this."

With the flair of a B-movie detective, Barberry raised the sword. Reggie leaned backward.

"I've never see that before, either. And I certainly didn't use it to cut off anyone's head."

Barberry snorted and turned to Swann, who had come up behind him. He handed off the sword and the plastic bag and looked back at Reggie as he reached for his handcuffs.

"You can put it all in a statement down at the jail," Barberry said. "You're under arrest."

Reggie's eyes widened, and he started to back-pedal, any indignation suddenly evaporating. Barberry grabbed his arm, and Reggie's eyes swung to Louis and Mel for help. Louis knew Reggie was one step away from having his face pushed into the concrete.

"Kent, relax," Louis said.

"But he's arresting me!"

Barberry spun Reggie around and shoved him toward a palmetto palm. Reggie stumbled, and Louis was going to catch him, but Mel was faster. He caught Reggie by the shoulders and held on to him as he threw Barberry a glare. Then he bent down and whispered something in Reggie's ear.

Breathless, Reggie nodded and slowly put both of his shaking hands behind his back. Barberry snapped on the cuffs and started a clenched-jaw recitation of Reggie's rights. But Reggie, head down and fighting tears, was listening to Mel's quiet advice.

"Come on, Kent," Barberry said. "Let's go."

Barberry dragged Reggie toward the unmarked cruiser, and Louis followed. He had a few things he wanted to say, but he needed to wait until Reggie was in the backseat.

Barberry pushed Reggie into the car and slammed the door. He knew Louis was hanging nearby, but he walked around the car to the driver's-side door and opened it.

"Detective," Louis called. "Can you give me a minute?"

"What for?"

"Got a question."

Barberry slammed the door hard enough to jiggle the car, making it clear he didn't want Reggie to overhear any of this. "Make it quick."

"Why didn't you tell us that you have twenty other suspects?"

"What the fuck you talking about?"

"The workers at the Archer Ranch. Twenty guys with whips."

"None of them cowboys killed Durand."

"And even if they did, you wouldn't break much of a sweat trying to make a case against them, would you?"

Barberry's upper lip curled. "You calling me a bigot or some kind of fairy hater?"

"I'm calling you a lousy cop with a real bad attitude."

Barberry stepped to him and poked a finger at Louis's chest. "Tough talk coming from a down-and-out colored boy with a paper PI license."

Louis flexed his hand, then inhaled slowly. "Someone ought to euthanize you and put you out of your misery."

"Huh?"

Louis walked away from him, a slow burn creeping up the back of his neck. As much as he wanted to deck Barberry and as good as he knew it would feel, he didn't want Mel worrying about getting two people out of jail.

"I hate that fucker," Louis said as he reached Mel.

"We need to help Reggie find a lawyer."

"You know one who will work for free?"

Mel shook his head and reached for his cigarettes. Louis had one idea about the lawyer, but he didn't want to mention it to Mel yet. It was a long shot, and he wasn't sure Margery Laroche would actually back up her affection for "poor dear Reggie" with a hundred grand for legal fees.

And in the end, even the best lawyer wouldn't be able to help Reggie Kent if there was no one looking for other evidence and other possible killers.

Louis looked to the house. The search was winding

down. Officers were closing the doors on the back of the county evidence van, and the uniforms were heading to their cruisers. The cop by the door was gone.

"Did you see where Swann went?" Louis asked.

"Back in the house."

Louis went inside. The place was empty, but it was clear it been searched. Most departments didn't require or even ask that the officers replace anything moved during a search, and Barberry's guys were no different. Rifled drawers hung open, books were dumped on chairs, and sofa pillows were strewn across the floor.

"Lieutenant Swann?" Louis called.

"Back here."

Louis followed the voice to a bedroom at the end of the hall. The room had lemon-colored walls and bright floral-print curtains. The cops had given the room a thorough toss. The spread was heaped on the terra-cotta floor, along with pillows, magazines, and books. Drawers were still open, the contents searched. Even the Haitian painting had been taken off the wall and flung into a corner.

There was a glass étagère on one side of the room. The top shelf held a variety of things: a colorfully beaded apple, a snow globe from New York, a green speckled bowl, a gold pen set, a crystal Eiffel Tower, and a wooden box.

On the other side of the room, the double closet doors stood open. There were some pastel shirts and slacks still hanging, but the cops had thrown most of the clothes onto the bed and had rifled though the shoe boxes on the closet shelf. A Vuitton duffel sat open in the middle of the floor. Louis noticed the tag said M. DURAND.

"Is this Durand's room?" he asked.

"Yeah." Swann picked up the painting, looked around for a place to hang it, and finally just carefully propped it up on the floor against the dresser.

"I thought we had an arrangement here, Andrew," Louis said.

Swann sighed. "I can't argue with a search warrant, you know that. I came along to make sure Mr. Kent didn't, either."

Louis did know that, but he wasn't going to cut Swann any slack. "What else do they have on Kent besides what they took out of here?" he asked. "Did Barberry tell you?"

Swann shook his head. "He walked into my office this morning waving the warrant and said I could come along or not. He didn't offer any more information."

Louis glanced again at the closet, noticing now that the bottom was bare. He was sure Barberry had taken all of Reggie Kent's shoes, and he had apparently taken all of Durand's as well. It was smart to take all of the shoes and hope for a match on something.

"Did you find that guy Labastide?" Swann asked.

"Not exactly, but I found his sister."

"Sister?"

"Yeah. You met her once. Rosa Labastide."

Swann's brows knit in confusion. "When?"

"Five years ago," Louis said. "She came to you to report her brother Emilio missing. She said you didn't seem interested and that you told her Emilio probably just went back to Mexico."

"I was just a patrolman five years ago," Swann said. "How does she know it was me?"

"She remembered your name. Said it first in Spanish—*Cisne*. That means—"

"Swan," Swann said.

Louis stared at him. "You speak Spanish?"

"Fluently."

"And you still blew this woman off?" Louis asked. "Even after understanding every word she was trying to tell you?"

Swann dropped down on the edge of the bed. Louis could almost see his mental rifling of memories, and, given the pained expression on Swann's face, his efforts to recall Rosa looked sincere.

"I think Emilio Labastide is dead," Louis said. "And I think he was murdered."

Swann looked up at him. "Then you did find him."

Louis took a quick look out the bedroom door to make sure all of Barberry's deputies were gone, then went back to Swann. It was time to bring him completely onboard the train or throw him under it.

"There was a decapitated body found over in Lee County in October of '84, a short time after Labastide disappeared," Louis said. "The man was buried without an ID, but I'm sure it's Labastide."

"How sure?"

"He matches the physical description, and he was found with a crucifix that looks a lot like the one his sister has."

Swann sighed and leaned his head in his hands. Louis looked out at the patio, watching the easy roll of waves over the sand.

Louis knew that cops lived with regrets, all kinds of them. From not spending enough time with their families to losing their tempers with mouthy suspects. But one of the worst regrets was that one time when you found yourself standing over a dead person you had met before. And you realized that at some time in the past, maybe a month or maybe a year before, you could've done something better. Made one more phone call, asked one more question, stayed one more hour at your desk.

Louis watched Swann, wondering how he could lure him completely over to his side. He couldn't help but think about that Officer of the Month certificate on Swann's office wall and Swann's "heroic act" of saving the drowning dog. Louis had no idea if Swann had the smarts or the mettle for a real homicide investigation. Or if he had the stones to buck his own chief.

Swann looked up at him. "What can I do to help?"

Hell, what did he have to lose?

"You ever wanted to be a spy?" Louis asked.

"Didn't every kid?" Swann said. "Who would I be spying on?"

"Barberry."

They met an hour later at a Dunkin' Donuts out near the airport. Mel paid for coffee and a bag of six doughnuts, three plain and three with sprinkles. They spotted Swann sitting in the back. As they slid into the orange plastic booth, Louis noticed Swann looking around uncomfortably.

"What's the matter?" Louis asked.

"Nothing," he said. "I've never been in a Dunkin' Donuts before."

"We weren't sure you'd even know what a Dunkin' Donuts was," Mel said. "That's why we gave you such detailed directions."

"Oh, I've heard about these places," he said. "This is where the real cops hang out, right?"

For about three seconds, the table was uneasily silent, then Swann broke into a grin. "Relax, guys. Let's get this meeting going. I've only got an hour."

"First, we need to know what Barberry has told you that we might not know," Louis said.

"I know he's still looking for that luxury car that was seen in Clewiston. He told me to ask around the island about cars Kent could have borrowed."

"Did you?"

"I questioned Kent, and he said he regularly borrowed cars from some of his 'lady friends,' as he calls them. They even give him extra keys. I checked and found out two of them are light-colored luxury cars that could match the one seen going through Clewiston. So I approached the two women at a party I was working last weekend and discreetly asked them about it. Both said Kent hadn't asked to borrow their cars in quite some time."

"That helps," Mel said. "Is there anything else we can use to eliminate Reggie as a suspect?"

"Not with regard to Durand's murder," Swann said. "But what about that other guy? Labastide? When was he killed?"

"The ME speculated he was killed two nights before he was found," Louis said. "That makes it October 31, 1984. But I don't think that will do us much good. What kind of person knows exactly where they were on a given night five years ago?"

Swann smiled. "I can tell you where Kent probably was."

"Where?"

"Margery Laroche's birthday party. Every year, she throws herself a Halloween birthday bash," Swann said. "We work security and parking. I'd bet my job Kent was there."

"Please tell me she keeps guest lists," Mel said.

"Even better. Most of the names would have been printed in the *Shiny Sheet* along with a slew of pictures. It's a big deal because everyone's in costumes. And knowing Margery Laroche, she would have kept a copy of the paper."

"Great," Louis said. "I'll go back and ask her about them."

"That's useful only if we can tie these two murders together," Mel said. "But for right now, we need to find something to clear him of Durand's murder."

"You guys know about the cowboys out at the Archer ranch?" Swann asked.

"Cowmen," Mel said.

"What?"

"They like to be called cowmen."

Swann just stared at him.

"We know they found Durand's body and that Barberry took all of their whips," Louis said.

"The reports said that none of the whips had any human blood on them, and Dr. Steffel said that the one used on Durand was leather. The ones Barberry confiscated were nylon," Swann said.

"Doesn't mean they didn't have leather whips somewhere else," Mel said.

"Did you get to read any of the statements Barberry took from them?" Louis asked.

Swann shook his head. "No. But as far as I know, Barberry never seriously pursued any of the Archer workers as suspects. Never even ran backgrounds on any of them."

"Jesus," Mel muttered.

"Did you two talk to any of them?" Swann asked.

"No," Louis said. He picked up a doughnut. It had lost some sprinkles, and he wet his finger to dab them up as he talked. "But we talked to the boss, a guy named Burke Aubry. He seemed sure none of them was involved. Said they wouldn't desecrate the ranch land like that."

"Not just the ranch land, Rocky," Mel said. "Devil's Garden."

"What's Devil's Garden?" Swann asked.

"The area of the ranch where Durand was killed," Louis said. "The family gave it to the state as a preserve."

"The guy found over in Lee County," Swann said. "How far is that from this Devil's Garden?"

"About thirty miles," Louis said. "But the weirder thing is, that body was found by a cowboy who worked for the Archers."

Swann's brow wrinkled. "That's a helluva coincidence. So, tell me again why we're taking this Aubry guy's word that his men are innocent?"

Again, Louis noticed Swann's use of the pronoun *we*. The guy obviously wanted in on this.

"We're not," Louis said. "But we could save ourselves some time if we had their statements so we could check them out for ourselves. Can you do that for us?"

Swann nodded. "No problem."

Louis pulled his notebook out again and flipped it

open to the first empty page. For a cop, it was easy to sit down at a computer and summarize a witness interview or input leads and have it all at your fingertips when the puzzle pieces started to fall into place. But as a PI whose cases had ranged as far as the northern woods of Michigan, he had learned to rely on notebooks with colored tabs.

He flipped to the back. "What's your home phone, Andrew?"

Swann reached into his wallet and pulled out a business card. Louis stuck it in his pocket.

"I guess the next thing we need to do is positively identify the body found in Lee County," Louis said.

"Get me his prints," Swann said. "I can match them to the ID card."

"Lee County screwed up and didn't take any," Louis said. "The only chance we have at an ID is digging him up and hoping there is enough of him left to compare."

"Then let's do it," Swann said.

"You don't know the asshole sheriff over there," Louis said. "He doesn't care about someone like Labastide, and he plays golf with the district attorney. If we want to dig Labastide up, we have to pay for it ourselves."

"It's a long shot, but I know a few people in the prosecutor's office over there," Mel said. "Let me give it a try."

"I have a question," Swann said.

"Shoot."

"Actually, I have a lot of questions." Swann lowered his voice. "You probably can guess I've never worked a homicide before."

Louis felt a twinge of pity for Swann. "You're working one now, Andrew."

Swann gave a small smile. "Okay, why would anyone in Palm Beach drive their victim all the way out past Clewiston to kill him? Why not just dump him in a canal in West Palm?"

Louis glanced at Mel. They had wondered the same thing, but without a suspect or a clear motive, there was no urgency to find the answer. But now, because they had two victims, it was time to give it some thought.

"We might be dealing with a serial killer," Mel said. "And they have unique ways of doing things—signatures, rituals, call it what you want. It's weird little details that only they understand that complete the act of murder for them."

"And being at that cattle pen could be some sort of sick staging?" Swann asked.

"Yeah."

"And the whip?"

"It may be important, but there was no indication in his autopsy report that the John Doe was whipped or tortured."

Swann looked confused. "Then why are we tying these two murders together?"

"Because there might be a relationship link," Louis said.

"Between who?"

Louis sighed. "I wish we knew."

"We're thinking this might be homosexual homicides," Mel said.

"Because of Kent?" Swann asked.

Mel shook his head. "No, because of certain patterns we're seeing. Both victims were similar in age and physical appearance. Also, both murders were extremely violent, what we call overkill. Both victims had their throats slashed. The throat is a sort of pseudo sex organ among gays."

"Ah, isn't that true of straight people?" Swann asked.

Mel glanced at Louis. *"Touché."*

Swann shook his head. "I still say, this just doesn't sound like Reggie Kent."

Mel was nodding. "I agree. When I was on the Miami force, I had some experience with this. I was one of the few cops who bothered to take the time to learn the psychology behind it."

Now Louis was listening intently.

"Reggie told us that he and Mark didn't really have a sexual relationship, that Mark was really straight," Mel said. "But Mark Durand was a hustler with the record to prove it. In my experience, these guys are often heterosexuals who agree to gay sex as long as certain rules are obeyed."

"And if someone breaks the rules?" Swann asked.

"Someone pays," Mel said.

"But Durand was living with Kent. He didn't need to hustle for money," Swann said.

Mel looked at Louis and shrugged. "I didn't say we had all the answers."

Swann was quiet, deep in thought. "So, was Labastide gay?"

"We don't know," Louis said.

Swann's eyes went from Louis to Mel. "Well, what the hell do you know?"

"Knowing that you don't know what you should know is the first step to knowing, grasshopper," Mel said.

Louis laughed.

Swann just stared at them, but then he smiled.

Louis flipped to a fresh page in his notebook. "Let's figure out our next steps," he said.

"Somebody has to go back to Rosa Díaz and ask her point-blank about her brother," Mel said.

"I'll do it," Swann said.

Louis finished writing in his notebook. He looked up and held out his hand to Mel. "Give me the receipt."

"For what?" Mel asked.

"The doughnuts and coffee. I'm keeping track of our expenses."

"I threw it away."

"Well, how much was it?"

"I don't know. Put down four bucks."

"You got a whole bag of doughnuts. It has to be more than that."

Mel rolled his eyes. "You're trying my patience here, Rocky."

"Good grief. It's my treat," Swann said. He tossed a twenty across the table to Mel. "And I've been meaning to ask you, why do you call him Rocky?"

"Rocky King was a TV detective back in the fifties," Mel said. "It's my term of affection for my friend here. I thought it sounded better than fuck-face."

Mel glanced at Louis. "You know, I think it's time to give our friend here a nickname."

"Mel—"

Mel gave Swann a smile. "Welcome to the team, Bat-zarro."

Swann frowned. "Bat what?"

But before Mel could answer, Swann's beeper went

off. He checked the number and quickly got up. He flashed his badge to the clerk and picked up the phone behind the cash register.

Swann came back and slid into the booth.

"We've got a damsel in distress," he said. He looked at Louis. "And she wants you to save her."

Chapter Sixteen

Margery was waiting for him in the lobby of the Palm Beach County jail. She was wearing a suit the color of eggplant and a matching wide-brimmed hat. A necklace of purple ice-cube-sized stones caught the light from the fluorescents as she spun to him. In the echoing tile cavern of the lobby—with its wanted posters, metal detectors, and rows of forlorn people sitting on metal benches—she looked like an exotic butterfly trapped in a dog cage.

"Louis! Thank God!" She exhaled a cloud of gin as she floated over to him. "What took you so long?"

"I got here as soon as I could," Louis said. "What's wrong?"

"They won't let me see Reggie," she said. She waved toward a man behind the Plexiglas. "And that horrible old bull won't take my check!"

"Check? What check?"

Margery popped open her big purse and pulled out a pink leather checkbook. "I am trying to pay Reggie's bail so I can take him home," she said, waving the checkbook toward the information booth. "And he won't listen to me."

The officer behind the Plexiglas wasn't smiling. Louis knew that the guys who pulled desk detail were usually low on the food chain. Margery had been here at least a half hour giving him shit, and he was probably one more insult away from arresting her for disturbing the peace.

"Margery, you can't bail Reggie out," Louis said.

"Of course I can. I don't care how much—"

"Number one, he hasn't even been arraigned yet, and number two, people who are charged with murder don't get bail."

Margery stared at him like he was lying—or just stupid—he couldn't tell. Then, to his shock, she burst into tears. Everyone was staring. He took Margery's elbow and steered her to a bench in the corner.

She dug in her purse for a handkerchief and dabbed at her eyes. A few long, shuddering breaths later, she was back under control. "I've really balled things up," she said. "I mean, first, I wasn't even home when Reggie called me. I was lunching with Dixie at the Colony, and it was past three by the time I got home, so I didn't know he had been arrested! Reggie, my poor, dear Reggie, had been trying to call me all day—Franklin must not have heard the phone—but thank God, I finally picked it up, and I came here, and they have been utterly beastly to me!"

Louis was afraid another outburst was coming. "Margery, you need to get Reggie a lawyer."

"I know that!" she said. "I called Harvey, but he's got some big case up in New York and can't get here until tomorrow." She grabbed Louis's hand. "Harvey is the berries, the absolute best money can buy!"

Louis nodded. "Good. That's what Reggie needs right now, the berries."

Margery's eyes drifted to the information booth. "They won't let me see him. I can't bear the thought of Reggie in there alone. My poor, dear old bunny. Do you think he'll be all right?"

Louis didn't want to tell her what he was thinking, that a man like Reggie Kent was dog meat in a place like this. Over on the island, Swann would have kept Reggie safe and comfortable. Here in a county jail, Reggie was just another animal in the zoo, a zoo where dear old bunnies were routinely dissected and devoured.

Louis glanced up at a sign by the intake window. Visiting hours had ended an hour ago. He told Margery to wait, and he went up to the Plexiglas.

"Yeah?" the beefy uniform said.

"I need a favor," Louis said.

"For her? No way, partner. That lady's got an ugly mouth on her."

Louis leaned in. "She's not herself. She's a little—"

"Nuts?"

Louis nodded. "Her son was brought in today. She's worried about him. Can you get her in for a few minutes?"

The uniform looked around Louis to Margery. "She told me to go iron my shoelaces."

Louis just nodded.

"You work for her?" the uniform asked.

Louis nodded again.

"Hope she pays you good, man." He hesitated, then gave a shrug. "Okay, you got ten minutes."

Louis quickly briefed Margery on what to expect and

made her promise to keep her mouth shut. She was silent and straight-backed as they went back into the jail's receiving area. The noise was deafening, a constant echoing barrage of banging metal doors as deputies and lawyers came and went. He had left his Glock locked in the Mustang's glove box, so once he emptied his pockets into a tray, signed the log, and got his visitor badge, he was waved through. But Margery wasn't about to hand over her purse.

"You can't take anything back with you," Louis said to her.

"Louis, this is a Birkin," she whispered fiercely.

"Margery, please."

She hesitated, then reached into the bag and pulled out three packs of Gauloises.

"You can't take those, either," Louis said.

"But they're for Reggie."

"He can't accept anything from outside," Louis said. The cop behind the desk was looking impatient. "If you want, you can deposit some money here in his name, and he can buy his own cigarettes."

With a sigh, she tossed the blue packs into the purse, snapped it closed, and handed the purse over. She accepted the badge the officer gave her, and they were buzzed in. Margery jumped as the heavy door closed behind them.

A uniform led them to a room with a row of standard cubicles divided with heavy Plexiglas stained with handprints, spit, and a thousand tearful kisses. Margery stood there, taking it in, her face white, her big red slash of a mouth slack. Louis realized she was as lost in this world as he was in hers.

He gently touched her back and motioned for her to sit in one of the plastic chairs.

A moment later, a door banged, and Reggie was led in, dwarfed by a huge cop in a green PBSO windbreaker. Reggie's eyes found Margery, and he practically fell into the chair on the other side of the Plexiglas.

His eyes brimmed, and he slowly brought up a hand and pressed it against the Plexiglas. Margery did the same.

"Oh, my dear, my dear old bunny," Margery whispered.

"I knew you'd come," Reggie said.

"Are you all right?" Margery asked.

Reggie started to say something, then just bowed his head. His shoulders shook as he cried. Margery started talking to him, her voice gentle but firm. Louis was trying to stand back to be discreet, but he heard her mention a lawyer and that Reggie would be out of there soon. He knew Margery had no right to promise him that, so he stepped forward.

Louis got his first good look at him. The guy had been behind bars for less than five hours, and he already looked like shit. The orange jumpsuit was too big, and the lighting brought out every line and blemish in his pink skin.

"You must be brave, dear, and don't get too grummy," Margery said, trying to sound upbeat. "Harvey will be here tomorrow, and Louis is working hard."

Reggie's eyes shot up to Louis. "When are you getting me out of here?"

Louis realized no one had told him that he wasn't getting bail. "It will take some time," he said. "You need to just hang tough and stay out of everyone's way."

"Hang tough," Reggie said softly.

The guard came up behind Reggie. "Time's up."

Reggie quickly pressed his hand against the glass again. The guard put a palm on Reggie's shoulder.

"You have to go," Louis said. "Don't make any trouble, okay?"

Margery put her hand up to the glass again. But the guard already had Reggie out of the chair and back to the door. They disappeared behind a metal door. Margery sat there, staring at the Plexiglas. Then she stood up, adjusted her hat, and walked quickly back out to the sign-in area. She retrieved her purse and, without a word or a look back at Louis, walked briskly back out to the lobby. Louis had no choice but to gather his belongings quickly and run to catch up.

When they were outside, she finally stopped. She closed her eyes and took three deep breaths, one hand against her chest.

Louis heard a car door and looked to the curb, where a black Rolls sat idling. Margery's beefy driver had gotten out and was starting toward them.

Margery waved him away. When she turned back to Louis, the steel was back in her eyes.

"Do we kiss now or later?" she asked.

"Ma'am?"

She snapped open her purse and pulled out the checkbook. "Do you need cash, or will a check do?"

"Ah," Louis said. They had never discussed any kind of payment for working Reggie Kent's case. Back at Taboo during their first meeting, Reggie had told Mel that he had money to pay them. But that, Louis now knew, was like much of Reggie's life: an illusion.

"I don't care how much it takes, Louis," Margery said. "I want Reggie out of that place, and I want you to have enough to prove him innocent of all this." She pulled out a pen and flipped open the checkbook.

"I'll sign it," she said. "You and Marvin decide how many zeroes you want."

Chapter Seventeen

The sign was still there above the door. DE MOR-TUIS NIL NISI BONUM. Of the dead, say nothing but good.

Louis and Swann stood in the hall outside the autopsy rooms at the Lee County medical examiner's office. Mel had stayed back at the hotel, again saying he had a headache.

The medical examiner, Vince Carissimi, was down the hall finishing up an examination of the newly exhumed John Doe. Louis hoped that they would be able to discover some bit of evidence that might tell them more about how John Doe died. But at the very least, he hoped they would be able to identify this fellow as Emilio Labastide.

How exactly that might happen, Louis wasn't sure. It would require that there be enough usable skin left on the hands to obtain clear fingerprints. Or, as a last resort and probably an option they would never take, there would have to be enough of a body left to be viewed and recognized by Rosa.

"What are we going to do if we can't ID him?" Swann asked.

Louis looked at Swann. His usual peachy tan glow was gone, replaced by the gray pallor of dread that accompanied someone's first visit to a morgue.

"I don't know," Louis said. "You got any other ideas?"

"You ever heard of DNA testing?" Swann asked.

Louis nodded. He'd read about it in forensics magazines and heard talk around O'Sullivan's. It was a new technology that gave cops a surefire ID off small amounts of human tissue. More important, it offered an indisputable genetic blueprint of whoever left tissue or blood at a crime scene.

"I know a little about it," Louis said. "But wouldn't we have to have some tissue from Labastide that we know is his, something we can compare this tissue to?"

"Sure," Swann said. "But in the absence of that, there's also a way to match him up with relatives at a lesser percent."

"Like Rosa?"

Swann nodded. "But we'd need a really large sample to do that. Plus, it would take months to get the results back, and it's very expensive."

"How expensive?"

"A hundred thousand dollars."

"Wow."

"A lot of money for something when the courts don't even allow it to be admitted." Swann shook his head. "Can you imagine how easy our jobs would be if we could swab up a drop of blood at a crime scene and match it up to some criminal whose genetic profile is already in the system?"

Louis could see a hard glint of interest in Swann's eye that he had never seen before. The guy had the heart of a true crime dog. That was the nickname Louis had given those studious guys on the force who loved poring over science files and psych profiles rather than being out on the street.

"I don't know many defendants who can afford that kind of testing," Louis said.

"Yeah, but it will get cheaper," Swann said eagerly. "Like video cameras. Remember when those came out, they were around a thousand dollars? I bought one last week for the department for under three hundred."

Louis was quiet. He'd been a PI for more than three years now and didn't want to admit to Swann that he'd only recently bought a Nikon with a telephoto lens. He hadn't even mastered all of the settings yet.

"Hello, gentlemen."

Vinny made his entrance. Tall and lanky, with a healthy head of gray hair, he wore a loose-fitting cotton shirt printed with the red tongue logo of the Rolling Stones. As always, a pair of headphones hung around his collar.

"Hey, Vinny," Louis said, extending a hand. "Good to see you. This is Lieutenant Swann of Palm Beach PD."

Swann stepped forward and, with an obvious hesitation, extended a hand to Vinny. Louis wondered if he was afraid Vinny had dead people's cooties.

"So, you're the big bucks behind this?" Vinny asked Swann.

"Me? No, I'm not paying for this."

Vinny looked to Louis. "Then who is?"

"I'll write you a check."

"*Semper letteris mandate,*" Vinny said, shaking his head.

"What?"

"He said, 'Get it in writing,'" Swann said.

They both looked at him.

"You speak Latin, too?" Louis asked.

Swann shrugged.

"My man!" Vinny said, holding up his palm. They high-fived. "*Latine loqui coactus sum!*"

They launched into a rapid-fire dialogue in Latin, laughing like two old golf buddies.

"Can we get on with business?" Louis said finally.

"Fine with me," Vinny said. "Let's go take a look at our friend."

He led them into the autopsy room. A familiar smell pricked Louis's nostrils: human rot, industrial-strength disinfectant, and that odd metallic scent of blood. There were three tables, two empty and the third covered with a limp blue sheet. It was only when Louis stepped forward that he could see the skeletal contour of what lay beneath the cloth.

Louis looked back. Swann hadn't moved from the door.

"First time?" Vinny asked.

"I saw an autopsy once in the academy," Swann said. "On film."

Vinny handed him a jar of Vicks VapoRub and motioned for Swann to rub some under his nose. Swann did as instructed, handed the jar back to Vinny, and followed him to the table. Vinny carefully pulled back the sheet.

Louis had to stifle a gag. He'd seen quite a few dead bodies, some as healthy-looking as they had been in life and others so decomposed that little remained but black sludge. This body was a weird combination of both. The legs tapered off into ragged black flesh; the bones of the ankles and feet were gone. There was a hollowed-out gut but an almost intact rib cage. There was no head.

Louis looked at Swann, wondering if he was going to have to pick him up off the floor, but Swann was staring at the remains with the awe of a kid seeing his first fireworks display.

"Come around here and look at the hand," Vinny said.

Louis and Swann stepped around the table. The dead man's hand was moldered and missing all of the fingers, but what remained was the ballooned stub of a thumb. And Louis knew why it was distended: Vinny had injected it with fluid to stretch the skin and get a clear print.

"Did it work?" Louis asked.

Vinny held up two fingerprint cards. One was the worker ID card from the old Palm Beach jail that they knew to be Labastide's. Louis had given it to Vinny the day they dug up the body. He recognized the other as one from the Lee County lab.

"Gentlemen, say hello to Emilio Labastide," Vinny said.

Louis walked to the end of the table and motioned to the decayed stump of the neck. "Can you tell us anything about the weapon used to decapitate him?" he asked.

"I can tell you it's not the same one that was used to stab him in the chest," Vinny said. "That was a small and narrow-bladed knife of some kind."

"Could he have been beheaded with a sword?" Louis asked.

"Sword? Why do you ask?"

"They took one from the suspect's house."

Vinny picked up several X-rays. As he slapped them onto the backlit panels, he started talking.

"Well, there were no X-rays taken originally," Vinny said. "I took these this morning of Labastide's cervical vertebrae. The only thing I can tell is that it was a large blade of some kind. There isn't enough tissue left for me to say exactly."

"So, it could be a sword?" Louis pressed.

Vinny nodded. "I can tell you that whatever was used, it was done with extreme violence. It's not easy to behead someone. Inexperienced killers would most likely try to saw a head off, especially if they were doing it to avoid identification."

"This happened in the middle of nowhere and likely in the dead of night," Louis said. "The killer probably had all the time he needed to do whatever he wanted with this body."

"Instead, he hacked away like a madman," Vinny said. "How big is this sword?"

"Maybe three feet long," Swann said. "It looks like an old saber."

Vinny crossed his arms and studied his X-rays. Louis could hear music squeaking from the little black foam pads on his headphones. It was Janis Joplin: "I'm gonna lay my head / On that lonesome railroad line / And let the 2:19 ease my troubled mind."

"One thing to keep in mind," Vinny said. "A sword is not an easy thing to use. If it's old, it's probably heavy and may not be sharp. I'm thinking whoever did this was standing upright and swinging downward. And even though he was in a rage, he had to have some strength and skill."

Louis stared down at the remains. At least they had a way now to connect Labastide to Durand—if the weapon was in fact a sword. But a more telling piece of evidence was still missing.

"Vinny, did you see any sign that Labastide was tortured?" Louis asked.

Vinny frowned and picked up the original autopsy report. He scanned it and shrugged. "Nothing here." He paused, looking down at the remains.

"Well, well," Vinny murmured. *"Minima maxima sunt."*

"'The smallest things are the most important,'" Swann said.

Vinny grabbed a magnifying glass off the shelf and used it to peer at the shriveled hand. He looked back up at Louis.

"The original autopsy was done by Thomas Cartwright, a.k.a. Careless Cartwright," Vinny said. "He wasn't the sharpest scalpel in the drawer and was known for going with what seemed the most likely. He noted a mark on the right hand, and because he knew the victim had been stabbed, he assumed it was a defensive wound."

Vinny motioned Louis closer and held the magnifying glass over the hand for him. Swann came, too, filling the space with a citrusy aftershave, which, given the stench from the table, was strangely welcome.

"Now, I ask you," Vinny said. "Does this look like a knife wound to you?"

Louis looked at the ashy, bloated hand. The furrow across the palm was clearly visible. He glanced down at his own hand, at the old knife scar that banded his palm like a strap. The line was white, flat, and razor-thin, nothing like the mark on Labastide's hand.

"That's not a knife cut," Vinny said. "I'd say that's a rope-burn-type mark, like the kind you'd get playing tug-of-war."

"Could it be a whip mark?" Louis asked.

Vinny raised a brow, then bent to examine the hand more closely. When he lifted his head, he nodded. "Sure could be."

Louis moved away from the table. His mind clicked back to the crime-scene photos he'd seen at O'Sullivan's, and suddenly it wasn't difficult to imagine the last few moments of Emilio Labastide's life.

Willingly or not, Labastide had been driven more than a hundred miles to the middle of nowhere. At some point, Labastide was overpowered by someone who stabbed him in the chest. He fought back and managed to get away. His attacker pursued him, maybe with the knife, but with a whip for certain. Labastide was young and strong, and despite the stab wounds, he managed to catch the tail of the whip in an attempt to wrestle it away.

But then he started to lose strength. Or maybe his killer came at him with a knife or the sword and hacked away with a madness that cops saw only in crimes that were intensely personal or blind rage. But were they looking at a lone serial murderer or a group motivated by pure hatred?

"You okay, Louis?" Swann asked.

Louis nodded.

There was no question in his mind that the murders of Mark Durand and Emilio Labastide were committed by the same killer or, quite possibly, killers. The links—the last known locale of the victim tied to Palm Beach, vicious decapitations, and torture with a whip—were too strong for even someone like Barberry to ignore.

Not that Louis intended to share any of this information with him. He knew Barberry would, beyond all logic, continue to dismiss any evidence that didn't favor his case against Reggie Kent.

If they wanted to make their case for a different killer irrefutable, they needed to offer the Palm Beach prosecutor not just circumstantial evidence but a believable motive for someone other than Reggie Kent.

Louis looked back to Vinny, who was pulling the X-rays off the clips. "Thanks for doing this, Vinny," he said. "We appreciate it. Can you hold the remains until we can notify his sister and find out where she'd like him reburied?"

"I can give you about three days," Vinny said. "Then I have to send him somewhere. Unless, of course, your benefactor wants to pay storage fees."

"We'll get back to you as soon as we can," Louis said.

Vinny pulled his headphones back on his head and covered the remains with the sheet. Louis and Swann left the autopsy room, walking quickly down the long hall in search of fresh air. Once outside in the sunlight, Louis paused on the sidewalk and took two or three deep breaths.

Swann came up next to him, hands in pockets, wearing Ray-Bans. "Are we going to see Labastide's sister now?"

"Yeah," Louis said. "We need to tell her we've found

her brother, and after you apologize to her, you need to ask her some tough questions."

"About her brother's sex life?"

"Yeah. You up for that?"

"Sí, jefe."

Louis stared at him.

"Yes, boss," Swann said.

Rosa was watering the red flowers outside her door when she spotted Louis and Swann coming up the stairs. Her look to Louis was warm, but when she recognized Swann, her brown eyes snapped with scorn.

Swann must have seen it, too, because he held out a hand in a gesture to stop Louis and moved slowly by himself to Rosa. Rosa set the water can on a small table and crossed her arms.

"Es usted. ¿Cómo se atreve a usted presentarle aquí?"

Louis didn't understand a word she said, but from the tone, it was not kind.

Swann stood close to her and began speaking very softly. Louis stayed where he was, a few feet from the open front door. Rosa's head was down, face hidden behind the thick curtain of ebony hair as she listened calmly to Swann.

"Su hermano está muerto," Swann said. *"Lo siento."*

Louis understood a few words—brother, dead, sorry.

Rosa's hands went to her face, and to Louis's surprise, she fell gently against Swann. He let her cry for a moment, then wrapped an arm around her shoulders and led her inside the apartment. Louis followed.

Swann took Rosa to the small table near the kitchen

window and sat across from her. She continued to sob, handfuls of Kleenex pressed to her face.

Louis sat on the arm of the sofa. For the next five or six minutes, he was quiet, listening to the soft murmur of Swann's Spanish and looking around at the meager Christmas decorations.

A small artificial tree stood on a table, draped with gold tinsel and decorated with three—only three—brightly painted glass ornaments in the shape of a sombrero-wearing *señorita*. Sitting on a plate nearby was a small array of what looked like gingerbread cookies shaped like the flowered decals of the hippie era.

A gurgle drew his attention to a blanket-draped playpen near the window. He went to it and looked down. A baby in a white T-shirt and an old-fashioned cloth diaper and rubber pants stared up at him, its brown eyes wide in curiosity. It was sucking tenaciously on a pacifier.

Louis heard the crinkle of a plastic bag and turned back to Swann and Rosa. She was calm now as Swann showed her the crucifix Burke Aubry had given them. Rosa touched it through the evidence bag, then gave Swann a nod and opened her blouse to show him an identical one around her neck.

Swann put the crucifix away and reached across the table to cover her hand with his. Then he said something in Spanish that brought a rise of color to Rosa's cheeks. She looked to the window, then lowered her head as she answered him.

Louis eased closer.

Suddenly, Rosa looked up at him and then back at Swann. "*¿Me pregunta usted si mi hermano fué homosexual?*"

"*Sí,*" Swann said.

Again, Rosa glanced at Louis. "*No,*" she said. "*No, era muy popular con las mujeres.*"

Swann looked to Louis. "She says he was very popular with the ladies."

"*Tuvo muchas novias.*"

"He had many girlfriends."

Rosa said something else. Swann nodded and then turned to Louis. "But that was when he was in Mexico. He changed once he came here."

Rosa's voice had dropped to a whisper. "*Tuvo una niña en Mexico,*" she said.

Swann listened intently, then turned to Louis. "He got a girl pregnant back in Mexico, and they had a daughter. That's why he came here, so he could make money to send home."

Rosa started to cry, and Swann took her hand in his and spoke to her softly in Spanish. It seemed intrusive to watch, so Louis turned his gaze back to the living room and, for want of something interesting, down to the baby.

It had lost its pacifier and started to kick and punch at the air and make those weird little snorty noises babies made when they start to get upset. Then it burst into a wail.

Rosa was there before Louis could pick up the pacifier. She swept the baby into her arms. The baby put its head against Rosa's shoulder, eyes wet and worried. It reminded Louis of the way the family dog looks at its owner when it knows something sad has happened to him.

"Thank you, Mrs. Díaz," Swann said, holding out his

business card to her. *"Gracias por decirme la verdad y por perdonarme."*

Rosa tucked the card into her pocket and looked to Louis. Her eyes were brimming with fresh tears. "I want to see Emilio's grave," she said. "Can you tell me where he is buried?"

Louis couldn't tell her that her brother was no longer buried anywhere but lying in a morgue cooler. He thought about Margery's check. He'd filled in the dollar amount for $50,000, with no idea of how much of that they'd actually use. Or if all of the costs would meet with Margery's approval. But this was going to have to be one of them.

"Do you have a cemetery here in Immakolee?"

Rosa nodded. *"Sí,* but I have no money to bring Emilio here. It must be . . . *muy caro."*

"Don't worry about it," Louis said. "It will all be taken care of."

Rosa thanked him and said something to Swann in Spanish before she took the baby to the bedroom. Swann watched her, ran a hand across his mouth, and left the apartment.

Down in the parking lot, Swann pulled his sunglasses from his pocket but didn't put them on. He stared toward the horizon, his eyes slightly pink.

"Just because he got a girl pregnant doesn't mean he wasn't gay," Louis said.

Swann looked back at Rosa's apartment and then to the ground. He seemed to be having trouble shaking the profound grief that had enveloped both of them upstairs.

"Yeah, I know," Swann said. "And I pressed her on that. She said she and Emilio had a gay cousin in Mexico and that he was okay with that, and had he himself been that way, he would've been open about it. But she was absolutely sure he wasn't. They . . . were really close."

Swann sighed and slipped on his sunglasses, seemingly grateful to have something to hide behind. Louis thought about their visit to the Lee County morgue and how Swann had stood over a rotting corpse without so much as wrinkling his nose. But faced with a young woman to whom he owed the mother of all apologies, he was nothing but mush.

"You need a drink, Andrew?"

Swann nodded. "Yeah. Sounds good."

They headed toward the Mustang, the sun on their backs. As he unlocked the car door, Louis glanced up at Rosa's apartment. There were two heavyset women waddling toward the open door, probably already sensing the bad news. He was glad Rosa would have people with her.

"Okay, I got a question," Swann said.

Louis looked at Swann across the canvas top of the car. "Go ahead."

"We now have no reason to think Labastide was gay," Swann said. "And we don't have much of a reason to believe Mark Durand was really gay."

"Right."

"In fact, both these guys, if the rumors prove to be true, were seeing married women," Swann said. "So where do we go from here?"

"Did you ever hear a rumor about Labastide, or anyone like him, being run from some woman's bedroom by a jealous husband?" Louis asked.

Swann shook his head. "Not a word. Who told you that?"

"Margery Laroche," Louis said. "But she wouldn't tell me the woman's name. Think you can get it out of her?"

Swann looked up at Rosa's door. "After that, I can face anything."

Chapter Eighteen

They were gathered on Margery's loggia. Louis and Mel were sitting on the rattan sofa. Swann was perched on an ottoman in the corner. Margery was ensconced on the lounge with the four pug dogs on her lap.

"I feel like Susan Hayward in *I Want to Live*," she said.

Louis stifled a sigh. Mel didn't bother.

Swann cleared his throat. "Mrs. Laroche," he said, "we're not interrogating you. We're just asking for your help."

She eyed them all and pulled the dogs closer. "Well, it feels like you're ganging up on me, and I don't like it," she said.

Mel rose suddenly and went to one of the arched windows, his back to them. Swann looked pained. They had been there for a half hour, trying to get Margery to divulge the name of the woman Emilio Labastide had allegedly bedded, but Margery refused to tell them. Louis knew that Mel was about one minute away from scaring Margery with an obstruction-of-justice charge, even though he had no authority.

And Swann? Louis glanced over at the guy. He

looked miserable, like someone was beating up on his mother.

"Margery," Louis said firmly, "I want you to listen to me very carefully."

"You, too, Louis?" she asked. There it was again, "Loo-EE."

"Margery, you hired us to help Reggie Kent," Louis said.

"But I already told you that he was at my birthday party that night," she said. "That's an alibi, right?"

"It's not enough," Louis said. "We can't help him unless we can prove someone else killed Mark Durand. You saw that jail. If Reggie is convicted, he will be sent away to prison. I've been to Starke, and it makes the Palm Beach County jail look like, like . . ."

"The Bath and Tennis Club," Swann said.

Louis glanced at him, then looked back at Margery. Her wide red mouth was still a hard line.

"You have to tell us the name of the woman Emilio Labastide was seeing," Louis said.

"Louis, dear," Margery said softly, "this is not like the real world. People here don't have jobs, so they have to find ways to keep busy. They shop, drink, do drugs, eat lunch, screw around, and gossip."

"Margery—"

"Let me finish," Margery said. "Everyone loves to hear the dirt. But they're afraid to death of being ostracized. If you talk too much, you're out. I told you before, this is a very small island."

She looked at Swann. "You know this," she said. "Just last week, one of your men had to go down to the docks and pick up a certain gentleman who was sitting there naked, zozzled on coke, wearing handcuffs and a purple bra. Your man didn't blink an eye, just put him in the backseat and drove him home."

Swann pursed his lips, his face reddening slightly. Mel had turned around and was listening.

Louis knew he had to try another tactic. "Margery, you said that everyone has affairs but that people here don't sleep down," he said. "So, why would this woman bother with a man like Emilio Labastide?"

Margery glanced at the other men before coming back to Louis. "Power is everything here," she said. "Men get their power from money. Women have to get it through their looks and who they marry. Well, that makes the women really jitzy—you know, anxious?"

"I need the name, Margery," Louis said.

She ignored him. "See, there are always young women coming here to find rich men," she said. "Every season, they swoop in like swallows, all these pretty-baby vamps with their fake blond hair and silicone boobs. It's quite a ridiculous spectacle, really, these horny old coots chasing after them and then ditching their wives for younger models. *Quel triste.*"

Louis slumped back on the sofa.

"You see, status is everything to women here," Margery said. "Where you sit at a ball, how big your jewels are, if you live north or south of Sloan's Curve, whether you get into the B and T or not. Women here will do anything to preserve their place, to avoid becoming substrata."

"Sub what?" Mel said.

"Not quite A-list," Swann interjected from his ottoman.

Margery nodded vigorously. "I mean, look what happened to Bunny Norris. Her husband, Hap, took up with that Samantha woman and gave Bunny the icy mitt. Well, Bunny had no choice but to endure a sordid divorce, take her money, and hightail back it to Newport."

Samantha?

Margery was prattling on. It took Louis a moment to catch up. Something about Samantha being "basically Boca" but that everyone accepted her as Hap's new wife only because he was "core people" and they adored him.

"And that weasel who's always on her arm," Margery said. "She tells people he's one of Hap's lawyers, but, well, really. How many lawyers 'live in' for days at a time?"

Margery sipped her drink. "Trash," she whispered. "You can dress it up in Dior, but it's still trash."

Louis was silent. He could feel Mel's eyes on him, waiting for him to press Margery further. He ran a hand over his face and leaned forward so he was only a few feet from Margery.

"I'll ask you again. Why would a woman bother with a man like Labastide?" he asked.

Margery's gray eyes held his. "It's the old double standard, ducky. The men can just set their little honeys up in a suite at The Breakers and hide it by charging it to the company. The women . . . well, they have to be creative."

She dropped dramatically back against the chaise cushions, sending the dogs into a frenzy of snorting and shuffling. "Are you sure you boys wouldn't like a little shampoo?" she asked.

"No, thanks," Louis said quietly.

He rose and walked over to Mel. They stood, staring out at the ocean.

"Time to take off the gloves, Rocky," Mel said.

Louis was silent, his mind on Sam.

"Louis?"

He looked at Mel.

"You want me to do it?" Mel asked.

"No, I'll do it," Louis said.

Louis went back to the sofa, but he didn't sit down. He picked up a manila folder from the table and stood over Margery.

"Margery, you knew Mark Durand, right?"

Margery stared up at him. "Not well. Reggie brought him to dinner once. He drank a little too—"

Louis pulled out an eight-by-ten photograph and tossed it onto the table.

Margery's eyes widened.

He tossed a second crime-scene photograph onto the table. "This is Emilio. What they found of him, at least. He was tortured with a whip and then beheaded. He has a sister who's been looking for him."

Margery's face had gone gray. She sat motionless, looking at the top photograph. Then she leaned over and picked it up. She stared at it for a long time.

Then she slowly set it, facedown, on the table. When she looked up, her eyes were brimming. "I think I need a drink," she said.

She brushed the dogs from her lap, rose, and walked stiffly to the door.

"Franklin!" she yelled. "Bring me the Hendrick's!"

She came back to the lounge and sat on its edge, her long, bony hands clasped in her lap. The four dogs sat at her feet, looking up at her.

She pulled in a deep breath. "The woman is Carolyn Osborn."

Louis heard a gasp and looked over at Swann. His mouth was hanging open as his eyes swiveled from Margery to Louis.

"Senator Carolyn Osborn," he said.

Franklin appeared and placed a silver tray on the table in front of Margery. She pulled a bottle from the ice bucket and picked up one of the glasses.

"Now, does anyone need a drink?" she asked.

Chapter Nineteen

The Osborn home was at the westernmost end of Worth Avenue. Margery had told him the home was one of the "significant" mansions on the island, set down in a neighborhood once known as Sue City, named after an heiress to the Listerine fortune whose family had once owned the entire strip of land on lower Worth Avenue.

Louis parked in the broad brick drive, his eyes taking in the four-car garage on the left side of the sprawling house. There was a blue Toyota Camry by the closed garage doors.

A maid let him into a bright entrance hall of white marble and pillars, where the only stab of color came from a flame-red orchid sitting on a mirrored table. As they passed through a high-ceilinged salon filled with antiques and sunlight, Louis's eyes were drawn to a twenty-foot white Christmas tree, decorated in silver and white like a department-store display and packed beneath with gifts in matching silver wrappings. His thoughts flashed briefly to Rosa Díaz's tiny tree with the three ornaments. No presents under that one that he could remember.

He was taken to a study of dark paneling and shadows, the windows hidden by plantation shutters, a sharp contrast to the blinding-white decor of the rest of the house. The maid told him to wait and stopped to switch on a lamp before she left.

As his eyes adjusted, the room's rich details emerged. A fancy carved desk on a zebra-skin rug. A full suit of medieval armor. A painted infantry drum. A glass display box filled with colorful medals. A spiked German helmet. Two cabinets in the dark corner filled with guns and knives . . .

Good God.

Louis moved closer to the desk. Above it hung a gleaming sword.

"Can I help you?"

Louis turned. The man at the door was tall, wearing gray dress slacks, a dark sports coat, and a white shirt.

"I'm waiting for Senator Osborn," Louis said.

"I'm Tucker Osborn," the man said. "And you are?"

"Louis Kincaid."

Louis came forward, holding out his hand. The man was around sixty, still vital and handsome, with searing blue eyes and a thick shock of dark hair with a feather of gray at the temples. He shook Louis's hand with an overly firm grip.

"You're that detective," Osborn said.

"Yes, I'm working for Reggie Kent," Louis said.

The fact that the name brought no reaction made Louis believe that to Tucker Osborn, a man like Kent wasn't even worth a blip on his mental radar. Substrata, as Margery would say.

"What is your business with my wife?" Osborn asked.

"I'm told she might know something," Louis said.

"About what? That Durand joker?"

Louis thought it was odd that Osborn had mentioned Durand with no prompting. But then, it was also damn odd that Osborn had an antique sword in his study.

"Actually, I need to ask your wife about a different man," Louis said. "His name is Emilio Labastide. He disappeared five years ago, October 31, 1984, to be exact."

A flicker of emotion crossed Osborn's face.

"I think I should talk to your wife, Mr. Osborn," Louis said.

"Out of the question."

"Suit yourself," Louis said. "But this is what's going to happen. I know that your wife had some kind of contact with Labastide. And I am, oh, maybe two steps ahead of the police. But once the fine fellows over at the sheriff's department find out what I have, they will be knocking on your door. And they won't be as quiet about it as I might be."

Louis had seen Osborn's face twitch at the word *contact*. He gave him a few more moments to think. "Now, can I talk to your wife?"

"She's not here," Osborn said.

"When will she be back?"

Osborn went to the desk, flipped open a silver box, and pulled out a cigarette. He offered one to Louis, who shook his head. Osborn lit the cigarette with a heavy silver lighter and drew on it so hard his cheeks went concave. He exhaled in a long, hard puff.

"What did you say your name was?" he asked.

"Kincaid. Louis Kincaid."

"Well, why don't you ask me the questions, Mr. Kincaid?" he said as he sat down in the leather chair behind the desk and switched on a lamp.

Louis caught a glint of metal. There was a tall Oriental vase in the corner. The hilts of five ornate swords were visible from its top. Louis looked back at Osborn.

"May I sit down?"

Osborn nodded at the chair opposite the desk.

"Five years ago, a man was chased from your house," Louis said.

"Oh, for God's sake, not this shit again," Osborn said.

"Again?"

"Look, that was an ugly rumor started years ago by one of my wife's political enemies," Osborn said. "It's bullshit."

Louis reached into his blazer pocket and pulled out a photo, tossing it onto the desk. "Do you recognize this man?"

It was a copy of the photo Rosa had given him of Emilio. Osborn's eyes flicked to it, and he shook his head. "Who is it?"

"The man your wife was supposedly having an affair with," Louis said. "The man you supposedly chased out of here."

Osborn stared hard at Louis. "Are you working for Morty Akers? Is that loser running again?"

"Who's Morty Akers?"

"I have nothing to say about this."

"Who is Morty Akers?" Louis asked. When Osborn didn't say anything, Louis leaned back and propped a foot on his knee. "You might as well tell me. I'm going to find out."

Osborn sat forward and snuffed the cigarette out in a crystal ashtray. "My wife was up for reelection five years ago. Akers was running against her. He's a slimeball, and he ran a sleazy campaign."

"What did he do?" Louis asked.

Osborn gave a snort. "You name it. He made these TV ads, taking every speech she did and editing it to make her sound like some Nazi brownshirt. He sent detectives to dig up shit on her family, her pastor, even her doctor because the guy's wife worked for the ACLU, for God's sake." He shook his head. "They call it 'opposition research,' you know."

"What does this have to do with the rumor about the man running from your house?" Louis asked.

"None of it was working, so Akers decided he needed to get personal." Osborn's jaw ground in anger. "About six years ago, my son got busted for having a couple of ounces of pot. No big deal here, but it happened down in Boca, and there was a police report. Akers claimed Carolyn engineered a cover-up with the cops. Plus, he hit her hard on the family-values shit." Osborn shook his head slowly. "My son was only fifteen. Yeah, he was stupid, but he didn't deserve what that asshole did, putting it on radio and TV."

Osborn pulled out another cigarette and lit it. He blew out the smoke in a slow stream, like he was trying to calm himself.

"Akers went to work on the household staff next," he said. "He tried to bribe them. And then he had private investigators hanging around with cameras wherever Carolyn went."

His icy blue eyes zeroed in on Louis. "How do you guys sleep at night?"

Louis met Osborn's stare. "So, Akers started the rumor that your wife was sleeping with someone?"

Osborn gave a hard nod. "Carolyn and I were separated at the time, and he must have found out. We were going through a rough patch and had decided it would be best if we lived apart for a while. I wasn't even living here in the house. This is a small town. Anybody here could verify that."

Louis had the sense the guy was overly touchy, like he was hiding something. Guys who had something to hide were always daring you to ask around. But those types were usually your everyday criminals, high on bravado and low on brainpower. Osborn didn't fit that.

Osborn drew on his cigarette and gave a wry smile. "Too bad you don't work for Akers."

"Why?" Louis asked.

"You could give him a message for me," Osborn said. "You could tell him thanks."

"For what?"

"When a guy is attacking your wife, you have a duty to hit back. If Akers hadn't done what he did to Carolyn, I might never have come home." He stabbed out the cigarette. "Ironic, isn't it? The asshole probably saved my marriage."

The phone rang. Osborn glanced at it but didn't pick it up. Someone in the house did. The extension button began to blink.

There was a soft knock on the door.

"Tucker?"

Louis turned at the sound of the woman's voice. She

stood outside the door, head poked in. She gave Louis a glance of curiosity and then looked to Osborn.

"I'm sorry," she said. "Am I interrupting something important?"

Osborn rose and came out from behind the desk. "No, Carolyn. We're finished." He looked at Louis. "Right?"

Louis rose. It was clear Osborn was not going to introduce him to his wife. Louis extended his hand.

"Senator Osborn, I'm Louis Kincaid."

She accepted his handshake with a cool smile, but her eyes darted to her husband for some sort of confirmation. She was a handsome woman of about fifty, tall and thin, in a dark blue pantsuit. Her hair was a silver blond, her face youthful but without the awful wind-tunnel stretched look that Louis had seen on so many Palm Beach matrons.

"You're the one who's working for Reggie," she said.

Louis nodded. "Yes, ma'am."

Her eyes lingered as her brows knitted, like she was trying to figure out why he was standing in her home. But she finally looked to her husband.

"Tucker, you really have to get started on your packing," she said.

"I don't think I'm going to be able to get away," he said.

"Tucker, you said . . ."

"We'll talk about this later, dear." He took her elbow and started to steer her away. But her eyes had dropped to the desk, to the photograph of Emilio. She quickly looked back up to her husband.

Louis picked up the photograph. "Senator Osborn, do you recognize this man?"

He was holding it out, but she didn't take it. "No," she said.

Then she gave him another smile. Louis wondered if politicians practiced their smiles in front of mirrors. How else could a human face so easily subdivide itself—warmth from the mouth and utter coldness in the eyes?

"Carolyn—"

Louis's eyes swung to the door. A young man in a suit and tie stood there, holding a leather binder.

"Yes, Greg?" she said.

The young man's pale face colored slightly. "Ah," he said, "I need a couple of minutes to go over your schedule, Senator."

"Of course," she answered. "I need to speak to my husband. Why don't you show Mr. Kincaid out?"

The man with the binder finally seemed to realize Louis was in the room. He hesitated, his eyes swinging between Carolyn Osborn and her husband. Then he closed the binder and gestured to the door.

Louis said his goodbyes to the Osborns and followed the young man out. The door closed behind them. Louis heard Tucker Osborn's voice rise, but he couldn't make out the words.

"This way," the young man said curtly.

"Sure, Greg. Whatever you say."

The man led Louis back through the big room with the Christmas tree and out into the white entrance hall. He walked fast, his gait as sharp as the part in his red hair.

He opened the door and stepped back. But Louis didn't move.

"Yes?" he asked impatiently.

"Greg, I was wondering—"

"Bitner," he said. "My name is Mr. Bitner."

Louis nodded. "And you work for Carolyn Osborn?"

"I work for the senator, yes."

"Assistant?"

"Personal secretary."

Louis nodded again. He pointed to the leather binder. "You keep track of where the senator is all the time?"

Bitner clutched the binder to his chest. "I make all of her appointments."

"How long have you worked for her?"

"Almost six years. Now, if you would—"

Louis held up the photograph of Emilio. "Did you ever schedule an appointment for this man?"

Bitner glanced at the photo. "No, he has never had an appointment with Senator Osborn."

"What about Mark Durand?"

Bitner's eyes narrowed. "Mark Durand?"

"Yeah, did she maybe let Durand escort her to a ballet or—"

Bitner tried to nudge him out the door. Louis shrugged off his hand.

"Greg, Greg . . . let's not get ugly here." He nodded at the leather binder. "How about we make an appointment for me to talk to your boss?"

"I'm sorry, but she's leaving soon for a family trip to Aspen," Bitner said. "After the holidays, she goes back to Washington. All questions from the media must be directed to her press secretary."

He whipped out a business card, and Louis took it. It

listed a name and an office in Washington. Louis pocketed the card.

"I'd rather talk to you, Greg."

Bitner's face reddened. "I must insist that you leave."

Louis shrugged and stepped out onto the porch.

"And please don't bother the senator again."

The door closed. Louis figured Greg Bitner would
have slammed it had it not been so heavy. He walked
slowly down the brick driveway. At the Mustang, he
paused to put on his sunglasses. He looked back at the
house.

Just sitting there in the den, he had counted eight
swords—seven in the holder and one on the wall. And in
a house this size, there were probably more.

He wondered if Tucker Osborn was missing one.

Chapter Twenty

L ouis found Mel at Ta-boo, sitting alone in the back,
bent over a plate of food that looked like something
from Vinny's autopsy table—paper-thin slices of red
meat drizzled with a nasty-looking yellowish sauce.

Louis stopped at the table and looked down. "What
is that?"

"Tuna carpaccio salad," Mel said.

"How much was it?"

"For crissakes, chill out about the money, would
you?" Mel said. "We just put fifty grand in the bank."

Yuba, the bartender, suddenly appeared. She looked

a little like an abstract work of art, with her raven-black hair tied with a white ribbon, smooth brown skin against a snow-white blouse, lips and nails the same flame red as the orchid in Osborn's house.

Louis stepped aside to let her fill Mel's water glass, discreetly appreciating the curve of her hips and the faint, sweet swirl of what had to be some exotic Indian perfume. When she asked him if he wanted a drink, he felt like he had been caught leering and could barely manage a "No, thanks." When she was gone, he turned back to Mel.

Mel had been given the assignment of chasing down background on the Archer ranch hands. Louis wondered if he had reached his confidential source at the Miami PD or even tried. From the looks of his deepening tan, maybe he had just wandered around the island all day. Lately, he hadn't been quite the same dogged investigator Louis was used to working with. Maybe they needed a long night at a quiet bar somewhere to talk about that.

Mel popped the last sliver of tuna into his mouth and talked while he chewed. "Did you know there is an antique weapons store right here on the island?" he asked.

"Antique weapons?" Louis asked. "Like swords and shit?"

"Swords, helmets, firearms, everything. The kind of stuff rich guys collect."

"Did you go in?"

Mel wiped his lips and discarded the napkin. "No, they were closed for lunch. But I got to thinking about what Reggie said about Durand getting that watch from one of his lady friends, and I started to wonder if maybe that sword Barberry took away was a gift. It would be nice for Reggie if we could connect that sword to some wealthy woman."

"Or her husband," Louis said.

"You know something I don't?"

"Tucker Osborn has a whole room full of that military stuff. It's like he thinks he's Sir Lancelot."

"Now, that's interesting," Mel said.

Louis looked at his watch. It was almost three-thirty. The store probably closed soon, and he wanted to get there before they locked up. It seemed especially cruel to waste an entire night waiting for the place to reopen with Reggie Kent in jail. Louis hadn't mentioned it to Mel, but he was worried about Kent's safety. Really worried.

"Come on," Louis said. "Let's go now."

"Cool your jets, Rocky," Mel said. "I saved us some trouble. Antique appraisers can't evaluate anything unless they see it." He held up a manila envelope. "I walked over to Swann's office, and he got us a good photo of the sword."

Louis pulled out the photograph. It was in color, vividly detailing every line of the intricate scrollwork on the hilt.

"Good job," Louis said. "Let's go."

"I got to hit the john," Mel said. "You go ahead, and I'll meet you outside."

Louis grabbed the lunch receipt so he could record it later and left Ta-boo. The wind was picking up, bringing a damp chill off the ocean and stirring up a cluster of storm clouds.

He waited, looking again at the picture, then peering into Ta-boo's large open window, wondering what was taking Mel so long. He spotted him standing at the end of the bar, talking to Yuba, heads tipped close, Mel's hand covering hers.

What the . . . ?

Then Mel gave her a quick kiss on the cheek, patted her hand, and started to the door.

Damn.

Was this what was keeping Mel busy on those days when he'd stayed in the hotel room feigning a headache? Was she the reason for the Ta-boo takeout and afternoon naps? Yuba had to be at least twenty years younger than Mel. What the hell did she see in him?

Mel emerged from the restaurant. "You ready?"

Louis just stared at him.

"Something wrong?" Mel asked.

"Uh, no."

"Well, let's go."

Louis looked to the window and then back to Mel. "You and Yuba . . . you got something going?"

Mel seemed to freeze. Louis stayed quiet, waiting for an answer. This was none of his business, but he wanted to know.

Mel finally sighed. "Yeah, we do. So what? You think someone like her can't see something in a guy like me?"

"Of course she can," Louis said. "But I thought—"

"You think she's some gold digger, looking to land some half-dead old fart for a husband."

Louis started to reply but closed his mouth. He had no defense.

Mel shook his head in disgust. "Yuba works on the island because she makes good money," he said. "She's saving her money so she can go to school. She's not looking to be someone's rich widow. Because you and I both know that no matter how pretty she is, there isn't one man on this island who's ever going to put a wedding ring on her lovely brown finger."

Louis felt like shit.

Mel shrugged. "And like I told you before, when your eyes go, other senses are sharpened. So, believe it or not, I still have something to offer to the ladies. Now, the subject of my sex life is closed. That okay with you, or do you need additional information?"

Louis shook his head. "Spare me, please. Let's go see the swordsman. If you'll excuse the pun."

Grande Armée Militaria was a small store tucked in a courtyard off Worth Avenue. Inside, it had the feel of a high-end jewelry store: creamy white walls, plush royal blue carpeting, and the usual mollifying Muzak that mysteriously made people speak in whispers.

An elderly, long-faced man behind a glass counter gave them a smile as they came in. Tall, with silver hair, he wore the uniform of the island: light-colored dress shirt, dress slacks, and navy blazer.

He was helping a woman who was examining a carved ivory chess set. Louis gave him a nod, then followed Mel toward the rear of the store. They paused in front of a wall of plumed military helmets and a row of what looked like Greek or Roman battle shields.

"My name is Chauncey Gillis. May I help you?"

Louis turned. The man had the soothing voice of an airline pilot and smelled like cedar and cherries, probably from the pipe in his breast pocket.

"My name is Kincaid," Louis said. "This is Mel

Landeta. We're private investigators working for Reggie Kent."

"Ah, yes. I heard Mr. Kent had hired someone to help him," Gillis said. "May I ask how things are going for him?"

"I'm afraid I can't share anything with you," Louis said. "But there might be something you can tell us to help him out a little."

Gillis's smile faded. "Well, I don't know . . ."

Louis pulled out the photograph of the sword. "Do you recognize this sword?"

Gillis took the photograph and walked back to the counter to get his glasses. He also picked up a magnifying glass and held it over the picture.

"This is a German prison officer's sword," he said when he looked up. "This is very rare, from the Clemen Solingen firm."

"You're sure?" Louis asked.

"Oh, yes, I'd know this anywhere." He pointed to the photo. "See the eagle's head? Its beak forms the hilt. And of course, here's the swastika in the gold. Lovely, just lovely."

"But it's a real sword, right?" Louis asked. "You could kill someone with it?"

"Of course," Gillis said. "Its beauty doesn't detract from the fact that it was manufactured with mayhem in mind. The balance is perfect for swinging. Definitely a working weapon."

Louis stepped to the counter. Apparently, Gillis hadn't heard that a sword had been taken from Reggie's home, or he would be more intrigued by the photo.

"Is it expensive?" Louis asked.

"Around five thousand," Gillis said.

"Is it rare?"

"Extremely," Gillis said. "This sword is museum worthy, a very important addition to any collection. I've only seen one pass through my store, and I've been here almost twenty years now."

"Do you remember who you sold it to?" Louis asked.

Gillis went silent. Louis could almost see the gears of his brain working.

"You sold it to Tucker Osborn," Louis said.

Gillis's face reddened. "I don't like to talk about my customers."

"I just came from Osborn's home," Louis said. "He told me to talk to you."

The bluff seemed to thaw Gillis some. "Well, if Mr. Osborn said it was all right."

"He sent me here. Said to talk to Mr. Gillis and only Mr. Gillis. When did you sell him the sword?"

"It was about five years ago," Gillis said. "Mr. Osborn has a magnificent collection of military paraphernalia."

"You're absolutely sure that this sword is the same one you sold Mr. Osborn?" Louis asked.

"I would stake my reputation on it," Gillis said.

Louis slid the picture back into the envelope. Gillis's identification of Tucker Osborn as the sword's owner was going to be crucial later, if Reggie was actually put on trial and if the sword turned out to be the murder weapon. And even more sweet was the fact that, as a jealous husband, Osborn could be assumed to have had motive. Nothing ever needed to be proven, but this was enough to raise some serious reasonable doubt.

Gillis suddenly bolted from behind the counter and hurried to Mel, who was holding a silver dome-shaped helmet.

"You got this in a seven and three-quarters?" Mel asked.

"Give me that, please," Gillis said, taking the helmet from Mel.

Gillis used a handkerchief to wipe the metal free of prints and carefully placed the helmet back on the blue velvet display stand.

Mel tossed Louis a grin as he came toward him. Gillis followed, still in a huff as he tucked his handkerchief back into his breast pocket. Then, as if something had suddenly sparked inside his brain, he looked up at Louis. His eyes held a flicker of apprehension.

"It just occurred to me," he said. "Do they think that Mr. Osborn's sword was used to behead that poor man who lived with Mr. Kent?"

Louis was sure Barberry didn't want to release the fact that a sword had been taken from the suspect's house, but hell, the information was probably already out there in whispered rumors. He might as well give it a stronger voice and let the grapevine do what it did best. Maybe he could stir up a reaction from the senator and her bastard husband.

"No one is supposed to know that, Mr. Gillis," Louis said. "I trust we can keep your confidence?"

"Oh, goodness, yes," Gillis said. "Discretion is my middle name, sir."

"Good," Louis said. "We appreciate it."

Louis turned to leave, but Gillis caught his arm. "May I ask if Mr. Osborn is a suspect?"

"I'm afraid I can't share any theories with you," Louis said. "Thank you for your help."

"Wait," Gillis said. "I just remembered something else. Do you have a photograph of Mr. Kent's deceased friend?"

"Not with us, no," Louis said. "Why?"

"Please excuse me," Gillis said. "I'll be right back."

Gillis disappeared behind a red velvet drape and returned with a copy of the *Shiny Sheet*. He had it folded to display an article on the murder of Durand. Gillis pointed to Durand's picture.

"I wanted to be sure before I said anything," Gillis said.

"Sure about what?" Louis asked.

"A few months ago, I had a young man come in and ask about the value of an antique sword," Gillis said. "He didn't have the sword with him, but he tried to describe it to me. Of course, I told him I would have to see it to offer an appraisal."

"Did he ever bring it in?" Louis asked.

"No," Gillis said. "And to be honest, I completely forgot about it. Until now. But I am almost positive the gentleman I spoke with was this man. This paper is old, but we keep them for wrapping things in shipping." He tapped the picture of Durand in the newspaper.

"You're sure?"

"I would stake my reputation on it," Gillis said.

"Did he mention where he got the sword?" Mel asked.

"No," Gillis said. "But I know that had he mentioned Mr. Osborn, I would remember that."

Louis glanced at Mel, still a little stunned at the day's events. First, Margery spills the name of a senator, then it turns out her husband not only collects swords but once owned the same sword found in the victim's house.

"Thank you, Mr. Gillis," Louis said. "Again, we'd appreciate it if you keep all this under your hat."

"Or your helmet," Mel added.

Gillis gave a tight smile. Louis was sure the minute they walked out the door, Gillis would be on the phone to anyone who would listen. Hell, Margery would probably know it all before she uncorked her evening bottle of shampoo.

They left the store and started walking. Louis was hungry, but by Palm Beach standards, it was far too early to eat dinner. No one sat down before dark.

"I had a thought," Mel said.

"Shoot."

"Reggie said Durand was sleeping with women. Women, plural," Mel went on. "Maybe they all gave him gifts. Maybe there's more than the watch and the sword."

Louis stopped walking, his brain tripping back to Durand's bedroom and the shelves of knickknacks. What had been there?

"We need to go back to Kent's place," Louis said.

"What for?"

"A treasure hunt," Louis said.

Chapter Twenty-one

The next morning, Louis and Mel went to see Reggie to get the keys to his house but also to check up on him. As expected, he wasn't faring well.

His pale skin held a gray tinge, and his silky yellow hair had lost its sheen. Head bent and hands clasped, Reggie asked if they could bring him his Paul Labrecque shampoo and the most recent issue of the *Robb Report*. Mel gently told him no and tried to update him on the case without giving him false hope that Barberry would suddenly see the light and get the charges dismissed.

When they asked Reggie if he could tell the jail to release his house keys to their care, Reggie agreed. Then he surprised them by insisting that they move into his house. Someone should enjoy the view, he said, until he got out of jail.

They packed up their suitcases and checked out of the Palm Beach Inn. There was something indecent about living in an oceanfront home owned by a man who was in jail. Even with Reggie's blessing, it still felt a little like freeloading. Still, as they unlocked the front door, Louis had to admit it was a relief to get out of the cramped hotel room.

Reggie's house, released by the police days ago, was spotless. It had been a disaster the day Reggie was arrested, and Louis wondered who had cleaned it up. He didn't like the idea of anyone being in there alone.

"This place smells like lemons," Mel said as he set his suitcase down.

Louis moved deeper into the living room. Every surface gleamed; every pillow was in place. He was thinking Margery had sent her cleaning crew over when he saw a handwritten note on the coffee table: *Mr. Reggie. I clean up after polise. You now owe me $300. You pay when you get out jail? Eppie.*

"Reggie's maid was here," Louis said.

Louis made a mental note to ask Margery if she wanted to pay Eppie and picked up his duffel. He was reluctant to settle into Durand's room before they had a chance to examine every item in it. Gifts were not always things displayed on shelves. There could be clothing, jewelry, credit cards, or even cash, things Barberry's men didn't deem important to proving that Reggie was a murderer.

To Louis's surprise, there were three bedrooms wedged inside Reggie's small home. He chose to settle in the middle one, a twelve-by-twelve square painted blue and decorated with a Haitian painting of cotton pickers under a bloodred palm tree. There was barely room for a twin bed and a small rattan desk. A single jalousie window opened into the branches of a bottlebrush tree, heavy with fuzzy red flowers.

He tossed his duffel onto the bed and left the room. He could hear the *clink* of plates from the kitchen and figured Mel was rummaging for something to eat since they'd skipped breakfast.

Louis stopped at the door to Durand's bedroom. Warm from the morning sun, the room was in perfect condition. The bed was made, the splashy green and yellow spread squared at the corners and dotted with throw pillows. The terra-cotta floor shone like it had been shellacked. The painting had been hung back in its place above the bed. A cool breeze from the open window gave the room a pleasant, beachy smell.

"You want some eggs?" Mel shouted.

"No, thanks."

Louis decided to start with a search for the Patek Philippe watch, since it was the one thing they could be sure was a gift to Durand. The police report had said there was no jewelry found on Durand's body. But Reggie had said Durand had the watch on when he left Testa's.

There was a green leather box on the dresser. Louis flipped it open and rummaged through the contents—cuff links, shirt studs, collar stays, a tarnished ring, two joints wrapped in foil, and a cheap Timex.

There was nothing of note in any of the drawers. Louis checked the nightstand drawer and gave the closet a once-over. Nothing. The Patek Philippe was not in this room. Where the hell was it?

He looked to the glass étagère. There was no sense in worrying about fingerprints, since he was sure Eppie had wiped away any evidence. But maybe he could figure out if something looked expensive enough to be a gift from an appreciative woman.

The gold beaded apple looked expensive, but there were no markings on it that offered any clues. The New York City snow globe was a cheap plastic thing, with a faded $4.99 sticker on the bottom. The green speckled bowl could be anything from a cheap carnival prize to a priceless piece of European dinnerware. The Eiffel Tower didn't look expensive, but Louis had to admit he probably couldn't tell Baccarat from glass.

The gold pen set was a Mont Blanc. No engraving and certainly something that would make a nice gift from a woman but not in the same league as the watch.

The last item was a wooden box. The wood was a light color, maybe rosewood, and looked old. The corners, hinges, and tiny lock were a matte-finish silver. Not so noticeable on the front was a small silver plate engraved with the initials RQL.

Louis opened the lid, releasing a pungent scent of a rich liqueur and aged tobacco. The silk-lined box had some odd dials on the inside of the top and was filled with a neat row of plump cigars.

"Do I smell cigars?" Mel asked from behind him.

"Yup."

Mel peered into the box, then plucked one of the cigars from it. He held it close to his eyes and then drew it sensuously under his nose.

"I have been blessed with physical pleasure more times on this trip than I deserve," Mel said. "But now . . . now I have truly gone to heaven."

"What the hell are you talking about?" Louis asked.

"These are Gurkha Grand Reserve cigars," Mel said. "Clearly the choice of discriminating—and filthy-rich—smokers everywhere."

"How much do they cost?"

"They make only about twenty boxes of these every year, and they run almost ten thousand dollars."

"Per box?" Louis asked.

"Per box," Mel said. He reached into his pocket and pulled out his Zippo. "Each one is infused with legendary Louis the Thirteenth cognac by Rémy Martin. You like Rémy Martin, don't you?"

"I love Rémy but not when it's been filtered through tobacco leaves," Louis said. "And give me that back. You're not smoking up the evidence."

"There's more in there," Mel said. "And besides, Mark Durand sure doesn't need them anymore."

Louis grabbed at the cigar, but Mel moved away from him and sparked his Zippo. Louis debated whether to fight with him over the damn thing and decided it didn't matter. There may have been twenty cigars originally, and who knew how many had been smoked?

"At least go outside," Louis said.

Mel obliged, and Louis turned back to the humidor, looking again at the engraved initials: RQL. Given the personalization and the fact that the plate looked as old as the box, it was a logical conclusion that RQL had been the original owner. Was the thing as old as it looked, and if so, had the plate been added years after? Or had the box been made to look like an antique?

He closed the lid and turned it over. There was a second plate, also silver but shinier, newer:

To Dickie, from Tink.
Happy Anniversary,
6-14-1979.

Well, "Dickie" could certainly be a nickname for "Richard," which matched the R. So, the owner could still be alive, and even better, he might be married to a young, adulterous wife who, for whatever reason, chose to give her boy toy an expensive present.

But why would Mark Durand want a cigar humidor? Reggie said Durand hated the smell of smoke so much that he made Reggie go out on the patio to smoke his Gauloises.

"Did you find the Patek Philippe?"

Mel was standing next to him, radiating an eye-burning stink, despite the fact that the cigar was stubbed out and in his pocket.

"No," Louis said. "But I did find something interesting. There are names on the bottom of this thing. Let's see if we can figure out who they are."

"Who you going to call?"

"No one," Louis said. "I have a *Social Register* Margery gave me. Anyone who can afford these cigars will be in there."

Mel followed him back to the living room. Louis dug into his duffel for the register and the Saks bag of *Shiny Sheet*s Margery had given him. "Here, look through these for anyone named Dickie or Tink."

"Tink? Good Lord," Mel said as he settled on the sofa with the newspapers. Between bites of scrambled eggs, Mel examined the newspapers with a magnifying glass.

Louis grabbed a glass of orange juice and sat down with the black book. The names were in alphabetical order, and Louis flipped to the L's. There they were. Right under the Kennedys: Tricia and Richard Q. Lyons.

Under the names was an address on the south end of the island, along with addresses for homes in New York and Paris. Under that was the name of what had to be a yacht: *SeaDuction*.

"Look for people named Richard or Tricia Lyons," Louis said.

"Hey, check this out," Mel said, holding out one of the newspapers. "You ever seen anything so obscene?"

"What?"

"The ice sculpture at the Cancer Ball," Mel said. "It looks like two people screwing."

Louis took the *Shiny Sheet* but never saw the picture Mel was talking about. His eyes were locked on a photograph in the lower right-hand corner.

A woman in a blue dress. Milk-white skin and carrot-red hair. On her arm was the same dark-haired ferret guy Louis had seen with her at Ta-boo and the ballet.

Louis read the caption: *Mr. Nesbitt Saban and Mrs. Arthur Norris.*

"How'd you like to see that thing next to the stone crabs?" Mel said.

Louis looked up quickly. "What?"

"That ice thing," Mel said, pointing to the newspaper.

Louis nodded and looked back at the photo of Sam. Everything that had happened between them that night was suddenly in his head, bringing a flush of warmth through his chest. But he was also hearing Margery.

Look what happened to Bunny Norris. Her husband, Hap, took up with that Samantha woman and gave Binky the icy mitt. Trash. You can dress it up in Dior, but it's still trash.

"What's wrong with you?" Mel asked.

Louis looked at Mel. They had been friends now for almost three years. Shared a couple of homicide cases, a few close calls, and a lot of beers. They talked about the Dolphins, their time in uniform, politics, and Mel's retinitis pigmentosa. But Louis couldn't remember one time they had talked at length about women. Hell, they never even discussed the fact that they had both dated Joe Frye, Louis's recent ex.

But for some reason, now Louis wanted to tell Mel about Sam. And about his phone call with Joe.

"I talked to Joe the other night," Louis began.

"Yeah? How's she doing up there?"

"She's busy."

"She's the sheriff. Even in a place like that, she's going to be busy." When Louis didn't say anything, Mel looked up. "You two have a fight or something?"

Louis wondered how Mel had picked up on it. "She told me she thinks we should see other people," he said.

Mel was quiet for a moment. "What'd you say?"

"I didn't say much."

"You never do, Rocky. Maybe that's part of the problem."

Louis's eyes shot up to Mel. But there had been no reproach in Mel's voice, just a sort of quiet acknowledgment that he understood Louis's nature. Louis realized in that moment that his friend had been sending small signals for a while now, trying to give him safe ways to open up and talk about what was eating him. But Louis had ignored them. Because, to be honest, he wasn't sure what was wrong. Joe was only part of it.

"You remember the night we checked into the Inn," Louis said. "And I didn't get back to the room until four?"

"Yeah."

Louis held out the newspaper and pointed to Sam's photo. "I was with her. In her house."

Mel stared at him for a moment, then picked up the magnifying glass and studied the newspaper. "Was this the same night you talked to Joe?"

Louis nodded, then realized Mel might miss it. "Yeah. Same night."

"How'd you hook up?"

"I was sitting at the bar at Ta-boo. She came up, made some small talk, and asked me to meet her outside in ten minutes." Louis paused, still feeling a rise of heat up the back of his neck. "I went. I left her in her bedroom without ever finding out her last name."

"You seen her since?"

"I saw her at the ballet, but she . . ." He cleared his throat. "She turned her back on me."

Mel tossed the *Shiny Sheet* to the table and leaned back against the cushions. For a few minutes, neither of them said anything. The only sound was the distant splash of waves on the beach. It made Louis a little homesick.

"So it was a revenge fuck," Mel said.

"Nice, Mel. That makes me feel a lot better."

"What? You're pissed that she didn't show you off to her friends?"

Louis shrugged. "No, but I figured I'd get a nod of the head or something."

"You did get something," Mel said. "You got a pretty piece of ass. You can't expect her to be your best friend the next morning."

Louis stared at the *Shiny Sheet,* hearing Margery Laroche's voice. *You can screw up and sideways but never down.*

"They were careless people," Mel said.

Louis glanced up at him.

"They smashed up things and creatures and then retreated back into their money or their vast carelessness and let other people clean up the mess they had made."

"Gatsby?" Louis asked.

Mel nodded.

Louis leaned back against the sofa. "There's something else," he said.

"I thought there might be."

"Something weird happened."

"At the ballet? You already said—"

"No," Louis said sharply. "In bed."

"And you're complaining?"

"God damn it, Mel, I'm serious here."

Mel was quiet.

Louis sat up, elbows on knees. "She passed out, man."

"You mean afterward, right?"

"Of course, afterward. Right after she came."

"What did you do?"

"I slapped her, and she came to."

Mel was smiling.

"I told you, this isn't funny. It scared the living shit out of me."

"I know, I know," Mel said. "I'm not laughing, believe me. It happened to me once. It's called *la petite mort.*"

Louis shook his head.

"The little death," Mel said. "That's what the French call an orgasm."

"Mel, she passed out cold," Louis said.

"Well, sometimes with intense orgasms, there's a decrease of blood to the brain, to the orbitofrontal cortex, to be exact. That's the part of the brain that is involved in behavioral control."

"How do you know this?"

"I told you, it happened to me once. The woman went out like a light, and I thought I had screwed her to death. After I got over myself, I did some research and found out I wasn't the big stud I thought I was."

Louis was quiet. He remembered something she had said while he was making love to her. *Die with me.* At least now it didn't seem so damn weird.

"Forget about it, Rocky," Mel said. "Forget about her. And you should call Joe back. A woman like her doesn't come around very often, and you'd be an ass to let her go. Believe me, I know."

Louis looked over at him. He had wondered a million times why Mel and Joe had broken up all those years back. Mel had said only that it was because she was a rookie just getting her start, and he was so much older and going blind and didn't want to be a burden on her. He was sure Joe felt nothing but friendship for Mel now. As for Mel's feelings, he had heard Mel talk with regret about only one thing in his life: the time his pride over his growing blindness had kept him behind the wheel of the squad car that had hit a kid and left him paralyzed. Mel had never before mentioned any regret about Joe.

Louis stared at the photograph of Sam for another moment, then his eyes went to the phone on the nearby table. But no words were coming, nothing that was an answer to Joe's words that had stung him most: *I want you to want something for yourself.*

Louis tossed the newspaper onto the table. He rose abruptly and went to the window, squinting as he stared out at the ocean.

"I called Vinny about bringing Labastide home to Immokalee," Mel said.

Louis was grateful that Mel had said something. "What did he say?" he asked, without turning.

"Vinny got a pretty good price from a friend of his who owns a funeral home. Think Margery will be okay with four grand?"

Louis turned. "How much was the exhumation and autopsy?"

"Seventeen thousand."

"Well, she said she liked the kid," Louis said. "I'll guess we'll find out how much."

Louis came back to the sofa and grabbed the social register. He started toward the door.

"Where are you going?" Mel asked.

"To find Tink and Dickie," Louis said.

"Do you want me to come along?" Mel asked. "We could stop for a drink on the way back."

Louis hesitated. "I think I want to go alone."

Mel shook his head. "Rocky, you've got to stop digging yourself deeper into this shithole funk." When Louis didn't say anything, Mel went on. "When you decide to put down the shovel, I'll be here for you."

Chapter Twenty-two

Richard and Tricia Lyons lived in an oceanfront monstrosity of a house. It was not one of those pretty Mediterranean Mizners that actually had some character. This was a new pastiche palace with Greek columns, gaudy chandeliers, and a grand arched entryway hung with faux-Versailles mirrors.

Carrying the humidor in the Saks shopping bag and led by a butler who wrongly assumed he was a pool guy named Marine Mike, Louis took the long walk through the canyons of the house. He knew very little about interior decorating, but there seemed to be little continuity in decor from room to room.

A white baby-grand piano basked in a rainbow of light from the cathedral-sized stained-glass window. A twenty-foot aquarium took up one entire wall, stocked with tropical fish and lobsters. An indoor Jacuzzi sat smack in the middle of a room filled with garden furniture. There was a twelve-foot marble statue of a Greek-gowned woman in one corner. The statue's toes were painted bright red.

Louis followed the butler outdoors to a jungle of palms and bushes with pink saucer-sized hibiscus blossoms. Beyond was a large kidney-shaped pool, its water the deep blue of the Electric Popsicle cocktail Louis had tried once down in Key West.

"Hello."

The voice was airy and unsure. Louis looked around and, seeing no one, ventured out from under the greenery and into the sun. A woman stood on the flagstone patio, a tawny-colored Afghan dog at her side. With its long, combed layers of hair, sagging face, and red-rimmed eyes, the dog had the look of an aging rock star after a long night.

Sadly, the woman resembled her pet. Wearing only a white swimsuit, she was rail-thin, with loose, deeply tanned skin cut with so many tiny lines she looked shrink-wrapped. Her hair could have been a wig created from the dog's hair, a long pageboy that wasn't moving in the breeze.

The woman sucked on a cigarette in a gold holder. "Hello," she said again.

"Hello," Louis said.

"You're not Marine Mike," she said.

"No, ma'am," Louis said. "My name is Louis Kincaid. I'm a private investigator working for—"

"Reggie," she said.

"Yes."

The woman blinked and glanced toward the house.

In profile, her long fake lashes protruded like fishhooks. Above them were streaks of green shadow. She was wearing a large teardrop ruby necklace.

The woman's aqueous blue eyes came back to him. "I should offer you a drink," she said. "I don't know where Gerald is. Did he tell you where he went? Should I call him?"

"I don't need a drink, ma'am," Louis said. "Thank you anyway. May I ask—"

She moved away from him, taking the long way around the lagoon to a small table in the shade. She picked up a glass, then, apparently seeing it was empty, reached for her terry-cloth robe instead. Her hands shook as she tried to find the holes for the sleeves.

He walked around the pool to her. "May I ask if you're Mrs. Lyons?"

She turned so quickly she seemed to lose her balance. "I'm sorry," she said. "I don't like people coming up behind me. I'm sorry."

"I apologize."

"No, it's I who should apologize. I should have introduced myself to you, and then you wouldn't have had to pester me for the information, would you?"

He was quiet, beginning to wonder if this woman was completely lucid.

She turned back to the table, picked up a silver cocktail shaker, and refilled her glass with a cranberry-colored liquid. "These are very good, you know," she said. "But they have the naughtiest name."

There were two empty glasses on a silver tray, and she picked one up. He was going to get a drink whether he wanted one or not and decided not to argue.

"They're called Sex on the Beach," she said, pushing the glass at him. "I had one at a party last New Year's, and I just fell in love."

He accepted the glass.

"Take a sip," she said, touching his hand. "Go on. Seize the moment, as they say."

He took a drink. As she watched him, her eyes lit up with delight. For a second, he wondered if she was going to break into giddy applause.

"Do you like it?" she asked.

"Yes."

The dog was suddenly between them, circling his mistress and licking the sweat off her bare legs. She murmured an apology to the animal, whose name was apparently Barkley, then set her glass on the ground. Louis watched in amazement as the dog lapped the glass dry. Its toenails, he realized, were painted the same red as the statue he had seen on his way in.

"Sit, please. Sit," she said.

For a second, he thought she meant the dog. "Me?" Louis asked.

She stared at him, her fishhook lashes fluttering as she gave a little laugh. It sounded like the tinkle of wind chimes. "Of course, you," she said, gesturing toward a chair.

He didn't move. "Mrs. Lyons, I'd like to ask you a couple of questions about a—"

"Tink. Please," she said. "I'm Tink to my friends. Been Tink for forty years now, ever since I was ten."

Christ, even Mel could have seen this woman was not fifty. Given the leathered skin, the bottle-shaped breasts, and the road map of purple on her legs, she was easily sixty-five, even if it was an expensively preserved sixty-five.

Louis set his drink on the table and reached into the shopping bag. "I'd like to ask you about something," he said. He withdrew the box and held it out to her. "Do you recognize this?" he asked.

Her eyes widened. "That's Dickie's humidor. Where did you get it?"

Louis hesitated, not sure how much to tell her. If the humidor had been a gift from this woman to Durand for his services, why did she seem surprised that it was missing from her home?

"You didn't give it to anyone?" Louis asked.

Tink placed a hand over heart, breathless. "Goodness, no," she said. "Dickie would kill me if I gave his humidor away. I would never. In fact, I'm not even allowed in his room."

Louis glanced at the house. He'd love to get inside Dickie's "room," but if his wife wasn't allowed, there was no shot for him.

"What else does he keep in his room?" Louis asked.

Tink suddenly turned, looking around for something. She seemed confused, whispering things Louis couldn't understand.

"Mrs. Lyons, are you all right?"

"Yes, yes," she said. "Is that my phone? Do you hear my phone?"

"No, ma'am."

"I'm sure it's ringing," she said, starting toward the house. "Harriet must be in the laundry. She can't hear the phone when she's in there."

The dog hurried after her. So did Louis, gently reaching for her arm to stop her. When she faced him, her eyes were wide and brimming with tears.

"Are you going to arrest me?" she asked.

He let go of her arm and took a step back. The right thing to do would have been to reassure her that he couldn't arrest her or anyone else. But he didn't care about making her feel better. He wanted answers.

"Why would I arrest you?"

She clasped the lapels of her robe and looked to the house, as if she was afraid they might be interrupted by someone.

"Mrs. Lyons, is your husband home?"

"No," she said softly. "He's out of town."

"Where?"

"I don't know exactly," she said. "He's hunting. He hunts those big awful pigs in the Everglades. They go every year."

"Who goes?" Louis asked. "Who does your husband hunt with?"

Again she looked to the house. Louis followed her gaze. A maid stood near the French doors, watching them.

"Harriet is watching us," Tink whispered. "She'll tell Dickie you were here. He won't like that."

"That's okay," Louis said. "I'll deal with your husband. Now, tell me, who does he hunt with?"

"Well, there's Bus Hamilton and George McMillan and—"

"Does he ever hunt with Tucker Osborn?"

Tink looked up, her eyes suddenly clear and bright blue, as if she'd just realized she was being interrogated and had said too much.

"You need to go now," she said. "You need to go and never come back. I haven't done anything wrong. I was only lonely. There's nothing illegal about being lonely. Now, go. Or I'll call Chief Hewitt to come and remove you."

Louis wanted to pursue her "loneliness," but he didn't need a confrontation with Swann's boss, nor did he need to be exiled from the island at this stage of the investigation. He backed away from Tink and bent down to slip the humidor back into the Saks bag.

Tink reached for it. "That's Dickie's," she said. "He'll want it back."

"Not yet," Louis said, pushing her hand aside. "It's evidence in a murder case."

"Whose murder?"

"Mark Durand," Louis said.

Tink stared at him, her faded pink lips agape.

"You remember good old Mark, don't you, Tink? I heard you two were real good friends."

"How dare you insinuate that I knew that despicable man," she said.

Hell, he had come this far. What did he have to lose?

"Oh, you knew him," Louis said. "Problem was, Dickie found out about you two. And he didn't like that very much, did he?"

Tink Lyons did her best to puff herself up with indignation, but there was a real look of fear in her eyes.

"Get out," she said.

Louis picked up the Saks bag, and with a small bow, he turned and started back through the jungle. He was almost back to the house when a spot of fire red caught his eye.

It was a good three feet tall, sitting on a table in the shade. The exact same red orchid he had seen in the Osborn house.

With a glance back toward the pool, he broke off one of the flowered sprigs and stuck it in his pocket.

He felt the weight of someone's stare and spun. It was just the Afghan. It was sitting three feet away, its sleepy eyes fixed on him.

Louis retraced his steps through the house, listening to the *click-click* of the dog's nails as it followed him. There was no sign of the butler. After a few false turns, Louis finally found the front door and let himself out. The Afghan came out with him and watched him every step of the way.

After leaving Tink Lyons's home, he headed straight to Clean & Green in West Palm Beach. He showed the owner, Chuck Green, the red blossom he had taken from Tink's patio. Green was surprised to see the orchid.

"You recognize it?" Louis asked.

"It's a vandaceous hybrid called *Renanthera diabolus,*" Green said.

"Is it expensive?"

Green nodded. "They're expensive because they're really rare. They used to grow wild in the Everglades, but the damn poachers nearly made them extinct. So, the state put them on an endangered list. Now, only a handful of growers are allowed to propagate them from seeds. I get good money for them."

"You have them here?"

Again he nodded, this time with pride. "I'm the only one in the county who grows them. They take a lot of patience and love. You have to wait a long time for them to bloom."

Louis thought suddenly of the red flowering plant

he had seen hanging over Rosa's front door. He couldn't remember if it was an orchid or not. "Mr. Green, could Emilio Labastide have had one of these?"

Green thought for a moment. "Come to think of it, he was really interested in orchids. It's possible I might have given him a *keiki*."

"*Keiki?*"

"That's a Hawaiian word for 'baby.' That's what we call orchid cuttings." He held up the sprig. "Where'd you get this?"

"From a home over in Palm Beach," Louis said. "Do you sell these orchids to anyone there?"

"Nope," Green said. Seeing Louis's disappointment, Green smiled. "But I do supply them to a flower shop on Worth Avenue. It's called Fleur de Lee. Talk to Bianca Lee, the owner. She's a regular buyer of my devil orchids."

Louis was writing in his notebook and looked up. "Devil orchid?"

"Yeah," Green said. "That's its common name. *Renanthera diabolus.* Devil orchid." He held out the sprig to Louis. "Look closely. The flower looks just like the devil's head."

On the drive back to Palm Beach, Louis had tried to make sense of it—three luxury items seemingly unconnected that were undoubtedly parts of a big puzzle. What the hell did an old humidor, an antique sword, and a rare orchid have in common? And maybe it was just a coincidence that the orchid had the same name as the place where Mark Durand had been murdered. But it was a damned intriguing one.

Fleur de Lee was a tiny shop not far from the antique

military store. Inside, Louis took off his sunglasses and stood perfectly still, afraid that if he moved, he'd break something. The place was stuffed with plants and flowers, including orchids of every size and color.

Except red.

As he waited for the owner, he pulled the sprig out of his pocket and stared hard at one of the tiny blossoms. Green was right. Its center looked exactly like a devil's face.

"Can I help you?"

Louis turned. The woman who had come out of the back was small and dark-haired, in her forties, and exotically attractive. She wore a green smock over dark slacks and a sweater and was carrying shears.

When she saw him, she stopped cold. Louis had gotten used to people staring at him here. But the look on Bianca Lee's face was different. It was just a flash, but it was there before the mask went up. It reminded him of the cheating husband he had caught last month coming out of the Days Inn in Fort Myers.

Busted. But for what? Selling flowers?

Louis palmed the orchid sprig. As he introduced himself, Bianca Lee nodded. "You're the one who's working for Reggie Kent," she said with one of those patented Bizarro World smiles. "He seemed like such a nice man, but you can never tell about people, can you? Imagine, cutting off a man's head."

"A man is innocent until proven guilty," Louis said.

"So they say," she said. "Now, what can I do for you?"

"I'm interested in orchids," Louis said.

"Really? Cut flowers or a plant? I have some lovely phalaenopsis that are quite reasonable."

"Do you have a devil orchid?" Louis asked.

Bianca Lee's smooth olive face went a shade lighter. She carefully set the shears down before she looked back up at Louis. "Devil orchid," she said. "I've never heard of it."

"Well, I don't know the fancy Latin name," Louis said. He uncurled his hand. "But it looks like this."

Bianca took the sprig and gave Louis a wide smile. "Oh, yes, *Renanthera diabolus*. I didn't know it had another name."

"Do you carry them?"

She nodded. "Yes, but we don't have any right now. I could probably order one for you. But it's frightfully expensive. I'm sure you would rather have—"

"Nope, I'm really interested in devil orchids."

Bianca stared at him, then held out the sprig. "Maybe you could check back later." Her smile was gone. There was ice in her voice.

"Maybe you could tell me who you sell these to," Louis said as he took the flower.

"Why would you need to know that?"

"I have my reasons."

Bianca shrugged. "Well, I have dozens of clients on the island. But I would never give out their names."

"Flower sales are confidential?"

"Privacy is everything here, Mr. Kincaid."

There was something about the way she said his name. He was close to snapping. He'd had it with these people.

"Look, lady," Louis said, "I can be back here in an hour with a county deputy and a search warrant for your records. Or we can do this nice and easy."

She just stared at him.

"How about if I name a few names and you just nod?" Louis said. "You know, like in that movie with Deep Throat?"

She didn't move. Louis could almost read her mind: The nice fellows at the pink police station would protect her. If she could just get to the phone.

"Okay, first name," Louis said. "Tucker Osborn."

Nothing. Not even a blink.

"Let's try again," Louis said. "Richard Lyons."

Still nothing. The woman was good.

Or maybe he was wrong. Maybe the orchid meant nothing. Maybe he was wasting precious time and needed to be concentrating on the humidor. Maybe it was time to go back to basics and see if the sword's blade matched the wound on Mark Durand's neck. It was possible that Dr. Steffel had something by now.

"Thanks for your help," he said, and left the shop.

Outside, he paused to put on his sunglasses. He was about to toss the orchid sprig but put it in his pocket instead.

He was almost to South County Road when a horn beeped behind him. It was a red BMW 325, not the newest model but shined to a gleam. Swann was behind the wheel. He pulled to the curb, and the window whirred down.

"I've been looking all over for you. Get in."

"Where we going?"

Swann couldn't hide his eager smile. "We've got a third body."

Chapter Twenty-three

It felt good to get off the island. Maybe it was just that he was sick and tired of doing the Bizarro World boogie-woogie, or he just longed for something plain and real. Whatever the reason, out here on the open highway, fifty miles west of Palm Beach, Louis felt freer than he had in a week.

Swann was a good driver, weaving the BMW through the truck traffic on US-80 like a cop used to car chases. Louis doubted Swann had ever had to push his police cruiser past forty over on his home turf. But the guy had changed in the last few days, taking to his role in Reggie Kent's case with the eagerness of a raw recruit.

Swann had found the third headless victim buried in the records of the Hendry County Sheriff's Office. Now they were on their way to find out if the body had any connection to their case.

As they drove, Louis filled Swann in about his visit to Tink Lyons. Swann was stunned into silence. Part of it was disgust, Louis suspected. But there was also something personal in Swann's silence, like he was angry at himself for being so naïve about the people who paid his salary. Or worse, he was feeling incompetent, eclipsed by a private investigator.

Finally, Louis broke the quiet in the car. "How'd you find this guy exactly?" he asked.

Swann glanced over at him then looked back at the road. "I've got a contact high up at the FDLE," he said. "Once I got somebody on the computer, it didn't take long. I just asked him to do a search for young male victims who had been decapitated or tortured."

Louis knew the Florida Department of Law Enforcement didn't jump at just anyone's request, and they sure didn't cough up information overnight.

"Must be somebody with some juice up there," Louis said.

Swann just stared straight ahead. "My father's a retired major for the state police. His name still carries some weight in Tallahassee."

Swann reached down and turned on the radio. He began stabbing at the buttons. Louis watched him, wondering how heavy that weight sometimes felt on Swann's shoulders. Heavy enough to flee all the way down to Palm Beach?

After a flurry of country music, sports talk and static, Swann finally gave up on the radio.

"How old's this one?" Louis asked after a few more minutes of Swann's silence.

"He was found three years ago, fall of '86," Swann said. "A couple of Seminoles found him in a swamp. Or what was left of him."

"What's that supposed to mean?"

"All they found was a torso with one arm," Swann said. "He was pretty chewed up by alligators. But there was enough for prints, and turned out he had a minor drug record in Fort Lauderdale."

"But we don't know if he was decapitated or a damn gator just bit the head off?"

"No, but when I found out he worked as a bartender in Palm Beach, I thought the connection was too big to ignore."

"How'd you find out he worked in Palm Beach?"

"County health records," Swann said. "You've got to have a card to work in the food and beverage business in Palm Beach."

"Good work, Andrew."

Swann glanced at him but said nothing.

The Hendry County Sheriff's Office was located in La Belle, a sleepy town of cracker houses, oak trees, and an old white courthouse on the banks of the Caloosahatchee River. The station on Bridge Street had two Hendry cruisers out front. But it was the third one that caught Louis's eye. It had the Palm Beach County seal on its door.

Barberry was in the detective's office when they walked in. He looked like he'd been caught on his day off. He wore baggy Bermuda shorts, white tube socks with loafers, and a Hawaiian shirt. His gold badge hung on a chain around his neck.

Swann's contact in Hendry County, a Detective Hernandez, stood nearby. He was a few years under thirty, with messy brown hair, a meager mustache, and an ugly polyester jacket that ballooned over his slender build.

Barberry was reading a file, but he must have heard the footfalls across the tile floor because he looked up. His sneer at Louis was expected, but his expression changed when he saw Swann. It registered disbelief, then he chuckled.

"Well, well, Andrew Swann," Barberry said. "Papa Hewitt know you're here, boy?"

Swann stopped in front of Barberry, but Louis could see he was having a hard time holding Barberry's eye. He had the same look that Bianca Lee had had in her fancy flower shop: busted.

Louis introduced himself and Swann to Hernandez. Hernandez mumbled a hello and looked at Swann.

"I'm sorry, Lieutenant," he said to Swann. "I had to call you back for something, and I thought you worked for the Palm Beach Sheriff's Office, but they told me they didn't know you, so I just asked for the officer in charge of the headless-corpse case, thinking he would be your partner, and then, well, they gave me to this—"

"Shut up," Barberry said. He looked to Louis and Swann. "What do you two jackasses think you're doing, calling people all over the state and getting them worked up into thinking we got a serial killer on the loose here?"

"We think we *do* have a serial killer," Louis said.

"On two lousy bodies that have nothing in common?"

Louis wasn't ready to tell him they had a third victim named Emilio Labastide or that they had already exhumed and examined the body, but he had to give Barberry something just so they would be allowed to stay in the damn room.

"They were both headless," Louis said.

Barberry gestured to the file Hernandez was holding. "Oh, for crissakes," he said. "This one here was probably made that way by a damn alligator."

"Well, now, Detective," Hernandez began. "That might not be accurate. If you'd take a look at the ME's report, you'll see that—"

"Shut up," Barberry said.

"Don't tell him to shut up," Louis said. "Go ahead, Detective Hernandez, what were you going to say?"

Hernandez stuck out his hand. "If I could have my file, sir?"

Barberry gripped the folder tighter, but even he knew the contents belonged to Hendry County and, more specifically, to this skinny, pimple-faced cop.

"Please, sir," Hernandez said. "Don't make me have to exert my authority and ask my guys to come over here."

Louis looked over Hernandez's shoulders. Apparently, his guys were the two uniformed officers lurking near the water cooler. They were watching the discussion with interest.

"Look, we're in a mess here," Hernandez said. "Our sheriff died suddenly, and the undersheriff was arrested last week for taking bribes. My boss is out sick, and our two other detectives are working 24-7 on a boat theft ring. Right now, we're looking out for each other. So, in other words, don't fuck with me here on my turf, okay?"

Barberry looked amused at the detective's bravado. He slapped the folder against Hernandez's chest. "Okay, I'm a stubborn sonofabitch, but I'm not stupid," he said. "Go ahead. Tell us what you got."

Hernandez opened the folder and cleared his throat. "His name was Paul Wyeth. He was twenty-three years old and employed as a bartender in Palm Beach." Hernandez looked up. "But you knew that, didn't you?"

"That's okay," Louis said. "Go on."

"Our Detective Cowell was assigned to the case but he passed away last year, so we won't be able to ask him any questions," Hernandez said. "But it looks like his theory was that the murder was drug-related."

"What makes you believe that?" Louis asked.

"Three reasons. First, Wyeth had a minor drug charge, and second, we found more than eight grand in cash in his apartment."

"What about his bank account?"

"Nothing to speak of."

"What's the third reason?" Louis asked.

"Wyeth was found in an area where drug dealers have been known to dump bodies."

"Where exactly?" Louis asked.

"In a spot called Turtle Slough. It's just north of Billy Swamp Safari, which is in the Seminole Indian reservation. The reservation police handed the case off to us."

"What's a slough?" Louis asked.

"A slough is a swampy kind of river that changes in size from season to season. They run from Lake Ocheechobee down to the gulf. Sometimes a slough flows fast, and other times it's nothing but mud."

Louis remembered seeing a stream on his trip to the cattle pen with Burke Aubry, and he wondered if it had been Turtle Slough. He noticed a Hendry County map tacked to the wall behind Hernandez. "Can you show us where this slough is?" he asked.

Hernandez picked up a pen. "Okay, here's us in La Belle," he said, marking a spot on the map with an X. He traced a path from the top corner of the county to the bottom. It crossed straight through the tiny green patch on the map named Devil's Garden.

"Where was Paul Wyeth found?" Louis asked.

Hernandez put an X on the line, just below the green box for Devil's Garden.

"How far is it from Devil's Garden to where Wyeth was found?" Louis asked.

Hernandez shrugged. "Maybe a mile."

"Could the body have floated that far without being attacked?"

"Possibly," Hernandez said. "But it wouldn't last much longer than that. That area's thick with gators and other critters."

"So, was the head chewed off or not?" Barberry asked.

Hernandez opened the file. "As you know, all we found was the torso and an arm," he said. "But according to our ME, there were marks in the neck bones that were consistent not with animal teeth but with a bladed instrument."

"And no head was ever found, right?" Louis asked.

"If you've ever been out in that area, you know that would have been impossible," Hernandez said. "Once all the meat had been eaten off it, the skull would be sucked into the muddy bowels of the Everglades, and there it would lie."

"Was Wyeth dressed?" Louis asked.

Again, Hernandez had to look in the file. "No, the ME was ninety-nine percent sure the torso was nude when it went in the water."

"Any sign he was whipped or tortured?" Swann asked.

This question seemed to surprise Hernandez, and he flipped through the reports. While he looked, Louis watched Barberry. He was quiet, hands shoved in his pockets, his stubbled jaw working on a wad of Big Red gum.

"No," Hernandez said, looking up. "The ME didn't note any whip marks or other defensive wounds. He just noted . . . let's see . . . over three hundred claw and brush wounds."

"Are there autopsy photos in there?" Louis asked.

"Sure." Hernandez handed him a stack of pictures.

Louis sorted through them quickly, looking for one of Wyeth's torso. The one he found showed a close-up of

Wyeth's bloated and ripped back. Louis knew only a doctor could tell for sure, but to his eye some of the lacerations looked similar to the ones he had seen on Durand's back. Which left the possibility, however remote, that Wyeth had been whipped, especially if he hadn't been wearing a shirt.

But Louis had to wonder if he himself was, as Dr. Steffel said, trying to fit the facts to an already-formed theory or letting them speak for themselves.

Still, it felt right: the M.O., the dump sites, similar victim profiles, the killer's "signature" of torture, degradation, and extreme rage. There was no way Barberry or anyone else was going to tell him they didn't have a serial killer on their hands.

Louis shoved the photo at Barberry. "You ready to admit you have the wrong man in jail?"

Barberry's eyes slipped to the picture, but he quickly raised them and Louis saw no concession in his face. It amazed Louis that this man could not get by his hatred of Reggie Kent long enough to allow himself one decent action.

"I'm not buying any of this yet," Barberry said. "Two bodies don't make this a Ted Bundy rerun. And what kind of sicko would kill off young guys if not some psycho queer like Kent?"

Swann came out of nowhere, shoving Louis aside as he grabbed a fistful of Barberry's shirt.

"You stop talking about Reggie like that!" Swann hissed.

Swann was an inch taller, fifteen years younger, and in far better shape than Barberry. Barberry could do nothing but push at Swann's tightly muscled forearm.

"Let go of me!" Barberry spat.

"You're a police officer. You treat people—*all* people—with respect. You hear me, Detective?"

Barberry broke Swann's hold and stumbled away, red-faced and breathless. Hernandez had backed himself against the map, the file clutched to his chest.

Swann finally moved away, calming himself by taking deep breaths. Barberry wiped his face and for a moment, no one seemed to know what to do.

"Look, Detective Barberry," Louis said, "you need to understand something here. We have information that will make your prosecutor look like a fool if he takes Kent to trial. And who do you think he'll take that out on?"

"What else you got besides this half-eaten corpse and a half-baked theory?" Barberry asked.

Louis didn't want to share things here, nor did he trust Barberry to strike a bargain in exchange for other information. He knew he'd have to cooperate at some level with this jerk, but there were a few things he wanted from him first.

"We'll tell you what we have if you'll tell us what the forensics are on the boots and sword and anything else you took from Kent's house," Louis said.

Barberry snorted. "No, you first or I'm not wasting one more minute talking to you. I don't need you. You need me."

Barberry wasn't right about many things but Louis couldn't argue with that.

"We have a third body," Louis said. "Same sex, same approximate age, same general appearance, same evidence of torture and decapitation, plus a connection to Palm Beach."

Barberry's bushy black eyebrows arched up. "Three, eh?"

"Your turn," Louis said.

"The boots we took from Kent's house are an exact match to footprints in the cattle pen," Barberry said. "The tread is really weird, so there's no mistake. And they aren't just any old boots. They're ostrich leather, some special things with air bubbles in the soles. Cost about six hundred bucks."

"What's the brand of boots?"

"Hell, I don't know," Barberry said. "Kangaroo Bobs or something like that. Some kind of fancy hunting boot."

Louis looked back to the county map, thinking. The fact that the boots found in Reggie's home were a match worked against Reggie, but it wasn't the final nail in the prosecutorial coffin. It could also reinforce Louis's idea that the killer might be a jealous husband, but he wasn't going to share that information with Barberry—yet.

"What about the sword?" Louis asked.

Barberry scratched his jaw, eyeing Swann. His loathing for Swann's professional betrayal was obvious. "Doc Steffel says the sword didn't match," he said. "Too thick, too dull, and it's double-edged. She says, in her opinion, the weapon was a single-edged sharp blade."

"Did she have any other ideas?" Louis asked.

"She's still researching," Barberry said. "Now it's your turn, Kincaid. Who is this third body and where was he found?"

"One more thing first," Louis said. "Give us your word you won't rat Andrew out to his chief. He's just trying to do the right thing for Kent, and you know how hard that can be when you have a politically sensitive boss."

Barberry snorted. "Deal. Now talk."

Louis gave Barberry a brief rundown on Emilio Labastide, explaining that the three men shared a similar victim profile. When he added that he believed none of the victims had been gay but that there still appeared to be a sexual element to the murders, Barberry's eyes glazed over with skepticism.

"Okay," Barberry said. "Even if I give you the fact that you might—and I say might—have a serial killer here, why is he running around killing straight guys? Don't serial killers target women?"

"We think he could be a jealous husband with a sadistic sense of retaliation."

It took Barberry at least fifteen seconds before he connected the dots. "So, these young studs were porking rich broads?" he asked.

Louis was silent, letting Barberry's mind chew on the possibility of such a motive and the nasty, invasive investigation that would ensue if it was true.

"You got suspects?" Barberry asked.

Barberry wasn't getting everything. "Not yet," Louis said, "but we're close."

"Give me what you got," Barberry said.

"No," Louis said. "You go back to your prosecutor and you convince him you were wrong about Reggie Kent and get him to dismiss the charges. I want Kent released. Then we'll talk."

"I could charge you with obstruction," Barberry said.

"Give me a break," Louis said. "Nobody does that anymore."

Barberry ignored him and held out his hand to Hernandez. "I'll take that case file, Detective," he said. "Looks like I'm a one-man serial-killer task force here."

Hernandez clutched the file tighter. "No disrespect, sir," he said, "but due to our current staffing issues here, I've been authorized to relinquish jurisdiction to any other agency that has a credible interest or jurisdiction in the case."

"And that's me," Barberry said.

Hernandez held up a finger. "But Lieutenant Swann here also represents a legitimate law enforcement agency, and seeing as how he was much kinder to me, I think I'll give the file to him."

Swann threw up a hand. "Thanks, Hernandez, but I can't take over your case," he said. "My agency doesn't have even the remotest jurisdiction over any of these crimes."

"Plus, you don't want to get your ass handed to you by your boss," Barberry added.

Hernandez sighed. "Then I guess it's yours, Detective Barberry," he said. *"Tu eres más feo que el culo de un mono."*

Barberry grinned and took the file. "Well, *gracias* there, Hernandez, to whatever you said. I'll make sure you get a mention when the collar's made."

Barberry walked away. The cops near the water cooler waited until he left the squad room, then disbursed.

Louis thanked Hernandez and followed Swann outside. It was not yet noon and the morning was unusually warm for December. Not a cloud in the sky or a breeze in the air.

"Hey, Swann," Louis said, "what did Hernandez say to Barberry when he gave him the file?"

"He said, 'You're uglier than a monkey's ass.'"

Louis laughed but Swann walked on toward the parking lot. He seemed lost in thought, sunglasses hiding his eyes.

"You going to be okay, Andrew?" Louis asked.

Swann shrugged as he stopped at his BMW to unlock the driver's door. "What can I do? I'll just have to wait and see if Barberry keeps his word."

They drove out of La Belle, heading back east on US-80. Swann was quiet, and Louis was worried about him. He suspected that any pride Swann felt over finding Paul Wyeth had been replaced by concern that he would lose his badge. Louis knew what that felt like. He had felt it himself years ago, standing in front of a state investigator, listening to him say that Louis would never work as a cop in Michigan again. Louis hadn't been guilty of any crime. But he hadn't stayed around to fight. And when the call came from an old friend to take a case in Florida, he had gone south. It took him two years to get the PI license. Like so many here, he had tried to reinvent himself.

He looked over at Swann. Maybe Swann would have to do the same. But Louis wondered if he'd be able to make it. He knew how a few ounces of tin was sometimes the only thing keeping you grounded.

They were almost back to Clewiston when Louis spotted the sign for the airstrip.

"Swann, do you have to get back to Palm Beach right now?" Louis asked.

"No, why?"

"The road to Devil's Garden is just ahead. I thought we could take another look at the crime scene. I could really use another cop's opinion."

Swann glanced over at him. Louis couldn't see his eyes behind the sunglasses, but Swann was smiling.

Chapter Twenty-four

Swann walked slowly around the cattle pen. His eyes lingered on the shred of yellow crime-scene tape that hung from one of the gray planks.

"Not much to see here," he said.

"I know," Louis said.

Louis looked back toward the gravel road. He could just see the red of Swann's BMW through the tall weeds and trees. He was trying to figure out what direction Burke Aubry had brought them in the last time they were here. They had crossed a stream, and if he was remembering things right, they had walked up to the pen from the opposite direction of the gravel road. And Detective Hernandez had said the Turtle Slough ran from north to southwest, which meant the stream was somewhere nearby.

"Andrew, let's see if we can find that stream," Louis said.

"Where Wyeth was found?"

"Yeah, I want to see how close it is to the pen."

They trudged south through the weeds. The red BMW was the only spot of color in the monotony of the greens and yellows, but they soon lost sight of it.

Louis was about to suggest they turn back when he heard the sound of water. They pushed through the brush and cattails, emerging on the edge of a fast-running brown stream.

"This has to Turtle Slough," Swann said.

Louis looked north. From this spot, he could again make out a sliver of red in the distance. They were only about fifty yards from the BMW and the pen.

"He could have been thrown in here," Swann said.

Louis nodded. "And drifted downstream, just like Hernandez said."

They were both quiet. A blur of movement caught Louis's eye. A giant blue heron was standing on the other bank of the slough, watching them.

"We'd better get back to the car," Louis said.

They found their way back to the pen, coming in the back way this time. Swann ripped down the last of the crime-scene tape and stuffed it into his pocket. But then he just stood there in the middle of the pen.

"Andrew?"

"This place is important," Swann said. He shook his head slowly. "I mean—this is going to sound stupid."

"Say it, Andrew."

"Something you told me that Aubry said. Something about this place being special to the cowboys?"

"No," Louis said. "He said it was special to Mrs. Archer. He called it sacred."

"Sacred? That's the word he used?"

Louis nodded. He knew where Swann was going with this. *Sacred* was the kind of word you used for battle-fields or burial grounds. They were too far north of the Seminole reservation for this to be significant to the Indians. And if there were any graveyards around here in this brush, there was no way he and Swann would find them.

"Come on, Andrew," Louis said. "We have to go talk to Mrs. Archer."

A dark-haired woman with a Spanish accent answered the door at the Archer Ranch. She wasn't happy about the idea of two strange men asking to see Señora Archer. She told them to wait on the porch and closed the door.

Ten minutes passed. Swann finally went and sat down in one of the rockers. "Maybe that place out there has something to do with her husband," he said.

"Husband? Why?" Louis asked.

"Aubry told us Jim Archer died in 1965. Maybe he's buried out there."

"It still doesn't explain why two men were murdered in the same area," Louis said.

"Damn, look at that," Swann said.

Louis turned to where Swann was pointing. Eight men on horses were coming up the coquina-shell drive-way. A pack of dogs trotted behind. All of the men wore denim shirts, jeans, and wide-brimmed hats. As they came closer, Louis saw that the big guy in the lead was Burke Aubry.

Louis and Swann came down off the porch as the men drew next to the red BMW and stopped. Aubry looked down at Louis through his mirrored sunglasses.

"All right, what's this about wanting to see Mrs. Archer?"

Louis heard the crackle of a radio and saw a walkie-talkie strapped on Aubry's saddle. He noticed that the other men had them as well.

"We need to ask her some questions about Devil's Garden," Louis said.

Swann came down off the porch toward Louis. Aubry's horse let out a loud snort and did a jerky side dance. Swann jumped back a good five feet.

Aubry calmed the horse. "Who's your friend?"

"Lieutenant Swann, Palm Beach Police Department," Louis said. "We came back because we have another man from Palm Beach who was found dead near here."

"In Devil's Garden?"

"About a mile downstream in Turtle Slough."

Aubry leaned on his saddle horn, head down.

"Does the name Paul Wyeth mean anything to you?" Louis asked.

Aubry shook his head. "That the dead man?"

"Yes," Louis said.

"What about the names Osborn or Lyons?" Swann asked.

"Don't ring a bell. They from around here?"

"Palm Beach," Swann said.

"That's another world, son."

"What about Devil's Garden," Swann said. "Why is it so special?"

Aubry stared down at Swann. "Special?"

"Mr. Aubry," Louis said, "the last time we were here, you said Devil's Garden was sacred to Mrs. Archer. It's really important that we talk to her, please."

Aubry turned to the other men. "You all can go back out. I'll catch up later."

Without a word, the men turned their horses and rode away, the dogs following. Aubry dismounted and tied his horse to the railing. He brought a ripe smell of sweat and horse with him as he came up onto the porch. Louis noticed that Swann was watching Aubry with awe.

"You don't need to bother Libby Archer," Aubry said.

"Mr. Aubry—"

Aubry held up a hand to silence Louis. "I can tell you everything you need to know."

Louis felt Swann come up behind him.

"Libby's son David died out there," Aubry said.

"When?" Louis asked.

"Twenty-eight years ago," Aubry said. "He was just eighteen."

Aubry didn't seem to want to go on. Louis had no choice but to press him. "What happened, Mr. Aubry?"

"It was an accident. His horse threw him. He hit his head on a rock and died."

Louis knew nothing about horses, and he guessed it could have happened exactly like Aubry said—a simple freak accident. But all of Louis's training, experience, and instincts forced him to distrust what seemed simple. Another young man dead in Devil's Garden. Even if it was nearly three decades ago, it wasn't something that could be ignored.

He looked at Swann. He was thinking the same thing. And Louis had heard something in Aubry's voice. Sometimes, the simpler the words, the more complex the emotions behind them.

"Mr. Aubry, were you working here then?" he asked.

Aubry nodded.

"You're sure there was nothing unusual about David's death?"

"The doc in Clewiston said it was a head injury, that his brain hemorrhaged before anyone could help him."

"Was there an autopsy?"

"Autopsy?" Aubry pulled off his hat and shook his head. "No, nothing like that. The Archers . . . they were, well, it was really a bad time. They just wanted to bring David home and bury him proper."

Louis knew how deaths were often handled in small towns, and twenty-eight years ago, things would have been even less sophisticated. Add to that an unassuming police chief and an ingrained trust of your neighbor, and it was easy to see why a fall off a horse would raise no questions. And maybe that's all it was, but Louis felt the need to press it.

"I know this is hard, Mr. Aubry," Louis said. "But can you tell me exactly what happened the day David died?"

There had been a dull kind of pain in Aubry's eyes before, like the man had long ago resigned himself to a life of backbreaking work and lonely nights. But at this moment, his blue eyes went almost colorless in the harsh light of the sun.

"You think David's death could have something to do with the men you're finding now?" Aubry asked.

Louis caught the break in Aubry's voice, and he almost didn't answer the question. But now there was something else he wanted to know more about: Aubry's obvious affection for this kid David Archer.

"It's a long shot," Louis said gently. "But we've discovered that sometimes, these kinds of killers get their start early, when they're very young."

"You mean a serial-killer-type fella?" Aubry asked.

Louis nodded. "Yeah."

Aubry gestured to the two empty rocking chairs. Louis and Swann sat down. Aubry leaned against the porch rail, his dusty hat still in his hand. "It was just before sundown when David's horse came back without him," he said. "We didn't get all fired up right at first, because we all knew David had just gotten the horse for his birthday and was still getting used to her."

"The horse was wild?" Swann asked.

Aubry smiled. "No, son, just full of piss and vinegar. Wouldn't have been the first time she throwed David, and we didn't think it'd be the last."

Aubry paused, the smile gone.

"Go on, please," Louis said.

"Well, Jim and me and the rest of us set out after him, thinking we'd find him sitting in the shade, laid up with a sprained ankle or something and waiting for us to ride up and take him home to supper."

Aubry stopped again and stared at his boots. Louis glanced at Swann. He had the look of a boy listening to a ghost story.

"Mr. Aubry?" Louis prodded.

"We found David in some heavy woods just north of the old pen," Aubry said softly. "I knew the minute I touched him, he was gone."

"What did you do then?" Louis asked.

Aubry cleared his throat. "Jim carried him on back to the house, and we called the doc. Not for David but for Mrs. Archer. I could tell she was going to need everything the doc, and maybe God, could offer just so she could make it through the night."

"So, no one ever took a closer look at David's head wound or the area where you found him?" Louis asked.

Aubry shook his head. "No reason to. Doc and the chief said it was an accident, and that's what got wrote down."

"The doctor and the police chief, they still around?" Louis asked.

"Both dead," Aubry said.

Louis pulled his notebook from his pocket, intending to ask Aubry to draw him a map of where this patch of woods was. He wanted to see the exact spot where David had fallen, although he didn't know why. The cattle pen had offered him no vibrations, so what could he expect from a plot of ground where a death had happened almost thirty years ago?

Swann leaned forward. "Mr. Aubry, what do *you* think happened to David that day?"

Louis looked to Swann, surprised not only that he'd spoken up but at the question itself. What had Swann heard that Louis hadn't?

"You said 'that's what got wrote down,'" Swann said. "We all know that sometimes what gets written down isn't always what happened."

Aubry walked a few feet across the porch, then turned back to them. "That same night, when we were sitting around the house trying to make sense of stuff, Jim started wondering out loud why David had been in those woods when he was supposed to be working on the fence line about a mile north."

Aubry's walkie-talkie crackled with a spurt of male voices. He listened for a few seconds, then turned it off.

"I knew what David was doing there, but I didn't tell Jim," Aubry said. "David liked to wander off and draw pictures. I was sure that's why he was there in those woods. It's the prettiest place on the ranch."

"Why couldn't you tell his father this?" Louis asked.

"Well, when David was thirteen, Jim found him in the barn drawing pictures of the horses. He got a little upset, told him only sissies did stuff like that."

"But David didn't give it up," Louis said.

"No," Aubry said. "He just couldn't seem to help himself. So, to keep peace, I told David he could stow his sketching stuff at my place. That's why the night we found David, I went to the barn to check David's kit and make sure there weren't any sketchbooks there. Jim had enough heartache that night."

Aubry pulled the bandanna from around his neck and wiped his face. The man was sweating, despite the cool breeze blowing in from the south.

"But I didn't find any sketchbooks," Aubry said. "I was thinking about that when I saw his whip was missing."

"His whip?" Louis asked.

"Yup. The saddle kit was still intact, but the whip was gone."

"Could it have fallen off when the horse bucked?" Louis asked.

Aubry shook his head. "But I took a trip out to those woods the next morning just to make sure. I didn't find anything."

"Could he have just lost the whip?" Swann asked.

"Cowmen don't just lose things off their saddles," Aubry said. "Our kit is as important to us as your police stuff is to you."

"Could David have loaned the whip to someone?" Louis asked.

Aubry shook his head. "No. His granddad Tom gave it to him, and that boy loved that whip like nothing else in this world. Waxed it himself, braided it himself. His initials were carved in the handle."

Louis thought back to the slashes on Mark Durand's bare back and the tiny piece of leather Dr. Steffel had retrieved from deep inside one of the wounds.

He looked to Aubry's horse, at the whip hanging on the saddle. It was a braided red and blue coil, not anything like the leather lash most people envisioned when they thought of a bullwhip.

"Did David's whip look like that?" Louis asked, pointing toward the horse.

"No," Aubry said. "We use nylon now. Holds up better in the wet weather. But David always used that old leather one."

"Is there a chance one of your cowboys stole it?" Swann asked.

"Cow*men*, son," Aubry said. "And no, like I told your friends when they were here before, no man of mine, then or now, would have stolen that boy's whip. Not from *that* boy and not that whip."

"Then someone had to have taken it from David that day in the woods," Louis said.

Aubry's eyes came slowly to Louis. There was a sad kind of reckoning in them, as if his twenty-eight-year-old struggle between what he hoped to be true and what he feared to be true was finally coming to an end.

"Is there a chance he could have encountered a

stranger out there and been robbed or bullied into a fight?" Louis asked.

Aubry shook his head. "You have to understand. This place is like an island. We all know each other. We protect each other. Strangers just don't wander onto the land. It's not their world."

"Then was it possible he was meeting someone?" Louis asked.

"I don't know who," Aubry said. "Everyone else was working. David should've been working. If he had a friend, he would have brought him to the house."

Louis glanced at Swann. They had both heard Aubry's use of the word *sissy* earlier and were probably thinking the same thing now: that David couldn't bring his friend to the house because he was gay.

But they had abandoned the theory of the victims' sexual orientation as motivation days ago. What the hell were they missing here?

Louis looked back at Aubry, knowing he needed to ask the question, but he just wasn't sure how.

Aubry must have seen something in his face. "I remember how that Detective Barberry was talking about that man who was killed in the cow pen," he said. "And now you're wondering the same thing about David."

"Mr. Aubry—"

"I ought to take offense at the idea that you think just because David liked drawing things, he was a molly-boy."

"I didn't say that."

"No, but you thought it."

Louis was quiet. Swann was staring at the porch, the squeaking of the rocker filling the stiff silence.

"But I won't take offense, because I know that you're

just doing your job the only way you know how," Aubry said. "So, I'll tell you this. David looked at pretty girls as much as any man on this ranch and even picked out the land where he wanted to build his home after he got married. Six kids, he used to say. Three boys, three girls."

He was quiet, staring Louis down.

"All that boy wanted was to have a family and live out his life here."

The sound of Swann's rocking chair stopped.

"Now, if you fellas don't have any more questions, I've got work to do," Aubry said.

Chapter Twenty-five

The first thing in the morning, Louis and Swann went to the county jail to see Reggie. When the guard brought him into the visiting area, Louis's heart sank.

Reggie had an ugly purple bruise on his cheek. Other details registered as Reggie dropped into the chair on the other side of the Plexiglas—a cut lip, a bandaged wrist, and vacant eyes.

"Kent?" Louis said.

It was a full ten seconds before Reggie raised his head.

"Oh, Christ, Reggie, what happened?" Swann said.

But Louis knew. Someone had beaten the shit out of him.

"Kent, listen to me," Louis said. "We're going to get you out of here."

Reggie's eyes brimmed with tears. "I can't do this," he whispered. "I can't stay here."

What could Louis say? He knew the only way to survive in these places was to be a power broker. But Reggie had no currency here, unless he was willing to provide drugs or sex. Reggie had no connections for the first, and from the looks of it, he had drawn the line at the second. If they didn't get him out soon, he'd be dead.

Louis glanced at Swann. He looked like he was ready to kill someone.

"Margery said she'd send a lawyer," Reggie said. "No one has come."

Louis had called Margery that morning. Her lawyer, Harvey, had been delayed on the murder case he was working in New York. She was frantic to get Reggie out somehow and had threatened to show up at the jail again. Louis had managed to talk her down off that ledge. He didn't need to be worrying about Margery getting arrested for creating a disturbance.

"We're working hard to get you out of here, but you can help us," Louis said.

"How?" Reggie whispered.

"I need to ask you some questions," Louis said.

Reggie bowed his head and ran a shaky hand under his nose.

"Kent, listen to me," Louis said. "You have to help us here."

He finally looked up and nodded.

"We found out who Mark was seeing," Louis said. "I need to ask you about them, but you can't tell anyone the names. Do you understand?"

Reggie nodded again.

"One of the women was Carolyn Osborn," Louis said. "Did he ever mention her?"

"The senator?" Reggie whispered. "Mark was . . . with the senator?"

"Yes. Did he ever talk about her?"

Reggie looked stunned as he shook his head slowly. "No, no, he never . . . he never even escorted her anywhere. Neither did I. She . . . she wasn't really part of our set. I mean, people liked her, but she was always in Washington. She just didn't go to the parties and things."

"You're sure?"

He nodded numbly.

"What about Tink Lyons?"

"Tink? Good Lord . . ."

"What?"

Reggie just shook his head, shutting his eyes. "She's . . . she's . . . I just can't imagine Mark with her. No, it's just not possible. No, no . . ."

Reggie was too kind to say what Louis was thinking. What did it take for a young man to bed someone like Tink Lyons? How much money was enough?

"I need to ask you something else," Louis said. "I found a humidor in Mark's room. Do you know how it got there?"

Reggie's pale face was a blank. "Humidor? Mark hated cigars."

"And you're sure you never saw that sword before the day the police searched your house?"

Reggie managed only a tired nod.

Swann leaned in toward the glass. "Reggie, what about the boots?" he asked. "Do you know where Mark got them?"

"Boots?" Reggie asked softly.

"The boots Barberry took from your house," Swann said. "You remember the boots?"

Reggie closed his eyes. "Yes," he whispered.

"Did they belong to Mark?"

"I don't know . . . I just don't know."

Swann looked at Louis in frustration, then back at Reggie. "What size shoe do you wear, Reggie?"

"What?"

"Shoes, what size are you?"

"Eight."

Swann looked at Louis. "The police report said the boots were a size eight and a half."

"That's close enough for Barberry," Louis said quietly.

"Reggie," Swann said, "do you know what size Mark wore?"

"I . . . Mark had big feet," he said. "I think he wore a ten."

Again, Swann looked at Louis. "The boots were custom-made. If they were a gift from someone, why weren't they made in Durand's size?"

Louis was quiet. The boots were the most damning piece of evidence in Barberry's case. As long as those boots were tied to Reggie, Louis would never be able to prove he was innocent. But even now, as he looked at the pathetic man on the other side of the Plexiglas, Louis couldn't help think that Reggie Kent was still holding something back.

The guard who had been standing back against the wall came forward. "Time's up," he said.

"One more minute," Louis said. "Please."

The guard took a long look at Reggie and backed off.

"I need you to think," Louis said. "We were able to trace two of the women Mark was with by the things he had in his bedroom. If there are more women, we need to find them, too."

"But I told you he never mentioned anyone by name."

"I know," Louis said. "But I need you to think really hard about anything Mark might have had that struck you as too expensive."

Reggie was still shaking his head, staring blankly at his hands. Louis glanced at Swann, then at the guard, as they waited for Reggie to reply. The guard tapped his watch.

"I'm sorry," Reggie said. "Except for that one time when I found the watch, I stayed clear of his room. He was very adamant after we . . . separated, that I respect his privacy."

The guard came forward again and touched Reggie's shoulder. Reggie looked up at him, fresh tears filling his eyes. His entire body seemed to wilt, and he could barely get to his feet.

Before Louis could ask anything else, the guard pulled Reggie away, and the two of them disappeared behind the steel door.

Louis and Swann left the jail, both silent until they were outside. Louis stopped walking and looked up at the jail. Then he let his eyes drift toward the boxy section of the complex where the sheriff's department was housed.

"Reggie will be dead in another week," Swann said.

"I know," Louis said. "You up to a visit to the Barbarian?"

Swann followed Louis's gaze toward the checkerboard of dusty windows. It had been only twenty-four hours since they had seen Barberry in Hendry County, and so far, it seemed he had kept his promise not to expose Swann's involvement to Swann's boss. But promises from Barberry were only as good as his mood, and Swann didn't need to aggravate that.

"I'll go up alone," Louis said.

"No," Swann said. "I'll go with you."

Barberry made them wait in the lobby for more than an hour. Louis paced for a while, then took a walk around the building, trying to get the image of Reggie's battered face from his mind. Every cop knew what happened when backs were turned and the lights went out in a large, understaffed county jail.

Not that Louis felt sorry for most of the bastards who inhabited the zoo. Most belonged there. But Reggie Kent didn't. And it seemed beyond depraved to keep him there.

"Louis, Barberry's ready for us."

Louis turned. Swann was standing outside the door, waving him inside. They found Barberry standing near his desk, working a wad of gum. He wore a polyester forest-green sports coat and a pea-colored tie.

"You got two minutes, Kincaid."

"You need to get moving on this case, Detective," Louis said. "Kent's getting kicked around pretty bad, and every day you waste gets him closer to getting killed."

"Well, jail ain't supposed to be The Breakers," Barberry said. "Maybe someone should tell him that."

"You have more than enough information to talk to

your prosecutor," Louis said. "You know Reggie Kent didn't murder Durand *or* either of the other two. What the hell is wrong with you?"

"Nothing's wrong with me," Barberry said. "I'm still looking into those other two guys, the bartender and the Mexican, like I told you I would. An investigation takes a lot of time. You know that."

"Have you even talked to your prosecutor about the possibility of a serial killer?" Swann asked.

Barberry turned to Swann. It was clear he still hadn't forgiven him for playing double agent between the sheriff's office and two rogue PIs.

"I ain't had time," Barberry said.

"Have you talked to anyone?" Swann asked. "Your chief of detectives? Your sheriff, for God's sakes? This is not just a routine homicide anymore."

Barberry glared at Swann, his jaw grinding hard on the gum. A small twitch fluttered the loose skin under his eye.

"You haven't told a soul, have you?" Swann said.

Barberry held Swann's eyes for another second or two, then turned slowly to his desk and picked up the phone. "Excuse me for a moment," he said.

Swann crossed his arms and looked away. Louis wondered who the hell Barberry was calling right in the middle of a conversation. Then, just as he heard a muffled male voice on the other end of the phone, it hit him.

"Yes, Chief Hewitt," Barberry said. "I appreciate you taking my call. I thought I should let you know that one of your officers has been wasting your department's time hanging around over here, trying to elbow his way into a homicide case we're trying to work."

Swann spun back to Barberry. A red flush crept up his neck as he listened.

"Swann," Barberry said. "Andrew Swann, that's right. Yeah. It's about that guy Reggie Kent. Yeah. Yeah, right. Well, I would appreciate it if you'd have a word with him."

Barberry held out the phone. Swann seemed frozen, the red in his neck now coloring his face.

"Your chief wants a word with you, Andrew," Barberry said.

Swann took the phone. Barberry didn't even give him the courtesy of some privacy. He stood close as Swann lowered his head and listened.

"Yes, sir, I understand. Yes, sir . . . yes, sir . . . yes, sir. Thank you, sir."

Swann hung up and, without a word, left the squad room. Louis looked at Barberry, who was unwrapping a stick of gum.

"You son of a bitch," Louis said.

Barberry laughed. "Yeah, well, like that little spic in Hendry County said, 'Don't come over here and fuck with me on my turf.' If and when any charges are dropped against Kent, you'll be the first to know. Now, go away and let me do my job."

Louis found Swann in the parking lot, leaning against the Mustang, head bent and arms crossed. He looked up when he heard Louis's footsteps. His cheeks were still bright with color.

"You okay?" Louis asked.

"I've been suspended," Swann said.

Swann made no move to get into the car. For a second, Louis couldn't read Swann's expression. Then he realized he had seen it once before, ironically on the face of a woman. He had been called out on a domestic abuse, and the woman had been sitting there, her face bloody, tears in her eyes, as she watched them haul her husband away. She said she had finally gotten up the nerve to leave him, and it was all there in her face—anger, humiliation, and relief.

"Come on, Andrew," Louis said. "Let's go home."

Chapter Twenty-six

Swann was silent on the drive back to Palm Beach. Louis didn't push it. He didn't know the guy well enough to give him advice about his job or his life, but he sensed that Swann had nowhere to go. So as they left the bridge and pulled onto Royal Poinciana Way, he asked Swann if he wanted to come back to Reggie's house for a beer.

Swann accepted quickly.

When they walked into the house, Louis stopped and stared. The main wall of the living room had been stripped of Reggie's beloved Haitian paintings. In their places were two large bulletin boards covered with papers and photographs. The small dining table had been pushed to the center of the room. There Mel sat, his head bent low, magnifying glass in hand.

"What's all this?" Louis asked.

Mel looked up. "Welcome to the pigpen."

Louis and Swann came forward. The bulletin board

resembled the displays Louis had seen in big-city homicide rooms for major cases, and when working with the FBI on a serial-killer case three years ago.

Separated into columns and color-coded, the board offered an easy-to-grasp visual blueprint of their complicated and increasingly confusing investigation.

On the right side were the victim's names across the top, with commonalities listed under each and linked in green marker. Under that were lists of physical evidence and subsequent leads formed. On the left side were the two women's names and those of their husbands, followed by what they knew about each person. A final column had the heading WHAT WE KNOW WE DON'T KNOW. It was blank.

On the second board, Mel had tacked up Swann's pilfered photographs of Durand's crime scene and close-up shots of the sword and the boots and all of the other items they had found in Durand's bedroom. Mel had even cut out pictures of Tucker and Carolyn Osborn and Tink and Dickie Lyons from the *Shiny Sheet* and hung them up.

"This is impressive," Swann said. "Why do you call it the pigpen?"

"That's what we called it back at Miami PD," Mel said. "Whenever we had a big case going, we'd put all the stuff in one room and we'd sit in there drinking bad coffee and eating cold burgers and throwing shit at the wall."

Louis knew it had probably taken Mel all day to put this together, given the trouble his eyes gave him with detail work. But Louis didn't want to deal with headless corpses right now. He was worried about Reggie. And Swann. That wasn't like him, to take the troubles of near strangers to heart. And no one here in Bizarro World was supposed to give a damn about anyone else.

Louis went to the kitchen to get a beer. But the only things in the refrigerator were a quart of milk, orange juice, and two bottles of Evian.

Louis grabbed the bottles of water and returned to the living room. Swann looked up.

"Sorry, Andrew, we're fresh out of beer," he said. He tossed a bottle and Swann caught it against his chest. Louis dropped down onto the sofa and kicked off his shoes.

Mel put down the magnifying glass and looked up from his spot at the table. "What's with the tone, Rocky?"

Louis opened the water and took a huge drink. "What tone?"

"We're fresh out of beer because Mel was too busy hanging out at Ta-boo again to go get some."

"Did I say that?" Louis said.

"You don't have to say it. I can still hear it."

"Give it a rest, Mel, will you?"

Louis looked over at Swann. He was standing at the bulletin board, staring at them both. He turned away, on the pretense of studying the photographs. Louis fell back against the cushions and closed his eyes. God, he wanted this case to be over. Nothing about it was making any sense, and every time he was able to empty his mind, Joe was there to fill it.

I want you to want something from yourself.

Right now, all he really wanted was to go home to his cottage and sleep in his own bed. He wanted to sit on his island, on his beach, and watch the sun melt into the Gulf.

"You ready to listen to what I found out today?" Mel asked.

"Go ahead," Louis said, without opening his eyes.

"First, I'm close to finding the private eye that Osborn said spied on his wife," Mel said. "Her rival, Morty Akers, died a couple years ago but I tracked down his former aide, who told me the PI's name was Barney Lassiter."

"Barney still among the living?" Louis asked.

"Yeah. He's got a current PI license out of Okaloosa County up in the Panhandle, but his listed employer, Sax and Sax Services, went out of business a few months ago. So, I haven't been able to zero in on Barney, yet but I got feelers out."

Louis swung up to a sitting position. "Osborn told me Lassiter did stakeouts and surveillance," he said. "What do you think the chances are he caught anything on film?"

"Not very likely," Swann offered. "If he had, he would have used it against the senator. I've never heard one piece of dirt on her. In fact, she's made her name drafting ethics reform and touting family values."

"That don't make her a saint, Andrew," Mel said.

"I never said she was," Swann said. "I'm just saying she seems like a pretty unlikely candidate for the kind of sleazy adultery we're talking about here."

"Let me tell you something, son," Mel said. "When it comes to sex, no one is an unlikely candidate. Anyone with working genitals can be enticed if the drought has been long enough."

Swann turned back to the bulletin board. Louis sensed that the conversation embarrassed him. Or maybe he had heard the slight condescension in Mel's voice. He forgot that Mel didn't know about Swann's suspension yet.

"Did you ever hear of those monkeys called bonobos?" Mel asked.

"Spare us," Louis said.

"They're a lot like chimpanzees," Mel went on unfazed, "but unlike chimps and gorillas, the bonobos are almost completely nonviolent and nonterritorial. And do you know why?"

"I said spare us."

"They're sex maniacs," Mel said. "They have sex at every opportunity, as a greeting, a goodbye, before they eat, after they eat. They can even be passing a strange monkey in the jungle and they'll stop and—"

"We get the picture," Louis said. "What's your point?"

"My point is, maybe if people were more like bonobos, they wouldn't find themselves curled in a fetal position on a therapist's couch. Or end up killing each other."

Mel's pontificating left the room in a tired kind of silence. Swann stayed at the board, studying the photographs with the expression of someone trying to figure out a piece of op art.

"I have something else to share," Mel said.

"Enough with the bonobos," Louis said.

Mel ignored him. "I found the manufacturer of those ostrich boots. It's a company called Safari Soles. I called their factory in Minnesota and although the lady was very nice, she told me we would need a warrant to get access to sales records."

"Shit," Louis murmured.

"You know any judges here we could convince, Andrew?" Mel asked.

Swann shook his head. "Not anymore."

Mel looked to Louis with questions, but Louis held up a hand, telling Mel not to push it. Mel shrugged and turned back to his notes.

"I've saved the best for last," Mel said. "I spoke with Dr. Steffel today. Since the sword didn't match the wounds, I wanted to ask her if she'd had any time to compare other blades and come up with something that was at least consistent."

"Did she?"

"She thinks it was a machete," Mel said.

Louis sat forward. "Like a cane machete?"

"She couldn't be that specific," Mel said. "But when she told me that, I had the same thought you're probably having. Who in Palm Beach would have a machete lying around the mansion?"

"Tucker Osborn has one," Swann said.

They both turned to stare at him.

"How do you know, Andrew?" Louis asked.

Swann let out a long breath. "About four years ago, I got called to a domestic there. The senator was crying, and Mr. Osborn was pretty drunk. He was waving a gun and yelling."

Swann got quiet.

"There's no such thing as privacy in a murder case, Andrew," Louis said.

Swann nodded. "I had to get Mr. Osborn quieted down, so I took him into his study. That's when I saw all the swords and stuff. He's got a closet full of them, including machetes."

"Who called you?" Mel asked.

"Bitner, her assistant," Swann said. "The senator would have never called."

"You got anything else about the Osborns you think we ought to know now?" Mel asked.

Louis heard the sarcasm in Mel's voice. He hoped Swann hadn't.

"Tink Lyons told me her husband goes hunting with some guys here," Louis said. "She didn't mention Osborn, but I got the feeling she knew the guy."

"You think Lyons and Osborn were in this together?" Swann asked.

Louis shrugged. "You know them. What do you think?"

"I don't think they know each other well," Swann said, shaking his head. "I just don't see it." He turned back to the bulletin board, studying the photographs. When he spoke again, his voice was soft.

"You really think these two men are capable of torture and decapitation?"

"With the right motivation," Louis said.

"Lots of women here cheat on their husbands. No one really cares," Swann said.

"A guy might care if the other man is a Mexican immigrant who can't even speak English," Mel said.

Now Swann was staring at the photograph of Emilio Labastide. "There's a five-year gap between Labastide's and Durand's murders," he said. "Are you saying this is some organized thing?"

"You ever heard of hunting clubs?" Mel asked.

Swann shook his head.

"There's this place up near Gainesville where rich

guys go to hunt safari-style," Mel said. "It's private land stocked with everything from African antelope to water buffalo and you pay based on how big a trophy you want. They even have corporate packages so businessmen can entertain their buddies. There's a big psychological element to hunting in a pack. Some guys really get off on it."

"You think we're dealing with some kind of murder club?" Swann asked.

"Like you said, Andrew, people here get bored easily."

Swann looked like his head hurt. "Are there other husbands in this club?" he asked.

Louis and Mel exchanged glances.

"We don't know," Louis said.

"Are there other women?"

"We don't know," Louis said.

They were all quiet again. Swann was staring at the photograph of the sword now. "If Tucker Osborn's sword wasn't the murder weapon, what was it doing in Durand's bedroom?" He looked back at Louis and Mel. "And why did he have Dickie Lyons's humidor?"

"We're thinking they were gifts, like the watch," Mel said.

"We don't know if Labastide or Wyeth got any gifts," Louis said.

"What about the gold crucifix?" Swann said.

"Sex and religion . . . not a good mix," Mel said.

They were all quiet, thinking. Louis laid his head back and closed his eyes. For a long time, the only sound came from the open sliding glass doors——the soft hiss of the waves breaking on the beach.

"Maybe they weren't gifts," Louis said quietly.

"What do you mean?" Swann asked.

Louis sat up, rubbing his face. "Except for the watch, the stuff Durand had didn't seem like anything he would really want. An antique sword that he couldn't sell. Ostrich boots two sizes too small. And expensive cigars that he wouldn't smoke."

Louis glanced at Mel. He could tell he had come to the same thought.

"He stole them," Mel said.

Louis nodded.

"But why?" Swann asked.

Louis locked eyes with Mel. He knew Mel couldn't read his expression but he suspected Mel could read his thoughts. "He knew that once he left that bedroom, he was nothing to them," Louis said. "It was his way of kicking them—and maybe their husbands—in the teeth."

Mel rose slowly and headed to the kitchen. Swann watched him, then turned back to Louis.

"So, the women paid these men for sex?" Swann asked.

Louis nodded. "Hernandez said they found eight grand in Wyeth's apartment. There's no proof it was drug money. Do you remember seeing anything in Durand's file about a bank account?"

"Yeah," Swann said. "But he had only about a hundred bucks in it. Maybe he stashed it somewhere around here."

Louis had been thinking the same thing. But Barberry's men had tossed the whole house and he himself had searched Durand's room pretty thoroughly and found no money.

"What about Labastide?" Swann asked. "Rosa sure doesn't have any money."

"Yeah, but she told you that Emilio had a girlfriend back in Mexico. Maybe he was sending cash home."

Mel came back, carrying a martini glass filled with orange juice. He set it in front of Louis.

"What's that?" Louis asked.

"Call it a peace offering. Enjoy it because there's no more vodka. But I promise I will go buy some tomorrow, dear."

Louis smiled and took a drink of the screwdriver. "I don't suppose there is any food in the house?"

"There's some French Muenster cheese in there," Mel said.

"I refuse to put something in my mouth that smells like a dirty jockstrap."

"I swear, Rocky, sometimes you're just—"

"Can I interrupt?" Swann asked.

Louis looked at Swann. He was holding the photograph of Rosa and her brother and looking like a man who needed to think about anything but facing his boss tomorrow morning.

"What is it?" Louis said.

"I've got one more question," Swann said. "Maybe we can link the men. But these two women have nothing in common. They aren't even friends. How the hell did they come to share the same lover?"

Louis glanced at Mel. Swann's question was one they had not yet asked themselves and at the moment, it seemed a glaringly stupid thing to miss.

He rose and went to the bulletin board. He looked at the photographs of Tink Lyons and Carolyn Osborn. One woman older and neurotic; the other attractive and successful. What were they missing?

He remembered something Margery had told him, about how easy it was for men to manage their affairs but how hard it was for the women to do the same.

Louis reached into his pocket and pulled out the orchid sprig. It was wilted, now the color of dried blood.

"What's that?" Swann asked.

"Our link," Louis said.

Chapter Twenty-seven

The first thing Margery did was to fling open the doors of a huge black lacquer armoire that held her vast store of prized liquor. They all helped themselves to their choice of "joy juice," as Margery called it.

Swann grabbed a bottle of Pasión Azteca tequila. Mel took his time and chose a Lustau amontillado. When Louis couldn't find any Courvoisier, he settled on a fat crystal bottle of Louis XIII de Rémy Martin. Margery stayed with the Hendrick's gin she had been cuddling up with most of the afternoon.

The second item on the agenda was food. Louis suggested they call out for pizzas, but Margery snorted and sent Franklin off in the Rolls. He returned with everything from the dinner menu of Ta-boo.

Now they were spread out in the loggia amid a wasteland of half-eaten steak tartar, cold poached salmon, Maine lobster, and portobello mushroom salad.

Everyone was drunk and, as Margery called it, "grummy." A pink-streaked sky was visible through the archways, but no one was looking. The phone was ringing, but no one was listening. The pug dogs were gnawing on leftover sirloin tips, but no one cared.

On the drive over, Louis had shared his theory with Mel and Swann about the devil orchid, which he believed was a symbol of something between the women. Swann had offered another tantalizing detail. He remembered that the red flowering plant outside Rosa's apartment was an orchid.

Louis was hoping that Margery could tell them how Bianca Lee—the only person on Palm Beach who sold the devil orchid—figured into the equation. Was she supplying more than just orchids?

But Margery had been less than helpful. To her, Bianca Lee simply owned a lovely shop on "Worthless Avenue" and did the flower arrangements for the best parties and all of the charity balls.

"Margery, are you sure you're not forgetting anything?" Louis asked.

"I told you, Louis," she said. "She's like, well, like a chiropractor or a policeman. You don't even notice them until you really need them."

Louis glanced at Mel. They both looked at Swann. He hadn't said a word in the last twenty minutes and was slumped on the sofa, slit-eyed, one of the pugs curled by his side. Louis wondered if he had even heard Margery's comment. Did he even understand that just like Franklin—that "utter ghost of a man"—Swann was invisible to people like Margery?

"Let's get back to Carolyn," Louis said.

Margery let out a dramatic sigh.

"You're sure Carolyn and Tink aren't friends?"

"Yes, I am sure," Margery said testily. "As I told you already, Carolyn doesn't mingle much. Her whole world is her political career."

"What about Tucker?" Louis asked.

"The Osborns are old money." Margery sniffed. "Tucker has never worked a day in his life. He's a charter member of the lucky sperm club."

Swann suddenly rose. "I need some air," he said.

Louis watched him stagger out through the archway. He turned back to Margery. "Osborn told me he and his wife were separated," he said. "Do you know why?"

Margery shook her head as she sipped her gin. "Years ago, there were rumors they were getting a divorce, but once she became a senator, well, that was out of the question. They have one of those make-believe marriages. He makes believe he's a good husband, and Carolyn makes like she believes it."

"Tell us about Tink Lyons," Mel said.

"Poor, sad Tink, banging around in that big, ghastly house," Margery said.

Louis waited for her to go on, but she fell silent again. He knew she was worried to death about Reggie. Her lawyer, Harvey, hadn't been able even to get Reggie moved to solitary to protect him. Their only hope was Barberry.

"What is their marriage like?" Mel asked.

Margery shrugged. "What can I say? The man is a pig. He made wads of money building ugly houses, and now he puts on these rock-and-roll concerts and monster-truck rallies over in West Palm Beach. The first time I saw him—good Lord, it must have been fifteen years ago—Tink brought him to a party right after they got married. He was strictly the full Cleveland."

"What?" Louis asked.

"He was wearing a brown polyester suit and this awful tie and brown shoes."

"We call it the full Barberry," Mel said.

"Why'd she marry him?" Louis pressed.

"Well, you have to understand something about Tink. Her family is old Philly Main Line but brittle stock. So when they all died off, she was alone." Margery heaved a big sigh. "She was forty-plus when they got married. I suspect Dickie was the first man ever to look at her twice."

Margery stared into her tumbler. "Poor Tink. I think she's a bit wobbly in the noggin."

Louis was quiet. If Tink Lyons was the doormat Margery was suggesting, it was hard to imagine her having secret trysts. But like Mel said, if the drought was long enough and the need for affection great enough, a person could do anything.

"Did Dickie Lyons hang out with Tucker?" Mel asked.

Margery shook her head. "There's a pecking order on the island, Marvin," she said. "At the top are the core people, the old guard. Then you have the A-listers like Tucker's family, who've lived here forever, get into the right clubs, and show up on the Fanjuls' Christmas-card list. Below that, there's a whole smattering of celebrities, dubious royalty, and Trump, of course. Then there's your basic parvenus and arrivistes—tolerated but still NOCDs."

"Come again?" Mel asked.

"Not Our Class, Dear. Tucker Osborn would never associate with someone like Lyons."

Louis's head was fogged with alcohol. He needed some fresh air. And he was worried about Swann. He rose and went out onto the patio. Swann was nowhere to be seen. The sun was almost gone, leaving a reflecting wash of pale pink over the ocean. Louis rubbed his face, and when he looked back toward the water, he spotted Swann down on the beach.

Louis went down the stone steps and across the lawn. At the road, he had to wait for a gap in the slow but steady stream of cars clogging South Ocean Boulevard. Bentleys, Rollses, Jags, and sleek Italian exotics. He was wondering who had died when he remembered that Margery had said there was a big event at Mar-a-Lago just down the road. Whenever Trump wasn't in town, he rented the place out to whoever could fork over big bucks, NOCD or not.

Louis crossed the road and went down onto the sand. Swann saw him coming.

"Hey, Louis."

"You okay?"

"I feel like I need to puke."

"Go ahead."

"Not allowed. If you even fart too loud in this town, you get a ticket."

"Andrew, you're the one who gives out the tickets."

"Not right now."

Swann walked to the water's edge, squatted, and splashed water on his face. When he stood up, his pink polo shirt was soaked, and his hair was spiked up.

"You're not much of a drinker, are you?" Louis asked.

Swann looked at him. "I've had my moments," he

said. "When I was twenty-four, I drove my car off a fishing wharf and almost killed myself."

"Were you drunk?"

Swann nodded. "Blood alcohol of one-point-nine."

"Jesus."

"It gets worse," Swann said. "The car was a Florida state cruiser, I was on the job, and it was intentional."

Louis took a step back, looking at Swann with new respect. Not that driving a ten-thousand-dollar cruiser into the ocean merited a reward, but it was so ballsy that it deserved *some* level of guy admiration.

"They fire you?" Louis asked.

Swann nodded. "My father, the esteemed Major Marshall Weston Swann, did it himself, in front of six other commanders. Guess he just decided that enough was enough."

"What do you mean?"

"The car was the last of a whole bunch of fuckups. I didn't show up in court half the time, slept with a woman I arrested, failed a drug test—"

"What for?"

"Cocaine," Swann said.

"Christ, Andrew."

Swann didn't answer. He lowered himself to the sand; Louis sat down beside him. It was quiet for a long time, just the sound of the waves rolling in at their feet.

"I always thought I wanted to be a cop," Swann said softly. "My mom died when I was three, and my dad raised me and my sisters. I was . . . in charge of the household, and every night when he came home, we had this ritual where I had to pass inspection."

"Lot of responsibility," Louis said.

Swann shrugged. "You know what I remember most?

Standing at his bedroom door, watching him take his uniform off. He'd unpin each medal and lay them in a row on the dresser. His badge was always last. He put it on a folded handkerchief next to my mother's picture."

Swann wiped his eyes.

"From the time I was nine, I attended every ceremony," he said. "Every police picnic, every funeral. I couldn't wait until it was me standing in front of that mirror. But when I got to the academy, I hated it."

"Everyone hates it," Louis said.

But Swann wasn't listening. "Freakin' hours of memorizing meaningless statutes," he said. "That stupid us-against-them mentality and that zombielike loyalty to complete fuckin' strangers just because they wore the same fuckin' uniform."

"Andrew, take a breath."

Swann lowered his head into his hands.

"Why didn't you just quit?" Louis asked.

"It took me a while to figure that one out," Swann said. "It was easier for me to get my ass fired than it was to tell my father that I hated doing the one thing he loved."

Swann blinked. "I left Tallahassee three hours after he fired me. For the next two years, I just bounced around the beaches trying to figure out what I wanted to do."

"How'd you end up here?"

Swann took a moment to answer. "Being a cop was the only thing I knew how to do," he said. "And I realized that I still wanted that badge back on my chest."

"You're not making any sense, Andrew."

"It . . . shit, this sounds corny as hell, but it gave me a sense of purpose and self-respect that nothing else ever could."

"Even here in Palm Beach?"

Swann sighed deeply. "Even here."

"How the hell did you get hired with your record?"

"My father sanitized my file," Swann said. "So, all Palm Beach saw was an average police officer who'd resigned for personal reasons."

Swann closed his eyes and leaned forward, elbows on knees. Louis had the thought that if the guy understood what a gift his father had given him, he didn't seem ready to acknowledge it. But then he remembered that Swann had asked his father to expedite that computer search that turned up Paul Wyeth. Had they repaired the relationship?

"Andrew," Louis said, "let me ask you something."

"What?"

"Would you consider calling your father and asking him to intervene with the prosecutor on Kent's behalf?"

Swann shook his head slowly, not looking up. "I haven't talked to my father in eight years."

"You said he helped you locate Wyeth."

"No, I said I threw his name around to get someone to help *me* find Wyeth. Dad was never involved. And I don't want him to be."

"Not even to get a shot at getting Kent out of jail?"

Swann just shook his head slowly.

Louis decided to let it go. Maybe he could bring it up again when Swann wasn't feeling so raw.

"You know, you shouldn't let what Margery said bother you," Louis said.

"Remember when you told me I wasn't part of their world?" Swann let out a tired breath. "I thought you were just being an asshole. But you were right. These people don't even see us."

Swann lay back on the sand and closed his eyes. Now it was Louis's turn to be quiet. Sam was suddenly there in his head. Margery had dismissed her as someone who dwelled on the same lower rung as Dickie Lyons. She was an outsider here, just as he himself was. But her snub of him still stung.

"Andrew, you awake?" Louis said.

"No."

"You know the name Samantha Norris?"

"Sexy Sam. Everyone knows Sexy Sam."

Louis was glad it was dark.

"What do you know about her?" Louis asked.

"Why do you want to know about her?"

"She was someone I met . . . the night Margery dragged us to the ballet. I thought she was interesting. Just wanted to know more about her."

Swann propped himself up on his elbows. "She's a climber," he said.

"Climber?"

"Yeah, she started out working as a home-care nurse for Hap Norris after he had his first heart attack," he said. "Then one night the starter wife, Bunny, caught them doing some physical therapy in the Jacuzzi, and all hell broke loose."

Louis was quiet, remembering what Margery had said about a sordid divorce.

"Happens all the time here," Swann said. "One minute they're pushing a wheelchair, and the next they're wearing diamonds."

Louis looked out over the dark ocean. Other questions were burning in his brain, but he was afraid Swann would hear something in his voice that went beyond idle curiosity.

"Yeah, but in the end, it was Sam who got the short end of the stick," he said.

"What do you mean?" Louis prodded.

"A couple years after they got married, Hap had a stroke. A really bad one."

A stroke?

"I haven't seen him in public since," Swann said, "but I heard he's pretty much . . . what do you call it when they can't move their arms or legs but their brain's still working?"

"I don't know," Louis said softly.

"Anyway, from what I hear, he's got his own medical clinic up there on the second floor of that old house," Swann said. "The best doctors, a steady supply of drugs, twenty-four-hour nurses to wipe his drool and change his diapers."

Louis was quiet.

"And a pretty wife just sitting around and waiting for him to die," Swann said. "Kind of sad, isn't it?"

The tide was coming in, and Louis watched the ebb and flow of the water.

"Sad isn't the word for it," Louis said.

Chapter Twenty-eight

It was almost time.

Would she be ready? Her heart was beating fast,

too fast. Could she stand it much longer? Of course she could. The moments just before were part of the experience. The tickle of palpitations in her breast, the shivers between her legs, the burn of her own skin when she touched herself. A lonely yet amazing kind of foreplay.

She moved across the room with a deliberate flourish, her steps soundless in the satin slippers, the brush of her white chiffon skirt like feathers against her thighs.

It was silly, she knew. The ruffles, the satin sashes, and the hours spent coiling her hair into sausage curls.

Oh, how long she had waited for this night. And this boy.

Bianca had promised he would be different from the last one. Bianca had promised he had learned the social graces, the art of a caress, and most important of all—and maybe as silly as the miniature bows but still important to her because it had never been important to Dickie—his breath would be sweet and clean.

Dickie . . . she wouldn't have to worry about him tonight. She had been so happy when he told her he had been invited to some big real-estate party at Mar-a-Lago. He didn't even care when she had begged off with a headache. She had sat at the window and watched him pull away in his ugly big Rolls, watched the parade of cars along the beach road going into Mar-a-Lago. And then, finally, she had gone to get her special room ready.

Tink turned on the small bedside lamp and admired her boudoir. The Hills of Provence vanity with its padded silk bench. The white antique iron canopy bed, draped in pink netting and covered by a satin comforter. And to complete the fantasy—and, of course, she understood that it was one—were her two beloved stuffed bears, Boo and Berri.

This was not the bedroom she shared with Dickie. That place—that awful place—had a dark four-poster bed, wider than even the biggest king and set on columns the size of redwoods. In the corner was a heavy dark armoire built to house three televisions and other pieces of electronic equipment. And as if the room needed topping off, Dickie had hung that trashy LeRoy Neiman painting of a bullfighter.

Tink closed her eyes.

Big ugly things for a big ugly man.

"Miss Tinkie?"

His voice came as tender as the hum of a fading violin. Was he early? Or was she late? No matter. He was here.

She started toward the bedroom door, then paused, hand poised over a wooden music box on the chest of drawers. It was a Nicole Frères, hand-made in 1814, an exquisite piece of lustrous black ebony with intricate ivory scrollwork.

Tink ran her finger across the lid. It had been sent to her from London on her tenth birthday, a gift from her beloved grandfather. It had been the last gift Poppy had sent her, and it was the only thing she had taken with her when she left her childhood home in Philadelphia.

Her hand went out to lift the lid, but she froze. She *so* wanted to play the music now as he entered, but she didn't dare. He might think her rude for not waiting, and there was no excuse for being rude, not even in sin.

"Miss Tinkie?"

He was standing at the door.

Slender and tall, with the soft white shirt lying against the hard muscles of his chest. His face was smooth and boyish in the glow of the lamp, his eyes as dark as her music box. He bowed his head and looked up at her from under a hank of silken black hair.

Tink smiled. He was shy. Could he be more perfect?

She lifted the lid on the music box and held out a hand to him. The melody of *"Un bel di"* filled the silence. His eyes slipped to the music box before they settled back on her. He seemed bewildered.

"It's from *Madama Butterfly,*" Tink whispered. "You recognize it, don't you?"

He set the orchid on the dresser, next to the music box, and turned again to look around the room. It was as if he just couldn't resist looking. Of course he couldn't, she knew. None of them could. Wasn't it every man's dream to have a virgin?

She moved to him and touched his face to bring his gaze back to her. Her other hand rested on his chest, her fingers inside his collar.

"Are you nervous, Byrne?" she whispered.

He lowered his head. She thought he would lean in and kiss her, but instead, he took her hand and held it firmly against his body. She pressed her lips to his cheek, wanting to feel the heat of his skin and breathe in his smell—his wonderful soapy smell—but he was steeled against her touch.

Something was wrong.

She drew back. He was looking at the bed again, a small twitch rippling his cheek, his eyes filmed with a dullness she had seen before.

He was repulsed.

She was the freak.

And if she didn't do something, he would leave.

"Please," she whispered. "Just close your eyes and pretend. We're sixteen. It's midnight, and we've just left the cotillion, and for the first time in days, we are alone."

He managed a small nod and closed his eyes, willing, she supposed, to put his mouth on her as long as he didn't have to see her. His lips were dry, his kisses without passion. He wouldn't carry her to the bed, as she asked, but walked her with no ear for the beautiful melody.

But she had asked him to be sixteen. Could she fault him for being so good at that?

He gently touched her breasts through the ruffled bodice of the dress.

"No," she whispered. "Like a boy, like a boy."

He hesitated. "I don't understand what you want," he said.

She wanted to cry in frustration. "I want you to be sixteen. Can you do that, please?"

"I don't know—"

"Like the first time you did it," she whispered. "Can you remember what that was like? That is what I want. Like we are sixteen, please!"

When he started again, it was different. This time, it was right. He pawed at her; he panted. He rubbed her, groped her, and finally, he hurt her.

And then, as she asked, he left her on her back, her lips raw from his hard kisses and her gown crumpled around her hips.

She lay there, listening to the rustle of his clothes as he dressed. When he was finished, she heard his footfalls as he crossed the room, then the soft click of the door as it closed behind him.

As the quiet returned, she realized that the melody in the music box was dying. Just *ping*s that became slower and slower as the cylinder made its last turns.

She was drifting, almost asleep, when a voice boomed from the hall, rocketing her to a sitting position.

"Who the hell are you?"

Dickie. My God, Dickie's home!

Tink jumped off the bed, ran to the door, and flung it open. Dickie stood on the landing, a giant blur of black-and-white tuxedo. He had Byrne crushed against the wall with a hand to his throat.

"Stop it!" Tink cried.

Dickie raised an arm to backhand her, but she ducked and retreated into her room. Tink watched in horror as he smacked Byrne with an open palm. Byrne tried to fight, but all he could hit were the thick slabs of Dickie's arms.

"Who the fuck are you?" Dickie shouted, bouncing Byrne against the wall. "What the fuck were you doing here?"

"I was invited!" Byrne yelled.

"Invited!" Dickie spat. His eyes swung to Tink and then down to her disheveled white dress. "What the hell are you wearing?"

"It's my gown!" Tink cried. "It's my special gown!"

Dickie pushed her back inside her bedroom and yanked the door closed.

She stood, eyes squeezed shut, hands over her ears. But she could still hear them. No matter how hard she pressed her hands against her head, she could still hear them.

"Get up!" Dickie yelled. "Get up on your feet!"

Byrne was crying now, mumbling things she couldn't understand. She couldn't bear it; she had to see what was happening. She opened the door and peeked out.

Byrne was on his hands and knees, gasping, the cream-colored carpet under his head speckled with blood. He was groping blindly for something to pull himself up with, but when he touched Dickie's pant leg, Dickie kicked his arm away.

"I oughtta make you crawl down those goddamn steps," Dickie said, "but I'm going to save you some time."

Dickie jerked Byrne to his knees and kicked him in the belly. Byrne screamed and started to crawl. Dickie kicked him again, catapulting him off the top step.

Tink put her fist at her mouth to keep from screaming, listening to the horrible thumping of Byrne's body hitting the wall as it tumbled down two flights.

Help him. You can help him, you stupid girl. There's a phone right here. Use it! Help him!

Hands shaking, she picked up the phone. But she couldn't remember which speed-dial button it was. She had been told a hundred times, but now she couldn't remember. Three. Yes, it was number three.

She punched the number and fell back against the wall. As the voice answered, her legs gave out, and she crumpled to the floor. She began to sob.

The woman on the other end of the line was telling her to calm down, to take a breath, that everything would be all right.

"No, it won't," Tink said. "He's going to kill him."

Chapter Twenty-nine

Y ou all right, Andrew?"

Swann took a moment to look up. The sunglasses hid his eyes, but Louis knew they were bloodshot. When he had roused Swann from the sofa back at Reggie's this morning, Swann's eyes had looked like a road map.

"I'm fine."

"You're a little green under that tan."

"I'm said I'm fine."

Louis leaned on the doorbell again. They had been standing outside the Osborn house for almost ten minutes, and so far no one had answered. In the driveway was a white Bentley, a silver Mercedes, and the same blue Camry Louis had seen on his first visit. The Mercedes, Louis noticed, had a government plate, so he assumed it belonged to Carolyn. Louis hit the doorbell again.

Swann let out a belch and a groan.

"Tequila will kill you, you know," Louis said.

"I'm okay, damn it. Let's just get this over with and get out of here, okay?"

The door clicked, and a face poked out. It took Louis a second to retrieve the guy's name from his fuzzed brain.

"Good morning, Greg," Louis said.

Bitner's eyes narrowed. "What do you want?"

"Greg, Greg, where's your holiday spirit?" Louis said.

"The senator isn't here," Bitner said.

"I'm not here to see your boss," Louis said. "We want to talk to her husband."

Bitner glanced at Swann. "Is this official police business?"

Swann nodded. "We just need to talk to Mr. Osborn."

Bitner hesitated, then opened the door. They stepped into the cool white entranceway. The red orchid was still there on the table.

"Wait here," Bitner said. "I'll go—"

Louis's eyes swung upward. Tucker Osborn was coming down the stairs. He was dressed in white shorts, shirt, and tennis shoes, his hair wet, his face flushed. He slowed as he saw them.

"What's going on here?" he asked.

Swann took the initiative. "I'm Lieutenant Swann, Palm Beach PD. We just need a few moments of your time, sir."

Osborn was looking at Swann, and Louis wondered if he recognized him from the domestic incident years before. Louis could almost see Osborn weighing his options. Finally, Osborn turned to Bitner.

"Go find something to do," he said.

Bitner reddened, his eyes flicking to Louis. Then, without a word, he turned and left.

"Now, what is it?" Osborn demanded.

"How about we go talk in your study?" Louis said.

Osborn stared at him for a moment, shrugged, and walked away. Louis and Swann followed.

The study was just as it was the first time Louis saw it, the heavy shutters closed, the lights off. Osborn flicked a lamp on as he entered. He went to the leather chair behind his desk and sat down. Swann assumed a position near the door, sunglasses in his hand, eyes in a squint, fighting the throb in his head. Louis took one of the chairs opposite the desk without being invited.

"Make it quick," Osborn said. "I have a tennis date in ten minutes."

It was an excuse; the guy looked like he had just gotten off the courts. But Louis wasn't about to let this asshole dismiss them like he had poor Greg.

Louis pulled the photograph of the sword from his pocket and laid it on the desk. "Do you recognize this?"

Osborn grabbed the photograph. Louis watched the guy's face, but there was nothing except impatience.

"This is a German officer's sword," Osborn said. "I have one—"

He froze.

"You have one just like it, right?" Louis said.

Osborn looked at Swann. "Yes, I have one."

"Can we see it?" Louis asked.

Something crossed Osborn's eyes, a cloud of confusion, maybe, but the irritation was close behind. He pushed himself from the chair and went to a dark corner of the large study. He hit a switch, illuminating the inside of the glass-faced cabinets Louis had noticed on his first visit. One cabinet held antique handguns, and Louis guessed that several were German Lugers. But the other cabinet held a display of bladed weapons.

Osborn opened the second cabinet and peered at the weapons for a moment before he turned back to Louis.

"It's not here," he said.

Louis rose and went to the cabinet. There were six swords mounted on brackets. There was one set of empty brackets. There were also four daggers, a bayonet—and two machetes.

When Louis looked back at Osborn, he couldn't tell if the guy was a great actor or genuinely surprised that the sword was gone. But Louis could almost see the gears in his head turning.

"I like your machetes," Louis said. "Can I take a look at them?"

"They're quite valuable," Osborn said.

"I'll be careful."

Osborn took the smaller of the two machetes off its brackets and handed it to Louis. It was a good eighteen inches long, and its wood handle was topped with a carving of a dog's head.

"Very nice. Where is it from?" Louis asked.

"The Philippines," Osborn said. "It's late-eighteenth-century."

"It's a military weapon?"

"The natives used it against their colonial invaders," Osborn said. "Now, if you don't mind—"

Louis swung the machete in a slow arc, making Osborn back away. "What's with the dog's head?"

"The head prevented it from slipping from the user's grasp," Osborn said tightly. "The end of the blade is rounded so that after it was embedded, it wouldn't get trapped in the opponent's body."

Louis glanced back at Swann. He was still standing by the door, looking even greener than before.

"May I have that back?" Osborn asked, holding out his hand.

Louis ignored him and set the machete back on its brackets. He lifted the second one out. It was very heavy, the blade more than two feet long and four inches wide.

Louis let out a low whistle. "What was this one used for?"

"It's Mexican," Osborn said. "It might have been used for clearing brush." He paused. "Or slaughtering cattle."

The machete felt awkward and too heavy and unbalanced to swing with one hand. Louis switched to a two-handed grip, holding the machete chest high, aiming it at the floor. He could almost feel the power such a blade would deliver.

He glanced at Osborn. The guy was sweating. Louis smiled and carefully set the Mexican machete back in its place.

Osborn closed the cabinet. "If you don't have any other questions, I have—"

"Just a few more, Mr. Osborn, and then we'll let you get to your tennis game."

Osborn just stood there, his eyes locked on Louis.

"Any idea where your sword went?" Louis asked.

"I don't have to answer any questions from you," Osborn said.

"Maybe not, but you'll have to tell the police here if you want to make an insurance claim."

Osborn looked at Swann and back at Louis. "Look, anybody could have come in here and taken the damn thing. The cleaning lady, the cable guy. You know how those people are. We've had things go missing from this house before."

"Maybe you should put some locks on your doors," Louis said.

"Maybe I will," Osborn said.

The phone rang. Osborn made no move to pick it up, and after three rings, it stopped. The button stayed lit and began to blink. Osborn glanced at it, then back at Louis.

"Do you know Dickie Lyons?" Louis asked.

"Lyons? Yes, I know him. Why are you asking me about him?"

"Is he a good friend of yours?"

Osborn gave a snort of disgust. "You're kidding, right?"

"Never more serious. Is he a good friend of yours?"

Osborn's eyes went to Swann, still standing behind Louis. When he looked back at Louis, he was smiling.

"Dickie Lyons is a turd."

"In what way?"

Osborn was looking at Swann again. "Maybe you can explain it, Lieutenant. Tell this young man how things are here."

Swann was silent.

"So, you don't have any associations with Lyons?" Louis asked. "No business deals, no little hunting trips with the boys."

"Hunting?" Osborn shook his head. "Look, I don't know what this is about, but I've never had anything to do with Dickie Lyons. He's a two-bit circus huckster who thinks he can buy his way onto the A-list."

The phone rang again. This time, Osborn pounced on it. He grunted a few impatient words into the receiver and hung up.

"Are we done?" he said.

Louis knew there was only one strategy left. It was the pigpen philosophy: Throw shit at the wall, and see if anything sticks.

"Do you know a man named Paul Wyeth?"

Osborn shook his head.

"You have any whips?"

"Whips? No."

"Have you ever been in Immokalee?"

"Good Lord, no. Why would I?"

"How about Clewiston? Ever tooled through there late one night?"

Osborn was quiet.

"You ever heard of Devil's Garden?"

"I think you should leave."

In the half-light cast by the lamp, Osborn's eyes were shadowed, leaving only his mouth visible. Nothing. There was nothing to see.

Osborn went to the door. He jerked it open and held out his hand. "Gentlemen."

Louis caught Swann's eye, and they left the study. The door closed behind them.

"I'm sorry," Swann said.

"About what?"

"I was no help."

Louis's head was pounding from his hangover. "Don't worry about it, Andrew."

They found their way back to the entrance hall and outside. Louis noticed that the silver Mercedes was gone. He wondered if the white Bentley could be the one that had been seen in Clewiston. Hell, he wondered about a lot of things right now.

As they were getting into the Mustang, the front door of the mansion opened. Osborn came out, dressed in the same clothes. Louis was tempted to ask him where his racket was, but Osborn put on his sunglasses, got into the Bentley, and drove off.

"Should we follow him?" Swann asked.

"Only if he had a machete in his hand."

Louis got in and started the engine. He unhooked the levers so he could put the top down, thinking they could both use the fresh air. As the top whirred down, Louis glanced into the rearview mirror. Greg was coming out of the house, clutching his leather datebook and keys. He went to the blue Camry, opened the door, and paused.

He came up to Louis's side of the car. He just stood there, face drawn, as he kept looking back at the house and then down the street.

"You got something to tell me, Greg?" Louis asked.

"I don't know," Greg said.

"Yes, you do."

Greg looked over at Swann, and when his eyes came back to Louis, they were anguished.

"They had a fight last night," he said.

"About what?"

"They've fought before, but it was bad last night."

Louis stayed silent. Greg wanted to talk, it was clear.

Greg's eyes went up to the house again. "He lied to you. He was here five years ago. You know, when all the stuff was going on with that private eye. Tucker was here. And he—"

Greg wiped a hand over his brow. "I don't want to see the senator hurt. I just . . ."

"Tell us what you know, Greg."

"He's not a good man," Greg said. "I've seen it. Five years ago, one night, I saw him push her down the stairs. She broke her arm." He shook his head slowly. "Last night, he was yelling at her, saying she wouldn't be where she was if it wasn't for him. And that she's never going to get any farther without him."

"What do you think he meant?"

"Tucker's always throwing it back in her face that she was nothing before he married her, that she never could have gotten elected to anything without his money, that he got her to the right people. He's always telling her that—that he made her what she is."

"Is that true, Greg?"

Greg shook his head. "He made her unhappy, that's what he made her."

Louis glanced at Swann, who looked stricken.

"Greg, I have to ask you something," Louis said. "Did she have a lover?"

Greg had been looking back up at the house, and his eyes swung to Louis. Louis saw a mix of emotions in the young man's face—loyalty, fear, conflict—and he knew that even if Greg Bitner knew the truth, he wouldn't tell.

"Did you ever hear her say the name Emilio?" Louis asked. "Or Paul? Or Mark?"

"I have to go," Greg said.

He went back to the Camry and got in, starting the engine. He pulled out and, without a look back at Louis, drove quickly away.

When they got back to Reggie's house, Swann disappeared into a bedroom. Louis found Mel sitting at the table by the pool with a tray of coffee, toast, and Bonne Maman strawberry preserves. He was reading the *Shiny Sheet* with his magnifying glass and looked up as Louis sat down across from him.

Louis picked up the last piece of toast, but the jam jar was empty. "You could have left me some jelly, you know."

"Try the cheese," Mel said, pointing to the box of Muenster cheese.

"I told you I won't eat that shit."

"Just open the box, Rocky."

With a tired sigh, Louis pulled the round box over and flipped off the lid. Inside was a big wad of bills bound by a rubber band.

"I found it this morning when I was looking for something to eat," Mel said. "There's twelve grand there. All in hundreds."

"Kent said he didn't have any money, so it must belong to Durand," Louis said.

"And it must have come from the women," Mel said. "So, where'd you and Andrew run off to this morning?"

Louis put the money back in the cheese box. "We went and saw Osborn," he said.

"What did he say about the sword?"

"He didn't know it was gone. But the guy has two machetes."

Mel raised a brow. "Could they be a match?"

"They were sharp and clean. One looked big enough to kill a cow."

Louis filled him in on the other questions he had asked Osborn, ending with the fact that Osborn claimed he had no dealings with Dickie Lyons.

"You believe him?" Mel asked.

"To hear Osborn say it, Lyons is scum. Why would he bother with a guy like Lyons?"

Mel sat up, swinging his legs to the ground. "Maybe he looked at him as someone who could provide a service." Mel picked up a notebook and flipped back a page. "I found Barney Lassiter today."

"The PI?"

Mel nodded. "He's still up in the Panhandle, but we had a long talk about the surveillance he did on Carolyn Osborn. The guy has logs of everyone who came and went at the Osborn home. Guess who shows up in his records?"

"Lyons?"

"Bingo. He says Dickie's company was hired by the Osborns to book the entertainment for Carolyn's election-night party five years ago. He's got a photograph of Lyons talking to Tucker Osborn out by the pool. The photograph was taken a week before Emilio Labastide disappeared."

"That doesn't mean anything. Like you said, Osborn probably looks at Lyons as hired help."

"Yeah, but maybe he was hired for something else."

Louis was quiet.

"I was thinking about what Andrew said about Carolyn Osborn and Tink Lyons having the same lover," Mel said, flipping to a new page in his notebook. "I did some calling around this morning to find out more about them. Like Margery said, Tink's parents died when she was in her twenties, leaving her with a small trust and an old house down here in Palm Beach. Tink rattled around in her crumbling house like one of those old Bouvier bags, until the bank managing her trust finally had to step in. She did a short stint in a psych hospital."

Louis shook his head. "How'd she hook up with Dickie?"

"Before he got into the entertainment business, he made his first millions in construction, building places like our tsarist dacha here." Mel gestured toward the half-built mansion beyond Reggie's bougainvillea bushes.

"Tink's trust hired him to fix up her house. I guess he figured that while he was at it, he could fix up his reputation by marrying an heiress."

"What about Carolyn Osborn?"

"Lassiter filled in a lot of those blanks," Mel said. "Carolyn's family owned orange groves and made money selling off their land to Disney back in the sixties. Carolyn got her law degree at Georgetown and did some legal work for the government. She got elected a Florida state representative in her thirties and was on the fast track, especially after she married Osborn. She won her election to the U.S. Senate pretty easily."

Louis was quiet.

"She's got a lot to lose," Mel said.

Louis rose suddenly. "Why the hell would she risk it all by screwing around?"

Mel started to say something but stopped, his eyes going to the sliding glass door.

Swann was standing there. His khakis were wrinkled, his pink polo shirt stained, his jaw stubbled with whiskers. But it was his expression that worried Louis.

"You sick, Andrew?"

Swann shook his head slowly. "No. I just called my answering machine. My chief is looking for me. He wants to see me this afternoon."

"Did he say why?" Louis asked.

Swann shook his head again. "I guess I better go home and get cleaned up."

His eyes, red-rimmed and empty, drifted toward the ocean. Louis knew he was thinking that when he came back, he might not have a badge.

He watched Swann walk away.

And what did a cop do when he couldn't make it even in a place like this?

Chapter Thirty

Swann waited in the hall outside Chief Hewitt's office. He wore clean khakis, a white dress shirt, and blue blazer. But this afternoon, for the first time since his job interview six years ago, he had a bright pink visitor's badge clipped to his lapel.

The chief's door opened, and Hewitt poked his head out. He was a small man, with trimmed salt-and-pepper hair and a narrow mustache so perfect in its shape and color that some of the officers joked that it was fake.

"Andrew, good of you to be on time," Hewitt said. "Come on in."

It was the largest office in the building, designed to make a tasteful but unquestioned statement about the importance of the man who occupied it. On one side of the room was a long glass conference table set with twelve high-back chairs of blue leather. The right side belonged to Chief Hewitt. The glass and chrome was standard in this place, but Hewitt had things that were uniquely his and, Swann realized, unique to this place, such as a framed photo of Hewitt and Prince Charles and a coat-rack with an array of "emergency" clothing: fresh shirt and jacket, a ceremonial dress uniform, and a tuxedo.

The walls held an arrangement of awards and certificates and the chief's cherished display of celebrity letters from Douglas Fairbanks Jr., astronaut Edgar Mitchell, and Jimmy Buffett, plus one of his most prized pieces, a note from Donald Trump, thanking the chief for providing security during the renovation of Mar-a-Lago.

"This situation saddens me greatly, Andrew," Hewitt said.

Swann looked back at Hewitt. His chief was standing near his desk, his hand resting on a green personnel file. The lettering on the tab was easy to read: SWANN, ANDREW T.

"It's unpleasant for me, too, sir," Swann said.

Hewitt pursed his lips, nodding as if he was mulling something over, but Swann suspected he was simply stalling. With a sliver of hope that he might remain employed, Swann stayed silent and tried to look relaxed.

"We do things a little differently on this island, Andrew," Hewitt said. "I thought you knew that."

"I do."

"The people here expect a higher standard of service than you might see elsewhere," Hewitt said.

"Pardon me, sir," Swann said, "but what could be better service than fighting to save an innocent man?"

Hewitt was quiet, his fingers dancing lightly on the file.

"Determining Mr. Kent's guilt or innocence isn't up to you."

"Making sure all the facts are brought to light is my job, sir," Swann said.

"The case is not in our jurisdiction."

"But Mr. Kent is," Swann said. "I couldn't stand by and watch that jerk in the Sheriff's Office railroad him because of what he is."

Hewitt's eyes were steady on his. Swann didn't look away. Somewhere from another part of the station, Swann could hear Muzak playing. Christmas carols.

"Before you came in today, I was having second thoughts about my decision to let you go," Hewitt said. "But given this new attitude of yours, I think this is for the best."

"May I ask exactly why I am being fired?" Swann asked.

Hewitt stared at him, as if that had been the last question he expected.

"Did I break a specific rule, sir?"

"It's more complicated than that," Hewitt said. "You failed to conduct yourself in a way that reflects positively on your department and your community."

"I was trying to be a police officer," Swann said. "I was trying to do what was right, not just what looked right."

Hewitt's mouth drew into a hard line. "I'm sorry this didn't work out, Andrew. I am a great admirer of your father. Please give him my best."

Swann looked at the wall of letters, then at the tuxedo hanging behind Hewitt.

"I need to have your keys, badge, ID, and gun," Hewitt said. "You know the gun's city property."

Swann pulled out his police wallet and keys and laid them on the desk. He unhooked his holster and set it next to his badge. Hewitt gathered them up and put everything in his desk drawer. He picked up a plain white envelope.

"Your final paycheck and two weeks' severance," Hewitt said.

Swann accepted it. "I need to get some personal things from my office," he said. "Do you want to call an officer in to oversee things?"

Hewitt shook his head. "Of course not," he said. "I trust you completely."

Swann shook Hewitt's hand and left. He went to his office. The drapes were still adjusted to where he liked them. No one had packed up his clock, his books, the picture of his dog, or the sweaters and jackets in the closet.

His in-box held a neat stack of yesterday's paperwork. Apparently, his admin clerk had not yet been advised to send the daily logs and reports on to someone else.

Let it go. Just pack and leave.

Swann found an empty box in the hall and packed up his things. He took his certificates and Officer of the Year plaque down, hesitating only a second before tossing them into the trash. He took a few minutes to go through his Rolodex and pull out a few personal numbers he wanted to keep. As he stuffed the cards into his pocket, he looked again at the daily reports.

Screwed or not by the department, he felt it wasn't professional to let the reports sit there. The detectives or the city attorney might need them to process a case, and if the reports sat too long, something might get misplaced.

Swann gathered them up and started toward the door, intending to return them to the clerk so she could redirect them to the right supervisor. Habit drew his eye to the activity log as he walked.

Out-of-service traffic light at South County and Royal Way.

Barking dog.

Intruder.

Swann stopped so he could read the details of the intruder call. False alarms and prowler calls were common enough, but few ever resulted in an actual person getting inside one of the businesses or homes.

> Time: 1:34 A.M.
> Address: 67 South Ocean Boulevard.
> Reporting party: Tricia (Tink) Lyons.
> Disposition: Intruder located and removed from property.

Tink Lyons?

Swann turned back and dumped the reports on the desk, looking for the separate report that would contain the details of the incident. He found it quickly. Across the top of the page was the officer's name, Gavin Mead, plus Lyons's address and the name and address of the intruder, Byrne Kavanagh.

Swann read on.

> I, Officer Gavin Mead, responded to a call of an intruder at a residence on South Ocean Boulevard. I encountered Mr. Richard Lyons and unknown subject in the front yard. Subject was unarmed, cooperative and provided ID in the name of Byrne Kavanagh. Mr. Lyons declined to press charges and I removed the subject Kavanagh from the premises and took no further action. End report.

Swann sighed. Patrolman Mead was young and, like all service people here, well trained. One of his skills as a cop was the art of knowing the difference between what he saw and what he was *supposed* to see.

And Swann had no doubt that Mead had seen a lot more than he had written.

He checked his watch. It was almost four P.M. and the swing-shift officers, including Mead, would be wandering in soon. Swann knew Mead was always on time and always got dropped off by his girlfriend across the street at Hamburger Heaven. Swann would wait for him there.

Mead saw him as soon as he shut the car door. With a glance at the station, he took off his sunglasses and came toward Swann. He had the look of a boy who'd just learned his father had been charged with a crime.

Swann understood. Like everyone in the department, Mead knew Swann had been suspended and maybe had already heard he'd been let go. It had to rattle the kid a little. Swann had been his training officer and then his boss for the last four years. If there was anyone to trust in that building, it was this kid.

"Did they fire you?" Mead asked.

"Yeah," Swann said. "But I'll be fine. You just need to keep going in there every day and do your job. Understand?"

"Yes, sir. Thank you for being here so you could tell me yourself."

"Well, that's not the only reason I'm here," Swann said. "I wanted to ask you some questions about a call you took last night at the Lyons house."

"Oh, wow," Mead said. "That was a weird one."

"I need to know exactly what the scene looked like when you walked up."

Mead's eyes slipped to the station across the street. "You sure I can tell you all this?"

"It's important, Gavin."

Mead nodded. "Well, you know it's a long walk from the cruiser up their drive. I was hustling, because Dispatch said there might be an altercation between the intruder and Mr. Lyons, but as soon as I got there, I saw Mr. Lyons already had the subject subdued and was trying to drag him somewhere."

"In which direction?"

Mead shrugged. "I wasn't sure," he said. "Maybe around the side of the house. It was hard to tell, with the place looking like a jungle and all."

"Was Kavanagh fighting him? Struggling?"

"No, sir," Mead said. "Mr. Kavanagh wasn't in any shape to fight anyone. Mr. Lyons had already kicked the crap out of him."

"What did he look like?" Swann asked.

"Who?"

"Byrne Kavanagh."

"I told you, he was beat up."

"No, physical characteristics. Clothing."

"Oh," Mead said. "He was wearing jeans and a nice white shirt, but it was all bloody. I recall from his stats, he was twenty-three, six foot, and one-sixty."

"Was he a good-looking guy?"

"Sir?"

"The kind of guy women would like?"

Mead shrugged. "He looked like the kind of guy you see in a catalogue."

"Where was Mrs. Lyons while you were in the yard?"

"She was hanging around the open front door," Mead said. "One time, when she came out into the porch light, I caught a glimpse of her. It was a little freaky."

"Why? Was she hurt, too?"

"No, but she was all dressed up," Mead said. "Hair ribbons and this ruffly white dress."

"A wedding dress?"

"No, it looked more like one of those old-fashioned doll dresses."

"Did Mrs. Lyons say anything?"

"She just whimpered and mumbled a lot," Mead said. "Mostly about making sure Mr. Kavanagh wasn't hurt—wait—she called him Byrne."

"So, she knew him?"

Mead looked away for a moment, then sighed. "I really hate assuming things, sir, and I know we're supposed to keep our thoughts to ourselves, but . . ."

"Say it, Gavin."

"I got the impression that Mr. Lyons had come home unexpectedly and interrupted Mrs. Lyons and Mr. Kavanagh playing some sort of . . . um . . . sexual game, if you get my drift."

"You don't think Mr. Lyons knew him?"

"Mr. Lyons was pretty drunk, sir," Mead said. "It was hard to understand most of what he was yelling, but I can say with some certainty that he didn't."

"Why are you so sure?"

"Because when I walked up, I noticed Mr. Lyons had Mr. Kavanagh's wallet in his hand. When I told him I couldn't leave without removing Mr. Kavanagh, Mr. Lyons threw the wallet down and said, 'It doesn't matter, I know who he is now, anyway.'"

"What happened next?" Swann asked.

"I asked Mr. Lyons if he wanted me to arrest Mr. Kavanagh for trespassing or anything, and he said no, just take him away. So, I helped Mr. Kavanagh to my cruiser and escorted him across the bridge to the Circle K."

Swann knew that the Circle K, a block from the bridge in West Palm, was their drop-off point for vagrants, drunks, and anyone else they wanted to throw off the island.

"Did Kavanagh say anything to you during the ride?" Swann asked.

"Not a word, until I asked him if he felt he needed medical attention," Mead said. "He said no, all he wanted to do was go home and make a call."

Swann ran a hand through his hair, trying to make sense of Mead's story. If this case was about what they thought it was, then Byrne Kavanagh would turn out to be the latest in a series of young men who were being employed by older, rich women for sex. And based on what they knew so far, at least two—maybe three—of the men who had come before Byrne had ended up dead.

"Sir," Mead said, "did I do anything wrong last night?"

"No," Swann said. "You did exactly what the department would expect us to do."

Mead stuck out a hand. "It's been great working with you, Lieutenant," he said. "You let me know where you end up, would you?"

Swann said he would, and Mead trotted off across the street. Swann stood there for a moment, then turned and went inside Hamburger Heaven. He got five dollars in quarters and stepped outside to the pay phone. He needed to call Louis and let him know what he had just found out.

But there was one other call he needed to make first. If not for Reggie, then for himself.

He dropped in eight quarters and dialed the number. On the sixth or seventh ring, he started to wonder if maybe he had misdialed it, but then a man answered.

"Hello?"

"Hello, Dad," Swann said. "It's Andrew."

Chapter Thirty-one

Byrne Kavanagh's apartment was at the end of an L-shaped building of pink stucco and blue doors. A rusty piece of tin mounted on the roof still tagged the place as the Breezy Palms Motor Court, but a newer and bigger sign near the driveway read CORONADO EFFICIENCIES—RENT BY WEEK OR MONTH.

Louis had the passenger door open before Swann put the BMW in park. When they stepped from the car, Louis unsnapped the holster on his belt and chambered a round in his Glock. He caught Swann looking at him.

Swann hadn't said much on the ride over to West Palm Beach, but Louis knew what he was feeling. He had just been fired. He had no gun, no badge, no legal authority to be here.

"You don't happen to have any plastic gloves in the car, do you?" Louis asked.

"Gloves?"

"Yeah," Louis said. "If Kavanagh doesn't answer, we're going in."

Swann went to his trunk. Louis looked up at the sky. It was only a little after six P.M., but it felt much later. Storm clouds were curling in from the west, billows of black and gray, made freakier by the lasers of lightning deep within.

Swann returned with two pairs of latex gloves. Louis couldn't help but notice that they were top-of-the-line, dusted on the inside with talc to make them easy to slip on.

Louis led Swann to apartment twelve and knocked on the door. They had stopped at the Lyons home before coming out to West Palm, hoping to grill Dickie on last night's altercation with Kavanagh, but there had been no answer. Mel had stayed back in Palm Beach, his assignment to keep trying to contact Dickie or Tink.

Their job was to find Kavanagh. Maybe to get some answers about how this prostitution ring ran and what had happened to the other three men. Even more important, they had to make sure Kavanagh himself wasn't going to become victim number four.

Louis knocked again. No answer.

Swann went to the window. The drapes were drawn, so he cupped his hands to peer through the slit between the panels.

"I can't see much, but I don't think there's anyone in there," Swann said.

Louis pounded on the door. "Kavanagh! You in there?" he yelled.

Nothing.

"Andrew, you know how to jimmy a lock?" Louis asked.

"Sure, don't you?"

Louis didn't answer him, not wanting to admit he'd

never gotten the hang of it. Swann dug into his pockets, and while he worked the lock with a Swiss Army knife, Louis scanned the parking lot. There were six cars, a van with a flat, and a pickup with a bed full of junk. Across the street was a liquor store and a café. Light traffic, no pedestrians, and no police cars.

The lock snapped, and Louis drew his Glock and looked back at Swann, indicating that he wanted to go in first. He didn't expect a confrontation, but there was always a chance that Kavanagh was hunkered down inside with his own weapon, so spooked he would shoot at anything that came through his door.

Louis eased the door open and stepped quickly inside. The room was gray with shadows, but he could see what he needed to see: bed, dresser, desk, nightstand. In the back of the efficiency was an exposed kitchenette. The bathroom door was wide open.

"It's clear, Andrew," Louis said.

Swann stepped in, closed the door, and hit the light switch.

If someone was paying Byrne Kavanagh good money for sex, he sure wasn't spending it on his living arrangements. The place was a classic cheap Florida rental: white walls, ugly green shag, tropical-print bedspread, and plastic bamboo lamp. Clothes were strewn near the bathroom door and across the bed.

A small cry broke the silence.

Both of them spun to the bed. At first, Louis saw only a heap of clothes; then the small orange and white ball of fur took shape. A kitten, looking at him the way his own cat did each time he walked in the door: relief that its human was home and food was on its way.

The kitten jumped off the bed, and Louis saw what it had been sleeping on—a dirty white shirt with red smears.

Louis held the shirt up so Swann could see it. The spatter across the torn front was definitely blood. The lapel said EMPORIO ARMANI. It was a good guess that this was the same shirt Kavanagh had worn last night.

"Well, we know he made it home," Louis said.

Swann nodded, holding up a pair of jeans he'd found on the floor. The knees were grass-stained, the thighs dotted with blood. Swann tossed the jeans onto the bed and turned toward the desk.

"Hold on a minute, Andrew."

Searching someone's correspondence was always a good way to learn more about them, but in this case, Louis wanted Swann to wait. It was important that they know what happened last night.

"Let's take a minute and walk through this like Kavanagh would have," Louis said. "I like to keep things linear."

Swann looked confused but nodded.

"Okay, Kavanagh was dropped off at the Circle K, a long way from here," Louis said. "Either he took a cab or hitched a ride. He probably didn't get home until after three A.M."

"Right."

Louis motioned to the bed. "So, he stripped off his clothes here and headed to the john."

Swann moved to the bathroom door and reached in to turn on the light. Louis stepped up next to him.

The room was a mess. Dried blood in the white basin, smears on the faucet handles, and perfect crimson fingerprints on the edge of the mirror where Kavanagh had opened the medicine cabinet.

The floor was littered with crumpled red tissues, bloody towels, and a bottle of aspirin, its contents scattered across the floor like beads from a broken necklace.

"Damn," Swann whispered.

"What's the matter?" Louis asked.

"Gavin should have done more," Swann said softly. "You don't just drop somebody who's hurting like this on the other side of the bridge and drive away."

The image of a police officer dumping a bloody Kavanagh on the street brought Mel's story to mind, the one he had told Louis about Reggie sitting on a curb in Miami, beaten and left by cops to find his own way home.

"Forget it," Louis said. "Nothing you can do about that now."

They returned to the main room and just stood there, staring at the bed. One side was heaped with clothes, and the other side was rumpled. Blanket pulled back, blood-streaked pillow bunched against the headboard.

"He slept here last night," Louis said.

Swann sighed and took a long look around. "But if he was in such bad shape, why did he get up today and go anywhere?"

"Maybe he went to work," Louis said.

"You saw that bathroom. Looks like he lost a quart of blood," Swann said. "And if he was getting money from the women, why did he need to work?"

"Well, from the looks of this place, I'd say he hasn't been in the sex business very long. Look through his desk and see what can you find."

Swann started sorting through envelopes and papers.

Louis opened the closet and sifted through the hanging clothes. A Sears sports coat. A pair of old Levi's and a windbreaker. Three pastel Italian shirts, a pair of Sergio Valente jeans, and two more white Armani shirts like the bloody one on the bed. Dumped at the bottom was a pile of dirty shorts, T-shirts, sneakers, and sandals. But there was also one pair of soft black loafers. Louis picked one shoe up. Bruno Magli.

"He's a yacht monkey," Swann said.

"What?"

"I'm sorry," Swann said. "That's slang for those guys who crew on yachts. It looks like his last job was for a yacht brokerage called Seven Seas. Here's his pay stub. This check is a few weeks old."

Louis looked back at the bloody pillowcase. He wanted to believe Kavanagh had gone to work today, but he was having a real hard time with the idea that the kid had the strength to get out of bed, let alone spend eight hours swabbing down a yacht.

"Should we call Seven Seas?" Swann asked.

Louis looked around the room. "You see a phone, Andrew?"

Swann looked around, then started moving clothes and pillows. He found a cord and followed it to the space between the bed and the wall. He came up with an old rotary phone and a black answering machine. The machine's red message light was blinking.

"Play it," Louis said.

Swann set the answering machine on the bed and pushed the tab. A female voice squeaked from the box, telling Kavanagh he had one new message. A male voice followed.

"Yo, Byrne, buddy, this is the boss. Where the hell were you this morning? Hey, look, I don't care that you're taking a better job. But you promised you'd finish this last run to Bermuda for me before you quit. Anyway, give me a call if you want your final check."

The message ended.

Louis suddenly remembered something he had seen outside. The pickup truck with the cluttered bed. "I'll be right back," he said.

The stuff in the back of the truck was boating equipment—heavy blue ropes, pulleys, cleaning equipment, a pair of old Top-Siders. Louis tried the driver's-side door, surprised to find it unlocked. The registration was in the glove box. The truck belonged to Kavanagh.

Louis searched through the stuff in the cab, looking for anything to connect Kavanagh to Dickie, Tink, Carolyn Osborn, or any of the men who had been murdered. But all he found was an empty 7-Eleven cup, half a bag of chips, and a pair of flip-flops.

He went back inside. "Kavanagh's truck is outside."

"Maybe some friends picked him up and they went out for a few beers," Swann offered.

Everything Swann was suggesting was logical. But something in his gut was telling him none of those things had happened. Kavanagh didn't pick up his last pay check. His drawers were filled with clean clothes, and his toothbrush was in the bathroom, so he hadn't left town.

Louis heard a cry and looked down.

The kitten looked up at him and trotted toward the kitchenette. Louis followed. The litter box in the corner held a couple days' worth of poop, and the plastic food dish was licked dry. So was the water dish.

Damn.

Louis opened the cabinet over the sink, looking for some cat food. He spotted a box of Tender Vittles in the back. When he pulled out one of the bags of food, an envelope fell out.

It was letter-sized, a heavy cream-colored paper. Louis slipped a finger under the flap and opened it.

Money. A thin stack of bills. But all of them hundreds.

"Andrew!"

Swann came up to his side. "Jesus. How much is there?"

"Two thousand dollars," Louis said.

"Payment from Tink Lyons?"

"Who knows?" Louis said. "Might be one night's work or a week's worth."

Louis turned his attention to the envelope, hoping for initials or something, but there was nothing. He was about to slip the money back inside when he saw the embossing on the back flap. The Scotch tape had damaged part of the design, and he had to hold the envelope up to the light to define the pattern.

It was a three-petal stylized flower tied with a band. A fleur-de-lis. The same image glazed on the door of Bianca Lee's flower shop.

"Get Mel on the phone," Louis said. "Tell him to get his ass over to Bianca Lee's flower shop and see if Kavanagh's with her."

"You think he'd go to her?" Swann asked.

Louis looked at the bloody shirt on the bed. "I don't know," he said. "But if she's his new boss, I wouldn't be surprised if that's where he went."

While Swann made the phone call, Louis took another look around the room to make sure they hadn't missed anything. Just in case Kavanagh had stashed more cash, he checked everything in the kitchenette, the bottoms of the desk drawers, the base of the lamp, and under the bed.

Swann hung up. "Mel says he's getting Yuba to drive him over there right now. I told him we'd call back in about thirty minutes to see what he found out."

Louis pushed to his feet. "Then let's go."

Swann pocketed the envelope, turned off the light, and followed Louis outside. It was raining now, big fat drops that hit the ground like small water balloons. Louis waited under the overhang while Swann fiddled with the doorknob to make sure it would lock again.

Suddenly, two gold eyes appeared in the window.

"Ah, shit," Louis whispered.

"What's the matter?"

"Don't lock the door yet," Louis said.

"Why?"

Louis headed back inside. "We have to take the cat," he said. "I have a bad feeling Kavanagh might not be coming home tonight."

Chapter Thirty-two

Bianca Lee stood at the window looking down at the courtyard. He was still there. What was the matter with him? Then she remembered some gossip she had heard. The guy was blind or something. Maybe he couldn't see the CLOSED sign she had put on the window of the flower shop.

She wondered where the black guy was. And why the hell was his partner banging on her door?

It was starting to rain. The bald guy looked up toward her window, pulled up the collar of his jacket, and scurried to a Honda waiting at the curb. Bianca caught a glimpse of the dark-haired woman at the wheel before the car pulled away down Worth Avenue.

Bianca let the drape fall and turned back to her small living room, to the man lying on her sofa.

"How's your head?" she asked.

He didn't look at her, didn't even move.

She sat down next to him and took the folded towel from his head. The gash on his scalp was deep, matting his dark hair with blood. His right eye was swollen shut, the ugly purple bruise spreading down his cheek. His lip was split and probably needed stitches. But she couldn't risk taking him to the hospital. She was almost shaking with anger as she looked down at Byrne Kavanagh's beautiful, shattered face.

God damn Dickie Lyons.

She had always known he was a brute, a man with no taste or appreciation for anything of grace. And sometimes she felt a twinge of pity for Tink, although the woman certainly brought on some of her own misery.

But this time, Lyons had broken something of *hers,* something she had invested a lot of time and money in, something she had made blossom into a thing of beauty.

She started to dab at his face with the towel, but

Byrne pushed it away. As he tried to sit up, he winced and held his right wrist.

"I think it's broken," he said.

She rose. "Let me get you another Percocet."

"No," he said quickly. "I just want to go home."

"I told you, Byrne, it's not safe. Tink said he's looking for you. She says he's got a gun."

She was lying; she had no idea where Dickie Lyons was, and she hadn't talked to Tink at all. The truth was, she didn't know what the hell was going on anymore. All she knew was that she had to keep Byrne here.

"What about my money?" Byrne asked.

"You'll get it, I promise."

"I just want my money, Bianca," he said. "I just want my money so I can get out of here. You told me this would be easy. You didn't say I'd get beat up. I don't want to do this anymore."

"Byrne, please, listen to me. Everything will be all right."

He closed his eyes and turned away.

She glanced at her watch. Where the hell was Carolyn?

When she called the Osborn house this morning, Greg told her that Carolyn was on her way to Aspen. But he had managed to reach her at the airport, and once Bianca explained what had happened, Carolyn had canceled her trip.

Calm down, Bianca. I'll take care of it.

You better, Carolyn. We can't let this happen again.

Bianca went back to the window and looked down on the street again. The rain was coming down hard now.

Damn, she didn't want to lose Byrne. He was special.

He was so sweet, much sweeter than the others. She had spotted him down at the yacht basin. It didn't take much to convince him; he was broke, and he was so trusting. He had been patient when she took him to the tailor, the stylist, and the manicurist. He was even willing to change what soap he used.

No more Lifebuoy, Byrne, it's Clive Christian for you from now on.

And when she had taken him to bed that first time— as she had done to evaluate all of the others—she knew he could service the fantasies of anyone.

He could have made so much money. That's why he had agreed to do this, so he could make enough to buy a sailboat and go off to Key West. He could have made a fortune, for himself and for her.

But now he wanted out. He wanted what he was owed for his night with Tink and wanted to go home and feed his cat. She could have just given him the two grand; she had enough in the register downstairs. She could have let him drift away just like all the others had after the season was over and the women had tired of them. But after what had happened to Mark Durand, she couldn't take any chances.

Bianca let out an angry sigh. She had really screwed that one up. She had misjudged him.

God damn Durand.

The first time she saw him sitting at the bar in Taboo, she hadn't been able to take her eyes off him. And she was desperate to find a new boy, because Justin had decided suddenly to go back to Los Angeles, so she had no one to finish out the season. She had approached Mark that same night, and on impulse, she had given him her special card, the cream-colored one with the fleur-de-lis and the private phone number. It was only later she found out he was trying to be a walker.

A walker . . .

Even now, it seemed ridiculous. Maybe Mark was living with that old fool Kent, but once she got Mark in her bed, it was clear he wasn't gay. It was clear, too, that he was willing to do anything to make money. If he was too rough, well, some of her women liked that.

She signed him up that night. She got greedy. She got impatient. She didn't vet him.

And then someone murdered him.

Bianca glanced back at Byrne. She couldn't let what had happened to Mark happen to Byrne. She had to keep him here, no matter what it took.

She looked again at her watch and back out at the rain. There was nothing to do now but wait until the others got here.

The blue Camry pulled up to the curb and stopped. Carolyn looked out through the driving rain to the door of Fleur de Lee.

"Do you want me to wait for you?"

Carolyn turned to Greg. "No," she said. "I don't know how long I'm going to be. And you know what to do."

Greg was gripping the steering wheel, his eyes intense. Carolyn reached over and put her hand over his. "Don't put this in my planner," she said softly.

"You don't have to tell me that," he whispered.

She smiled wanly. "I know."

"I never put any of them in your book."

"I know that, too."

Greg looked out the rain-splattered windshield.

"Everything's going to be all right," Carolyn said. "Please don't worry about me."

"What about—?"

Carolyn glanced over her shoulder. Tink was curled in the corner of the backseat, staring vacantly out the window.

"I'll take care of Tink," Carolyn said softly. "We don't know where Dickie is. I don't want her to go home right now."

Greg nodded. Carolyn reached over and touched his cheek. "Thank you," she said. Then she pulled up the collar of her raincoat and got out of the car.

She opened the back door and helped Tink out. Huddled together, they hurried through the rain.

There were no lights on inside Fleur de Lee, and the CLOSED sign hung in the window. But the door was unlocked, and Carolyn slipped inside, ushering Tink in ahead of her. In the dark, there was nothing to see. But the smell was overwhelming: the sweet, heady scent of hundreds of flowers.

Tink stayed by the door, a thin figure in a too-large trench coat, arms wrapped across her chest, like she was trying to hold herself together.

Carolyn shut her eyes, like that would help her hold herself together as well. Because that was what she needed to do right now. If she didn't, the whole thing was going to blow up.

Tink was weeping.

"Tink," Carolyn said softly. "Stop crying."

"He's gone. He's never going to come back, and he was the only one, the only one that I loved, and he's never coming back."

Carolyn let out a tired breath. There was no sense in trying to reason with Tink when she got like this, when she got confused and started talking about the men like they were from her past. It was better if she knew nothing about Byrne right now.

"What took you so long?"

Carolyn turned and spotted Bianca standing in the far shadows.

"I had to go get Tink. She's in bad shape," she said.

Bianca looked at Tink and back at Carolyn. "Why did you bring her here?"

"I couldn't leave her at home," Carolyn said. "I couldn't be sure she wouldn't call the police again. And I don't trust Dickie."

"What about Tucker?"

"I don't know where he is."

The smell of the flowers was giving Carolyn a headache. She glanced back at the door. The rain was coming down hard, and she doubted anyone was out on the avenue tonight, but they couldn't take any chances.

"Let's go in the back," she said.

Tink didn't seem to be listening, so Carolyn linked her arm through Tink's, and they followed Bianca to the small storage room in the back. Bianca closed the curtain that divided the back room from the front of the shop.

Carolyn led Tink to a chair, and she dropped down onto it, hanging her head. Bianca switched on a small lamp, and when Carolyn saw her face, she realized Bianca was scared. It was unexpected in Bianca, and it made Carolyn angry. She had trusted this woman, given her control of everything. And control was not something she gave easily to others.

Except Byrne.

A splash of red caught Carolyn's eye. There was a potted red orchid sitting on a workbench.

How had this happened? How had she allowed it to get so out of control? How had something so normal turned into something so ugly?

Normal . . . was that even the right word?

She stared at the orchid.

Was finding comfort in a man's arms normal? Was trying to feel beautiful normal? Was feeling wanted and needed normal?

Was sex normal, if you had to pay for it?

She wondered if Tucker ever thought of things like this when he was with one of his women. No, it was different for men. They had their affairs, hid the costs in the company books, and left no tracks or traces. Even if they got careless, there were snickers in the cabanas and whispers in the banquettes of Au Bar but no one was ever kicked out of the fraternity.

But the women . . . they couldn't ever be careless.

They couldn't just book at room at the Brazilian Court.

They couldn't just write a check.

They couldn't do it alone.

So, they had formed a sorority. They shared lovers, and they shared the secret. Bianca funneled the women's checks through her florist shop books under the guise of a charity, taking a handsome cut for her trouble. They called it the Orchid Society.

Five years, five men. A new one each season. Bianca found the men, checked their backgrounds, groomed them, dressed them. Bianca knew what each of the women liked. She knew what the men could do, because she had bedded each man herself.

And by the time a man walked into one of the bedrooms on the island, he was as rare and perfect a specimen as the red orchid he carried.

Carolyn looked away from the orchid to Tink. She had to take control again.

"Where's Byrne?" Carolyn asked quietly, moving away from Tink.

"Upstairs," Bianca whispered.

"Is he all right?"

Bianca gave a tired shrug. "I gave him a couple of Percocets."

"What did you tell him?"

"I told him what you told me to say, that he'd get his money and he could leave." She paused. "But I think we need to do more for him."

"More? Like what?"

"More money," Bianca said.

"How much?"

"Fifty grand."

Carolyn just stared at her. "Are you insane? Why should we give him that much money? He didn't even make it through the season, for God's sake. He's trying to blackmail us."

Bianca shook her head. "All he wants to do is take his cat, go buy a boat, and start over somewhere."

"What makes you think he'll keep his mouth shut? What makes you think he won't be back here in six months asking for more money?"

"He's not like Mark, Carolyn. He's a good kid."

Carolyn was silent. She had been with Byrne only

once, and he did seem harmless enough. Maybe he would be content just to drift away like Paul and the others had. But there was no way to be sure, no way to know she could trust him. And after what had happened with Mark, she had to be certain.

As for Bianca, she wasn't sure she could even trust her anymore. Even if they managed to get fifty grand in cash together tonight, how could they be sure it wouldn't end up in Bianca's bank account?

No, there was no room for error now. There was no room for trust.

A soft groan drew Carolyn's eyes to the corner. Tink . . .

They should never have allowed her into the society in the first place. She certainly couldn't be trusted now. Maybe they could convince her that Byrne had simply left, but Carolyn knew Tink was too fragile mentally. And now that those detectives were on Dickie's trail, they would be after Tink. And if Tink was pushed, she would break. She would tell them what happened to Mark.

A sound in the front part of the shop made Carolyn jump. The door opening and closing. She felt Bianca come up beside her, and they both looked toward the curtain.

It parted, and a woman stood there, hands on hips. She jerked off her rain hat and shook out her red hair.

"All right, which one of you bitches called this meeting?" Sam said.

Chapter Thirty-three

As usual, Barberry made them wait. They were sitting on a bench in an empty hallway a short distance away from the double doors of the Violent Crimes squad room. The background noise was a familiar mix of radio chatter, men's voices, and distant sirens.

Louis had just gotten off the pay phone with Mel. There had been no lights on in Fleur de Lee and no answer at the door. Mel told him he also called the shop, hoping the business phone might be forwarded to Bianca's home, but there had been no answer.

Since none of them had any law-enforcement authority, there was no way to locate a home address for Bianca or issue an APB for Byrne Kavanagh. They had no choice but to come back begging to Barberry.

Louis watched two deputies come down the hall. Their yellow slickers were dripping. Evidently, it was still raining like hell.

Swann was hunched forward, elbows on his knees, his hair still dripping water into the collar of his shirt. Louis had his head back against the wall, eyes closed. The kitten was in the Mustang, sleeping peacefully in a pillowcase. It was a trick Louis had learned a few years ago when he had to transport Issy to the vet and couldn't find the cat carrier.

The bang of a door drew Louis's eyes up. Barberry came toward them, an ugly tweed jacket slung over his shoulder and a pack of Camel cigarettes in his shirt pocket. So much for willpower, Louis thought.

Barberry kept his eyes on Swann as he came forward, taking obvious pleasure that there was no badge on Swann's chest or belt.

"Guess things didn't work out for you so well over there on Fantasy Island, huh?" Barberry asked.

Swann crossed his arms, and Louis watched the two of them stare at each other. Swann had come close to slugging Barberry once, and that was when he still had a job to worry about. Now that he didn't, Louis wasn't sure how much he was going to take from this dimwit, and he didn't need Swann tossed in jail on an assault charge.

"Detective," Louis said, "we need your help."

Barberry turned to Louis. "What for?"

"We have a young man who's missing," Louis said. "He fits the same victim profile as the others, and he got the crap beat out of him last night by a jealous husband."

Barberry sighed. "And I care about this why?"

Louis drew a slow breath before he went on. "Look, Detective," he said, "we have three guys we think were fooling around with married women. They're dead. Now we have a fourth man who was doing the same thing, and he's missing. All we want from you is help finding him before *he* ends up dead."

Barberry pulled at his chin. "Okay, I'll give you a few minutes to convince me to call out the troops, but this time, I want to know *everything* you got on this. Everything."

Louis had no faith that Barberry would do them any favors, but he also had no choice but to give him what he wanted and hope he had a sliver of decency. Finding Kavanagh would take a statewide APB, massive man-hours, and some legal authority to bust open a few doors. Things only Barberry could do.

"Talk, Kincaid."

As Louis recapped the entire investigation, Barberry listened, his brow arching with interest at the mention of Senator Carolyn Osborn but then furrowing with skepticism when Louis tried to explain Bianca's role as a madam.

But even as Louis wound his story down, he saw from Barberry' superior expression that he had just surrendered whatever leverage he had.

Suddenly, Louis understood the man. Barberry wasn't stupid, incompetent, or small-minded. He was just plain lazy, wanting others to do his work for him and then pissing on them so he could take the credit.

"I've listened to you," Barberry said, "but now you explain one last thing to me. Why do the tracks left at that cattle pen exactly match those custom-made boots I took out of Kent's house?"

Louis just stared at Barberry. He didn't know the answer. Even if he did, he would never tell this asshole.

"Detective," Louis said, "we came here to get your help. If you refuse to do your job and Byrne Kavanagh dies, you will regret it. I promise you."

Barberry moved his jacket off his shoulder and took a notebook from the inside pocket. "You say you checked this flower store to see if this Kavanagh guy was there?"

"Place was dark," Louis said.

"What's the owner's name again?" Barberry asked. "I'll run a DL and get her address for you."

"It's Bianca Lee," Louis said.

"Don't be surprised if no one turns up under that name," Swann said. "She probably changed it."

Louis turned to look at Swann.

Swann took a wipe at his wet hair. "If your name is too . . . if it—"

"Ends in a vowel?" Barberry said with a smirk.

Swann ignored him. "People come to Palm Beach to reinvent themselves, and that includes their names. Reggie's real name is Kaczmarek. When he first got to Palm Beach, he legally changed it."

Barberry gave a chuckle and wrote something in his notebook. "I don't suppose you dickheads have any idea where we can start looking for this Kavanagh clown."

"I'd send a couple of deputies over to the Lyons house to see if Dickie knows where he is," Louis said.

Barberry snorted. "You want me to go knocking on a man's door, with no probable cause, and ask him if he's got his wife's stud boy tied up in his kitchen?"

"I told you, he beat the shit out of Kavanagh last night."

Barberry glanced at Swann, that nasty twinkle in his eye. Louis knew that going to the Lyons home was one thing Barberry wasn't going to do.

"Why don't you ask Papa Hewitt to help you out there, sonny? It's *his* island."

Swann turned and walked to the end of the hall. Louis watched him, then looked back at Barberry. He was probably going to blow any chance of getting Barberry's cooperation, but he suddenly didn't care.

"Look, you piece of crap," Louis said, keeping his voice low. "I ought to take that fucking badge of yours and shove it down your throat and hope you die trying to shit it out."

Barberry chuckled. "You know it's against the law to use profanity against a cop."

"You're no cop," Louis said. "That guy over there is twice the officer you'll ever be, whether he ever puts on a badge again or not."

Barberry lifted his hand and made an exaggerated gesture of looking at his watch. "You got thirty seconds to disappear from this hall, or you'll be bunking with Kent." He grinned. "Then again, maybe you'd like that."

Barberry walked away, back toward his squad room. Louis stood there, feeling the burn creep up the back of his neck. He realized his fist was clenched.

"Louis, you okay?" Swann asked, coming up next to him.

Louis turned and left. Swann hurried to keep up as Louis went through the lobby and shoved open the glass double doors.

It was raining and windy. He stopped, fists clenched and rain stinging his face as he stared up at the halyards clanging on the flagpole. He looked down at the waxy bushes that circled the flagpole's base.

Fuck!

He kicked at the nearest bush, scattering dirt and almost losing his balance. Then he jerked one of the plants from the ground and, in a spray of dripping mud, flung it toward the station doors. It smacked against the glass, stuck there for a second, then slid down the door to the sidewalk.

"Louis, stop!"

He spun toward Swann, chest heaving.

"We're going to see Reggie," Swann said calmly. He glanced back at the station doors. "And we need to go now."

• • •

If Louis had ever seen a more pitiful image, he couldn't remember it. Reggie behind the scratched Plexiglas, his hair pruned into a bad buzz cut, his eyes glazed, his lip swollen to the size of a plum.

Swann took the lead, slipping into the chair. "How you doing, Reg?" he asked.

Reggie wiped a hand under his nose. "I'm okay," he whispered. His voice was rusty with a cold. "I need money."

"Money?" Louis asked. "You mean you need to buy things at the commissary?"

"Not *things,*" Reggie said. "I need cash to buy protection. They want money."

Reggie put his hands over his face. His knuckles were raw, his nails dirty. Through the tinny speaker embedded in the glass, Reggie's breaths sounded like a rattling of his rib cage.

"We'll take care of the money," Louis said. "But right now, I need to ask you some questions. Can you pull yourself together for me?"

"Yes. Yes."

"What do you know about Bianca Lee?"

"The flower lady?" Reggie asked. "She . . . she does nice parties."

"Did Mark Durand ever mention her name?"

Reggie closed his eyes, coughing softly. "Not that I can remember."

"Did you ever see a red orchid in Durand's possession?" Louis asked. "Or in your home?"

For a long time, Reggie just sat there, eyes closed, fingers laced at his forehead. It was so quiet all they could hear was the hum of the fluorescent light. Then the white noise of the jail started again—hollow male voices and the buzz and clang of steel doors.

"The night Mark met me at Testa's," Reggie said, "he had a red orchid with him. He dropped it during our fight."

Reggie closed his eyes again, grimacing as if in pain.

"What else happened?" Louis asked.

"I was upset about him seeing those women," Reggie said. "I asked him if he had a date that night and if the flower was for *her*."

"What did he say?"

"He said yes, and I got mad."

He went silent again, eyes closed.

"Reg, tell us everything," Swann said. "We need to know everything you said that night."

"I told Mark he didn't understand," Reggie said. "I told him that no matter what those women told him when he was with them, no matter how many gifts they gave him, he was no better than anyone else who provided a service to them."

"What about the orchid?" Louis pressed.

"That's when he got mad, and he told me I was wrong, that he was part of their world in a way I would never be. He said he was a member of the Orchid Society."

"The Orchid Society? That's how he described it?"

Reggie nodded again. "I thought he was lying, like people do when they tell you they belong to the Bath and Tennis."

"But he never mentioned Bianca Lee as part of that society?"

"No."

"Did he ever mention any other women we haven't talked about yet?"

"No."

"Did he ever mention the name Byrne Kavanagh?"

Reggie coughed and shook his head.

Louis looked at Swann. What else was left?

Swann leaned forward. "Reggie, remember the last time we were here, we talked about the expensive things in Durand's bedroom?"

Reggie nodded.

"We believe Durand stole those things from the women he was with."

Reggie sighed. "I'm not surprised."

"You need to think, Reggie," Swann said. "What else showed up around your house that didn't seem like something Durand would buy himself?"

Reggie shut his eyes again. He was listing to the right, and Louis hoped he wasn't going to fall off the chair.

"Come on, Reggie," Swann said. "We don't have much time here."

"There was a Hawaiian shirt once, but I think he ended up using that for a . . . oh, wait." Reggie rubbed his face. "There was that god-awful painting."

"Painting? What kind?"

"This horrible landscape," Reggie said. "I found it in the back of his closet."

"Do you think he could have stolen it from one of the women?"

Reggie shook his head slowly. "I doubt it. It was very amateurish, not anything the women I know would own. I thought maybe he bought it for me as a gift. So I stuck it back in the closet and prayed I'd never have to look at it again."

Louis remembered seeing a Haitian painting in Durand's room, once right after the search and again when he and Mel moved in.

"We need to know exactly what this painting looked like," Louis said. "Was it Haitian?"

"I told you, it was an amateur thing," Reggie said. "It was this vulgar cowboy painting with dogs and horses . . ."

"Cowboys?" Louis leaned in closer. "You need to think hard here. Did Durand *ever* tell you where he got that painting?"

"No, but I can tell you the name of the artist," Reggie said. "It was signed in the corner. Archer."

Louis looked at Swann. He looked like someone had just given him a kick in the gut, but the intensity in his eyes told Louis that Swann's mind was already racing toward the cattle pen in Devil's Garden.

"We need to go," Louis said. "You hang in there, you hear me? I promise you, it'll be over soon."

"One way or another," Reggie whispered.

Chapter Thirty-four

A single yellow floodlight was the beacon that led them through the driving rain to Aubry's bungalow. His old Jeep was parked next to a small stable.

Louis and Swann hurried up to the porch. Louis

knocked, the sound drowned out in the clamor of the
rain beating on the tin roof. Finally, the door opened.

Aubry stood there, holding a beer. "What the hell?"

"Mr. Aubry, we need to talk to you," Louis said.

"Must be pretty damn important for you to come all
the way here on a night like this."

"It is, believe me."

"Well, get in here, then."

They stepped into a dimly lit room, warm from a
blazing fireplace and pungent with the scent of fresh
pine. Next to the coral-rock fireplace was a Christmas
tree decorated with carved wood ornaments and old-
fashioned bulb lights.

Louis stayed by the door, dripping on the plank
wood floor, Swann shivering behind.

"Come on in and sit down," Aubry said. "You aren't
going to get anything wet that I care about."

Louis sat on the edge of a lumpy sofa covered with a
blanket. A small yellow mutt with large pointed ears and
a long snout looked up at them from its place in front of
the fire, then laid its head back down.

Aubry came out of the kitchen and tossed each of
them a towel. "I'd offer you a beer, but this is the last
one," he said, holding up his bottle. "I was thinking of
going up the road to Mary Lou's for a six-pack."

Louis dried his face with the towel. "We're fine."

Aubry sat down in a beat-up lounger by the fire. "So,
what's this about?"

"We have another missing man," Louis said.

"Dead?"

"We don't know. We're hoping he's still alive."

"Well, you're not going to find anyone out there in

that rain tonight," Aubry said. "So, I don't know what help I can be."

"Louis?"

Louis looked over at Swann. He first saw the gun rack with two rifles, but then his eyes found the spot of color on the wall next to the rack.

It was a framed painting of men on horses roping a red steer, with yellow dogs running in the green grass.

Louis turned back to Aubry. "You said David sketched. Did he do paintings, too?"

Aubry nodded toward the painting. "That's one of his over there. I've got others. Why you asking?"

"One of his paintings turned up in Palm Beach," Louis said. "And we have to find out how it got there."

Aubry was silent.

"The last time I was here, we talked about David's friends," Louis said. "Could David have given one of his paintings to a friend?"

Aubry shook his head slowly. "David was pretty private about his art stuff. He never thought they were much good, and I told you Jim was funny about it."

"Is there any chance some of his paintings could have been left in the house and his father or mother gave them away?" Louis asked.

"No," Aubry said. "David was getting ready to go off to University of Florida, and he asked me to keep his art stuff. He wouldn't have left any paintings inside the house for his father to find."

"I know I'm grasping at straws here, Mr. Aubry," Louis said, "but can you think of anyone who was around this ranch twenty-eight years ago who could have found their way to Palm Beach?"

"You never know what paths people are going to take," Aubry said, "but the folks who were around here back then, especially those close to the family, they aren't the kind of people who'd feel at home in a place like Palm Beach."

Louis didn't know where else to go with this. Why couldn't he see the connection between David Archer's world and Mark Durand's? Who or what did they have in common?

"Louis," Swann said, "we need to head out to the pen."

"You fellas aren't going anywhere in that fancy car you got," Aubry said. "You'll be caught in the mud for sure."

"Will you take us?" Louis asked.

"Why? You think your missing man might be laying out there already dead?"

"It's been twenty-four hours since he disappeared," Swann said. "Two of the three victims were killed the same night they vanished."

Aubry set the tray down and disappeared again down a hall. He returned wearing a rain slicker, boots, and a cowboy hat. He had a second rain parka for Louis.

"Don't have another slicker," Aubry said to Swann.

"No problem. I have one in my trunk."

"You armed?" Aubry asked.

"I am," Louis said, patting his belt beneath his windbreaker. "Andrew's not."

Aubry pulled two bolt-action rifles from the rack, made sure they were loaded, and handed one to Swann. Louis tried read Swann's expression as he took the rifle.

He knew the academy trained recruits in all weapons, but he doubted Swann had shot any type of gun for a good many years.

Louis put on Aubry's slicker, and they left the house. Swann got his bright yellow raincoat from the BMW's trunk.

It took them about ten minutes to get to the pen. For the first half-mile, the old Jeep slid over the sloppy ground with seemingly no traction. Then the tires hit something solid, and Louis knew where they were. Aubry was taking them in via the gravel road he and Mel had used on their first visit just two days ago.

Aubry brought the Jeep to a stop a few feet from the fence, the blackness before them pierced only by two foggy beams from the headlights. Between sweeps of the wipers, they stared at the labyrinth of fences.

"Let's take a walk," Aubry said.

They grabbed flashlights and stepped into the rain. Louis pulled up the hood of his parka. When he looked back at Swann, the fluorescent stripes on his raincoat sleeves and the words PALM BEACH POLICE stood out even in the dark.

They split up, Aubry and Swann heading to the left, Louis to the right. It was hard to hear anything over the steady beat of the rain and just as hard to see anything in the flashlight's beam.

Louis walked slowly, sweeping the light over the dirt, searching for anything that looked out of place. A hump on the ground, a glint of a metal buckle, a gleam of pale, wet flesh. But there was nothing to see. Nothing to hear but the *plink* of rain and the occasional creak of a rusty gate in the wind.

Louis paused at the fence of the largest pen. He had a decent view, but he couldn't see every inch, nor could he see what was on the other side of the small lean-to.

He looked around for the gate that he had heard, and when he didn't see one, he slipped through the rails and into the pen. The ground was mucky, and there was a smell in the air that seemed to grow stronger with every step.

Halfway across, Louis paused, struck with one of those weird feelings that he was being watched. He leveled the flashlight and made a slow turn, but he saw nothing but the cage of wood fencing.

"Andrew?" Louis called.

"Out here," Swann said.

Louis saw him waving his flashlight, took a breath, and walked on. There was nothing in the lean-to and nothing on the ramp, ground, or rails to indicate that anyone had been here recently. He headed back to the Jeep.

Aubry was waiting for him, sitting in the driver's seat with the door open and shaking rain from his hat.

"Where's Andrew?" Louis asked.

Aubry gestured toward the darkness south of the pen. Swann's light was a fading prick of white.

"Where's he going?" Louis asked.

"Said he wanted to look at the stream," Aubry said. "I tried to tell him that in this rain, his little stream was gonna be more like a lake, but he was intent on going anyway."

"Christ," Louis said. "I'll be right back."

He caught up with Swann on the muddy edge of a surging swamp. Swann had his rifle in one hand and was making slow sweeps of his flashlight with the other across the surface of the brown water. The hood of his coat had blown down, and his head was soaked.

Louis stopped about six feet behind him, on higher ground. "Andrew, get your ass back up here before you get eaten by a fucking alligator."

Swann turned and trudged from the water. He pushed past Louis without saying a word or lifting his head.

"Andrew."

Swann walked on.

Louis watched him for a few seconds, then looked back at the water. It was running fast to the south, carrying branches that floated downstream like gnarled brown fingers.

Louis pointed his flashlight downward. But even as the beam skated across the brown water, he knew that if Byrne Kavanagh was in there, they'd never find him tonight. At least, not the three of them alone.

Louis swung the flashlight over the brown water one last time, then headed back, using the beams of the Jeep's headlights to find his way out of the darkness.

Chapter Thirty-five

Sam eased off the gas as the sign for Clewiston came into view. The last thing she needed now was to be stopped for something as stupid as a speeding ticket. She had to be careful this time.

Not like that time five years ago, when, in her anger and impatience, she had sped through town in Hap's big old silver Bentley. She had been lucky that night, lucky that no cop had stopped her; lucky, too, that Emilio had been so trusting.

Stupid boy . . .

Still, that was what had attracted her to him in the first place. He was beautiful, yes, but he wasn't very smart, and that was what had led her to take him into her bed. He barely spoke English, but she didn't want a man to talk. He didn't want to stay and hold her, but she never wanted a man to linger after sex. He never asked about her life, but she didn't want to have to tell him about her invalid husband. And best of all, he didn't flinch when she asked him to put his hands tight around her neck during orgasm.

He never asked her for anything. So, she bought him an expensive gold crucifix to replace the cheap one he always wore. She had been angry when he told her he had given it to his sister. And when she bought him the second one and demanded that he always wear it during sex, she had enjoyed his embarrassment. He had been embarrassed, too, about the money when she offered it. But he always took it.

Stupid, stupid boy.

In the end, she was the one who was stupid. Getting giddy over martinis that day with Carolyn at Ta-boo, too impressed that she had been invited to sit at a coveted table by the fireplace, too needy that a woman like Carolyn would even have a drink with her. And then, brassy with booze, asking Carolyn if she had ever experienced "a little death" during sex. St. John Knitted-up Carolyn, whose husband—everyone knew it—had been cheating on her for years. Cautious, controlling Carolyn, who had never had the guts to take a lover of her own but had listened to Sam's stories about Emilio with animal eyes.

She brought Emilio to the Osborn house that same night. Lots of wine, a dimly lit bedroom. But Emilio, when he realized he was expected to bed two women, had balked and bolted from the house.

Stupid boy. How dare he embarrass her like that in front of a woman like Carolyn Osborn?

When Emilio came to her the next night, saying he wanted out, she said she understood and offered to drive him home to Immokalee. But her anger built the farther west they drove, until finally, she steered the Bentley down a deserted road, and while seducing him one last time, she stabbed him. When he tried to run, she whipped him and, in a blind rage, cut off his head. She put the head in the trunk of the car.

Hands red with his blood, her body burning with a sexual rush, she drove back to the island, eased the Bentley into the huge old garage, and dead-bolted the door. The old car had stayed there for the last five years, untouched.

Sam turned left, heading south now through the narrow streets of the black neighborhood they called Harlem. Then the little houses fell away, and the lights of Clewiston dwindled to blurs in the rearview mirror. Now there was nothing but muddy pastureland, not even a rutted service road or trail. But she knew exactly where she was going.

She hunched over the wheel and peered up at the dark sky. The rain had stopped, and the last of the clouds were drifting east, leaving a pitch-black sky and a full moon.

Light. Yes. There would be light now. The cattle pen would be lit up like a stage.

She glanced over at Carolyn in the passenger seat, one hand braced against the dashboard, the other clutching the handgun. A striking image, Sam thought, Carolyn's perfect red nails against the cold steel of her husband's Luger.

Carolyn had begged her to keep this one simple, just find a deserted place in West Palm, put a bullet in Byrne's head, and walk away. But that seemed so tame, so unimaginative. Why kill the boy if there was no pleasure to be derived from it?

"Sam, where are we going?"

Carolyn's voice sounded funny, like she was straining to be heard through a static-jammed microphone. Sam knew what it was. This woman, this powerful woman, who had destroyed careers for the smallest political slight, who had sat across tables from world leaders, was not in charge. For once, she wasn't the one in control, and taking away control, Sam knew, was like depriving Carolyn Osborn of air.

"I told you where we were going," Sam hissed.

"This isn't the same way we came before."

"Don't worry about it."

A whimper came from the backseat. Sam glanced at the rearview mirror. It was too dark to see anything, so she fumbled for the switch to turn on the dome light. It was important to know what that loony bitch was doing every second.

Tink was cuddling a drowsy Byrne, stroking his hair and whispering nonsense.

"Tink, shut up," Sam said.

"Leave her alone," Carolyn said. "You know how she feels about him. Why did you even bring her?"

It was a good question. Tink had been a loose link in this chain, but Carolyn had always had a soft spot in her heart for the poor old thing.

Can't we find a man for her?

Good God, Carolyn, who would want her?

We can pay someone, can't we?

It was Carolyn who had the idea that they find a way to organize and hide their affairs. It had been easy to lure Bianca into the proposition by giving her a healthy percentage. It had been easy, too, to find other women on the island willing to pay for sex, but it always came back to the three of them—Sam, Carolyn, and Tink.

The young men. There had been a succession of them over the last years—lifeguards, pool boys, waiters, personal trainers—it was never hard to find them in the island's orbit. When the season ended and the mansions were shuttered and the women headed north to their summer homes, the men were sent on their way with bonuses.

And then, every fall, when the women returned, Bianca had a new bright shiny thing for them to play with.

Paul Wyeth had been an exception. He had gotten greedy and tried to blackmail them, threatening to expose Carolyn. Sam hadn't hesitated. He was a coke addict, so it had been easy to lure him out to Devil's Garden and kill him. Cutting off his head before she dragged him into the slough—she had done that only because there had been a certain symmetry to the act that appealed to her.

Sam never told Carolyn why Paul disappeared. Carolyn never asked. But Sam knew she would someday collect on that favor.

Tink was crying again.

"He needs a doctor! Where are we going?"

Sam pressed down on the gas pedal, answering Tink with a roar of the engine. The Bronco lurched forward, fishtailing crazily before the tires caught harder ground. Carolyn let out a gasp. Byrne groaned.

Sam ignored them, more interested in the land before her as the emerging moon vanquished the darkness.

To the west, she saw nothing but swaying grass, rolling brush, and an occasional silhouette of an umbrella-shaped oak.

Far off to the east, she could see the lights of the sugar refinery. Even with the windows rolled up, the smell was there, that stink of burnt sugar.

With the bad smell came the memories.

Papa, limping from the old truck, his lunch pail in his hand, his bottle of rye tucked under his arm, his overalls drenched in the sugary, wet steam of the refinery. He never looked at her, never waited for an answer, but still, every day, he asked the same question.

How was school, Sosie-Mosie?

Mama, standing at the stove, her face still flushed and her mouth still raw from her afternoon visit from Mr. Cooley, the widower across the street with the retarded son. Or Mr. Thomas, the pig farmer who brought them chops for Easter. Or any one of her mother's men, whose grunts and groans had stayed in her head long after their faces had faded.

Don't tell your daddy. This is my secret, Sosie, our secret. You hear me?

The stink of the sugar was finally receding. The air grew clean, and the knifelike blades of the cane changed to soft grass and old trees.

David was there in her head now.

They were on his horse, riding through pastures, taking a different cow trail every time but always to the same destination, always to their secret place.

Do you love me, David?

Yes, Sosie, yes.

Why was he with her so vividly tonight? Over the years, he had come and gone, usually like a pale ghost, sometimes like flesh and blood. And in those moments, like tonight, she could feel the hard muscles of his back as she clung to him on the horse, see his sky-blue eyes and feel his soft, sand-colored hair. He had taught her to ride. He had taught her to use his whip so she could flick a tin can off a fence post. But it had been his hands she could remember best. Gentle enough to cradle baby chicks, powerful enough to wrestle a steer, skilled enough to bring his world to life on canvas.

And eventually, sweet enough to please her.

God, Sosie, I want you so bad.

Do you love me, David?

A loud groan drew her back. Tink was crying. Sam slapped the light on and looked in the rearview mirror. Byrne was awake now, trying to get out of Tink's arms.

Sam reached into her jacket and dug out Bianca's vial of Percocet. She tossed it back to Tink.

"Give him another pill."

"No," Tink said. "He's already sick."

"Give him another fucking pill!" Sam yelled.

The Bronco hit a large rock and reeled sideways,

spraying mud across the windshield. Sam hit the wipers and slammed on the brakes. The Bronco slid to a steamy stop a few feet from a live oak.

Carolyn spun to Sam, her hand still on the dashboard. "You could've killed us," she said.

Sam didn't look at her. She stared out the window, gripping the wheel. She knew exactly where she was.

"Stay here," Sam said.

She pushed from the Bronco and slammed the door. It was windy and cool. She pulled her jacket tighter around her and trudged through the mud, her feet lost inside Hap's stiff-ankled hunting boots.

She entered a dark tunnel of live oaks and stopped. This was the place, the exact place. But things were different now.

Cool, not hot.

Dark, not daylight.

She was forty-five, not seventeen.

The wild red orchids that he had scaled the trees to pick for her were all gone.

Sam dropped to her knees and closed her eyes. The tears burned hot.

I'm leaving tomorrow, Sosie.

But you said we'd stay here together.

I have to go to school.

David, you promised . . .

I never promised you anything, Sosie.

Things coming fast now, all of those memories, the bad ones now, coming in a mad rush, just like everything had come in a rush that hot day so many years ago.

The trembling of her hands as she buttoned her blouse back up. The sticky ache between her legs. The hammering of her head. The nervous whinny of a horse. The rough feel of the jagged rock in her hand. The sight of his hair curled against the back of his tanned neck.

The crunch of the rock against his skull.

Red. Red. Red . . . a slow river of it on the green grass.

David? David?

One moment of blind rage. Then his lips gone cold. Her life gone cold. Everything frozen now, her heart and her head. Everything erased, the future, the past, and the fragile line she had always drawn between love and hate.

He had made love to her.

She had killed him.

And now, somehow, she had to forget him.

The horse stared at her with wild eyes. She moved to it slowly, placed a hand on its heaving neck. It stood still long enough for her to take the whip off the saddle's horn. Then it jumped back and disappeared into the trees. Cradling David's whip to her chest, she walked out of Devil's Garden.

"Sam?"

The voice snapped her back. It took her a moment to make out Carolyn's form at the edge of the trees.

Sam rose, wiping her muddy hands on her jeans as she walked to Carolyn.

"Let's get this over with," she said.

Chapter Thirty-six

They left their shoes, rifles, and raincoats on the covered porch. Aubry delivered a fresh tray of hot coffee and went to work on injecting new life into the dying fire. The room swelled with warmth and the smell of burning wood.

"Mr. Aubry," Louis said, "may I use your phone?"

"Certainly," Aubry said.

Louis dug into his wallet for the number and called the Palm Beach County Sheriff's Office. Since leaving Barberry, he had discovered only two new pieces of information: the Orchid Society and David's painting. Louis hoped it would be enough to persuade Barberry to spare some deputies and a couple of four-wheel drives for a thorough search of Devil's Garden.

Barberry was off duty, and the swing-shift commander sounded stressed, mumbling something about an armed robbery and a chase, then telling Louis he would try to find Barberry when things calmed down. Louis tried two more supervisors, and after fifteen minutes of being on hold while one tried paging Barberry, Louis hung up.

"You could try Chief Hewitt," Swann said.

"Not his jurisdiction or his case," Louis said. "And I don't think he gives a shit, anyway."

"You need some fellas to search for your victim?" Aubry asked.

"Yeah."

"My men could do that," Aubry offered.

Louis looked up. The thought of putting civilians out

there in this weather to search for a body, with the remote possibility of also coming across a killer, was crazy. But these were tough guys who knew their land and their rifles. And Aubry had that same look on his face now that Swann had that day back at Dunkin' Donuts. He wanted to help.

"How many you got?" Louis asked.

"Twenty."

"We'd appreciate anything they could do, Mr. Aubry."

Aubry picked up the phone and dialed. Louis heard him ask for a man named Mike, and then he said, "Get the crew ready for a search. We got a lost man out there."

Louis looked to Swann. He was watching Aubry, clearly still impressed with the man's command of his world.

"I can't keep them out too long," Aubry said when he hung up. "Don't want to put them or the horses at risk, but I can give you a few hours."

"Thanks," Louis said.

Aubry set his walkie-talkie on the table by the fireplace and disappeared into the kitchen. Swann, too restless just to sit and listen to it, went out onto the porch. When Louis went out to the BMW to get Byrne's kitten, Swann was sitting in one of the rockers, staring off into the darkness.

The house was filled with the smell of chili cooking when Louis went back inside. He installed the cat in the bathroom with its litter box and dish of food.

By the time Aubry came out with a tray with three bowls, Swann had come back inside and was warming by the fire. Louis realized neither of them had eaten all day.

Too hungry and too tired to talk, the men ate in silence, sopping up the chili with corn bread as the chatter of the walkie-talkie played in the background.

Every so often, Aubry would pick up the walkie-talkie to answer one of his men's reports. The men had divided into teams of two, methodically checking each pasture. One team was checking the slough. But Louis knew the Archer Ranch was four thousand acres, and two of the bodies had been found off the ranch. The chances of finding anything were near zero.

Just before eleven, a report came in from one of the men that a horse had been injured and that the area around the slough was becoming too dangerous in the dark.

Aubry looked at Louis and keyed the walkie-talkie. "I don't want anybody stranded out there. Bring them back in," he said. "We'll try again at dawn."

Louis went in to check on the cat. When he returned to the living room, Swann was back at the wall, staring at David's painting.

"That's my favorite one," Aubry said.

"Where did David do his painting?" Swann asked.

Louis thought it was a strange question. Aubry looked surprised, too.

"They're oils," Swann said. "Between that and the turpentine to clean up, it's messy and smelly."

"I let him set up a work space out in my stable," Aubry said. "David stayed over here a lot."

Louis turned back to the fire, for the first time noticing the three framed photographs on the mantle. The first was Aubry on a horse, the second a middle-aged couple and a small boy—Louis figured they were Jim and

Libby Archer with a young David. The last was a hand-tinted portrait of a young man in a western-style dress shirt and string tie. Clear blue eyes, sandy hair, strong jaw, and cleft chin.

He picked up the frame and turned to Aubry. "Is this you?" he asked.

Aubry hesitated and shook his head. "David. Last picture taken," he said softly. "Libby loved that picture best."

Louis put the photograph back in its place. He heard again that love in Aubry's voice, for both the boy and his mother. He saw again the sadness in the man's eyes. Anyone could plainly see that David Archer was the image of Aubry. Louis thought about asking the question that had been in his head for days, but how did you ask a man you barely knew if he was the real father of another man's boy?

"You want to see his sketchbooks?" Aubry asked.

Louis caught Swann's eye. There was no reason to look at David's work. No reason at all, other than to let Aubry share something he had kept to himself for almost thirty years.

Aubry went to a battered footlocker tucked in a corner and came back with an armful of notebooks. He handed Louis a tattered tan book that cracked when opened to the first page. It was lined, like it was meant for practicing penmanship, but it was filled instead with childish doodles of horses and dogs.

The second book was an old wire-bound red book. Its plain pages, edges tinged yellow with age, showed more drawings of horses and cowboys, but the craftsmanship had grown more assured. As Louis flipped through the pages, he could almost see the boy becoming the artist.

The other books were more of the same, the sketches becoming increasingly mature as David graduated from pencils to charcoal and, in the last book Aubry gave Louis, to pastel chalks.

There were a few portraits—leather-skinned cowboys, a Seminole woman in her rainbow-colored native blouse, and a good likeness of Aubry in a blue shirt that matched his eyes.

But the best drawings were of the land. A pink spoonbill in a blue stream. Russet cows against green palmetto palms. A lilac and dove-gray sky at dawn. A spiky green air plant lodged in the fork of a black-branched live oak. And a long-stalked plant with sprigs of red flowers, each blossom's tiny devil face carefully rendered.

Louis turned the page. The portrait stopped him cold.

Red hair. Upturned nose. Haughty tilt of the chin. The face was younger and rounder, but the eyes, so cunning and clear, were the same.

God. Sam.

He held the book out to Aubry. "Do you know this girl?"

Aubry peered at the page. "That's . . . what's her name? She was the little gal who worked at Mary Lou's."

"Please try to remember, Mr. Aubry."

Aubry scratched his head. "It was Susie or Sasha. No, I remember. Sosie. That was it. Sosie."

Louis looked back at the picture, Swann's voice in his head. *People come to Palm Beach to reinvent themselves, and that includes their names.* He turned to ask Swann if he knew anything about Sam's past, but Swann had gone back out onto the porch.

"Did David know her?" Louis asked, turning back to Aubry.

"I suspect so, since he went down the road to Mary Lou's often enough, and she was a pretty little thing," Aubry said. "But if you're asking if she was special to David, I'd have to say no. She wasn't the kind of girl a boy like David would bring home."

"Do you know anything else about her?"

"Her dad was a cutter in the cane fields but sliced his leg up in an accident and went to work in the refinery. I remember he got pretty sick with drink, so Sosie had to drop out of school to take care of him. That's why she was working at Mary Lou's."

Louis had a memory of the sad houses outside Clewiston and of that little girl standing in the dusty parking lot of Mary Lou's.

He could almost imagine what had happened. A pretty girl took up with the local prince. David couldn't bring her home, so he met her in secret. What had happened that summer in Devil's Garden, maybe no one would ever know. But David had died there, and Sosie had made it all the way to Palm Beach and transformed herself into Samantha Norris.

Had Sosie killed David? Had Sam killed the others?

But was a woman strong enough to behead a man? Then he remembered what Dr. Steffel had said when he asked her how much strength a decapitation would take. She had told him that if the blade was sharp and the person skilled, "a guy didn't have to be Conan the Barbarian."

Louis had been thinking about Reggie at the time. Now he was remembering the fierce power of Sam's arms wrapped around his back as he made love to her.

He knew women could be cold-blooded killers, just like men. Battered women pushed to their limit. Women who partnered up with violent men. So-called black widows who murdered husbands for money. Even women who killed their own children.

But a woman who killed men out of pure bloodlust? A woman who tortured and decapitated with cold-blooded precision? There was nothing in any police academy book that talked about that kind of psychopathy. And nothing in his own experience as a cop.

Louis looked back at the drawing of the red-haired girl. The face morphed, and he was looking down into Sam's flushed face as he entered her.

Die with me.

"You all right, son?"

Louis looked up at Aubry. "Yeah," he said. He closed the sketchbook. "I need to use your phone again."

He dialed Reggie's number, arousing Mel from sleep. "Hey," Louis said. "You awake enough to listen?"

"Yeah. Yeah. Go ahead."

"I think Samantha Norris is our killer."

"Who?"

"The redhead in the *Shiny Sheet*," Louis said. "You know. The woman I was . . ."

"Wait, wait . . ."

Louis could hear Mel fumbling. When he came back on, his voice was steady. "Jesus. You think she killed them all?"

"Yeah. It started with a boyfriend twenty-eight years ago," Louis said, glancing at Aubry. "I don't have time to explain it all right now, but I need you to go over to her house and—"

"I can't see shit at night. You know that."

Louis let out a breath. "Mel, is Yuba there?"

"Yeah."

"Have her drive you to Sam's house. It's on South Ocean. I don't know the address. But there's a big iron gate and this old Spanish castle house—"

"Rocky, take a breath," Mel said softly.

Louis ran a hand over his face and started again, giving Mel directions as best he could remember. "She's probably in the guesthouse," Louis said. "Just sit outside the gate and make sure no one leaves. Andrew and I are on our way."

When Louis hung up, he realized Aubry was staring at him. He had heard everything. But Swann still didn't know.

Louis went out to the porch, but there was no sign of Swann. The BMW was still parked in the drive.

Louis turned to go back in to see if Swann had slipped inside to go to the john. He froze. Swann's raincoat was gone. So was the rifle.

Chapter Thirty-seven

Was it possible to go to hell twice in one life? What a stupid thing to think about now. But that was what was ricocheting around in Carolyn's mind as she watched Sam pull Byrne from the Bronco. She hadn't wanted to come to this place that first time—*God, had it been only two weeks ago?*—but it had taken all three of them to handle Mark.

She didn't want to think about that night. And she had been able to stuff the memories in a box somewhere deep inside her, put on her public face, and go on. But now, back here in this place, it was all there again.

Mark Durand had been a mistake. The first time he had been in her bed, she had known that. His idea of seduction was to get drunk on Tucker's bourbon, then bed her with a quick pawing and brute force. One night she caught Mark in Tucker's office and called Bianca, telling her to cut him loose.

But Tink was on his appointment book for the next night. And that's when everything went wrong.

The call had come to her private phone at midnight. It was Tink, wailing that she had killed him by hitting him with a lamp. Carolyn arrived to find Sam trying to calm a hysterical Tink. Mark's half-naked body was on the bedroom floor. He wasn't dead, but then Sam said something that made Carolyn's blood go cold.

Well, maybe the bastard should be.

The details spilled out of Tink. He had called her vile names and said he couldn't stand the feel of her wrinkled skin or the "old dead woman" smell of her body. Sam reminded them both that Mark had been demanding more money and that she suspected him of stealing a painting from her bedroom. But it was when Carolyn spotted Tucker's Patek Philippe watch on Mark's wrist that even she became convinced that he needed to be punished.

They tied him with Tink's old Hermès scarves and dragged him outside. By the time Durand came to in the backseat of the old Bentley, they were in Clewiston. They let Sam do all the talking.

Where are you bitches taking me?

You've been a bad boy, Mark. But you do your job to-night, and you'll get a nice big bonus.

Carolyn had felt a tingle of excitement as they drove past the dark cane fields, like she was in some grand adventure. But when Sam slowed the Bentley and Carolyn caught her first look at the old fence, she knew it was no game.

Sam prodded the groggy Durand into a pen and ordered him to strip. When he refused, she pulled out a whip and, with one quick move, cracked it across Durand's back. Carolyn backed up against the fence in horror.

But Tink . . .

Doped up on her Valium and vodka, she had watched with fascination at first, then broke into cheers when Sam started to crack the whip repeatedly across Mark's back. Before it was over, Tink had wrestled the whip from her and took her own turn. By the time Mark had stopped moving, Tink had collapsed in the dirt, half laughing, half crying. Sam ordered Carolyn to take Tink back to the car and wait.

They sat silently in the dark of the Bentley. Sam finally emerged from the pen, the whip coiled around her shoulder. As she slid in behind the wheel, Carolyn saw her hands, red with blood.

Sam, what did you do?

Never mind. Let's go.

It was two days later that Carolyn read the story in the newspaper that Reggie Kent had been questioned in the murder of Mark Durand. When Reggie was arrested, Carolyn finally called Sam. That was when Sam told her she had put a pair of Hap's boots on Reggie's patio.

Don't worry, Carolyn. It's all under control.

A moaning sound brought Carolyn back to the present.

Byrne was lying in the mud, holding his head.

"Keep the gun on him," Sam said to Carolyn as she started toward the back of the Bronco.

Carolyn kept the gun down at her side. She had shot a gun before, back when her father took her out in the groves to practice on cans and bottles. But that was a lifetime ago. Tucker's gun felt heavy and slippery.

Carolyn heard a thud and saw Sam coming around from the back of the Bronco. She was holding a whip in her left hand and a machete in her right.

"No, Sam," Carolyn said.

Sam smiled. "I don't think you have any bargaining chips here, Senator."

She stuck the machete into a leather sheath hanging from her belt and looped the coiled whip over her shoulder. She pulled out a nylon cord and, kneeling next to Byrne, bound his hands in front of him. He screamed as the cord tightened around his broken wrist.

Tink dropped down into the mud next to him, crying.

Carolyn closed her eyes. There was nothing to do but go through with it now. She just had to get through this night and get back to the protection of the island. That was her plan, to do whatever she needed to do to survive tonight.

Tink started to wail. Carolyn's eyes shot open.

"God damn it, shut up!" Sam yelled.

Suddenly, Sam stood up and looked at Carolyn. "Shoot her."

"What?"

"Shoot the bitch! Now!"

Carolyn shook her head and started to back away. Sam lunged at her and wrenched the gun from her hand.

"No!"

A flash, a boom. Tink fell back into the mud.

Carolyn couldn't move, couldn't even pull in a breath. She stared at Tink, hair splayed in the mud, a small dark hole in her forehead. Her eyes were still open.

The jab of the gun butt in her stomach jolted her back.

"Take it," Sam said.

"No, I don't want—"

"I don't care what the fuck you want. Take it!"

Carolyn took the gun with shaking hands. She watched through tear-blurred eyes as Sam went back around the Bronco and yanked Byrne to his feet. He stood there, wavering, his face white and slick with sweat in the moonlight.

Suddenly, Byrne swung his bound hands up. His fists caught Sam in the jaw, and she fell backward. Byrne began to run.

Sam stumbled to her feet, holding her cheek, her eyes raking the brush and trees. Carolyn saw what Sam saw: the white blur of Byrne's shirt disappearing into the darkness.

Chapter Thirty-eight

Swann shifted the rifle from one hand to the other and kept walking. He could see nothing behind him but the shrinking yellow glow of Aubry's stable light. And he could see nothing in front of him but darkness. But he walked on, his step surer than it had ever been.

He didn't know why he was going back to the cattle pen. He just knew he couldn't sit there one more minute listening to the cowmen's voices on the walkie-talkie.

A sliver of light moved across the ground in front of his feet. He stopped and looked up. The last of the clouds were drifting east, unmasking a full bone-bright moon.

He pushed off his hood. The cool air brought a clarity he hadn't felt all day, and he realized that the hangover he'd woken up with that morning was finally gone.

Jesus, was that only twelve hours ago?

He moved on, grateful for the asphalt when he got to the two-lane road. He used the butt of the rifle to tap the mud from his shoes and looked down the road. It wasn't far to the gravel road that led to the pen. Maybe ten minutes on foot.

The moon disappeared, cloaking Swann again in darkness. He stopped and reached into his raincoat pocket for his flashlight, but before he turned it on, the moon reappeared. He could see the sparkle of gravel ahead.

Pop.

He froze. Was that a gunshot?

He wasn't sure. It had been a good ten years since he'd heard a gun fired outdoors. Qualifying in Palm Beach was done at the indoor range, where the padded ear protectors and concrete walls made the noise sound like bullets ricocheting inside an oil drum.

God. He was a cop. How could he not know something like this?

He took a quick look behind him and then broke into a trot toward the cattle pen. He was far closer to it than he was to Aubry's, and he wasn't wasting time going back. It might only be one of Aubry's men taking pot shots at something, but if it wasn't, then somebody was in trouble.

The moon disappeared again as he drew close to the pen. He stopped at the first fence to catch his breath and raised his flashlight. The beam moved with a nervous shiver over the gray wood. Nothing. He scaled the fence and wound his way through the maze, stopping as he tried to figure out where the central pen was.

"Hello?" he called.

Silence, then a low moan. Or was it just the groan of an old wooden gate?

Swann kept moving, his eyes alert for the slightest movement, ears tuned to the smallest sound. He saw and heard nothing, but still his veins were starting to burn with a trickle of adrenaline.

Another fence. He stuck a shoe on the lower rail and climbed over, dropping quietly to the ground on the other side. He was in another small pen. He stood, holding his breath and listening again for the moaning sound. He heard nothing but the dripping of water.

"Hello?"

Then the sound came, guttural and pained.

Swann hurried to the far fence and stepped up onto the rail to give himself the best view. The beam of his flashlight bounced wildly, and he had to force himself to steady it.

It was the main pen. There, near the rear . . .

A man on his back, his face turned away from

Swann's light. It had to be Byrne Kavanagh. And if he was moaning, then he was still alive.

Swann vaulted the fence and started across the pen, then stopped. His first instinct had been to run to Kavanagh, but that same adrenaline that moved him forward now stopped him cold.

Where was Kavanagh's attacker?

Swann leveled the flashlight and made two slow sweeps, peering hard into the darkness beyond the reach of the beam.

Another moan.

Swann swung the light back to Kavanagh. The collar of his white shirt was soaked in red, the skin above it slashed and oozing blood.

Swann hurried to him and dropped to his knees. For a few seconds, all he could do was stare at the gaping wound in Kavanagh's neck.

Don't freeze. Not now. Stop the bleeding.

He set the rifle down and ripped open his raincoat to get to the handkerchief in his pants pocket. It was small and thin, but he had nothing else. How was he going to get Kavanagh back to the house? Why hadn't he brought a radio?

A sudden blur in the corner of his eye. A flash of silver coming down in an arc.

He threw up his arm and ducked away. The machete blade sliced through the sleeve of the raincoat and into the meat of his shoulder. The pain seared through his muscle as he tumbled backward.

Jesus! Get the gun! Get the damn gun!

But he couldn't reach it. Couldn't even see it. All he could make out were dark legs and boots and the blur of movement as the blade slashed the air above him.

He rolled and crawled and finally struggled to his feet, falling twice in the mud before he reached the fence.

The fence. He'd have to jump it.

A *crack-zing* of the rifle. The scorching rip of a bullet through his thigh. It crippled him like a crowbar to the back of the knees. He stumbled forward, too weak to grab the rail. He collapsed, his back against the fence, his lungs burning.

She came into focus slowly. The pale khaki jacket. The dark pants. The flaming red hair.

Oh, God . . .

"Damn, damn," she hissed. "Goddamn it."

Sam Norris stood a few feet away, the rifle propped clumsily against her hip as she tried to work the bolt action to load a second cartridge. He could tell by the rattle of metal against metal that the rifle was jammed.

Time. That gave him time, but how far could he get?

She heaved the rifle across the pen and drew the machete from the sheath on her belt. She started toward him.

Dark eyes. White face. Nothing there but rage.

Chapter Thirty-nine

He heard the crack over the grind of the Jeep's engine.

"Rifle," Louis said.

"Near the pen," Aubry said.

Aubry gunned the engine, bypassing the road and cutting diagonally across the open land toward the pen. Louis leaned forward, trying to see ahead of them, but the headlights were dirty and old.

First, he saw the wood of the fence, and beyond that the faint outline of the slanted roof of the lean-to. Then Aubry made a small turn, and the lights swept left, washing over a woman standing in the pen. She spun toward them, frozen in the white glow.

Khaki jacket. Dark pants. Flaming red hair. A machete in her hand.

She bolted, running away from them toward the darkness beyond the pens.

"Burke, find Andrew!" Louis shouted.

He pushed from the Jeep and ran toward the pen. The gates were too far away; he had no choice but to jump the fences. He misjudged the first, toppling over it into the mud and scrambling back to his feet. He sailed over the second without losing a step.

Away from the headlights, everything was fuzzy and black, but he pushed forward, catching a glimpse of a body lying in the dirt. A small part of his brain registered it as not Swann but Kavanagh. But even that thought vanished when he caught sight of a red tail of hair slipping through an open gate—only one of many in the maze, he knew. She'd have to zigzag through them. He could vault over the last fence and catch her in the open field beyond.

But the last rail was rotted, splintering under his weight and sending him again into the mud. He struggled to his feet, trying to catch his breath as his eyes scoured the darkness. The moon gave him a fleeting flash of her jacket far ahead.

He threw off the bulky slicker and sprinted forward, praying that the ground stayed level and the moon stayed bright. His mind was racing with questions. Was Swann dead? Did Sam have his rifle? Was she the only killer? Was she the only one out here? And where was she running to?

Suddenly, she was gone again, swallowed up by the looming black shadows. He slowed, then stopped and stared.

Trees. Lots of them.

He glanced over his shoulder, then back to the woods, every second he stood here ticking off in his head as wasted time.

Go. Go after her.

He leveled his Glock and walked into the woods, up a sloped and rocky path. The moonlight vanished. The air smelled thick, green, and dirty. The trees felt close, tightening around him like the press of an anxious crowd.

Take a breath.

He made his way up the path, turning from left to right and back again. The sounds were soft, floating on the air like broken leaves. It was hard to tell which direction they were coming from. The rustle of a branch. Was it behind him or ahead? The *plink* of raindrops. Close or far away?

Crack!

Something snapped across his back, ripping his shirt and stinging his skin. He ducked and spun, not sure where to point his gun, not sure what the hell had hit him.

Crack!

His sleeve was slashed, his skin on fire.

Crack!

The whip ripped across his knuckles, tearing the gun from his hand. He heard it hit the blanket of leaves, but he couldn't see it.

Crack! Crack!

His hands were soaked in blood.

Crack!

"Stop it!" he screamed.

Crack. Crack. Crack. The whip swirled through the darkness like a lasso, snapping thin branches and splattering up dirt like the kick of a bullet. There was nowhere to go, nothing to hide behind, and he couldn't run. He couldn't leave his gun for her to find.

Crack!

A snap across his legs.

Crack!

The tail of the whip sliced into his face like a hot wire. Stunned, he cried out and dropped to his knees, teeth gritted, tears blurring his eyes. *The gun . . . find the gun.*

He threw a hand into the leaves.

Crack!

His fingers touched steel, and he came up in a spin, searching for that sliver of khaki in the tall, dizzying shadows of black and brown. For a second, it was still, the only sound the rush of his own breath.

Then the milky oval of her face took shape. A white mask with scorched black eyes.

His mind tripped with three thoughts.

Shoot to kill.

Shoot to wound.
Shoot to kill.
He aimed for her heart and fired.

Chapter Forty

The dawn sky was lilac and dove-gray. A fog hovered low to the ground, making the live oaks look like they were floating in the air.

The drone of the generator suddenly quit, and for a moment it was silent. Then came the morning song of the birds.

Louis looked over at the deputies who were starting to dismantle the floodlights. Hours ago, the cattle pen had been lit up like a garish arena. Now it had returned to its blur of bleached wood and weeds.

From his position sitting in the passenger seat of the open police cruiser, Louis watched the processing of the scene. They would go on all day, this careful army of deputies, detectives, and technicians, even though the bodies had been taken away hours ago.

Louis had watched as the two black body bags were loaded into the county van. He had been the one to identify them. Tink Lyons, found out by the Bronco. And Samantha Norris, lying under the giant oak in Devil's Garden.

Byrne Kavanagh had been taken out in an ambulance, his throat slashed, half his blood gone from his body, but still alive.

And Swann . . .

Louis hadn't even seen him as he raced through the dark after Sam. It was only as he walked back, holding his ripped cheek, that he saw Aubry cradling Swann in the high weeds. Swann's shoulder had been slashed, and he had a bullet in his thigh. But by the time the sheriff's deputies arrived, Swann was already trying to talk his way out of going to the hospital.

"Coffee?"

Louis turned. A tall man in slacks, dress shirt, and jacket was standing there holding a Styrofoam cup. There was a gold badge hanging from his breast pocket. His name tag above it read MAJOR GENE CRYER.

"Thanks, Major," Louis said, taking the coffee.

Cryer looked out over the pen and the trees. "Lot of land," he said.

"Four thousand acres," Louis said.

Louis looked over to where Burke Aubry stood with three deputies. He had a map of the ranch open on the hood of the cruiser and was helping direct the search.

They had questioned Swann, Aubry, and Louis. Cryer himself had grilled Louis for more than an hour.

They had taken the rifle and Louis's Glock; it was routine in any investigation. But after Louis had told them what had happened and that he hadn't shot Tink Lyons, they had begun a search for a second gun. They were also looking for other victims. No one, not even Louis, could be sure there weren't more.

"I've had some time to go over everything," Cryer said. "And right now, I am inclined to believe you're telling the truth."

"What about Carolyn Osborn?" Louis asked.

"We'll check her out." He paused. "She's a senator, you know."

"Yeah, I know."

"What makes you think she had anything to do with this?"

Louis was quiet for a moment. "I just know."

"Well, senators are printed for security clearance. So, if she was in the Bronco, we'll find out."

The crunch of gravel drew Louis's eye to the road. A tan sedan pulled between the cruisers and stopped. A bulky man got out and looked around.

"Christ," Louis muttered.

Barberry spotted him and came toward the cruiser, his badge on its chain bouncing on his belly.

"Hey, Major," Barberry said. He didn't even give Louis a glance.

"Where the hell have you been?" Cryer said.

Barberry finally looked at Louis and ran a quick hand through his messy hair. "I was home in bed all night," he said. "Got a damn stomach thing going on."

Louis could smell the medicine stink of Listerine from where he sat.

"Why didn't you respond when Kincaid called you last night?"

Barberry gave a shrug. "Nobody called me."

"I checked the logs, Ron. You were paged four times. You never answered."

Barberry looked at Louis. "Look, I don't know what this asshole's been telling you, Major, but I've been all over this case from day one. You can check my reports."

Cryer stared down at Barberry, then turned away, his jaw grinding. "Get out of here," he said.

"What?"

Cryer looked at Barberry. "Just get out of here."

Barberry shot Louis a final glare and stomped off. Louis watched the tan sedan back out and disappear down the gravel road.

Cryer tossed out the last of his coffee in disgust. "I've been looking for a reason to unload that guy. Maybe I can get him demoted to warrants."

"Well, he looks good in puke green."

Cryer managed a smile. "You're from Fort Myers, right?"

Louis nodded.

"Somebody said you're hoping to go home soon."

Louis nodded again. He was dog-tired, and the wound on his cheek hurt like hell, even with the antiseptic and butterfly bandage.

"I'll try to move your Glock through the pipeline and get it back to you in a couple days," Cryer said.

"Thanks. I appreciate that."

Cryer was surveying the scene, and when his eyes got to the brown spot in the pen's sand where Byrne Kavanagh had been slashed, he let out a breath. Then he shook his head and walked over to one of his deputies.

Louis rose slowly from the cruiser. He was stiff, his muscles still releasing their adrenaline high. Beneath his bloody shirt, his skin hurt, but he couldn't tell exactly where, so it felt like a million bee stings.

He shivered, looking around. There was no reason for him to stay here anymore. He saw Aubry coming toward him. He had taken off his denim jacket and held it out to Louis.

"Better put this on, son."

Louis didn't object. The jacket smelled like horses and was stained with Swann's blood, but it was warm.

"That young fella gonna be okay?"

"Andrew's going to be fine."

Aubry gave a nod as he looked back at the cattle pen. Louis realized he was staring at something on the fence. It was the small sign that said ARCHER PRESERVE. He suspected Aubry was thinking about how he was going to tell Libby Archer what had happened here.

When Aubry turned back, Louis was surprised to see tears in his eyes. "I don't have any way to thank you," Aubry said.

"For what?"

"The truth."

Louis just nodded.

"Come on, I'll drive you back, and you can pick up your friend's fancy little car." They were halfway to the Jeep when Aubry paused. "I almost forgot. What about that kitten back in my bathroom?"

Louis closed his eyes. He'd forgotten about the damn cat. He couldn't take it home.

"How about I keep the little fella?" Aubry said.

Louis smiled. "You're a lifesaver, Mr. Aubry."

Chapter Forty-one

Byrne Kavanagh was going to live. He would have a hell of a scar across his throat, and it would be months before he could talk, and even then, the doctors said his voice would likely sound as if his throat were lined with sandpaper.

Louis stepped from the elevator on the fourth floor of the Palm Beach County Hospital and walked down the hall toward Room 456. Louis had been here every day for the last three days, but so far, Kavanagh had been too weak or too drugged to make any kind of statement.

Louis hoped things would be different this afternoon. The extra days spent sitting around Reggie's house waiting to wrap things up felt long and unproductive, despite the trickle of information that was still coming in.

The deputies had found four sets of footprints near the Bronco: Sam's, made by the oversized boots she was wearing, which proved to be custom-made for her husband before his stroke and identical to the pair found in Reggie's home.

Tink Lyons's, made by her beaded slippers.

Byrne Kavanagh's, made by brand-new loafers.

And a fourth set that led from the Bronco south toward the cattle pen, then veered straight west toward the asphalt road, where they simply stopped. They were made by a woman's dress boot, size eight. Louis believed, without question, that it was the wearer of those boots who took the gun, fleeing the scene after Tink was killed. How she got back to Palm Beach was still a mystery.

Although she wasn't Louis's prime suspect, they had to check out Bianca Lee. It took the sheriff's office only an hour to find out that she had hung a sign on her shop door that said CLOSED FOR THE SEASON and was boarding a plane to Madrid at almost the exact moment Louis and Aubry were racing toward the cattle pen. The unidentified boot prints could not be hers.

Which left Carolyn Osborn.

They had enough evidence to question her: her fingerprints in Sam's Bronco and the bullet removed from Tink's head, which turned out to be a German 9mm, made for a Luger or a P38, circa World War II. The deputies never found the gun, but everyone knew that Nazi militaria was the cornerstone of Tucker Osborn's collection.

But Major Cryer was a cautious man, and, like Louis, he knew Carolyn Osborn would claim that as a friend of Sam's, her prints had been left in her truck at another time. As for the German handgun, it had probably been dropped in a drainage canal by now, its brackets in Tucker Osborn's gun cabinet mysteriously empty.

Which is why Cryer wanted to hear what Kavanagh had to say before he knocked on a senator's door and started talking murder.

Kavanagh was the only person who could place Carolyn Osborn out at the cattle pen that night, making her as guilty as Sam of kidnapping, torture, the murder of Tink Lyons, and the attempted murder of Kavanagh. And if Louis could tie Carolyn to Kavanagh's attack and the Orchid Society, he could link her to Mark Durand.

And Durand's murder—premeditated and involving torture and decapitation—made the senator eligible for the death penalty.

Louis stopped at the door to Kavanagh's room. There was a deputy seated outside, leafing through a magazine. Normally, there would be no reason to assign a cop to guard a victim, but Cryer's cautiousness didn't stop at the idea of ruining a political career without due cause. He reluctantly yielded to Louis's insistence that not all of the killers in this case were dead and assigned the guard until Kavanagh was released.

The deputy outside Kavanagh's room got up from his chair as Louis approached.

"Has Major Cryer been here?" Louis asked.

The deputy shook his head. "Not today. He had a long night and asked me to call him only if the guy was awake and talking."

"Nothing yet?"

"No, sir. But if he says anything, let me know, okay?"

Louis nodded. "Will do."

Kavanagh was awake, the bed elevated. His face was still bruised from Dickie Lyons's assault, but it was his body that was jarring to see. He was bare to the chest, his skin marked with a web of cuts. An air tube protruded from the turtleneck of bandages that wrapped his throat.

Louis stepped to the side of the bed.

Kavanagh's eyes slid to him, teary with pain.

"My name is Kincaid," Louis said. "I'm an investigator. You up to talking to me?"

Kavanagh motioned weakly toward a small dry-erase board and a marker on the night table. Louis gave them to Kavanagh.

With everything the guy had been through, Louis didn't want to be insensitive. The best thing to do was to keep his questions pointed so Kavanagh could supply one- and two-word answers.

"Who did this to you?" Louis asked.

Kavanagh wrote something and angled the board so Louis could read it.

DONT KNOW

"I'm sorry?" Louis said. "What do you mean you don't know?"

Kavanagh underlined his answer. <u>DONT KNOW</u>

"Okay," he said. "Maybe this will help. You were found out on a ranch near Clewiston with your throat cut. Do you know how you got there?"

NO

Louis stared at the board, baffled. He had seen a lot of victims in his life, some so traumatized it took them weeks to put together a cohesive story. But they were usually visibly shaky and barely able to begin reliving the event. Kavanagh looked tired but in control. In fact, he seemed mildly annoyed.

But maybe his reluctance to talk was something else. He was only twenty-three, paid to provide sex to rich older women. Maybe he felt humiliated that he had been overpowered and almost killed by those same women.

"Look, Kavanagh," Louis said. "You have nothing to be embarrassed about. And if someone has a gun on you, you do what you're told. I understand that. So will everyone else."

NOT EMBAR

"Then tell me who took you to the pen and attacked you," Louis said.

Kavanagh erased the board with his hand and wrote in hard slashes.

DONT KNOW

Louis glanced at the door, wondering if he should find a doctor and ask if Kavanagh had suffered some form of amnesia. Then he decided against it, not wanting some nurse to force him to leave. He'd find out himself what this kid remembered.

"Do you know who and where you are?" Louis asked.

BYRNE. FUCKIN HOSPITAL

There was nothing wrong with Kavanagh that a little pressure wouldn't fix. He'd start with something Kavanagh couldn't pretend not to remember.

"We know you were at Tink Lyons's house the night before you were taken to the pen. Do you remember getting beat up by her husband?"

NO

"Do you know why you were at her house?"

Kavanagh stabbed at his board to reiterate his answer.

"Do you even know Tink Lyons?"

NO

"Do you have any idea how you were injured?"

NO

What the hell was going on here? Was it possible Kavanagh's brain *had* shut completely down? Had the women given him a powerful drug that blocked his memory? Is that how they had subdued him?

But if that was what had happened and he really didn't remember anything, why wasn't he asking Louis questions? What kind of person wouldn't want to know?

"Okay, Kavanagh," Louis said. "I'll leave you alone, but you're going to be getting visits from lots of other people. Cops. You need to think about telling them the truth."

Kavanagh stared at his board.

Louis turned to leave, then caught a glimpse of something on the windowsill, a potted flower. It wasn't red; it was white. But it was definitely an orchid. He went to the window. No card or label, nothing to tell him what shop it had come from or who had sent it. He looked back at Kavanagh.

"Who brought this orchid to you?" Louis asked.

DONT KNOW

"Did Senator Osborn come to see you this morning?"

WHO THAT

"Did anyone come to see you? A guy named Greg, maybe?"

NO

Louis looked back at the orchid. It was the most bizarre thought he'd ever had, but he knew it was true, because the evidence was right there in front of him—and in Kavanagh's preposterous lapses of memory.

He looked back to the bed. "How much did she pay you?" Louis asked.

Kavanagh turned his head only enough for Louis to catch the flash of guilt in his eyes. Then he looked away.

"How much?" Louis pressed.

Kavanagh scribbled on the board.

DONT KNOW WHAT U MEAN

Louis walked back to the bed. "These women killed three men before they tried to kill you," he said. "You were nothing to them but a toy that they got tired of and threw away."

Kavanagh had his head down and a white-knuckled grip on the marker.

"Good God," Louis said. "That woman left you for dead in a stinking cow pen. You're going to let her get away with it?"

Kavanagh's head came up, and he looked slowly to the orchid, his eyes dull. For a long time, the only sound in the room was the wet rasp of air through his tube.

Louis studied Kavanagh's profile, trying to imagine what he might have looked like when he walked into

Carolyn Osborn's bedroom in a white Armani shirt, carrying a red orchid.

But now . . .

Split lip, broken nose, one eye pooled red, deep cuts stitched closed with knotted black thread. And forever with the voice of an old man. If he could speak at all.

How much was that silence worth?

Louis turned to leave, but as he reached the door, he could hear the squeak of Kavanagh's marker moving across the board. He turned back.

Kavanagh held up his board.

WHERE MY CAT???

For a moment, Louis felt a twinge of pity. But it evaporated when he thought of Rosa Díaz, Burke Aubry, and all of the nameless people waiting for the young men they loved to come home. He was tired of these selfish people whose only concern was for whatever money and comfort they could wring out of other people's lives. And that now included Byrne Kavanagh, who was willing to shelter a murderer so he could make a few bucks.

Kavanagh punched the board.

WHERE MY CAT???

"Don't know," Louis said, and left the room.

Chapter Forty-two

Carolyn picked up the pencil and leaned toward the mirror. She carefully outlined her top lip but then her hand began to shake, and she let the pencil fall to the dressing table. She pressed her palms to her forehead and bowed her head.

She didn't hear Tucker come in and pick up the pencil from the floor. When he set it in front of her, she looked up.

"You've got to stop this, Carolyn," he said.

She looked up into his eyes in the reflection of the mirror.

"It's barely noon," Tucker said. "How much have you had to drink?"

"Nothing."

He gave her a look of disgust.

"I told you, I am not drinking," she said.

"Are we going to go through this all over again?"

She shook her head, closing her eyes.

"Carolyn?"

Silence.

"Carolyn, look at me. We were able to keep it quiet last time, but I don't know if I can—"

"Tucker, just leave me alone," she whispered.

Tucker was quiet. She hoped he had moved away. But then he said, "We're leaving in fifteen minutes."

She didn't open her eyes until she heard the bedroom door close.

Finish your makeup. Get dressed. Go downstairs. Get in the car. Go on.

But the woman in the mirror didn't want to move. The woman in the mirror was still back there in the dark, crouched in the weeds, watching, watching, watching.

Running to the cow pen and watching Sam slit

Byrne's throat. Then hiding behind the fence, clutching the gun but unable to bring it up and point it at Sam and do what needed to be done. That had been her plan, to go along with what Sam wanted, let her kill Byrne, and then just kill her and get away. That had been her plan from the moment she got the call from Bianca to come to the flower shop. Because she knew that everything had fallen apart and that she had to take control of the situation.

But then the cop in the yellow raincoat had appeared, and she watched in horror as Sam shot him. She didn't know why the cop was there or what was happening. Then the other man had appeared, that black man who had been at her house, the one who had been asking all those questions all over the island. She had watched as he chased Sam into the dark.

She had heard the *pop* of a gun somewhere back in the woods, but she was too frozen to move. Then the black man emerged from the shadows, and she watched him walk into the headlight beams, face bleeding, gun at his side.

She knew Sam was dead. There was no one left to talk, no one left to betray her, no one left she needed to control. So as the moon emerged from the clouds, she used the light to find her way out to the asphalt road. She ran with burning lungs down the dark road to the cinder-block store with the name MARY LOU'S over the door.

Greg's blue Camry was parked in shadows. It had all been set up before they got to the flower shop, because by that point in this whole mess, she couldn't be sure what Sam was capable of doing. Greg said nothing when she got in his car, just put the gun under the seat and drove north on the deserted road.

They were ten miles east of Clewiston by the time they passed the first Palm Beach County Sheriff's Office cruiser going the opposite way, lights blazing, sirens wailing.

The next morning, Greg had brought her a copy of the *Palm Beach Post*. It was the front-page story, bumping the big news of the day—a train hitting a truck—down the page. It took two days for the *Shiny Sheet* to catch up, with a small story on the front page, leaving out most of the details. But there was a color photograph of Tink and Dickie Lyons taken years ago at the Cancer Ball.

Tink, poor Tink.

Carolyn had always understood she could never control Sam. But she was certain that once everything was over, once they got back to the island, she could bring Tink under her sway.

Poor, sad Tink.

But sometimes sacrifices had to be made.

Carolyn gathered up the last of her makeup, put it into its bag, rose slowly, and went to the bed. The Vuitton train case was open and she put in her makeup tote and snapped the case shut.

She went back to the dressing table and picked up the crystal bottle of perfume. She pulled off the stopper, closed her eyes, and took a drink. She opened her eyes and wiped the scotch from her lips. She put the stopper back and carefully set the bottle back in its place on the dressing table.

All she to do was act normal and just get away. That was all. Get away and hope that when Tucker realized his gun was missing, he would blame it on the servants, fire someone, and go back to just leaving her alone.

"Senator?"

She looked up. Greg stood at the door. The sight of him was strangely reassuring. His trips back and forth to the car with luggage had kicked up the cowlick in his hair.

"Your schedule is clear today for travel," he said.

She nodded as she pulled on her suit jacket.

"Tomorrow, you have a ski lesson at ten, your sons arrive at noon, you have a phone meet at two P.M. with Governor Martinez, and then Mr. Denver's cocktail party at eight."

"Yes, thank you," she said. "You can take that case now, please."

Greg closed his appointment book and crossed the bedroom to pick up the case. But he seemed in no hurry to take it downstairs.

"Is there something else?" Carolyn asked.

"I just wanted you to know," he said softly, "that I reserved an hour for us tonight at eleven."

She turned to him slowly. "Excuse me?"

"Just one hour, Carolyn." Greg gave her a small smile and walked out of the bedroom.

What had he meant—one hour? And why had he called her Carolyn?

The little bastard. How dare he make any assumptions?

She turned and looked to the perfume bottle, but she didn't reach or it.

The hell with him.

Once she got away, away to the clean snow and air of Aspen, she could forget all this, get the drinking under control, get back to Washington, get her life back under control.

Voices . . . outside.

She went to the French doors and looked out but there was no one there except the pool boy skimming leaves.

Greg. It was Greg and another voice she didn't recognize, coming from the front of the house. She went to the other window, which looked down on the driveway.

Through the palm fronds, she could just see the back of the Bentley. The trunk was open, several Vuitton bags still sitting out on the bricks. Then she caught a glimpse of Greg's red hair in the sun, but she couldn't see whom he was talking to.

Then the other person moved into her view.

It was the black private eye. He was talking to Greg, and Greg was shaking his head, holding up his hands.

Suddenly, the black man looked up, right at her window. He was wearing sunglasses so she couldn't see his eyes, but she knew he had seen her. Greg looked up, too. Her heart began to hammer and she pulled in a deep breath. She couldn't trust Greg; she had to go down there and take control.

Louis heard the front door open and looked beyond Greg's shoulder.

"Looks like your boss has better manners than you do, Greg," Louis said.

Greg spun toward the house just as Carolyn emerged. She came down the driveway to stand beside him at the back of the Bentley.

"Can I help you?" she asked.

"Your assistant here tells me you're leaving," Louis said.

"Yes, we always go to our home in Aspen for Christmas. It's a family tradition."

"So you're not hanging around for the funeral today?" Louis asked.

"Funeral?"

"Tink Lyons."

Carolyn didn't blink. "I'm sure all her friends will be there."

Greg edged closer to Carolyn's side. "We have to get going, Senator, if you want to make your flight."

Louis took off his sunglasses and stared at the guy, but Greg wouldn't look him in the eye.

"I just got back from the hospital," Louis said. "You were there, weren't you, Greg?"

Greg stayed silent, but a flush of red began to creep up his neck. Carolyn's face, Louis noted, remained a perfect mask, and for a second he felt a begrudging kind of respect. He had seen a lot of liars in his job, but she had it down to an art. A quote—some long-lost fragment from the Bible school his foster mother Francis had made him attend—flashed into his head. Something about liars and murderers having to suffer a second death.

"I left my briefcase in my office, Greg," Carolyn said. "Go get it, please."

Greg gave Louis a final look, then walked back to the house. He paused at the front door, watching them.

"He's such a good little puppy," Louis said.

"What do you want?" Carolyn asked.

"I know you were out there," Louis said.

"Out where?"

"The cow pen."

"I don't know what you're talking about."

"Your prints were in her Bronco."

"Whose Bronco?"

"Sam Norris's."

Carolyn didn't blink. "I've been in her car many times. We were good friends."

"No, you weren't."

Louis looked to the front door of the mansion. Greg was still there. He looked back at Carolyn.

"What'd you do with the gun, senator?"

"Gun?"

"The one you used to shoot Tink."

Carolyn was silent.

"The one you probably were going to use to kill Sam."

"I really have to go."

"The bullet they scraped out of Tink's head," Louis said. "It was nine millimeter, a German antique. Doesn't your husband have a thing for Nazi stuff?"

Carolyn stared at him. "You can't prove anything," she said.

"And you can't control everything, senator."

She turned away.

"Bianca Lee? You got her under control?"

Carolyn started toward the door.

"You got your husband under control, senator?"

She kept walking.

"What about Greg, senator? You got him under control, too?"

Greg was standing there at the open door, staring at Louis.

"What about Byrne Kavanagh?" Louis yelled. "How much did you pay him? And how long before he comes back asking for more? You got *him* under control, senator?"

Carolyn turned, and to his surprise, came down the driveway and stood in front of him.

"I think you should go now," she said. "I think you should get off our island and leave us all alone."

A blur of movement at an upstairs window caught his eye. Tucker was up there, looking down at them.

"Oh, I'm going home, all right," Louis said. "I can't wait to get out of here. But I'm not going to forget what you did. I can link you to Mark Durand through your husband's sword. And I promise you, senator, I will find a way to link you to that German gun if I have to visit every antique dealer in this state."

She tipped up her chin. Her expression held the same smugness he had seen on almost every face he had encountered in this place.

He leaned toward her, finger raised. "And you can tell your little puppy over there that I'm going to watch him, too. Everywhere he goes, everything he does, I'll be watching. I'm guessing he knows exactly what happened last night, which makes him an accessory to murder. I'm also guessing that someday he's going to get tired of you and your games and decide you're not worth protecting anymore."

Carolyn had gone pale. "Get out of here before I call the police and have you thrown off the island."

"With pleasure, lady," Louis said.

He put on his sunglasses and walked down the driveway to the Mustang.

Chapter Forty-three

When Louis arrived at Margery's mansion, he was surprised to see Margery herself answer the door.

Louis was almost afraid to ask. "Where's Franklin?"

"Franklin?" Margery waved a hand. "Who knows?"

"I thought for a moment he had finally become a true ghost of a man," Louis said with a smile.

"Oh, God, no, the old thing will outlive us all."

She linked her arm through his and led Louis into the hallway. As always, it was as warm as a hothouse, but the air grew cooler as Margery steered him out to the loggia.

Reggie was lying on the old rattan lounge, wrapped in a white terry-cloth robe and surrounded by the four pug dogs. The table next to him held a stack of newspapers and magazines, some prescription bottles, and a large bottle of Pellegrino in a silver wine cooler. Reggie put down the *Shiny Sheet* and gave Louis a smile.

"Louis," he said softly, "I'm so glad you came."

Reggie had been out of jail only two days, but already he looked better than the last time Louis had seen him. Still, he had lost his tan and a good ten pounds. With his jail buzz cut and thinner face, he bore little resemblance to the man Louis had met that first day in Ta-boo.

"Can I get you anything, dear?" Margery said, sitting on the edge of the lounge and stroking Reggie's head.

"Franklin is making me some tomato soup."

Margery bent over and gently pulled Reggie's head to her breast. His face disappeared in the billowing sleeves of her caftan.

"My poor old bunny," she said. She released him and rose with a sigh. "Will you watch him for a moment, Louis? I have to go upstairs."

"No problem."

"I'll be right back, dear," she said to Reggie. And she was gone, three of the pugs in her Shalimar wake.

"How you feeling?" Louis asked as he sat down in the chair near the lounge.

Reggie gave a small shrug. "Margery said I could stay here until I get back on my feet."

"Thanks for letting Mel and me stay in your house. Eppie came by and gave it a good go-over. Everything's ready for when you move back in."

"So, you're leaving?"

Louis nodded. "Yeah, we're splitting this afternoon. It's time for me to get home."

"Mel didn't say anything about you leaving when he was here yesterday."

"I just decided this morning," Louis said. "It's time for me to get back to reality."

Reggie nodded numbly. His stomach let out a rumble, and he looked with hope toward the archway. "I think Franklin forgot my soup," he said with a sigh.

"Want me to go see if I can find him?"

Reggie nodded. "And tell him not to forget the dough balls."

"Dough balls?"

Reggie gave a small smile. "When I was a boy back in Buffalo, my mother would make me Campbell's tomato soup whenever I got sick. She used to dig out the insides of Wonder Bread and roll it into balls and put it in my soup."

Louis rose. "Be right back."

It took Louis a while to find the old tile kitchen in the maze of hallways, but when he finally did, it was empty. But there was a simmering pot on the stove and a silver tray. The familiar red, yellow, and blue ballooned loaf of bread was on the counter.

Louis figured Franklin had disappeared again, so he ladled some soup into a beautiful blue and white bowl and set it on a silver tray along with a linen napkin and an ornate silver spoon. He wedged a few slices of the soft white bread under the bowl and took the tray back to the loggia.

"No Franklin. But I found the soup."

Reggie looked down at the tray as Louis set it on his lap, then up at Louis.

"You gotta do your own balls, man," Louis said.

Reggie picked up a slice of bread, dug out the middle, and rolled it into a ball. He placed it in the soup and poked at it with the spoon. He took slow, careful sips of the soup, the swelling of his lip making him wince with each attempt.

Finally, he set the spoon down with a sigh. "I can't even eat soup," he said softly.

"You'll be all right, Reg," Louis said.

Reggie went quiet, his hand tucked under his chin as he stared out at the blue sky beyond the archways. When he turned back to Louis, his eyes were moist.

"That's the first time you called me by my first name," he said.

"It is?"

Reggie nodded.

The lone pug that had stayed with Reggie laid its head on his leg. Reggie stroked its ear.

"I know you think I'm ridiculous," Reggie said.

"I don't—"

Reggie silenced him with a hand. "That's okay. You get used to it, you know."

Louis's eyes wandered to the archway, hoping Margery would appear and save him. But from what? Truth was, he had thought Reggie Kent was ridiculous. And from the start, he had wanted to distance himself from this man, like shaking his hand or just saying his first name would somehow suck him into a world he didn't understand and wanted no part of. But this week, a lot of little worlds had been turned upside down within his larger one.

"You shouldn't get used to it," Louis said.

Reggie had been looking out at the ocean again and turned back. "What?"

"You should never get used to people treating you like shit because you're maybe a little—"

Reggie smiled. "Queer?"

"I was going to say different."

They were quiet again. A phone was ringing somewhere deep in the house. Louis and Reggie both looked at the mute extension phone, but neither made a move to pick it up.

Louis saw a shadow pass over Reggie's bruised face and wondered again what he had endured in jail. A part of him didn't want to know, no matter how much he figured Reggie might need to talk about it.

"I was in jail once," Louis said.

Reggie looked at him in surprise.

"Eight years ago, I had to go back to the town where I was born in Mississippi," Louis said.

"You're from Mississippi?"

Louis nodded. "Some shit happened there, and I ended up in jail. One of the guards put a noose around my neck and tried to hang me."

"Good Lord," Reggie whispered.

"Yeah, he was a real piece of work."

They were quiet again.

"Do you think about it a lot?" Reggie asked.

Louis hesitated. "It left a scar around my neck, but it's faded a lot. Now I only think about it every time I shave."

Reggie gave a wry smile and stroked the pug.

"You'll be okay, Reg," Louis said.

He gave Louis a long look and heaved a big sigh. "That's not my real name, you know."

Louis nodded. "Andrew told me you changed it."

"Ronald Barnabas Kaczmarek, that's my real name. How can a person be taken seriously with a name like that?"

"Sounds like a perfectly good name to me."

"Not in this town."

The pug jumped off the lounge and trotted off. Reggie picked up the *Shiny Sheet* and held it out to Louis. "It's all here, you know, every sordid detail. Tink Lyons's funeral is today. The jackals are having a field day picking at the carcasses."

"Why don't you leave?" Louis said.

Reggie folded up the *Shiny Sheet* and set it on the table. "Where would I go? Back to Buffalo? Please."

Louis was quiet.

"I know this is a horrible place in many ways," Reggie said. "But it is also quite lovely, and it is my home. There's no way you'll ever understand, but I feel safe here. I don't think I can survive anywhere else anymore."

Louis understood perfectly. With Margery at his side, Reggie Kent would resume his place on the island. His phone would ring again. His ladies would embrace him again. He would return to the ballet, to caviar on his patio, and to his coveted table by the fireplace in Ta-boo.

The snorting of pugs made them both look to the archway. Margery came in, her Pucci caftan a floating rainbow cloud.

"I just got off the phone with Harvey," she said. "You would not believe what that man is charging me for all this."

Reggie looked away, embarrassed.

"He got the charges dropped against Reggie," Louis said.

Margery grimaced. "Okay, he hit on all sixes, but he still cost me some heavy sugar. Lawyers . . . the world would spin so much better without them."

"Can't say I disagree with that," Louis said. He rose. "Well, I have to get going."

Margery stared at him. "Going? Going where?"

"It's time for me to go home."

"Is Marvin going with you?"

Louis nodded.

"But I thought he was canoodling with that lovely bartender at Ta-boo?"

Louis had ceased to wonder how word got around the island so fast. "Marvin's leaving, too."

Margery let out a big sigh and looked down at Reggie. "Well, say your goodbyes, dear. I'm going to walk him out."

Reggie looked up at Louis. "How can I thank you?" he said softly.

"Just be happy, Reg."

Reggie nodded.

"Let's ankle, Louis," Margery said.

Louis followed Margery out of the loggia and into the hallway. The pugs followed them outdoors. Louis watched them as they rolled and snorted in the grass. Louis spotted Franklin over by the coral fountain, ladling out leaves with a small aquarium net. A van pulled up to the mansion across the street and dislodged a crew of three women in uniforms who disappeared behind a servants' entrance gate. Two brown-faced Hispanic men in long-sleeved shirts and wide-brimmed hats were perched on ladders, trimming the twelve-foot hedges.

Margery was watching the blue swells rolling in from the Atlantic. She pulled in a deep breath and closed her eyes.

"Things are changing," she said softly.

Louis was quiet.

"When I got here, there were rules, and everyone knew how to act," she said. "But now . . . the world is too much with us on our little island."

She turned to Louis. "I was reading the papers today," she said. "About Mark Durand and everything. But there was nothing about Emilio." She paused. "Did you ever find out what happened to him?"

Louis didn't feel like going into any of it now, but he knew Margery would find out everything eventually. "He was murdered," he said.

Margery looked back toward the ocean. "He was a nice boy," she said softly. "I had this little fantasy about him."

She sensed Louis staring at her but kept her eyes on

the ocean. "Not like you might think. It's just that, well, I couldn't have any babies, you see, and my Lou did so want a son."

She was quiet for a long time before she turned back to Louis. "Didn't you tell me that Emilio had a family?"

Louis nodded. "He has a sister in Immokalee."

"A sister. What is her name?"

"Rosa. Rosa Díaz."

Margery hesitated, then dug into the pocket of her caftan. She came out with her pink leather checkbook. "Oh, futz, do you have a pen, dear?"

Louis padded his jacket and produced a Bic.

"Turn around, love."

Louis did as instructed, and Margery used his back to write. She ripped out a check, and he turned back around.

"Give this to her, would you?" Margery said.

Louis looked at the check. It was for $50,000.

"You don't have to do this," he said.

"Of course I don't, ducky. But it makes me feel good."

She dug into her caftan again and pulled out a second check. "This is for you."

Louis unfolded the check. It was for $250,000.

"Margery, this is too much," he said.

"Half is for Marvin, you foolish boy," Margery said.

Louis folded the check and put it in his pocket. "Margery, you're a right gee," he said.

She grabbed him and planted a huge kiss on his lips.

When she pulled back, her red slash of a mouth was a smudged smile. "Now you're on the trolley, Lou-EE."

Chapter Forty-four

When Louis got back to Reggie's house, he found Mel in the living room packing up the pigpen. Mel had scrounged up some file boxes and already had them labeled with the victims' names and the contents.

Keys still in his hand, Louis stood in the middle of the room watching Mel as he stuffed reports into manila envelopes. Mel finally noticed him.

"What's wrong?" Mel asked.

"Do me a favor," Louis said. "Before we drop this stuff off with Major Cryer, make copies for us."

"I already did."

Louis just stared at him.

"I know you," Mel said. "If Kavanagh croaks, I know you aren't going to let that bitch go free."

"Kavanagh's going to live," Louis said.

"Is he talking?"

Louis shook his head. "Carolyn Osborn bought him off."

Mel rose to his feet. "When? How?"

"This morning."

"He admitted it outright?"

Louis shook his head. "No, but there was an orchid in the room. I asked the cop on my way out why he let anyone in there, and he told me the only person who went in was a redheaded delivery guy."

"Greg."

"Right."

Mel looked around at his boxes, then back at Louis. "Well, hell, maybe Kavanagh looked at it like this," he said. "He could put Carolyn Osborn in jail and go back to being a poor guy with an ugly scar, or he could keep quiet and be a rich guy with an ugly scar."

"I get that," Louis said. "But I'm not going to let this drop." He looked at Mel. "Thanks for making the copies."

Mel tossed the envelope into a box and gestured to the sliding glass doors that looked out over the beach. "Andrew stopped by to bid us farewell," he said. "Better go tell him the news. He's outside with Queenie."

"Queenie?"

"His dog."

Louis looked out the window. Against a blended blue backdrop of ocean and sky, Louis saw Swann. He was wearing baggy denim shorts, a lemon-yellow T-shirt, and, on his thigh, a thick white bandage that contrasted sharply with his tan. Queenie was an Irish setter, the same dog Louis had seen in a picture on Swann's desk.

"Give him this for me," Mel said.

Mel was holding a comic book. The cover showed a Frankenstein face looming over a puffed-chest Superman. The title was *Escape from Bizarro World.*

"I don't think he'll appreciate the joke," Louis said.

"Yes, he will," Mel said.

Louis took the comic book and walked out to the beach. Queenie was in full gallop after a stick, Swann watching her with pride. Queenie snagged the stick and started back to them, her body lithe and graceful as she bounded across the beach. In the slanting afternoon sun, her copper fur shone like wavy silk threads against the canvas of white sand.

"She's a beautiful animal," Louis said.

Swann heaved the stick again and faced Louis. "Yeah. I fell in love with her the first time I saw her."

"Where'd you get her?"

"She found me," Swann said. "I was sitting in a park reading, and she just wandered up. No tag, no collar. I put ads in the paper, but when no one claimed her, I kept her."

Louis nodded and looked at the two crutches in the sand, then at the second bandage on Swann's left shoulder.

"You're crazy to be up on that leg so soon," Louis said.

"I know, but I wanted to come over and say goodbye to you and Mel."

Queenie came back and dropped the stick at Swann's feet, then started a dance around his legs. Swann gave her another throw and looked at Louis. His eyes paused for a second at the thin scar on Louis's cheek.

"So, when do we arrest the senator?" Swann asked.

"We don't."

"Why not?"

Louis told him the story, including the face-to-face outside the Osborn home. Swann listened but in the end seemed less surprised than Mel, if that was possible. Maybe that's what happened to normal people who stayed there too long, Louis thought. They became shock-proof.

"You know," Swann said, "the worst part is that without a prosecution of Carolyn Osborn, we'll never find out *why* they did it."

"Samantha Norris was a psychopath," Louis said softly.

"That's a legal label for a very complicated personality," Swann said. "What about Tink Lyons and Carolyn Osborn? What was going on in their heads that made them vulnerable to someone like Samantha Norris in the first place?"

Louis was quiet, watching Queenie.

"Did you know there's not been one documented case of a female serial killer using the level of violence we saw here?" Swann said.

Louis sighed.

"And what few female serials there have been have almost always used poison or some other impersonal method of murder. They don't kill for lust or thrill," he said. "That's what makes Samantha Norris so fascinating. I mean, think of how much we could learn if—"

Louis looked down at the sand.

Immediately, Swann felt silent. Queenie was back, nuzzling his leg, but he didn't seem to notice her.

"Christ, I'm sorry," Swann said.

"Forget it."

Swann finally noticed Queenie and gave her another run with the stick.

"I've been thinking a lot about Burke Aubry," Swann said after a long silence. "I was thinking how lucky he is."

"Lucky?"

"Yeah, the guy hasn't got anything, no money, no family, lives in that broken-down house with only a dog for company."

Louis didn't say what he was thinking, that Burke Aubry still had a woman he had loved for decades, and the memory of their son.

"But that man loves what he does." Swann paused,

squinting out at the ocean. "My dad is like that. I used to hate him for it. Now I think I envy him."

They were both quiet, watching Queenie chase a flock of gulls.

"I sent away for an FBI application," Swann said.

Louis turned to face him. "The FBI?"

Swann nodded. "I got the idea when I was reading about the serial killers. I speak four languages and have a degree in psychology. Maybe I can be useful there."

Louis nodded. "I know someone up there in the Behavioral Science Unit," he said. "I can give her a call and try to open some doors for you."

Swann smiled. "That would be great. I'll need some help explaining why I got fired here."

"You were fired for the right reason, trying to do your job. Sometimes they like hearing that kind of honesty."

Queenie came back, and Swann tossed the stick again.

"Did you tell your father yet?" Louis asked.

"I'm going to wait until I'm accepted. That way, it'll be easier to finally thank him for cleaning up my record all those years ago."

"I think he'd appreciate that."

The silence flowed in again.

"So, what about you?" Swann asked.

"I'm going home, sit on my beach with a beer, and wait for the next case to come along," Louis said.

When Swann didn't say anything, Louis looked over at him. Swann opened his mouth to say something, then looked out over the water.

"What?" Louis asked.

"Nothing."

"You want to bust my chops one last time about how PIs are just pieces of shit?"

"Are you kidding?"

"What then?"

Swann shook his head. "I just don't get it. You're really good at this stuff. Why'd you give up the badge, man?"

"I didn't have a choice," Louis said. "I was run out of Michigan."

"Why not try again here?"

Louis kicked at the sand, wishing this rusty box hadn't been opened. When Queenie returned with her stick, Louis picked it up and gave it a hard throw. He watched the dog lope down the sand.

"Hey, I know how hard it is to start over," Swann said. "But you can't just sit on the beach waiting for shit to come to you."

Louis couldn't look at Swann. Queenie brought the stick back and dropped it in front of Louis. He picked it up and held it out to Swann. "I've got to get going," he said.

Swann took the stick. "Well, listen," he said, "it's been great working with you. I mean that."

"Same here, Andrew."

"And thanks for getting me fired."

Swann stuck out his hand. Louis shook it. "Good luck, Andrew."

"Say goodbye to Mel for me."

"Oh, that reminds me." Louis pulled the comic book from his back pocket. "Mel wanted me to give this to you."

Swann unrolled it and chuckled. "I looked it up, you know."

"What?"

"Batzarro. I know he was a fuckup."

"Mel has a warped sense of humor."

Swann rolled up the comic book and smiled. "Tell him I'm going to frame this and hang it on my wall at Quantico. It'll be something to help me remember you two assholes."

Chapter Forty-five

When Louis came back in from the beach, Mel was finished with the pigpen. He handed Louis the black *Social Register*.

"You want this?"

"Toss it."

Mel put it in the plastic garbage bag at his feet. He put the lid on the file box that held all of the case information they had accumulated in the last eleven days.

Mel picked up the box and set it by his suitcase at the front door. Louis's own duffel was there, his rumpled blue blazer draped across.

"You okay?"

Louis nodded. "Is there any beer left?"

"Might be one still in there."

Louis went into the kitchen. It was spotless, burnished to a gleam by the invisible Eppie. Louis yanked open the refrigerator and peered in. Someone had stocked it with Perrier, two bottles of Veuve Clicquot, and a fifth of Rodnik vodka. There were fresh eggs, orange juice, and two tins of osetra caviar.

But no beer.

Louis went back to the living room. "Where'd the groceries come from?"

"I figured Reg could use some goodies when he got home. So Yuba and I hit the Publix this morning. And yes, I kept the damn receipt so you can write it in your little notebook."

Louis smiled.

"Are you smiling?"

Louis dug in his jeans and pulled out Margery's check. He gave it to Mel.

"What's this?"

"Our payment."

Mel brought the check up to his eyes and squinted. "Twenty-five hundred bucks? Not too shabby."

"Add some zeroes."

"Twenty-five thousand?"

"Add another zero."

Mel stared at Louis.

"We have to split it. And if it's okay with you, I'd like to give Andrew fifty grand."

"Hell, he earned it." Mel smiled. "And maybe now you could break down and buy a decent blazer."

Yuba came out of the back bedroom carrying a suitcase. "All packed," she said. "You sure you're okay with this, Louis?"

Louis had been surprised when Mel said he wanted to bring Yuba back to Fort Myers. She had quit her job at Ta-boo and still had plans to go back and get her degree. But for now, she was going to move into Mel's little apartment. No promises, she had told Mel. None expected, he had told her.

"At least I'll have someone to talk to on the drive home," Louis said with a smile.

He watched as Yuba linked her arm through Mel's and gave him a kiss on the cheek. He started toward the bedroom.

"Where you going?" Mel asked.

"Final walk through," Louis said.

He went through each of the rooms, but they were spotless. In Mark Durand's bedroom, he paused. All of the items were still there on the étagère, and the pastel shirts were lined up in the closet like mints in a box.

The spot of red and green on the wall above the bed caught Louis's eye. It was David's painting.

He went over and took it off its hook. He was certain Reggie didn't want it. He was certain, too, that Burke Aubry wouldn't mind if he took it.

When he went back out to the living room, Yuba and the suitcases were gone. Through the open front door, he could see her putting them in the trunk of the Mustang.

Mel was gathering up the pile of *Shiny Sheet*s and stuffing them into the garbage bag. He paused, peering down at a page.

"What's that?"

Mel held it out.

Louis took it. It was the page with the photograph of Sam and the lawyer. Flowing blue dress, milk-white skin, and carrot-red hair.

"You okay?" Mel asked.

"Yeah."

"You hit her in the heart."

"That's what we're trained to do."

"But it was a woman this time."

"I'm fine, Mel. Let's just get out of here."

Louis crumpled the paper, stuffed it into the garbage bag, and hoisted the bag. He followed Mel outside, making sure he stopped to lock the door. Then he slipped the key into a flowerpot as Reggie had requested, put the garbage bag in the trash can, and got into the Mustang.

They headed south, passing the velvet greens of the country club and the geranium-bedecked entrance to the Breakers hotel. At the old stone Bethesda-by-the-Sea Church, Louis had to stop to allow the long line of cars to exit. He had no choice but to pull the Mustang behind the funeral cortege that was taking Tink Lyons to the cemetery.

At the Palm Beach police station, Mel and Yuba waited in the car while Louis went in and paid his "ugly car" fine. When he got back, Mel had put the Mustang's top down and was slumped in the passenger seat. Yuba was in the back, face turned up to the sun.

"Let's go home, Rocky," Mel said.

They drove west on Royal Poinciana Way and across the bridge. After a quick stop to drop off the file box with Major Cryer at the Palm Beach County Sheriff's Office, they headed due west on US-80.

Louis's mind was racing ahead. And there was a lightness in his chest, like he could breathe for the first time in a week. No, for the first time in years.

Maybe it was Andrew's questioning. Maybe it was the firmness of Major Cryer's handshake and the respect in his eyes. Maybe it had been there, buried inside him for a long time now, and had only taken Joe's words to bring it out.

I want you to want something for yourself.

Whatever it was, he had made a decision. It had come to him suddenly as they left the sheriff's office parking lot, hitting him like a sharp stab to his heart.

He wanted to get back in. He wanted to feel the weight of a badge on his chest. Even if it meant going to Lance Mobley and begging, he was going to try once more.

He couldn't wait to get home. The first call would be to Mobley. But he knew he had to make a second call to Joe. He needed to try once more with her, too.

The strip malls and gas stations disappeared, and they were out in the scrublands. Soon they reached the swaying green curtains of the cane fields.

Mel was slumped in the seat, asleep. Louis glimpsed Yuba in the rearview mirror. Her head was back, her eyes closed, her lips tipped in a secret smile, long black hair fanned out behind her.

Louis looked back to the road, squinting hard into the sun.

He had made love to her

He had killed her.

And now he had to forget her.